The Swans of Lorraine

by

Phillip Varady

The Swans of Lorraine

This is a work of fiction.
Any similarities to persons living
or dead is purely coincidental.

Copyright 2008 by
Phillip Varady Sr.
ISBN 978-0-6152-1504-4

Other works by this author:
Shadow In My Eye
The Stonebearers
Sepik

Phillip Varady

PREFACE

The setting for this novel is in France and begins in Saint Mihiel in the *département* of Meuse and ends in Laxou in the *département* of Meurthe et Moselle. Both are in the former *province* of Lorraine. This troubled land has seen more than its fair share of war and deprivation being on the border of two great European powers. These two *départements* are in the western part of Lorraine and were spared the worst of the troubles that their eastern neighbors experienced but when things were at their worst, their eastern neighbors fled west into their bosom. More than once when the refugees had the opportunity, they declined to return to their former homes with an historic sense of the future repeating the past.

No matter which nation governed this land nor whatever political subdivisions were created, external pressures have never erased the idea of being *Lorrain* even though it has been more than two centuries since there has been a political entity named Lorraine. The will of the people to live in peace with themselves has overcome long-standing differences in spite of occasional outbursts of what might be termed a mixture of patriotism, nationalism, chauvinism and self determination. The result today is an area, almost unique in Europe, where multi-culturism is on-going and successful.

Lorraine was formed in 843 when Charlemagne's empire was divided among his three grand-sons. The central portion

The Swans of Lorraine

was then ruled by King Lothaire who gave his name to the land which later evolved to Lothringen in German and Lorraine in French. Because of its critical geographic position between culturally and linguistically different groups it became a constant arena of wars and invasion. Through years of battles, physical and political, the kingdom was reduced to a duchy having lost much of its territory. In 1552, France occupied the chief cities: Metz, Toul and Verdun. A devastating time followed the onset of the Thirty Years War which began in 1618 when the casualties of that war and plague decimated the area.

In 1663 the duchy was again invaded by French troops and also in 1670, after which French control became total. By the Treaty of Ryswick, King Louis XIV restored the duchy to Duke Leopold who had been in exile in Austria. By then the population had been reduced by half and eighty villages had ceased to exist. This occasioned a wave of immigrants, mostly from Germany, Switzerland, Burgundy and Savoy. In 1702 and again in 1714 the French sent troops into Lorraine in an attempt to conquer it but Duke Leopold managed to get international recognition for neutrality. His son Francis Stephen married Maria Theresa of Austria and later became Francis I of the Holy Roman Empire. In a bizarre bit of politics he swapped the Duchy of Lorraine for the Duchy of Tuscany. Stanislas Leszczynski who was forced to abdicate as king of Poland became the new Duke of Lorraine, thanks to his father-in-law Louis XV. At the death of Stanislas in 1766 Lorraine finally became a part of France, his daughter and heir Marie being the queen of France.

In 1790 Lorraine was divided into four *départements*: Meurthe, Meuse, Moselle and Vosges. A small area was ceded to Prussia in 1815. Village populations were again ravaged by a cholera epidemic in 1832. In the following decades, under Prussian leadership, German nationalism sparked a series of aggressive actions to create a new nation. The last of these was the Franco-Prussian war of 1870. After a quick victory and with their army occupying part of France, and using the pretense of the large German speaking population along their common border, the newly unified Germany annexed the department of Moselle, a small part of Vosges, and Alsace. A flood of French speaking refugees left the annexed territory because they refused to live under German rule. In an attempt to ameliorate the loss of Moselle the name of the *département* of Meurthe was changed to Meurthe et Moselle. It was never changed back.

The loss of more than 150,000 French speakers increased the percentage of German speakers in what was now a *Reichsland* called Lothringen. In an effort to re-populate the area the German government encouraged Germans to take advantage of the plethora of vacant farmland with only limited success. They then invited Italian workers to seek employment in Moselle's many mines.

The process of germanization began with the prohibition to schools to teach in any language other than German. In France an analogy of the situation was made as of a mother and daughter being separated. By the time Lothringen again became Lorraine after the conclusion of the First World War in 1918, two whole generations had grown up speaking only German; at least in public. When the transfer of sovereignty was made official by the Treaty of Versailles in 1919 France forbade the use of German in an effort to francosize its new citizens. The resistance of the German speaking population created animosity which continued for years between the two ethnic groups. Over 100,000 ethnic Germans were expelled from Lorraine and Alsace. Families of mixed ethnicity faced bitter choices. The expulsion created a labor shortage and workers were invited to come to the area. When few French returned to their former homeland, foreign workers were invited, the majority of which were Poles from the area around Poznan, which was in Germany until the end of the war. Others came from Czechoslovakia, Hungary and Slovenia. These had been under Austrian rule and all had some knowledge of German but not French. Often it was not until the second generation that these immigrants learned the language of their new nation.

Bitterness and charges of unpatriotic activities lead to endless and pointless debates about what a *real* Frenchman was. Teachers were required to begin teaching in French – cold turkey – when they themselves were not fluent in that language. A separatist movement began seeking cultural and political autonomy, exacerbated by the French government's recalcitrance. Grudgingly the government relented and allowed some teaching in German in the schools and for religious education. Just when Lorraine had learned to live in peace with its diverse ethnicity, the Second World War brought the re-annexation of its eastern portion to the Third Reich. This time the area was combined with Saarland and the perceived oppression of ethnic Germans was thought to have ended. Many ethnic French were expelled from the area and again many German speakers were brought in to re-germanize it.

When General De Gaulle organized the Free French armed forces they chose as their symbol *La Croix de Lorraine* to counter *La Croix Gammée*, the swastika. The majority of the people, regardless of ethnicity, considered the Nazi regime repugnant. Those that changed their allegiance during the occupation suffered most when the battle front passed through it in the fall of 1944. The majority of the *Lorrains* considered the Americans as liberators.

In 1873 when the last Prussian soldier left that part of Lorraine that would remain French, a broken Cross of Lorraine was placed in the basilica of Sion, 20 km south of Nancy, with the inscription in the unique dialect of Lorraine 'Ce n'a me po tojo' (C'est n'est pas pour toujours) – 'This is not forever'. When Lorraine was re-united with France in 1918 a new inscription was added. 'Ce n'ato me po tojo.' (Ce n'était pas pour toujours) – 'This was not forever'. In 1946 the broken cross was replace by a new one with a new inscription. 'Estour inc po tojo' (Maintenant c'est pour toujours) 'Now it is forever'.

The author had the distinct pleasure of spending two years of his youth in Lorraine, falling in love with the inhabitants and the amalgamation of cultures that make it unique in France. The experiences and friendships of this time centered mostly at my workplace in Toul and after hours having a few *Kronenbourgs* at Le Café Deux Hémisphères in Nancy or Cyro's in Toul. It was a wonderful time of my life.

Phillip Varady

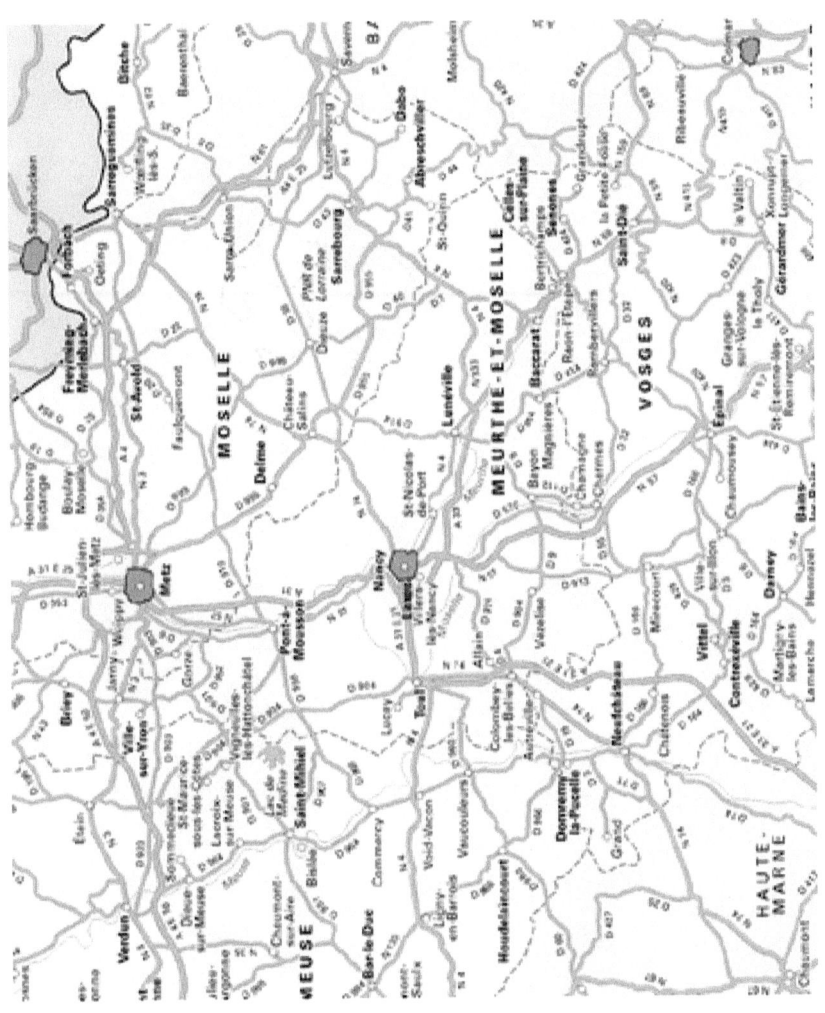

The Swans of Lorraine

Phillip Varady

Chapter 1

My first memory ever was of me standing in the doorway of my parent's bedroom, watching as my father motioned to me to come forward into the room. He never spoke much because he would always wind up coughing. He was coughing then but when he stopped there was a smile on his face as if he was about to give me a surprise. After taking a step or two he signaled me to stop and picked up a rifle that was lying on the floor, putting the muzzle under his chin. I remember the sound as it fired and I remember the wall behind him being splattered with blood. I remember screaming. I do not remember being only four years of age.

Next, I remember Monsieur Dosé, one of my teachers, kneeling in front of me in the headmaster's office.

"Édouard, are you feeling better now?"

"Yes, Monsieur Dosé. I feel quite well now. May I go home?"

"We've sent for your mother, Édouard. She should be here any moment," the headmaster said. "What happened to cause this, Max," he asked Monsieur Dosé.

"I don't know, Sir. He was reciting and suddenly went into a trance of sorts. He seemed not to be aware of anything around him but when I took his hand he willingly came along with me here. He seems different now . . . somehow."

My mother arrived, very distraught that someone should summon her to the school. She rushed to my side and sat next to me on the bench.

"He seems to be all right now, Madame Jannot," the headmaster said.

Not trusting his evaluation she quickly looked me over to determine if I had suffered any physical injury, having been told nothing of my condition. She squeezed my shoulders and elbows and felt my head, for I bump I supposed. When she could find nothing apparent she turned to the two men and was about to speak. I stood up and took her hand.

"I'm well now, Maman," I said.

She didn't understand.

"What happened?" she asked them.

"Maman, it's over," I said, smiling. "I'm well now."

Whether Monsieur Dosé and the headmaster knew about my father, I was never certain. I always thought that everybody knew and for some reason they never mentioned him. But my mother now knew my meaning and without a word we left the school and went home. We spoke no more of it. It was October of 1925, one month before my seventh birthday.

My childhood in Saint Mihiel was difficult. The boys my age treated me differently, as though I *were* different. I was once, but I am no longer as I used to be. The more I tried to be like them the more they thought that I was pretending. After a few years I gave up trying and accepted my . . . I cannot call it isolation; I was never excluded . . . it was more of never being *in*cluded but being tolerated, still being able to call them my friends. I often wondered how much of this was because of my father's decision to end his life or my reaction to it.

My best friend was my sister Eliane who was born shortly before my father's death. She became aware of how my friends treated me and would often volunteer to keep me occupied when I was left alone. We decided to teach ourselves Latin and went about it quite determinedly until someone who knew that language heard us speak it and informed us of how badly we were pronouncing everything. We gave it up in favor of chess. I constantly told myself how content I was with the way fate was leading my life; Eliane and I could not have been happier with each other. The rest of the world did not matter all that much.

On my fourteenth birthday my mother called me into her bedroom to show me something. From the pages of a book she removed a photograph and handed it to me. It was a picture of a young man in uniform, not a French uniform; at least not one that I had ever seen. He was seated in a chair at an angle to the camera but his face was fully forward. He was very stern looking, a handsome man, clean-shaven with his hair combed flat atop his head.

"Who is this?" I asked.

"His name is Rheinhold Popp."

I stared at the photograph thinking 'S*o, this man is Rheinhold Popp . . . and why . . . ?*'

"He's your father!"

Just like that she made my sister my half sister. I threw the photograph on the bed and ran from the room. I had nowhere to go so I wandered into the woods until I came to the slope that dropped away from the town on two sides. From this location I could see nothing of civilization except the railroad tracks below. I sat there for a long time thinking about what all this really meant; how it would change anything; how it would affect my love for Eliane. I thought it odd that I was more concerned about my relationship with my sister than I was about which absent man was my father. When I realized that I had a hunger to know more, I returned to the house.

My mother was preparing supper. She heard me come in but did not turn around. I stood there waiting for her to face me but she would not. What anger I had gave way to curiosity. In the end I succumbed.

"May I see the photograph again, Maman?"

"It's where you left it, Édouard."

I was surprised, thinking that she would have hidden it away, never to allow me to see it again because I had reacted so badly. *She was forcing the issue; she wanted me to know this and more.* I retrieved the photograph and studied it closely, looking at every detail of his face. I went to a mirror to compare his features with mine. With honest impartiality I had to admit that there were similarities. I looked next at a photograph of my parents and saw no such similarities between me and . . . the man next to my mother. I placed the two photographs side by side and returned to the kitchen.

"Are you going to tell me about him?"

"Yes. What do you want to know?"

"Everything! Why did you wait until today to tell me?"

"Where is Eliane?"

"I don't know. She's not in the house."

"I don't want her to know. If you feel that you must tell her, I cannot stop you."

"I won't tell her."

She dried her hands at sat at the table. I sat opposite her. She leaned back in the chair, folding her hands on the table and looked into my eyes. I could not discern any emotion in her voice or on her face.

"Your father. . . *Eliane's* father was conscripted when it was obvious that war would come; we were married only two months, I was only sixteen years old. Within months the town was in German hands. The first time I met *your* father was two years later when he came with some other officers to Grand-père's butcher shop. There were other butcher shops in Saint Mihiel but they came here because Grand-père spoke perfect German. Your father was a Lieutenant in the artillery. I spoke German well enough but he spoke very good French . . . the only one of all his comrades. They had been coming to buy once a month; they were very polite and paid in silver. Grand-père didn't mind but Uncle Richard spoke against it. After a few visits he and I would chat about things. He would ask about my life and family and I about his. It was about this time that a wounded soldier, a neighboring farmer, was allowed to come through the German lines; he had lost both his legs. He said that he thought that my husband had died in the same battle, but could not say for certain."

"Suddenly my brother saw my casual conversations with Rheinhold in a different light. He began accusing me of things that were untrue; Grand-père quickly put a stop to it. 'So what if your sister is nice to our customers . . . business is business', he said. A few days later your father came into the shop and Grand-père congratulated him in German because he saw that he had been promoted to Captain. It pleased your father that he understood German, but in speaking with us he had learned that Uncle Richard did not have the same skill. What he didn't know was that my brother hated Germans and refused to learn anything of that language when our father tried to teach it to us. We both remember the stories that Grand-père told us of the hardships that his family suffered after the Franco-Prussian War when they chose to leave St. Avold. When Rheinhold came the next time, Grand-père was sick and had stayed at the house. He asked me in German if he could see me that evening. I didn't answer but I think he knew that I wanted to but was too afraid to say yes. Months went by and he never made mention of it again."

"We all knew that there were several taverns where female company could be had, so I didn't think of him that way. Finally, I wrote a note and kept it with me until he came again. When I wrapped the meat that he bought I slipped it inside. It was late when he came and he left just before dawn. We were together almost every weekend for the next year but after the Americans liberated the city, I never saw him again. I was seven months pregnant but we both suspected that my husband was still alive."

"What did your husband say when he saw me?"

"He thought it no excuse that I assumed that he was dead. He accused me sleeping with one of the farmers that we knew. I denied it and after a few days he chose a different one to accuse. Another denial was followed by another accusation until he had named everyone he knew. I never told him the truth. He had lost a part of his foot in the war and his lungs had been damaged by the gas. It took him a year before he could work again. By then he had accepted you but everyone knew that you were not his."

"Why did he do it?"

"He was in pain every day because of his lungs and often spoke of wanting to die. I thought if we could have a child he would stop all that talk. After Eliane was born the worst of his friends teased him that the mystery father had struck again. He threatened to kill me unless I revealed the name. I was very scared; I believed that he would hurt me. He had turned most of his friends into enemies through his wild accusations. He would go everywhere with his rifle. I showed Rheinhold's picture to him and he just laughed. Five minutes later I heard the shot."

"Why did *you* do it?"

"I'll tell you anything you want to know about your father but the rest is none of your affair. When you get older you will know the answer."

I stood up. I wanted to know more but right now I needed to be alone. As I was leaving the room she called to me.

"Find your sister; we will eat in fifteen minutes."

My sister, yes, my half sister! That thought took away some of the joy that I was experiencing from knowing that my mother's husband was not my father. How could I tell Eliane how glad I was to learn that the bastard that fathered her was not *my* father? I wanted to know more . . . about him, about Germany, about being German . . . well, half German. Never again would I share the sentiment that everyone else in this area had, *we taught those bastards a lesson, didn't we!* But I was still French, this was still my home, these were still my people. W*ould there come a time when we could forget all that and live in peace, side by side?*

I saw Eliane as she was coming home from her friend's house; I hurried to her. When we were together, I took hold of her hands. She said nothing . . . but then she was accustomed to my showing some sign of affection. Her straight brown hair fell over her shoulders, her bangs framed her face. The few freckles that she had when she was younger were mostly faded away. Her face was a bit long but what one noticed most was the fact that even when she wasn't smiling, it appeared that she was about to. From our features one could not say 'She looks French but you look like a damn German.' We both looked just like everyone else in Saint Mihiel. I still loved her more than any other person in the world . . . except of course . . . no, more than any other person in the world. I put my hand on her cheek.

"Give me a kiss," I said as I knelt on one knee in front of her.

She kissed me politely on the lips and I hugged her.

"What is this all about?"

"I think you are the best sister in the world and I am very happy to be your brother. I love you Eliane."

She gave me another kiss and smiled at me.

"Are you up to something?"

"No," I said and left it at that.

I stood up and we began walking toward the house. I looked at Eliane; she was looking at me. She accepted my answer without another thought or question. She took my hand in hers and squeezed it.

That summer I worked part-time in the shop with Uncle Richard, one of my cousins and my mother; Grand-père was not well. He advised me to continue my education as much as I could and not think about becoming a butcher; Uncle Richard had three sons. In the evenings my mother would take Eliane and me to see her father and tend to his needs. I took the opportunity to question him about the war and particularly about the Germans. I became fascinated with his recollections but was careful not to express any admiration for the Germans or limit my inquiries to them. My mother was aware of what I was doing and how I felt.

When Eliane was elsewhere, I questioned my mother about my father; sometimes asking the same questions days apart hoping to hear different answers or more of what may have been once forgotten information. There came a point when she could tell me no more . . . or decided to put an end to this. It was about the same time that Grand-père died. My cousin Jacques-Henri began to work in the shop full time when I went back to school. Uncle Richard wanted to give my mother only one third of the income but after a heated quarrel they agreed on forty-five per cent.

I took my grandfather's advice and gave up all thought of ever working in the shop. My grades had always been good but now I determined to excel. Eliane and I would test each other on our lessons at the expense of play or socializing with our friends. The boys that had once tolerated me became distant; I had not gained their admiration for my good grades but instead their envy and displeasure. My interest in the war led me to investigate its causes and results and the more that I learned the more I realized that I had to go farther afield to understand the whole story. I became so deeply involved in it that one day I was aware that I had found my life's calling.

When I completed my studies at the lycée, first in my class, everyone was surprised to hear that I had been accepted at the Sorbonne; it didn't surprise me a bit. My mother allowed Eliane to accompany me to Paris when the time came to register. I could have done it through the mail but there was another matter to consider . . . my subsistence. The registration process took only a few hours and then we investigated notices offering assistance that were posted in the hall. Not finding anything decent the first day, we rented a cheap room on the boulevard Saint Germain. It was two days and many other equally bad situations later that we came to the home of Monsieur Thouvignon. His offer was for a room and meals in return for tutoring his child. It seemed like a wonderful position.

His home was on a busy street, the rue Descartes, with many restaurants and shops. At street level there was a curio shop selling artifacts and trinkets from the Far East and India. We rang the bell and waited; Eliane gave me an encouraging smile. The door was opened by a dark skinned young lady wearing a scarf about her head. I could not determine her origin but thought that her speech would offer some clue.

"May I help you?" she asked in perfect French.

"I would like to speak to Monsieur Thouvignon concerning the position he advertised for a tutor."

"Come upstairs, please."

She gave Eliane a curious look, no doubt wondering why a young girl would accompany me in a search for a position. At the top of the stairs she turned to us.

"Please wait here," she said and hurried off.

Presently a woman came to the door, very fashionably dressed with her black hair held together by many combs. She stood some distance from us and eyed us carefully before she spoke.

"I am Madame Thouvignon. Will this be your first year at the Sorbonne?"

"Yes, Madame! Is the position still available?"

"We have had many applicants but as yet have not decided."

I stared at her mouth. Her pronunciation caught my ear and it led me to believe that she was not French. When she spoke again she was staring at Eliane.

"What is your name and who is your pretty companion?"

"I'm sorry. I am Édouard Jannot and this is my sister, Eliane. My mother allowed her to accompany me to register for school. Neither of us has ever been to Paris before."

"What is your birth date, my dear," she asked Eliane.

"The first of June, 1922, Madame."

"Wonderful! Come along; Monsieur Thouvignon will be home shortly. You may wait in the parlor for him. I will send Laure-Anne down to meet you both. She is two days older than you, Eliane."

We sat on two elegant chairs in front of the windows that overlooked the street. On the walls were several portraits of very well dressed gentlemen—no women. The tables were all topped with marble and the carpet was Persian. Eliane made some hand gestures and facial expressions to indicate that she was duly impressed with her surroundings. Madame Thouvignon re-entered the room.

"I have just discovered that my daughter is not at home. A few phone calls will find her. It shouldn't take long."

She went on about her business and presently the flash of a person went by us in the hallway toward the kitchen. We waited another few minutes until a young girl entered the room and stood before me. I was surprised that she was only fourteen; she looked older. She was not wearing her school uniform but had on a dress that a young lady might wear to some event. Her dark wavy hair fell over her shoulders, front and back, and her dark eyes drew my gaze. She was very attractive but it was her eyes, the way they animated her face that made a lasting first impression on me.

"Nice to meet you, Monsieur Jannot. I am Laure-Anne."

She smiled and extended her hand to me as I got up and we shook briefly. I could not help staring at her; seeing a young woman, not a fourteen-year-old girl. She turned to Eliane.

"I'm so glad that you could come along with your brother, Eliane. Having a brother is a luxury that I miss. You must love your sister very much," she said to me, "to want her with you on your first trip to Paris."

How very grown-up she seemed, in her outwardness and the insinuation that I think she made. I was impressed that she knew our names; I suppose that her mother supplied them. I felt a bit defensive and just smiled nervously in answer to her statement. She asked me which subjects I excelled in and after I told her I asked about those in which she needed the most help.

"All of them," she said unashamedly. "I don't like school."

"Your father expects that a tutor will improve your grades. Do you think so?"

"My father wants me to go to a university but I know that will not happen. It's all so boring. My schedule for the next term requires me to learn German. Who needs that?"

"Really? Me too! I'm eager to learn another language. Eliane and I tried to learn Latin on our own but gave it up. I think German would be easier."

Eliane joined our conversation, recalling those days and the three of us shared stories about our schools. After a few minutes Monsieur Thouvignon appeared and Laure-Anne took Eliane and left us alone. He was quite a bit taller than me and held himself erect, which gave him an impressive air. His suit looked expensive and I had the impression that he had never gotten his hands dirty at work.

"Please sit down, Édouard. Do you drink coffee?"

"I have had some . . . yes. Yes, I drink coffee, Sir."

"Fariza, bring some coffee and pastis for us," he called out to his housekeeper.

"Yes, Monsieur Thouvignon," she answered from outside the room.

He settled into his chair and leaned back and crossed his legs.

"Do you have your bac with you," he asked.

"Yes Sir." I extended my hand with the graduation certificate in it. If he had extended his hand a bit more he could have taken it but he did not make that effort and I had to come out of my seat to reach him.

He looked it over carefully; he could not help but notice that I was awarded the highest honors. With admiration and a bit of surprise, he handed it back to me. He asked many questions concerning my abilities, especially my ability to be effective in my dealing with a fourteen-year-old girl. I mentioned Eliane and suggested that he might question her to determine that. He seemed satisfied.

"And what shall be your field of endeavor, Édouard?"

"I intend to be an historian, a university professor and later a writer. Perhaps, also, an advisor to our government on our relations with Germany."

"Do you have any advice for them at present?"

"Yes. The treaty of Versailles was so harsh that it allowed Chancellor Hitler to use general disdain for it to rally popular support around himself and his Nationalist Socialist Party. He has made known his desire to overturn every one of its provisions and regain every loss suffered by Germany including the re-annexation of Alsace-Lorraine. Now is the time to stop him militarily; he will only get stronger if we do nothing."

"Mmmm, very astute, Édouard. I agree with you but I doubt if our government or the British government will have the backbone to act. Do you think a future war will be a repeat of the Great War?"

"No, Sir. Germany has built an all-new military, faster tanks, faster aircraft, and a more mechanized force. We have merely patched and repaired ours and still rely on fixed defenses to keep them in check."

"Do you have a prediction then?"

"The Schlieffen Plan would have worked if von Moltke had executed it correctly. I believe that they will use the same plan with success this time. They will have us in months."

Monsieur Thouvignon was standing at the window with his back toward me. I could not tell if it disturbed him to hear an eighteen year old predict the overtaking of our homeland by a hated enemy in so short a time. He remained silent for minutes.

"What sort of work does your father do?"

"I have never met him, Sir. He was called away near the end of the war, just months before I was born. He was a captain in the artillery; he never came back."

I felt something that I had never felt before; I'm not sure if it was pride or a lack of guilt. I had finally acknowledged my real father.

"A shame, a real shame. My sympathies, Édouard. Too many good men were no more than cannon fodder. I too fear that war will come again. So, then your sister is . . ."

"Her father is Jannot. My mother never told me about my real father until I was fourteen and asked that I not tell Eliane. I have respected her wish."

Fariza returned with the refreshments and was serving them when Madame Thouvignon popped her head in the room.

"Are you finished, Jean-Marie? If so I will join you," she said.

"Yes, we are finished. I think we have an excellent candidate in this young man."

As she was exiting the room he called after her.

"Nathalie, bring Laure-Anne downstairs but don't say anything."

I watched as Monsieur Thouvignon poured his pastis into his coffee; I did the same. We sipped the hot anise flavored brew as Fariza brought another serving for Madame who reappeared directing the two girls in front of her into the parlor.

"What do you think of this one, Laure-Anne?" Monsieur Thouvignon asked.

"He's the most intelligent and least pretentious, Papa . . . and we will both be studying German next term."

"So then, you would like me to choose Monsieur Jannot?"

"I would like you to choose Monsieur Jannot, Papa," she said.

"Very well, Édouard. You have a position here that will last as long as your effectiveness and good behavior does. Understood?

"Yes, Sir. I understand perfectly."

I thought that Laure-Anne's little formality had something to do with a prior understanding between father and daughter but I did not let it concern me. I was elated and Eliane was also, more than obviously. Monsieur Thouvignon had Fariza show me my quarters on the third floor—across the hall from hers. It was not a bad room; about four meters square with windows facing the rear courtyard.

Monsieur Thouvignon insisted that Eliane and I stay at his house until Saturday before we returned to Saint Mihiel. He drove me to the hotel on boulevard Saint Germain to retrieve our possessions. Eliane shared Laure-Anne's room and I spent a restless night listening to the rain bouncing off the mansard in my new quarters. The next morning, while it was still dark, there was a tapping on my door. I opened it to discover Fariza wearing only a thin cotton nightgown, which the light from her room turned nearly transparent. Her dark curly hair hung almost to her waist.

"Would you like me to call you with the others when breakfast is ready?"

"Yes, if you would, please. Thank you."

She turned to go, stopping half way around, allowing me to see the shape of her breasts through the garment, then turned back to me and stood very close.

"If ever I can do anything else for you, do not hesitate to ask, eh?"

"I will. Thank you Fariza."

I took a slight step backward and folded my hands in front of me to hide my embarrassment. She smiled, knowing what I had done. She turned to go but walked very slowly as if waiting for me to engage her in further conversation. I felt obliged to say something.

"Fariza, is that an Arabic name?"

"It is Berber. I'll wager that an intelligent young man like you will be able to tell me the difference, or perhaps if you don't know you will be curious enough to find out by the time you return," she replied without turning around.

We both returned to our rooms. I waited until I heard her go downstairs before I came out to use the WC and then washed and dressed. Thankfully, others were up and about when I entered the dining room.

My benefactor gave us a tour of Paris on Thursday and Friday afternoons, and drove us to the Gare de l'Est Saturday morning to catch our train. Away from his daughter's hearing he instructed me to keep my opinions and observations concerning a future war to myself, to confine my thoughts to her school's curriculum. Eliane and Laure-Anne had become very good friends—lifelong friends. On the train coming back home Eliane was very quiet and I suspected very sad.

"What is this," I asked, pointing to a small white paper bag that she was clutching.

"Oh," she exclaimed, and her sadness disappeared. In turn she brought out three articles, describing them briefly. "Whole black peppers from Zanzibar, paprika from Hungary and Olive oil from Spain."

"Why do you have them," I asked.

"They are gifts, samples, Madame Thouvignon called them."

I knew there was more to this but could not imagine what.

"Read the bottom of the labels," Eliane suggested.

Printed on each one was the formula 'Imported from …… by Sachs, Thouvignon & Cie.'

"So, he is in the import business."

"That's not all," Eliane gushed. "Madame Thouvignon was born Nathalie Sachs in Prague, Czechoslovakia. Her father is a Jew but Laure-Anne says that her mother never was. Her grandmother was Catholic and also married a Jew but was allowed to raise her mother Catholic because she never had a son."

"Did she tell you why it's Sachs, Thouvignon and not Thouvignon, Sachs?"

"Monsieur Sachs's suppliers were more valuable then Monsieur Thouvignon's markets. Perhaps as part of the bargain he married his partner's daughter."

"Was it an arranged marriage?"

"Laure-Anne says it was but swears that they are devoted to each other."

"Hmmm, how do you like Laure-Anne?"

"Oh, she's very nice. She's like an older sister but she is so considerate. She knows so many things."

"What things?"

"Girl things. Don't bother asking; it's none of your business."

"Oh, *those* kinds of things. Don't worry; I won't say a word to Maman."

"It's not *that!* You're getting the wrong idea."

"Well, I suppose then that you had better correct me."

Eliane wasn't fooled by that ploy and just smiled at me. She put a hand behind my neck and pulled my head toward her, giving me a kiss.

"Édouard, you're so . . . You know what you are, don't you?"

"Wonderful?"

"Yes, I'll give you that. But don't let it go to your head; you have flaws, you know."

"Me? No. I'm perfect. You told me so yourself."

"Well, Laure-Anne saw you staring at Fariza and was willing to bet that the girl would have you in bed within a week."

I was suddenly very warm and unable to respond.

"Oh, Édouard! You've done it already?" Eliane exclaimed, covering her mouth with her hand as she giggled. She wasn't condemning me; rather she thought it was amusing.

"No," I protested. "I haven't laid a finger on her, I swear."

"Ooooh, how very modern we are! Going to the Sorbonne and having a mistress and only eighteen years old. Maman will be so proud . . . or amused, eh?"

"Eliane, I swear. It never happened."

She looked at me in my distress and believed me. We never lied to each other and she knew it. She patted my cheek sympathetically.

"Well, don't give up hope. It hasn't been a week yet."

I suggested that she write to Laure-Anne as soon as we returned home and ask our mother about spending the summer in Paris next year if it was acceptable to Monsieur Thouvignon. As it turned out, everyone was pleased with that arrangement and Eliane would be permitted to go to Paris if her grades were satisfactory. Her grades were always superior. Our three-way relationship would grow very close; we cared for and respected each other immensely.

By being patient and inventive, I slowly aroused some sense of self-improvement in Laure-Anne and she gradually took interest in her studies. There was not an immediate correlation between interest and better grades however. That next summer she and Eliane formed a bond that surprised yet pleased me. It also proved to be a great benefit to me, one that would have gone unappreciated except for the openness and total honesty that Eliane and I shared. She told me that she had reminded Laure-Anne that I would hold my position only as long as I was effective.

Near the end of my second year at the Thouvignon's, a change came over Laure-Anne. Mostly it was an interest in my personal affairs and a constant desire to know my thoughts on different matters. She convinced her mother to allow her to have her long hair cut to make it more like some of the fashionable dos that were so popular in the cinema. She would ask my advice on personal things which she had not previously sought. Most tellingly she would ask very roundabout questions concerning Fariza which were only thinly veiled attempts to discern the extent of our relationship.

Fariza continued to tempt me with her near nudity, acting as though it was quite normal for mature people to comport themselves in such a manner. After a while it *did* seem normal and we would talk together most mornings in the hallway, I wearing only my shorts. One Sunday morning Laure-Anne came up to the third floor to get Fariza for some chore (something she was forbidden to do, she should have called to her from the floor below). This morning Fariza was late, which is probably why Laure-Anne was sent to get her. I had already dressed.

"Fariza," Laure-Anne called out as she neared the top of the stairs, "is that appropriate attire to be wearing in front of Monsieur Jannot?"

"It could not be helped, M'am'selle. We both came out of our rooms at the same time," she lied. "I will try to be more careful in the future."

"My mother needs you immediately in the kitchen."

Laure-Anne seemed to dismiss the matter as Fariza returned to her room to dress. I too would have gone back to my room except that Laure-Anne began to question me about her schoolwork. We continued speaking until Fariza started down the stairs. After taking a few steps she turned.

"Does Madame know that you came up to the third floor, M'am'selle?"

"No she doesn't, Fariza, but if she hears of it she shall also hear of what I discovered here. You'd best hurry; she's waiting."

Laure-Anne waited until she was out of sight and then turned her attention to me.

"Is she sharing her bed with you yet, Édouard?"

"She is trying very hard to make it so but I have resisted so far."

"Really? Has she kissed you?"

"She has come very close on occasion."

"This close?" She put her hands on my shoulders and standing on her toes, brought her face very close to mine.

"Closer." I said nervously.

She brushed her lips against mine.

"This close?"

"No."

She moved her hands slowly around my neck and pressed her lips to mine. I held her gently until she finished, unable to hide my arousal.

"Wait for me Édouard . . . please. Will you do that?"

"I . . . yes." I did not want to say more; I wasn't entirely sure what she meant.

She quickly descended from her forbidden zone and I waited a bit before joining the Thouvignons for breakfast. I was pleased that Laure-Anne did not act childishly by making little gestures or knowing looks. The talk this morning centered on the intentions of Chancellor Hitler in the matter of Germany's claim on the Sudetenland. I commented only briefly not being able to focus on the subject; I was becoming more and more delighted with Laure-Anne's show of affection. I had no idea what there was about me that could have precipitated such an action.

"What are your plans for today?" Monsieur Thouvignon asked me.

"I thought that I would rummage through the book stalls along the Quai Saint Michel. One never knows what one might come across."

"May I go with him, Papa? " Laure-Anne blurted out, ". . . if you had no other plans."

Madame Thouvignon's face showed instant displeasure.

"I'm sure that Monsieur Jannot would enjoy at least one day a week away from you. Isn't that so Édouard?" she said, almost forcing me to agree with her.

"I don't mind Madame, and besides, we could practice our German for her exam next week."

"No!" Monsieur Thouvignon snapped. "You may go but no German in public."

"Really, Jean-Marie, don't you think that . . ."

Monsieur Thouvignon held up his hand and Madame Thouvignon held her tongue. He looked at her over the rim of his coffee cup but spoke to Laure-Anne.

"And you will insure that Monsieur Jannot delivers you promptly at noon at your grandfather's house. We will be spending the day there."

"Thank you, Papa. When did you plan to go, Monsieur Jannot?"

"We could leave right after breakfast. There is this Greek gentleman who owns a restaurant just a street away from the Seine who tells me such fascinating stories from the war about the Turks and the British and the Italians . . . not to mention the Bulgarians. I think you will enjoy meeting him."

We were on our way in ten minutes, taking a half hour to walk to the rue de la Huchette where my Greek historian had his place of business. Not once did either of us refer to this morning's event. It was only when we were standing in front of the restaurant, deciding whether to go inside or stay in the cool sunshine that Laure-Anne took my hand when she saw the proprietor approaching.

"Ah, good morning Édouard. How's it going today?"

"Very well, Théodore, and you?"

"Well, I think my day will be a bit nicer now that you bring such a lovely companion to my establishment."

"This is Laure-Anne. She is my . . ." I hesitated, thinking which word would best describe our relationship.

"You don't have to tell me what she is. Her eyes tell me. Am I right Mademoiselle? I am, I am; only a blind man would miss it. Come inside, sit!"

We took the table furthest from the entrance; we were the only patrons inside.

"Coffee and . . . coffee?" he said, looking at Laure-Anne.

"No. A *panaché* please."

"A *panaché?* You?" I asked, very surprised.

"If you think it is inappropriate I will have a coffee."

"Well . . . no, if that's what you want. What would your father say?"

"He allows me to have a little beer now and then."

I nodded to Théodore and he left us.

"Thank you," Laure-Anne said quietly.

"Are you feeling grown up today?"

"Yes, very mature. Did you notice?"

The Swans of Lorraine

She glanced at Théodore who had his back to us, then leaned toward me and kissed me, placing her hand on my cheek. I returned her kiss. I was thrilled.

Théodore served us and pulled another chair to the table to join us.

"Did I ever tell you about the time I met this Churchill fellow?"

"Yes, Théodore. Now that you've impressed the young lady, tell me about the Bulgarians and Macedonians and why they got involved in all this?"

Théodore's story lasted for three coffees and two panachés. We thanked him and strolled to the Quai Saint Michel hand in hand. Although we looked at some books, we were for the most part, looking at each other. Later at her grandfather's house we kept a respectful distance lest someone was watching from a window.

"I will be thinking of you all day," she said in German when the housekeeper answered the door.

"Be careful," I warned her in the same language. "Your mother will have me out in a minute if she knew. And I will be thinking of you."

Walking back to the rue Descartes I wondered about the wisdom of this morning's actions. To say that my position would be more secure if none of that had ever happened was obvious but I would not have missed it for the world. What am I to do? *Be careful, very careful!* I know that I could remain above suspicion in my day-to-day dealings but I had some misgivings as to Laure-Anne's ability to do the same. I must stress to her the many ways in which one reveals one's feelings: unknowingly, unwisely and sometimes with abandon.

On my return to the house I went into the basement, which was beneath the curio shop, where Monsieur Thouvignon maintained a wine cellar of sorts. I found a bottle of Chablis and went upstairs to the kitchen, opened it, took a glass and retreated to my room. I would have to find my own dinner with the Thouvignons dining at his father-in-law's home and Fariza on her afternoon off. I poured a half glass and swallowed it in large gulps. It was cool and very refreshing; I refilled it. I smiled to myself at my unusual behavior. *Are you feeling grown up today, Édouard?*

It was the warmest day of the year so far, so I stripped down to my underwear and began to compose a subject review for the exams that Laure-Anne would have next week. About an hour later and with nearly half the bottle emptied, I began my own for the three weeks of exams that I would have following hers. There came a knock at my door. It could only be one person.

"Yes?" I called out without rising from my desk.

Fariza entered the room, dressed as any young woman in Paris in 1938 would have looked. She seemed very different, very alluring, and even had on a bit of make-up. She approached my desk and sipped some wine and smiled at me.

"When the cat's away . . ."

"I have permission," I said feeling very smug. "And who are you to accuse me. I didn't know you were permitted to go out in public without your scarf."

She finished the glass without comment and handed it to me.

"May I have more?"

I thought that since we were alone in the house, this might lead to something. I poured the glass full not really believing that what I had just imagined might actually happen but I was a bit curious and was in the frame of mind to play this game with her. She drank half of it and sat on my bed.

"I have a problem, Édouard, and only you can help me."

"What is it?"

"My employment here may end shortly. I have just come from my father's house and he informed me of his intention to have me marry a friend of the family. The man is of the same age as our employer. I know him well and do not like him one bit."

"Will your father force you to marry him?"

"Yes, I'm afraid so; but I have a plan and that's where your help is needed."

"I'll do what I can but what might that be?"

"If I was living in my father's home, his word would be accepted concerning my virginity but as it is . . . the groom's female relatives will examine me to determine that. If I am no virgin there will be no wedding and I will continue here . . . just as I wanted. Do you understand what I require of you?"

I did and was instantly fearful of jeopardizing my relationship with Laure-Anne. I did not want to do this and had only the minimum of sympathy for Fariza's plight. When I looked at her I knew that she could read my thoughts.

"Is there no one else that you know better that would do this?"

"The men that I know better would not dare to do it for fear of being murdered by my father. You are the only one that can keep this misery from me. I need your help, Édouard. Please do this for me."

"I'm sorry, Fariza, but there is more at risk for me than you know. I cannot jeopardize everything. I hope you understand."

"There's no need to apologize. I know that this is a strange request and that you are already risking your position by your involvement with Laure-Anne."

She smiled at me with a knowing look. She came back to my desk and finished the wine and extended the empty glass toward me. I refilled it wondering if she was making a threat. I was not quick to confirm or deny what she implied but sought to glean a bit more from her.

"What makes you think that there is anything improper in our relationship?"

"Ah ha! There is! You would have denied outright if it were not so. So, have you taken her to bed yet?"

"You are totally mistaken. There is nothing, absolutely nothing between us."

"Édouard, I have nothing to lose by making an accusation at the dinner table. I will certainly be let go immediately, but then I would have to give up my position if I married anyway. If there is anything at all, the guilt on that young girl's face will confirm my suspicions. Do you want to risk that?"

I was angry to be played this way. I was afraid to risk her threat of confrontation. I felt so helpless, so . . . pitiful.

"Come on, Édouard. Am I so ugly that you are repulsed by me?"

"No, not at all. You don't understand."

"Ah, you are in love, is that it? She need never know. She *will* never know."

Fariza slipped out of her skirt and removed her blouse. She stood before me in her slip and put her arms around me, resting her head on my chest. The smell of her hair brushing against my nostrils evoked a strange feeling in me, one of a dashing cinema hero reaping a reward of sorts for some momentous feat. Then there was the feeling of mischievousness for tasting some forbidden fruit. My hands found their way to her buttocks; the slip was all that she was wearing.

With the utmost care I created memories of the way her flesh felt in my hands as I raised her slip, of the unveiled beauty of her breasts as she pulled it over her head, of the taste of her skin as my lips found what seemed to be their natural place. We proceeded slowly, both of us knowing what to do but neither of us having had the experience. It was an afternoon of discovery, of adventure, of pleasure. When we were exhausted we finished what little wine was left and began again. In all that time I never once thought of Laure-Anne.

Later as Fariza and I sat in the kitchen eating our evening meal, the Thouvignons arrived. As soon as I could, I prepared Laure-Anne for her French exam and went over her essay submission. We were very proper sitting in the dining room as her parents listened to the radio in the parlor. When we were finished I rushed upstairs hoping to find Fariza's door open but it was not. I tapped lightly but received no response. I went to bed.

In the morning when Fariza awakened me I sought a bit of amorous play but she would have none of it and wagged her finger at me as if I were naughty. I took it as a good sign for something to come in the evening. My schedule that day was hectic as we prepared for the end of the school year. I arrived home just in time for our meal, having no time to prepare Laure-Anne for her German and history exams on Tuesday. Fortunately those were her best subjects. The conversation at the table turned from the normal politics and business.

"Has anyone noticed a change in Fariza?" Madame Thouvignon asked. "She seemed so cheerful today, almost joyous."

"She spoke yesterday of resolving some difficulty with her father," I volunteered.

"Her father has been dead for four years," Monsieur Thouvignon said. "That was when we took her in; her mother is the Sachs's housekeeper."

"I suppose that I misunderstood her then," I flustered.

My error was overlooked but apparently my expression was not.

"Monsieur Jannot, do you have time to clarify something about Louis XVI's policies before you retire?" Laure-Anne asked.

"It's late, Laure-Anne," Madame Thouvignon chided. "You will have to get by with what you know. History is your best subject; you shouldn't have any difficulty."

"It won't take but a minute, Maman."

They both looked at me and I nodded. Laure-Anne left the table and returned with her lesson book but sat in the parlor. I excused myself and joined her. She placed the book on the table between us so that we both could read what she was pointing out with her finger. It had nothing to do with Louis XVI.

"She tricked you, didn't she?" Laure-Anne asked quietly, rhetorically. "She finally found a way to overcome your resistance . . . and she *did* overcome it, didn't she?"

I could not answer; I was so ashamed. Tears filled Laure-Anne's eyes.

"What did you think I meant when I asked you to wait for me."

"I wasn't sure. I didn't think you meant this. I'm so sorry."

"Édouard, we have lost something. We can never be those two innocents who discover the beauty and wonder of the act of love for the first time."

I was devastated. I was amazed at how deeply she loved me when for me it was only a pleasant feeling.

"Stand in front of me," she said.

"What? What do you mean?"

"Stand in front of me! I don't want my parents to see me."

I got up and blocked her parent's view of her as she wiped away her tears.

"Thank you, Monsieur Jannot. I understand perfectly now," she said as she rose and retook her place at the table.

I bid them all goodnight and went to my room. The next morning when Fariza awakened me, we chatted in the hallway for a moment as though the events of Sunday afternoon happened to two other people. That evening when I prepared Laure-Anne for the next day's exams she did not once look directly at me. Wednesday evening was the same. Thursday was her final day of school. Eliane arrived on Saturday.

It troubled me greatly to know the hurt that I caused Laure-Anne but I needed to study for my own exams. I was either at school or isolated in my room, sometimes skipping meals or having Fariza bring me scraps after the family had eaten. There was only one day in the following three weeks that I had a chance to be with Eliane and I could tell that Laure-Anne had confided in her because she was very cool to me, the only time in her life that she was like that. When my exams were completed I said good-bye to the Thouvignons and boarded a train to Saint Mihiel. I purposely avoided seeing the girls.

August was hot that year but that was the only time that I had to spend with my mother. She had made a deal with her brother to decrease her share to forty per cent in return for working only five days a week. She also had income from her husband's farm, which she rented to a neighbor. I thought that she would do better in a rented room in town but she could not bring herself to leave the only home she had known for twenty-four years. She made a promise that in two more years when both Eliane and I would be out of school, that she would reconsider my suggestion.

Things were not going well between my mother and Uncle Richard. He was bitter that his oldest son, Jacques-Henri, was taken out of the shop to join the army and my next cousin, Michel, had to take his place. My uncle had hoped that Michel would go on to university but my mother thinks that he did not have the qualifications. It seemed not to matter to him that Jacques-Henri was two years older than me and that I was not receiving any special consideration because I was a student.

The days that I spent at home were boring when my mother was working. I had no desire to visit with my so-called friends and longed to be back in Paris, even if I were not at the Thouvignons. Evenings we would sit in the garden, she, inquiring about my life in Paris and me, trying to learn more about my father. In a week we had run out of conversation and she would increasingly visit her friends while I spent all my time reading. The last Saturday in the month Eliane returned home and, happily for me, she was as warm and wonderful as ever. I did not have an opportunity to speak with her alone at length until Monday when our mother went to the shop.

Phillip Varady

"Coffee, Monsieur Jannot?" Eliane asked as she sat on my bed, awakening me.

"I'm glad that you are not mad at me still."

"I was never mad at you. I was disappointed that my brother could be such a cold-hearted bastard, destroying the love of someone who lives for only you."

"You know that Fariza tricked me," I said, sitting up and taking the cup from her. "I didn't want to do it, you know."

"Yes, yes, that's what any man would say."

I had no defense, no way to convince her of the truth of my alibi. After allowing my agony to fester a moment or two she patted my cheek sympathetically.

"I believe you, Édouard; I just can't believe that you could be so stupid."

I put one arm around her and hugged her, placing my mouth at her ear.

"Then you wouldn't mind getting me a piece of buttered bread, eh?"

Eliane laughed and pushed me away almost spilling the coffee in my lap.

"If you are typical of the men in France, I think that I shall never marry."

While she went off to the kitchen, I wondered if Eliane's forgiveness was matched by Laure-Anne's. I finished my coffee and joined her, taking a seat at the table.

"Do you think Laure-Anne has forgiven me?"

"I will tell you what I am permitted to tell you if you will answer a question for me. I promise that it will remain a secret between us."

"I need to know. Yes, I will answer anything you ask."

She placed the bread in front of me but put her hand on mine to prevent me from eating it. She looked me in the eye with a great seriousness, real or pretended, I could not tell.

"Did you enjoy it?"

God in heaven, I have been tricked again! I am no match in a contest of wits with a female. All that was left was for my mother to turn on me. I knew that I had to answer and knew also that she would know if I lied. I made her wait while I thought of the best way to reply, reliving that afternoon in my mind. Suddenly I burst out laughing.

"Yes! Yes, dear God, it was wonderful, unforgettable. It was . . . it was . . ."

"Tell me about it," Eliane said with a smile."

"What? Certainly not! Not to my sister!"

"You promised!"

"You said one question."

"Yes but you volunteered to answer anything."

"Well, I won't."

"Then I won't tell you about Laure-Anne."

"That's not fair. You promised."

"Did you take all your clothes off?"

"I don't want to talk about it . . . yes; we took all our clothes off."

"Did you kiss each other all over?"

"Enough! Are you perverted?"

"Did you do strange things . . . you know, like . . ."

"It was the first time for both us. We didn't know any strange things. You're terrible, you know. How can you ask me these things?"

Eliane shook her head and made a face that lead me to believe something was wrong. Reluctantly, I disregarded my better judgment and asked.

"What? Why are you shaking your head?"

"It wasn't Fariza's first time. Why do you think Laure-Anne thought that it wouldn't take a week for her to get you in her bed?"

"Oh my God! No wonder she was so good," I moaned.

"Did she have an orgasm?"

"Yes."

"Every time?"

"Yes."

"How many times did you do it?"

"Just twice."

"Just twice? In two years . . . just twice?"

"What two years? One afternoon! She lied to me and made a fool of me.

"Édouard, look at me! You're not a fool; it's just that women are cleverer than men when it comes to that sort of thing. You will be pleased to know that Fariza is no longer employed by the Thouvignons."

"How did that come about?"

Eliane wagged her finger at me and smiled conspiratorially.

"Let's just say that some women get very protective of their men."

"So, it was revenge then? Has she forgiven me?"

"She told me to tell you that you would be welcomed by all and that when she had a chance to speak with you privately that she would discuss the matter with an open mind. She said that you should not be fearful of such a meeting."

"Did you stand up for me? I know you did. You're so loyal to me; I love you for it. Is there anything more that you can tell me?"

"She . . . no! She is a very strong person. She will get exactly what she wants."

"Can you tell me if . . ."

"No more! I've got to get dressed. I have so much to do before school begins."

Eliane left the room and I ate my bread and had another cup of coffee. I was just going back to my room when she was about to leave the house. She gave me a great hug and kissed me.

"Édouard, you're such a wonderful person. You should think better of yourself. You worry too much."

If that was encouragement, it was very welcome. It was all I had to go on as I returned to Paris the following Saturday. I didn't know what to expect as I entered the Thouvignon's home. I was met at the top of the stairs by a thin woman, about thirty years old, who had a terrible accent. She had been expecting me and informed me that the family would be home late and if I wanted something to eat that I had better let her know now because she had the evening off as well as Sunday afternoon. I informed her that I was hungry and would appreciate whatever she could prepare for me. After putting away my things I came to the kitchen to eat.

"Monsieur," she said as she placed my meal before me, "seeing as we share the same floor and facilities, I will tell you this. I will tolerate no behavior from you less than that of a perfect gentleman. Is that clear?"

"Yes . . . Madame, or is it Mademoiselle? Or would you prefer that we use each other's Christian names?"

"It's Madame. I suppose that we need not be so formal; I am Odète Dumez."

"Édouard Jannot," I said, and stood to shake her extended hand.

"Yes, Madame Thouvignon mentioned your name, your Christian name, but not your surname. I know a family named Jannot back in Picardy. Do you have relations there?"

"No. We are all from Lorraine. So, you are from Picardy? What brought you to Paris?"

She stood there without answering for a moment or two and I thought perhaps that I should not have asked. She sat down opposite me, still without answering as I began to eat.

"My husband beat me once too often and I left him. A man ought to be tender with a woman; don't you think so, Édouard?"

"Yes, absolutely. You did the right thing."

"Are you a tender man, Édouard? I hope that you are; you seem so understanding, so nice."

"I like to think so. I have always treated women with the greatest respect."

"That's very comforting, Édouard. We must speak again about this but at the moment I am pressed to meet a friend. I shall see you in the morning."

"Enjoy your evening, Odète. I'll see you in the morning then."

I finished my meal and went to the cellar and took a bottle of Moselle. I was nervous about meeting Laure-Anne and thought that a good night's sleep would help. With Odète out of the house there was no way for them to know that I had arrived short of coming to my door, and I doubted that any of them would do that. I began to read and sip and when sleep beckoned I submitted. I was asleep in a minute once I lay down. I don't know how long I had been sleeping when I heard my name spoken softly, directly in my ear.

"Édouard, wake up. We must talk." A hand was pushing my shoulder.

"Laure-Anne? Have you lost your mind? What are you doing here?"

I rolled over on my side, propping up my head with my arm. All that I could see of her was the silhouette of her head as she knelt at my bedside.

"We must come to an agreement . . . tonight."

"If your parents catch you here it will be the last time you shall ever see me."

"Then let's get it over with quickly."

"What do you want?"

"Do you think that I'm still a little girl?"

"No, of course not."

"Do you think that I have only an infatuation with you?"

"No, I know it is more than that."

"Do you think that I'm a woman?"

I hesitated. If I say no, she will accuse me of treating her like a child and if I say yes she will . . . what? Before I could answer she stood up and got into my bed, rolling me on my back and partially lying on top of me.

"If you are in doubt," she whispered in my ear, "put your hands on me."

I could feel her bare breasts against my chest. I put an arm around her. She rose up a bit and spoke in a normal tone.

"That's not what I meant and you know it."

"Be quiet," I cautioned quietly.

"Do it," she said, again much louder than I.

I let my hand slide down her back to her buttocks. She turned on her back, pulling my hand until it was between her open legs. She pulled my head down to her breast and I kissed it. She stretched her body out on mine and spoke in my ear.

"Am I a woman, Édouard?"

"Yes, you are every bit a woman."

"I want to make love to you but not tonight. Will you wait for me this time?"

"Yes."

"You promise? A solemn promise?"

"Yes."

She got off me and gave me a passionate kiss. I responded, allowing my hand to explore her breasts. She slid her hand into my shorts and I throbbed at her touch. She giggled and kissed me more passionately.

"Do you know which night I have chosen, darling?"

"No, *darling,*" I replied, mocking her.

"Our wedding night, *darling!*"

She got out of the bed and put on her nightgown, stooping to kiss me one more time. She would have gone but I caught her hand and she sat next to me.

"Are you going to tell Eliane what happened here tonight? Or does she already know? Oh, my God, she does, doesn't she?"

"Yes and yes. But now I have details to give her. I love you, Édouard, do you love me?"

I didn't answer; I wasn't sure.

"Eliane said that you wouldn't answer that question. Whether it is true or not will you say those words for me, just once?"

I hesitated . . . too long. Laure-Anne put her head next to mine and whispered in my ear.

"You don't have to say it. Your sister advised against forcing you to."

I could feel her warm tears on my cheek. Who was I that someone as wonderful as she should fall in love with me? What were the odds that this would ever happen again in my entire life? I began to weep, silently at first but once seeing the great depth of my feeling, it became audible. My body began to tremble and great sobs came from deep inside me. She put her hand on my mouth to quiet me. When at last I regained control of myself, she removed her hand.

"Laure-Anne, I love you. With everything that I have, with everything that I am, I love you."

Now it was she who could not control herself. I cradled her face against my chest and stroked her hair. When she quieted down I kissed her eyes.

"I should go before I change the night I have chosen," she said with her lips on mine. "I'll do it if you want . . . anytime."

"I will wait. One thing . . . I know that you tell Eliane everything. Don't tell her about this part. Will you do that for me?"

I waited for a reply but there was none. I wished that I could see her face; I couldn't imagine what the difficulty could be.

"At least . . . don't tell her that I cried."

"I would never do anything to hurt you, my love."

She kissed me and rose from my bed and was gone. I waited until I was sure that she was safely back in her own room then turned on my light. I poured a glass of wine and looked at myself in the mirror. I was grinning like a fool. I toasted myself and drank it down at once.

So, Édouard Jannot, a little girl has awakened the man in you. Will you awaken the woman in the little girl or have you already done that?

Chapter 2

The first two or three weeks were awkward for Laure-Anne and me as we learned how to interact without revealing our feelings in front of her parents, or in front of Odète, who turned out to be a bit like Fariza, in that we determined that she was looking for some close attention by a willing young man. We think that she found such a person because she would go out every Saturday evening and would be there every Sunday morning without anyone ever hearing her return home.

I would pretend to misunderstand her veiled offerings or misinterpret them as something innocent, much to her frustration. She must think that I am a dunce. If she ever makes it plain I will have to plainly reject her. I will not break my promise to Laure-Anne. Although she made reference to it only once it is well understood that we will marry. The earliest would be two years distant and it does not make much of an impression on me. I have changed nothing of my plans for the future.

Late in November as I was returning from school, a bit earlier than usual, I came upon Laure-Anne some distance from the house, with a group of girls from school. I was on the other side of the street and as I drew abreast of them, she called out.

"Hello, Monsieur Jannot. How are you?"

"Hello, Laure-Anne. I'm well, thanks. See you at the house."

I continued to walk. I was pleased that she didn't call me over to her friends to introduce me, as though I were some trophy. So grown up, so proper, so wise.

The following Sunday as we were having breakfast Laure-Anne proved Eliane to be correct when she said that her friend was determined to get what she wanted.

"Papa . . ." Laure-Anne began, "is it true that respect of others is a good indicator of maturity?"

"Yes, I would say so . . . but not the only one."

"I asked Monsieur Jannot if he thought it disrespectful if I began calling him by his Christian name. He said that I have shown greater respect by honoring the teacher student relationship, by faithfully doing my lessons and getting good grades. He suggested that it was a matter for you to decide, being a reflection of my parent's standards. So, Papa, do you think it would be a matter of maturity or familiarity?"

Laure-Anne should write novels. That was a wonderful piece of fiction. Even Madame Thouvignon thought so as she covered her smile with her napkin. I think that her father had anticipated a day such as this because his answer was instantaneous, sounding as though he had practiced delivering it.

"In the house, among ourselves, it is proper but in public in front of others, whether he is present or not, he will remain Monsieur Jannot."

"Yes, Papa," she said dutifully, then turning to me, "Édouard, have you ever been to Les Invalides. There is a photographic exhibition there about the Battle of Verdun. Papa fought in that battle. We are going this morning; would you like to join us?"

"We are not going this morning," Monsieur Thouvignon interjected. "I forgot to tell you, Laure-Anne, but your Great-uncle Milan arrived this morning from Prague and we have urgent company business to discuss with him and your grandfather and Uncle Shlomo. It will have to be another time."

"The three of us could go, if you would like, Madame," I offered.

Madame Thouvignon looked at me with a slight smile as she considered the offer but after a minute she declined.

"Why don't you two go? I know that Édouard is fascinated by all things historic. Is that agreeable, Jean-Marie?"

"What? Oh, yes, of course. They may even see a photograph of me there."

Laure-Anne and I were delighted and managed to show not a bit of it. Later, as I was waiting alone for her in the parlor, Madame Thouvignon approached me.

"I am not so far removed from being a young girl like my daughter that I would forget how easy it is for someone like her to develop an infatuation for an older man like a teacher . . . like you. That supposed conversation about respect was pure fiction, wasn't it?"

"Yes, Madame. I had no idea she would do that. I had no part in it."

"Don't worry; I know my daughter. She is growing up and has no idea how to do it. She is only experimenting. Remember that, Édouard; I will only warn you this one time. You know what I mean, don't you?"

"Yes, Madame. You are perfectly clear."

"Good! Enjoy yourselves and . . . here." She pushed some folded-up banknotes into my hand. "For lunch . . . and don't mention it to my husband. I wouldn't want him to think that I'm encouraging this sort of thing."

"Yes, Madame, and thank you." I put it into my pocket as I saw Laure-Anne coming through the dining room.

"Are we ready, Monsieur . . . Édouard? It will be hard to break old habits."

She was such a good actress; I think she even fooled her mother.

"Have a good time, love." They kissed cheeks and Madame Thouvignon left.

"After you, Mademoiselle."

"Not just yet. Papa wants a word with you before we go. He'll only be a minute."

And so he was, entering the parlor waving away Laure-Anne.

"Wait downstairs, dear. I want to speak to Édouard in private."

As she was leaving he put his hand on my shoulder and drew me to the window.

"I respect you very much, Édouard, and your opinions too. When you are done at Les Invalides I would like you to come to my father-in-law's house and meet some people. You will be the youngest man there. Do not be quick to offer opinion or advice."

"Yes, Sir. Thank you."

"And I am putting my trust in you concerning Laure-Anne. Don't disappoint me."

"No, Sir; I won't."

"Good . . . good. And here . . . taxi fare," he said, as he put a banknote in my hand. "And maybe lunch, too," he said, as he put another with the first. "And no mention of this to my wife. I don't want her to think that I'm encouraging this sort of thing, you know. Try to be there about five; we'll have dinner later."

"Thank you very much, Sir. You're very generous."

"Go ahead. She's waiting for you." He waved to her through the window.

I rushed downstairs and wanted to take her hand but was not that rash or impatient. I purposely placed her between the house and myself so that I could glance upward to see if her father was still watching at the window. I did not see him nor could I detect a place where the curtains were pulled aside slightly if he wanted to remain unseen.

"That was very bold of you to take it upon yourself to invite me," I said.

"And that was very clever of you to invite my mother. What would we have done if she had agreed to come?"

"I think that we would have had a very good time at Les Invalides . . . and *she* would have paid for lunch."

"You have money for lunch?"

"Certainly! Being a student is not the same as being a pauper. Come on, I think that I shall surprise you more than once today."

We turned right instead of left and at the next street went down the hill.

"This is not the way to the Metro," she protested.

"I know. This is the way to the nearest taxi stand."

She said no more about my apparent display of wealth but once on our way she leaned over to me and whispered.

"If you need it, I have a few francs."

It was all I could do to keep from laughing and I'm sure she misinterpreted my smile but I thanked her all the same and gave her a kiss.

At Les Invalides I was amazed how intently she regarded the exhibits. I know that she had an interest in history and that it was one of her better subjects; would that she had a passion for it like me.

"Édouard, Look! Here he is."

Laure-Anne was excitedly pointing to one of the photographs. It was a battlefield scene of a few ragged men and their artillery. All their faces were somber, their uniforms filthy and it looked as though they resented having to pose. I read the caption below. 'When victory was finally achieved, fourteen men and three howitzers were all that remained of Captain Jean-Marie Thouvignon's . . . .'

"There! There he is! Doesn't he look mean? He taught those bastards a lesson, I'll bet."

Her face was so animated, her voice so full of pride, both for her father and for being French. I think that my secret will forever remain just that.

"I wonder if it was the same lesson they taught *us* in 1870," I said, quite intentionally to make a point. It almost went unnoticed.

"What are you saying?"

"Come on, let's go."

"But there's more to see," she protested.

"I've seen enough."

"But I want to see more."

"As you wish. I'll meet you outside," I said quietly and walked away.

I waited outside for at least five minutes before Laure-Anne joined me.

"That wasn't very nice of you," she said angrily. "I don't like being treated that way. Was it such an imposition to ask you to stay a bit longer?"

I totally disregarded her little tantrum.

"What can you tell me about the faces of the men in your father's photograph?"

"Don't change the subject. I want an explanation."

"If you answer my question you will see that I am giving it to you."

It took a few moments for her to see that I was not going to respond directly to her anger. Her face then became studious as she tried to remember what she had seen.

"They looked mean, very serious. So what?" She answered defiantly.

"Why weren't they jubilant, celebrating? After all, this was a major victory."

"I don't know," she said more quietly.

"Fourteen men from a company of over a hundred. How many were standing?"

The discontinuity of my question changed her demeanor. She suddenly became my student again, realizing that I was teaching her something that she had totally missed. She closed her eyes, trying to picture it in her mind.

"All but one," she said correctly. "The man on the right was on the ground. He was leaning against the wheel of one of the guns. Why?"

"He was not standing because he had only one foot. No one was treating him; there was no emergency. He did not consider the loss of a foot sufficient cause to be removed from the battle. He was there because he wanted 'to teach those bastards a lesson.' He'll go home and father a litter of healthy boys who will teach the next enemy's boys another lesson . . . and it won't be too long from now.

The Germans wanted to bleed the French white and the French didn't care how many of their sons died; they would not let them have the town. Some accounts say seven hundred thousand died at Verdun. Think, *seven . . . hundred . . . thousand!* Isn't that staggering? Can you imagine that many corpses . . . that many wives or sweethearts mourning, that many children growing up without a father? And we haven't learned shit! French or German! The leaders in both countries are no better than schoolyard bullies, smashing each other's toys. Each one wanted to . . ."

I couldn't go on. My eyes were full of tears and I was afraid that I would begin crying aloud. Laure-Anne suddenly had tears in her eyes, crying for me rather than the situation. She held me close.

"Édouard, I'm sorry. I had no idea how you felt about it."

"Nor I," I said, amazed at myself.

We stood there like that for some time until we were both composed.

"Have you ever heard your father speak of those times?"

"No, he *never* speaks about it."

"Ask him why, sometime."

Laure-Anne smiled her assent and we began walking west, following the Seine. We passed under the Eiffel Tower without even noticing it and stopped in the middle of the Champs de Mars. I took off my coat and spread it on the grass and we sat. She removed her shoes as I lay back, putting my hands under my head. She lay beside me with her head on my chest and one hand on my shoulder. Not a word was spoken for a half hour. Then she pulled herself up and placed her face directly over mine. I formed my lips for the expected kiss but she spoke instead.

"When shall we marry?"

What a question from a sixteen year old! But a legitimate question nonetheless. I pushed her shoulders back a bit so that I could watch her eyes. She was too close for me to focus.

"If we waited for your parent's permission or blessing . . . I would say never. When do you want to marry?"

She pulled at my wrists and I released her. We kissed and when we separated she said without emotion, "Today."

We both smiled and then laughed. She took my face in her hands and kissed me again pushing her tongue through my lips. It was a long kiss.

"If you persist in that," I said jokingly, "I had better turn over to avoid embarrassing myself."

She agreed and we switched positions and continued. She immediately slid her hand under my thigh and forced me to sit up to prevent her from attaining her goal.

"How did you get to be so naughty?" I asked.

"I must be associating with the wrong people."

"Yes, I agree. And one in particular named Eliane."

We joked and laughed and touched and kissed and an hour went by and we would have stayed there forever except that hunger intruded into our thoughts. We walked back to the Eiffel Tower and found a vendor selling crêpes and had two apiece. Next we settled in a corner of a café and ordered a half bottle of red and took two hours to drink it.

"We should be going," I said.

"Did my father tell you to bring me home at a certain time?"

"Not quite. He wanted me to bring you where he would be by five and then have dinner with him."

"But he's at my grandfather's." She was clearly unhappy with this.

"Exactly. Why the concern?"

"Nothing. Let's get it over with."

"What are you not telling me?"

She would not answer and in the taxi she would not even speak. When we arrived and I rang the bell, Laure-Anne was standing off to one side.

"Well, hello, Édouard. Nice to see you again."

It was Fariza! I was speechless . . . but for only a few seconds before I came up with what I thought was a brilliant response.

"Nice to see you too, Fariza. Have you worked out that difficulty with your father?"

"There's no need to pretend, Édouard. Everyone knows. Hello, M'am'selle. Please come in, your father is expecting you both."

Fariza was wearing what I assumed to be more traditional Berber clothes, not at all like the housekeeper's dress that she wore at the Thouvignons. As we walked through the door Laure-Anne spoke the word 'bitch' quite loudly and I am sure at least some of those present heard it. I stopped her by taking hold of her arm and turning her to face me.

"What did she mean *everyone* knows?" I said in a harsh whisper.

"Everyone! Do you not understand *everyone*?" she answered angrily.

"Who's included in *everyone*?"

"Jeder man! Verstehst du jeder man? Ist das besser?"

"You mean your parents? And who else?"

"Are you an idiot? Everyone! Everyone in this house and probably, by now, even my great uncle Milan from Prague. She probably had it published in the newspaper."

Laure-Anne stormed off but was quickly intercepted by her father. They spoke a bit and she continued on; he approached me.

"Ah, Édouard, right on time. How was your day?"

"The exhibit was very moving. We saw a photograph of what was left of your company. We both cried afterward."

He stared at me with a look that I had never before received from another person in my life. He made a motion with his hand for me to continue.

"I think that Laure-Anne will be asking you some questions about it. I know you asked me not to go beyond what her school taught but I could not help myself and I expressed my view about the stupidity of it all."

"That's fine, Édouard. She's more mature now and I think she can understand it better, especially with your perspective. She's quite angry with me for inviting you here . . . that thing about Fariza. But don't worry, she very content with the outcome."

"Who? Laure-Anne?"

"Oh, no. She's still angry. Fariza, of course. The child will be taken care of."

"The child? My child?"

"She didn't tell you? I expressly told her to inform you so as to relieve any anxiety you might have over the matter. A student is certainly not capable of maintaining a child. But, come on. I want you to meet some people."

I couldn't believe what I had just heard. I'm going to be a father and Monsieur Thouvignon dismisses it as just something to be 'taken care of.' I could understand Laure-Anne's unwillingness to tell me; she didn't want me to develop a sense of obligation to the child and especially to Fariza but to withhold that information from me . . . I didn't want my life to become entangled with Fariza and a child but it angered me that she refused to tell me, that she was managing my affairs. In spite of how I felt I still wondered about the anxiety she must be experiencing. I dutifully followed Monsieur Thouvignon from the entry through the parlor and into the dining room.

We approached three men, very well dressed and groomed, who immediately turned their attention to us as we neared them. They had been standing in a circle of sorts but moved to form a line to greet me.

"This is the young man I spoke of earlier," Monsieur Thouvignon said. "Édouard, I would like you to meet my father-in-law, Anton Sachs . . ."

He extended his hand to me and once I had grasped it he put his other hand on mine and shook it heartily.

"Welcome to my home, Édouard. Jean-Marie has fed me crumbs about you, little bits and pieces for the last two years, and I am very pleased to finally see you in the flesh. There is much that I would like to talk to you about."

"Thank you, Sir. I hope that I have not been promoted above my capabilities."

"I'm sure that is not the case," he said and gave my hand a solid thump before releasing it.

". . . and my wife's uncle and Monsieur Sachs's brother, Milan who has just arrived from Prague this morning."

"Édouard . . ." He nodded and shook my hand.

"Nice to meet you, Sir."

". . . and my brother-in-law Solomon, whom we all call Shlomo."

"A pleasure, Sir."

This last one smiled warmly and shook my hand vigorously but said nothing.

"Jean-Marie, leave the young man in our care for a few minutes and send Dihya to me. Don't hurry back," Anton Sachs said.

"Certainly!" He smiled a curious smile as though he was a party to some prank.

"So, a student at the Sorbonne. That's an accomplishment in itself. An historian, eh? So, what does an historian aspire to? What do you see as your future?"

My first instinct was to express my thoughts as desires or hopes but when I opened my mouth to speak they came out as predictions.

"After a mandatory apprenticeship as a teacher in a lycée, I will move on to a professorship at a university. I am still unsure as to whether I shall devote my time and energy to being a government advisor or an author. I firmly believe that hard work will be rewarded."

"Well, you are right about that but there are other factors that one should consider. We will have a chance later to speak of them. Ah, here comes my housekeeper."

I stiffened, knowing that this was Fariza's mother. Was she included in the *everyone*? I'm sure she was.

"Dihya, I don't believe that you've met young Édouard."

"A pleasure to meet you, Sir."

"The pleasure is all mine, Dihya," I managed blurt out.

"Dihya, bring us some cognac, please. We will be in the sun room."

Our host ushered us to a room off the dining room whose rear wall was all windows. I could tell from the setting sun that it faced south and imagined how comfortable it would feel on a cold winter afternoon. We took seats on upholstered chairs around a glass-topped table.

"So, Édouard, from an historian's point of view . . . what do you see in the near future, for France, for Europe?"

"War, Sir. Without a doubt."

The younger Sachs, sitting opposite our host and me, was speaking quietly to his uncle, probably translating.

"And what brings you to this conclusion?"

"Due to Germany's late consolidation as a nation they had a great disadvantage in the world marketplace and yet they made great strides, competing with and in some cases surpassing both the French and English. For those two nations this was intolerable and threatening. The Great War deprived Germany of its gains and the Treaty of Versailles humiliated her. But the German spirit was still alive and now they want it back, all of it, everything that was taken from her."

"And you think that they will go to war to get it."

"Absolutely! If we don't stop them immediately we may never stop them."

"We stopped them before. Why do you think we will not be able to do it again?"

"The British let France bleed on the battlefield. Sure, they helped but it was France's blood that made the greatest sacrifice. Now it is Chamberlain who waves a piece of paper, not Daladier. He thinks that the English can stay out of it by throwing the dog a bone but the dog wants our hand. We French know better! It was the British who gobbled up the German empire and the German markets. The other allies got crumbs, the Americans got nothing. Why would any of them come to our aid when it is British policy and cowardice that will bring us into another war? Germany will go after all the territory that they lost or territory that they can make a claim to because of a large German population, starting with the weakest. I assume that your brother is here because of the occupation of the Sudetenland. Poland, Denmark and Belgium will be the next victims. If they attack France and we cannot overcome them immediately, which I don't believe we are capable of, we will negotiate a truce with concessions. The French people don't want another million casualties."

"What concessions would France be asked to make?"

"Access to markets in North Africa, South-East Asia, the return of Togo and the prize . . . the reunification of Alsace-Lorraine with the Fatherland."

"The reunification . . . Fatherland? You say that the way a German would say it. I would call it a re-annexation by our enemy!"

Fear ran through me. He was absolutely right . . . I said that like a German; I didn't mean to . . . it just slipped out. *Think, Édouard!*

"I know that offends you, Sir, I meant to. That is exactly the way they will propose it to us. They will want us to know what humiliation is; they will rub our nose in the dirt. If you can remember the conditions that the Versailles treaty imposed on Germany, think of how they will use the same conditions, and will say that it is in all fairness, to inflict on us a lesson never to be forgotten,"

"Are you aware of the events of two days ago?"

"The pogrom? Yes, I try to keep up with current events; they are tomorrow's history. Do you know more that what was reported in the newspapers?"

His brother began a very animated conversation with him, in what I assumed was Czech, and then after a brief exchange he explained it to me.

"My brother is impressed by your astuteness in calling the events in Germany and the Sudetenland a pogrom. We think that it has also occurred in Austria. News by telephone indicates that thousands have been placed in camps because the jails had not sufficient space. It is curious how they knew that they would need camps."

"It's part of the larger scenario of the scapegoat. They will continue to blame every ill on the Jews until they either run out of ills . . . or run out of Jews. I know that thousands have already fled."

"You paint a very bleak picture, Édouard."

"Yes, I know. I wish it were not so; I wish our leaders were more courageous but that is not the case and we have only ourselves to blame for electing them."

I saw Dihya approaching and I determined to study her face for an indication of her feelings toward me. She came to the table with her tray and placed a glass in front of each of us, never taking her eyes off her hand. At the very last second, as she was turning, her eyes but not her head shifted to me and she smiled . . . and she was gone. The sound of quiet laughter brought my attention back to the others. It seems that in my brief distraction I had missed something. Perhaps they thought that I was rambling.

"Gentlemen, to our continued good fortune and safety, *l'chaim*," the grandfather said.

We brought our glasses together and they, all still chuckling, stared at me. It became apparent when our glasses touched—mine had twice the cognac as theirs. So the future grandmother approves of me! We took a good taste and settled back in our chairs.

"That was very insightful, Édouard. There are many in government that share your feeling and your concern but they are not in the majority. But," he suddenly said, loudly, "there is a matter I wish to ask about that only you can tell us."

"What is that?"

He leaned forward and the others followed his lead. I too leaned forward expecting a question of the utmost importance.

"How did you . . . ah . . ." he made a motion with his hand as if he wanted me to answer with only this little part of the question spoken. I had not the slightest idea what it was that he expected me to intuitively know. My puzzled look forced him to ask a more complete question.

". . . you know . . . how did you like the little Berber girl?"

The three of them leaned close like a bunch of schoolboys waiting to hear the exploits of one of their own. I didn't know if I should be wary or discreet, flippant or offended. I began to sweat. I thought I knew what they wanted to hear and decided to give it to them. I looked each of them in the eye in turn, and then smiled.

"I thought that I was in heaven," I proclaimed and laughed as heartily as the rest of them. Only the uncle seemed a bit subdued and turned to his nephew as the grandfather slapped me on the back.

"Was?" the uncle asked.

"Er hat gesagt daß es Himmel war," the nephew replied.

"Good, eh?" he said in French.

"Die beste," I replied whether in German or Yiddish or both, I do not know but they began to laugh uproariously and raised their glasses. We all swallowed down what remained. My chest felt warm and I forced myself to breathe deeply to cool down. The others envied me; I know they did.

My last reply was misleading. 'Best' requires the comparison of a minimum of three, good, better . . . so I was lacking two experiences. They seemed to accord me some status because of it all and I let them, fraud that I was. Into this camaraderie walked Monsieur Thouvignon and Laure-Anne. I could see that she resented the good time that I was having; she looked miserable. She suddenly put on a bright smile as she approached her great uncle.

"Es ist sehr gut dich wieder zu sehen , Oncle Milan. Hast du ein gute reise gehabt?" Laure-Anne asked in as good German as *I* knew to speak.

As they continued their conversation, Monsieur Thouvignon led me out of the sunroom and asked a difficult question.

"I know they asked about Fariza and you. What did you tell them?"

"I told them what they wanted to hear."

"And what was that?"

"Please, Sir. My answer would have been different if you were present and they knew it. You know these men better than I; you know what I said."

I believe that he wanted to hear it as much as they but had to remain above all that in order to maintain some distance between us. He was not my comrade.

"You're clever, Édouard, but honest. Clever and honest, a rare combination."

We returned to the sunroom where I was asked many more questions by Anton. He insisted that I call him that, 'Too many Monsieur

Sachs' here', he said. He seemed to be testing my knowledge of different fields and I think that I impressed him. Laure-Anne left after a few minutes in order to allow us to continue our all male gathering. After an hour or so we were called to dinner before which I met the three gentlemen's wives and received some strange but not disapproving looks. 'Everyone' included them also. Fariza served the opposite side of the table and throughout the meal did not once look my way. Laure-Anne was watching her more closely than I and by dessert had lost her anger.

Shortly after dinner, Madame Thouvignon said that we were ready to leave and asked Laure-Anne and me to wait in the car. After we made the rounds to bid all a good night, Dihya saw us to the door. Fariza was standing in the doorway of the dining room, facing us, patting her belly. When Laure-Anne noticed her, Fariza smiled. Hatred flashed across Laure-Anne's face. I took her arm and pulled her away toward the car. Once inside I began to act out the scenario I had planned earlier.

"How dare you not tell me that I was to be a father," I screamed at her.

Her anger turned to despair. She began to sob loudly. I let her go on for a while, letting her think that she had lost me forever. When I thought that my student had suffered sufficiently to receive the lesson that I wanted to teach her, I pulled her hands away from her face and spoke very gently to her.

"There is nothing . . . there is no one . . . in this world that will ever separate me from you. I love you beyond belief. Why do you have so little faith in me?"

I said what I said because that is what she needed to hear. I wondered if it was so; I hoped that it was. For a few seconds she was absolutely silent and then she began to cry ever more loudly. She grabbed at my neck so tightly that I had to pull at her arms to breathe. Fortunately her parents were slow to leave and when they finally came out they seemed to be involved in some personal matter and paid no attention to us at all. At one point Laure-Anne rested her head on my shoulder and it was some time before I realized it and shrugged to make her aware of what she was doing. I don't know if Monsieur Thouvignon saw it in the rear-view mirror.

Two weeks went by quite normally. It was the last Sunday in November and we were at breakfast when Monsieur Thouvignon surprised me.

"Édouard, are you free to join us at my father-in-law's for dinner?"

"Yes, certainly. I would very much like to speak with him again."

"Good! We will also be having a holiday dinner there on Christmas and would like to invite Eliane but thought that it would be unfair to leave your mother alone . . . if she would be alone. Would she?"

"Yes. I don't think my Uncle Richard would invite her; even if he did, she would probably refuse. He resents having to share the business with her."

"What business is that? I don't believe the subject ever came up."

"Ha! They are new customers of yours. They do business as RGC Farinet. My Uncle Richard, my Aunt Gèsele and my mother Claudine are butchers although my aunt never goes to the shop. She does all the paperwork and my cousin Michel is an apprentice as I was one summer."

"Imagine that! Why have you never mentioned it before? I would have given them a discount price. Which products do they buy?"

"It isn't much. Peppercorns, some herbs and seasonings for the sausages and Greek olives and some Dutch cheeses. They had to take the olives and cheese to make a minimum order and it was only because they were close enough to a distributor in Bar-le-Duc that their order was accepted."

"Are they pleased?"

"Your prices are about the same as their previous supplier but they are selling lots of olives. No one else in Saint Mihiel sells Greek olives."

"I'll send them some other products on consignment. Perhaps I will make grocers of them. There will be no financial risk, you understand. If they don't sell they can return them. Will you tell them? Will your mother accept my invitation?"

"She doesn't have a phone but the shop does. I'll call her tomorrow."

"Good! Please impress upon her my earnest desire to have her share the holiday with us, and to stay three or four days."

"I will, Sir. I would enjoy that very much myself."

I was buoyed with enthusiasm and expectation at the prospect of having our families meet. At Anton's that evening I was included in a business discussion at which I said not a word and was not asked a single thing. Later, Monsieur Thouvignon explained that his father-in-law wanted me to get a feel of the business and its day-to-day problems. I met Shlomo's children, who had not attended the previous dinner, his son Charles, who treated me in a very condescending manner, and his daughter Louise who seemed to be an idiot. Laure-Anne later confirmed that the poor girl had some mental disability. Anton hardly spoke to me due to some supposed urgency in liquidating their holdings in Czechoslovakia. Milan had sent for his family and was looking for a house in Paris. It would be a permanent move he said.

At midday on Monday I called the shop. Michel answered and we had a strained conversation for a minute before he gave the phone to my mother. He didn't tell her who it was on the line.

"Hello, it's Claudine."

"Maman, it's me, Édouard. How are you?"

"What's wrong? Are you all right?"

"Yes, I'm fine. Everything is fine. How would you like to spend Christmas in Paris, you and Eliane, as guests of Monsieur Thouvignon?"

"Oh, that would be nice. Will he come and get us? Or must I go broke paying for two railroad tickets?"

"Maman, you have enough hidden away that you could buy the bank. Are you going to let a few francs keep you and Eliane from enjoying the holiday or would you rather spend the day at Uncle Richard's?"

"Sure! That might happen . . . right after I sprout wings. Why did he invite us?"

"Well, I could say because the shop is a customer but I think it's because he likes me and because Eliane is such a good friend of Laure-Anne and he didn't want you to be alone for the holiday. I didn't mention that he invited Eliane first, did I?"

There was a silence, which I attributed to contemplation but it lasted far too long.

"Maman? Are you still there?"

"Yes, I'm still here. Yes, I will come. Will I look like a peasant to them?"

"They're not like that. We will be having Christmas dinner at the grandfather's house, so bring your fanciest dress."

"The Jew? You're having Christmas dinner at the home of a Jew?"

"They're very modern, Maman, you'll enjoy it."

After another long silence she finally agreed.

"Maman, I have to tell you this. Two years ago when Monsieur Thouvignon asked about my father and I told him that he was a captain in the artillery . . . that he went away and I never once saw him. I purposely gave the impression that he died in the war. He may bring it up because he also was a captain in the artillery . . . just thought I'd tell you."

"Do you know why I love you so much, Édouard? You make life so interesting. Is there anything else that I should know? No, no, don't tell me. Just let me go from moment to moment, thrilled by the suspense. When shall I come?"

"I don't know yet. I'll call you back when I do. Thank you, Maman. I love you."

"Yes, yes. Don't push your luck. I love you too . . . I suppose. Good-bye."

I called her back a week later. She was to arrive on the 23rd and return on the 27th. The spare room between Odète and me would be furnished for my mother, and Eliane, of course, would share Laure-Anne's room. I wondered how my mother survived these last sixteen years; was it because she was strong or was she barely clinging to sanity. Her only social contacts were the wives of our neighbors. How would she function in a real family setting? I suddenly felt guilty for not being the son I could have been; I think that I shall try to rectify any shortcomings I may have.

When the doorbell rang that day, I was in the parlor with the family. I raced down the stairs and flung the door open. Blissfully my mother was in front; I think that I would have brushed by Eliane to get to her. I hugged her with a great intensity, so much so that she must have wondered about my state. We separated and she gave me a kiss on my lips, something rare. Her smile showed me that she was duly impressed . . . and pleased.

"Well, that in itself was worth the trip," she said.

"I missed you. How are you; how are things going?"

"Life goes on. It's good to see you, Édouard. Are things going well?"

"Yes. Wonderful! Come on, come in. Eliane, give me a kiss."

She kissed me and when we separated she had such a smile, just short of laughing out loud, that I suspected that two young women were controlling my life. As we got to the top of the stairs, the Thouvignons were lined up to greet us. Laure-Anne came forward immediately and shook my mother's hand.

"It is so nice to meet you, Madame. I feel such an urge to call you Claudine; is that all right?"

"Oh, yes, please. Only strangers call me Madame. I have longed for this opportunity to meet you, Laure-Anne."

"Maman, may I present Jean-Marie and Nathalie Thouvignon. My mother, Claudine Jannot."

Madame Thouvignon came forward and embraced her, exchanging *les bises*. I was very surprised at this show of familiarity. Monsieur Thouvignon shook her hand warmly and invited us all into the parlor. Laure-Anne and Eliane embraced and for a moment I could not tell if they were laughing or crying. When they turned round to face us I saw a curious joy on their faces.

"Odète," Monsieur Thouvignon called out, "please take Madame Jannot's bag to her room and Mademoiselle Jannot's to Laure-Anne's room."

My mother was about to protest but I discretely held up my hand to stop her. She had never been in a household with a servant.

"We will be ready for coffee when you return," he continued. "Is that your pleasure . . . Claudine, or would you prefer something else?"

"Oh, no. Coffee will do just fine."

Monsieur Thouvignon came to my side and spoke quietly to me.

"I hear that the Café sur la Colline serves a wonderful hot fruit punch. Why don't you take the girls there for an hour or so while we get to know your mother."

He placed a five-franc note in my hand and patted my shoulder. Laure-Anne and I got our coats and the three of us danced down the street. We found a table in the café near the fireplace and stood before it several minutes until the waiter brought our drinks. Eliane had the hot fruit punch but Laure-Anne and I had crème de menthe.

"Will someone tell me what's going on?"

The two girls smiled and laughed then pulled me forward and kissed my cheeks.

"Are we going to be married, Édouard Jannot," Laure-Anne asked excitedly.

"Yes, we will marry, Laure-Anne Thouvignon," I answered in the same vein.

"And I am a witness," Eliane exclaimed. "The deed is done! All that remains is for those in power to give their . . . approval?"

"No. Acknowledgement," Laure-Anne corrected.

"What are you talking about?"

"Why do you think Maman was invited here," Eliane asked.

"Are you serious? Do you know for a fact or are you guessing?"

"Well . . ." Eliane hesitated, "why do you think you were not thrown out on your ass when you . . . ah, . . . serviced the servant?"

I was stunned. Eliane's assessment would certainly explain many things but I could not understand why this whole chain of events had ever started.

"Why would your parents ever consider me as a suitable husband for their only child," I asked Laure-Anne.

"Because I asked them to," Laure-Anne replied.

Eliane put her hand on Laure-Anne's arm and gave her a sad look. Laure-Anne seemed unaffected by that action, almost defiant. She gave me a weak smile.

"Because she threatened them," Eliane said.

"With what?" I asked.

Neither of them was willing to answer.

"Come on, I want to know."

I waited while each of them wrestled with something inside themselves but to no avail. My angry face and wild hand gestures finally got to Eliane. Just as she was about to tell me what I wanted to know, Laure-Anne stopped her.

"Please don't say," she pleaded. "I'll tell him one day, I swear. Please, Édouard, don't pursue this now. Please."

I did not pursue it. We sat in silence for a long time until it became embarrassingly painful. I told them that I wanted to get a breath of air and would be outside for a few minutes. Presently they came out and suggested that we go back to the house. It was much too early if we were to give them an hour, so we wandered up and down the street looking into shop windows, the two girls in front and me behind by a few steps. We walked as slowly as we could so as not to interrupt our parents and their negotiations, if that's what they were doing. As we entered the hallway, Monsieur Thouvignon was just coming up from the basement with two bottles of red and a white.

"Ah, excellent timing," he said, waving the bottle of white above his head. "Let's go upstairs. How was the punch?"

"Oh, it was so tasty . . . and very warming," Eliane said.

She continued to chat with Monsieur Thouvignon as they climbed the stairs. I did not move; Laure-Anne was at my side. My anger and frustration slipped away as I looked into her eyes. I didn't know what to expect upstairs, maybe *she* did. She held out her hand to me and we went up. Odète had set out some glasses and was opening a bottle. We put our coats on the rack and entered the parlor to take seats but my mother drew me back toward the door.

"How involved are you with this girl?" She spoke softly; there was no anxiety or accusation in her voice.

"I love her."

"Have you been to bed?"

"No. We agreed to wait until we married."

"You asked her to marry you, then?"

"We sort of came to an agreement . . . decided that we would. We just knew that we would, it seemed so logical. We love each other."

"So, she didn't ask you to marry *her* . . . or did she?"

"No." My recollection was hazy, I wasn't sure if she had ever done that. "Why?"

"Laure-Anne seems to get what she wants and she wants you."

"Well then, that's a good thing, Maman, isn't it?" I detected the beginnings of an unwanted protectionism.

She didn't respond. She was aware that from this point on, if she continued, we would be on opposite sides of the matter. She gave me a kiss on the lips, a token I would say, of what was in her heart.

"Yes, that's a good thing. I've had you long enough; time to give someone else a chance," she joked and put her arm in mine.

We took our places in the parlor. We were facing one another, the Thouvignons on one side and the Jannots on the other. He sat between wife and daughter and I between mother and sister. Odète had finished pouring the wine and left. Six glasses of red; I didn't particularly like red. What a thing for a Frenchman to say . . . but then . . .

Something was not right. Things were moving along; everyone else seemed to know what part to play. It was as though they had all just finished reading a novel and were discussing the story and I was not sure if I had the same book.

"Claudine . . .?"

Monsieur Thouvignon seemed to be offering or requesting something from her. Of course, the results of her confirmation of the facts presented to her by the prospective in-laws concerning the victim, poor fellow.

"Go ahead, Jean-Marie."

"Good . . . good. Well, we all know what is happening . . . and what might . . . what your intentions are. Laure-Anne has been reluctant to give us many details preferring to have Édouard answer our questions."

What a mistake that will be! Of everyone present I think that I know the least. A glance at Laure-Anne revealed nothing; she sat expressionless. Has she really put the whole thing in my hands? That seems out of character for her but if that's what she wants then I shall handle it.

"What would you like to know, Sir?"

"When were you planning to marry?"

"In June . . . of 1940, after we have both completed our education."

Monsieur Thouvignon made a disapproving sound to let me know that it was not his intention that Laure-Anne's education should be complete at that time but he continued.

"And where will you live?"

"I don't know. I will be assigned a teaching position. I will have some choice as to the region but not the specific city."

"Would you stay in Paris?"

"That's a possibility but Laure-Anne and I have not discussed it. In this matter we cannot please both families. We cannot live close to both of them. A place half way between Paris and Saint Mihiel will please neither. Much will depend on the positions available."

The questions from this point on were senseless; all could be answered by 'I don't know' or 'maybe.' In all this time no one had taken a sip of wine. While Monsieur Thouvignon was pondering yet another question, I sought to put an end to it.

"Sir, is the wine for a toast?"

"Yes, a toast. I thought . . ." He left his thought unspoken.

So, the outcome was already decided; then what is it we are awaiting? My mother picked up her glass and looked to the rest of us. One by one the glasses were taken in hand. I don't think the father of the bride was quite ready to give up asking questions and certainly was not ready to propose a toast. He hesitated.

"May I do it?" Eliane asked.

Monsieur Thouvignon made some condescending gesture with his hand, as though he was being gracious but I knew it was because his heart was not in it. Eliane was smiling broadly, relishing the opportunity. I wonder if she had planned this.

"To the future Monsieur and Madame Édouard Jannot. May they prosper and be in health all their days."

The Swans of Lorraine

They all smiled and made appropriate remarks and took great swallows of the wine. Laure-Anne placed her glass on the table and gave her father a long embrace. I imagined, not incorrectly I'm sure, that she was whispering in his ear the whole time. It seemed odd to me that not once was the subject of permission brought up. It was neither asked nor given as though the outcome of this meeting was a foregone conclusion and only the details required attention.

My mother stood up and turned to me. I rose and embraced her. She said not a word but I felt her tear on my cheek and waited until she wiped it away before I released her. Laure-Anne came and embraced her next and I felt obligated to give my future mother-in-law the same. I would have made it only a cursory thing but she held me closer and longer than I would have imagined. She said something in my ear, which I did not understand.

"It's Czech," she said. "It's what we say when we wish someone good fortune."

Her eyes were moist and I thought that she was only a breath away from total loss of control of her emotions. I put my mouth to her ear.

"There will never come a day in Laure-Anne's life that she will lack the love of her husband and there will never come a day in yours that you need be in doubt as to her well being."

As I straightened up she put her hand to her face and with a slight nod, fled from the room. Damn! I have done it! Instead of calming her down I have put her over the edge. Monsieur Thouvignon watched her go but remained for a moment to embrace me and give me a few solid thumps on my back. He excused himself and attended to his wife. My eyes settled on Eliane. No one had embraced *her* yet but she waited patiently. I took her in my arms and held her for a while. When we relaxed a bit she kissed me, on the lips, as was our habit, but this time a bit longer than ever before. Laure-Anne stood to the side and placed a hand on each of our heads and we arrived at a place where our three foreheads were together.

"We did it!" Eliane exclaimed quietly.

Yes, we did. But what did we do? I didn't want to know. I felt as though I had been manipulated, not that I was displeased with the outcome. When I looked in Laure-Anne's eyes I knew that the end justified the means. I could see into the depth of her soul and see the unbounded love that she had for me. I envied her; I wished that I could feel what she felt. I loved her without a doubt, with all that was in me. It

Phillip Varady

was just that she had more in her than I. Or did I have as much and it was only a matter of time until it found its way through the dark pathways and locked doors? Was my heart cauterized when I was a child or will her love be the balm that makes me whole?

My lips found hers and we exchanged our hearts with this simple action. I know that Eliane's face was only centimeters away, watching unashamedly. A second hand rested on my shoulder . . . my mother's. I finally understood why she had risked everything to be with my father.

The Swans of Lorraine

Chapter 3

On Christmas Eve we all went to church. We walked rather than rode; it would have been crowded having all six of us in the Citroën anyway. Odète was given two days off with pay; she chose Christmas and the day following. We would have to fend for ourselves in her absence, my mother assuring them that we would survive 'just fine.' I'm sure that meant that she was volunteering to be the new housekeeper. The church that the Thouvignons attended was Saint Severin's, near the boulevard Saint Germain. I know that there was one closer to the rue Descartes and I concluded that this was his childhood church when his family was not so well off.

A priest stood outside welcoming the parishioners; we were treated with no special recognition, with a generic greeting. I suspected that the Thouvignons rarely attended. The Jannots were not much different—all the major holidays and feasts, and then rarely when we turned to God as the supplier of last resort. Inside the church I had a twinge of claustrophobia; the ceiling seemed low, the windows few and the glow of candlelight encapsulated the congregation in a finite sphere of reality surrounded by a cocoon of darkness.

We sang and listened and prayed, or at least pretended to. If the experience was to produce a good feeling in us, it succeeded. For the others I cannot speak but for me the removal of guilt for my sparse attendance left me in a much better state. I could easily make it to Easter without sinking into condemnation. As we walked slowly through the quarter we stopped often to examine the offerings of the local merchants. The thought struck me that I had bought nothing for Laure-Anne. For the first time that I can remember, I lied to her.

"I have a gift for you but it was not available immediately and may be several days before the merchant has it in his shop. I hope you won't mind waiting."

"No," she said with a smile. "I'll hold on to my gift for you so that we can exchange them together."

"Sure. That would be nice."

We walked behind the others; even Eliane walked with them. We could finally walk holding hands without disapproval.

"Did you like that church?" she asked.

"It was gloomy, too small . . . poorly laid out."

"Yes, it is all that. That's where we will be married."

"I would prefer just the civil marriage, the Jannots are Protestant, you know."

After an outright lie why not a slight fabrication to teach her a lesson about taking things for granted and being a bit too self-centered. She stopped dead in her tracks and faced me, more annoyed than surprised.

"Why didn't you tell me?" She did not hide her annoyance.

"Why didn't you tell me you were Catholic?"

"Well, what did you think we were, Buddhists?"

"*Well,*" I replied, mimicking her tone, "with a family that speaks Yiddish, I could not be sure."

"Eliane told you about my family. You knew!"

"Yes. You made sure that Eliane passed on the information that you wanted me to know. Did you make her report to you?"

"You're making this sound like a conspiracy?"

"Your words, not mine! What would you call it?"

"I would call it a serious case of distrust or perhaps paranoia. Do you think we are plotting against you?"

"Plotting, certainly but I would not go so far as to say that it was against me. It was more that you were making decisions without me, decisions for which you should have had the decency to ask my opinion . . . or didn't it matter to you as long as you got what you wanted?"

"I don't see how I can continue in our relationship if you think so badly of me."

She was bluffing. This was a challenge for supremacy. I know she loves me enough not to carry this to an unfortunate conclusion.

"What are you saying?"

"I can't give my life to a man who doesn't trust me. Perhaps we should reconsider our marriage plans."

She's bluffing! So it has come to this; I would die without her but I cannot be the man she would like me to be.

"As you wish." I said.

She stared at me then walked away to rejoin the others. She's bluffing! She still had that annoyed look, not a sad one. She will apologize later and I will also and it will be all right again. I caught up with them and walked silently back to the house. Later we all engaged in polite conversation but Laure-Anne and I did not speak. I went to bed very fearful. She was bluffing. *Dear God, please let her be bluffing.*

When morning came I realized that it was over. I would have thought that she had so much of her life invested in me that she could do nothing else than continue in our relationship but apparently I was wrong. I pulled my luggage from under the bed and began to fill it with my belongings. I thought that I could do anything, be anything . . . for her, but that wasn't so. She could have my soul, my life . . . but she could not have this. A knock came upon my door. My expectations were all negative as I answered it.

"Édouard, about last night . . ." Eliane stopped in mid sentence. "What are you doing?"

"I'm packing. As much as I love her I just can't be the man she wants me to be."

"But she loves you and you love her."

"I love her, yes, but she loves a man she's created in her mind and I'm not that man. I look like him, talk like him and for the most part I do the things he does but her man does one thing that I cannot."

"What is that?" She asked, genuinely puzzled.

"He licks her boots. It doesn't have to be every day . . . and it will never be in the presence of others, but every now and then he will have to show that he will bow to her as a demonstration of his love. I think, at her age, that she is amazed that she has this power and as for me at my age, I am amazed that I have allowed it for so long."

Eliane showed no sign of surprise . . . curious. So, she herself must have been aware of what her friend was doing.

"Why did you lie to her and say that we were Protestants?"

"What did she threaten her parents with?"

"That has nothing to do with this."

"Neither does your question." I was suddenly suspicious. I took hold of Eliane's hand and pulled her into the room. "You can come in too, Laure-Anne!"

A few seconds went by before she showed herself. She eased into the room, her face to the floor. At least she wasn't defiant.

"Will you really leave?"

"I'm not the man you want."

"Édouard, I love you. Please don't go."

"Eliane, could you leave us alone for a minute?"

"She can't be up here alone. I promised."

"Go sit on the stairs."

Eliane walked into the hall and turned to face us. I waited as she delayed sitting, thinking, do doubt that she could put her ear to the door when I closed it. She sat.

"Stay there!" I said sternly.

As soon as the door was closed, Laure-Anne attempted to embrace me but I wouldn't allow it and sat on the bed, pushing my suitcase aside to make room for her. She sat with her hands in her lap.

"Why do you treat me this way?" I asked her.

She knew. She just didn't want to say. I waited for a minute or so but realized that she would not answer. I stood up and put the last of my clothes in the bag.

"I don't want to end up like my mother," she said quietly.

I sat down again, taking hold of her hands.

"And how has she ended up?"

"She's so afraid of my father, so obedient. She's not allowed to make the slightest decision. I know every time he makes love to her, which is not often. He does it as a reward for her good behavior. I can hear them sometimes; I can see it in her face the next morning."

"So, you would prefer to be like your father instead, is that it? And I will be the one to be rewarded for *my* good behavior?"

"I wouldn't be like that."

"You are already like that. If you don't see it you will never be able to change. Do you see that you are like that?"

She sat silently. I wanted to tell her that I would stay; that I could love her no matter what but I didn't believe it myself. I was desolate that she could not answer whether through stubbornness or ignorance.

"I don't think I am like that," she finally said, "but I would rather be like him than her. I could never be like my mother."

"I would never ask you that . . . and I would never be like your father because . . ."

"We're coming," Eliane shouted from the hallway. She popped her head in the room. "We're ready to go. Are you coming, Édouard?"

I did not want to go. Nothing had been resolved. Laure-Anne had not the slightest intention of changing. I was weakening as the moment of truth arrived. If I did not go with them, I would not be here when they returned. We stood and she tugged my hand as she took a step toward the door. If she tried to make this decision for me, I would be gone. Perhaps she realized what she was doing and released my hand.

"Please, Édouard. We can finish talking later."

I welcomed the delay; I had not capitulated; I merely deferred the decision while I gathered more data. Yes, a very wise move; give her a chance to do . . . something.

I nodded and made a gesture with my hands for them to proceed. No one was smiling; we all knew that the decision could be reversed for one word, one action. We squeezed into the Citroën for the five-minute drive to the Sachs's, putting on our masks, our smiling faces, once we entered the house.

Only Anton and Vlasta (Madame Sachs) were there from the family. I didn't expect Milan; he had already expressed his opinion about mingling Jewish traditions with those of the 'goyim.' He assured me that the word carried no pejorative meaning, it simply meant non-Jew. Shlomo apparently shared his uncle's sentiment, which was a good thing for me; I didn't like him much.

My mother and Vlasta formed an instant bond when it was mentioned that she was a butcher. It seems that Vlasta's father supplied chickens for a kosher butcher in Prague. They went into the kitchen . . . as a gathering place for women. I wound up in the sun room listening to Anton speak about 'Kristallnacht' and the huge fines levied against the victims. It was interesting, it was history in the making but my thoughts were elsewhere and I wished I were also.

Anton signaled to Fariza and handed her a slip of paper when she came.

"This should be sufficient," he said. "You can set the white on the kitchen doorstep. That should chill it a bit, eh, Édouard?"

Fariza read through the list of wines to bring upstairs, one hand resting unconsciously on the bulge of her belly. She was only five month pregnant but . . . .

"Will you help me, Édouard?"

I didn't know if that was proper, both of her to ask and for me to go to the cellar with her but I nodded my assent. I watched as she left us and then it struck me. It was all so simple, so clear. Without even excusing myself I went to the kitchen and found Laure-Anne there with all the other women in the house and took her hand and pulled her toward the cellar door.

"Come with me," I said quietly.

She didn't resist but was totally perplexed. I stopped half way down.

"When we get downstairs, stand just outside the wine room. Don't make a sound, just stand there and listen. Understand?"

She nodded and we continued down. We could hear the clink of bottles as Fariza was pulling them from the rack. I left Laure-Anne at the door.

"How have you been, Fariza?"

"Very well, Édouard. I like it here. There, just there is a basket; he has ten bottles selected. And how have you been?"

"Good. Things are going well."

"I'm glad to hear it. Are you and Laure-Anne . . . you know?"

"I'm not sure what you mean but I think the answer is 'no.' "

"Ah, too bad. Poor boy."

"How's the baby doing?"

"Very well. My mother says all the signs are good."

"If it's a boy will you name it after its father?"

"Mmmm. I might," she said, giving me a big smile. "But my mother says it will be a girl. I think I would like a girl."

"Then you could reverse the name, eh?"

"What?"

"Instead of Jean-Marie you could name it Marie-Jean."

"I can't believe he told you. Was he bragging?"

"Actually he never said a word. I guessed and was right. You're too big for five months. How many is it?"

"Six . . . six and a half. You won't say anything, will you?"

"I won't if you tell me whether or not he sent you to attack me."

"Attack you? You didn't act like a victim. Yes, he told me to hurry before it would be obvious to you that you couldn't be the father. It was already too late. Are you sorry that it's not yours?"

"No, I'm delighted."

"Oh, I'm heartbroken but then poor students are better off with no children, eh?"

"What does your mother know?"

"Nothing. Only three of us know the truth."

Four of us, dear Fariza. I put the wine in the basket as we chatted a bit more. Laure-Anne was long gone when we came out of the room. Upstairs, I found her with her father and Anton. She seemed to be listening intently to their conversation but I suspect that she was looking at, or should I say looking into, the man that I exposed. Everything went quite well that afternoon; we all acted normal.

Anton and Vlasta got Laure-Anne and me aside after dinner to congratulate us on our engagement. I never asked why Monsieur Thouvignon didn't make an announcement at dinner but I really didn't care. By my acknowledgement without comment, Laure-Anne knew that I was not leaving. My ego . . . or pride, found a convenient excuse to stay.

My mother went home content; she liked Laure-Anne very much in spite of her first impression. Unknown to me at the time, they would write each other occasionally. Laure-Anne became withdrawn although she continued to do well in her studies. We spoke every day but little of it was personal. Then I noticed that she seemed to be with her mother more often, which was neither good nor bad but to me it meant a recovery from whatever depression she was in.

The first Sunday in February we were again at Anton's when he presented Laure-Anne and me with engagement gifts— pair of wristwatches. It was a catalyst that got us talking about the future, our future. When we were securely on a wedding path and all else was behind us, as we sat alone in the sunroom she asked a hard question.

"Why did you expose my father's indiscretion to me?"

"Because I love you. Because I couldn't let you turn out like him. I'm sorry it had to be him but . . . I don't care who it may be, no one will come between us."

"That's a very good answer. Just what I thought you would say."

"And so . . .?"

"And so, I've been the child, the bitch, the dull witted one and you've been the rock, the mentor . . . the better example. I'm someone else now . . . better, wiser and I love you more. Now it's not only my body that tells me so, but my intellect also. Do you understand? Do feel the same way?"

"Turn your back to me."

"What?"

"Put your feet up on the cushion and sit sideways with your back to me."

She did as I asked. I undid the top button of her blouse and slid my hand under her slip and cupped her breast. I gently rubbed, squeezed and pinched it. She said nothing at all but put her head back to rest on my shoulder. I looked around casually at the others who were here and there enjoying each other's company. This was so daring, so wonderful. After about five minutes, reason overcame bravado and I withdrew my hand. Laure-Anne buttoned up and turned to face me.

"What does your intellect tell you about that?" I asked.

"I'm so happy that I will be the only one to bear your children. What does your body tell you about that?"

She was perfect. She could handle me; we could handle each other. There was such a trust that had grown between us that we always put the other first. If either of us wanted to carry this into the bedroom the other would have gone without question or regret. Why neither of us did so remained a mystery; I suppose that we each assumed it would be more selfish than giving, so we waited.

March was not a good month. German troops occupied all of Czechoslovakia and the fate of many of the Sachs's friends and relations was in doubt. Milan was so grateful to have followed his instincts. He bought a house where many other émigré Jews lived in the eighteenth district. He saw Anton often but not the Thouvignon's.

Toward the end of May I thought to give Laure-Anne something for her birthday but had little money. The Christmas gift that I never bought and Laure-Anne's gift for me that was never given were both forgotten. In my poverty I thought that a token would express my feelings; she would appreciate it, I was sure. One evening as I was coming home from school I noticed the proprietor in the window of the curio shop where we lived and I thought I might find something different, something sentimental, something cheap. I went in.

"I'll be right with you," he shouted from the window as he tried to extricate himself. "Hello, how are you?" he said when he finally stood before me.

"Good evening, Sir. I'm looking for something special to give my fiancée for her birthday. Something that will always remind her of these days."

"Well, we can start with a diamond pendant . . ." he pointed to a section of the display, "or a bracelet with other precious stones . . ."

I allowed him to run through it all, down to those thing that could be classified as arts and crafts. While there, as he was trying to influence me with some trinkets I spotted a necklace. It had no stones, just gold work.

"May I see this?"

He brought it out and laid it on a piece of red velvet. It seemed to be worked from a solid piece of gold. It was about five or six centimeters across, with the chain connected to an unseen fastener behind. It was two birds facing each other in a circle of gold, one with its wings extended behind it and its neck stretched upward. The other had its wings folded and its head touching the breast of the other. I picked it up by the chain to look at it more closely. The birds' feet had black enamel on them; their bills also with small patches of yellow beneath their eyes. As I held it very closely I could see individual feathers engraved on it. I wanted it.

"How much?"

He turned it around to reveal a small tag. He didn't speak the price, so as not to frighten me, I'm sure, but it was more than I could ever afford. I shook my head and he put it back into the case.

"Perhaps something made by a native artist?"

I removed the wristwatch that Anton had given me and laid it on the counter.

"I'll trade you this for the necklace."

"We are not a pawn shop, Sir."

"It's a bargain. Look at it; you can't go wrong."

He picked it up, examining front and back.

"Do you know what this is worth?"

"Certainly," I lied. "Much more than this trinket."

"This 'trinket' is solid gold."

"So you think the watch is brass?"

"No, I'm not saying that . . ."

He hesitated; I began putting it back on my wrist but he put his hand on it. He motioned for me to let him see it again, going through the same examination. Without a word he placed a small box covered with purple velvet on the counter. He reached for the necklace, removed the price tag and carefully coiled the chain in the box, placing the birds on top. With a snap he closed it and handed it to me.

"She will love it."

I smiled and stuffed it in my jacket pocket. I quickly left the shop lest he change his mind, and raced upstairs, my heart pumping wildly. Laure-Anne was not home yet from a friend's house so I deposited this treasure in my room. I wanted to give it to her immediately but it was only Thursday and her birthday was Tuesday next. I was burning with anticipation; I could not wait that long.

Monsieur Thouvignon had relaxed somewhat his restrictions on his daughter's activities with me since our engagement and it became our habit to spend Saturday night at a local dance hall where my much more modern fiancée tried to bring me out of the dark ages of waltzes and foxtrots. I would say that she only partly succeeded. Sunday afternoons also we were allowed to do as we pleased.

This Sunday I had Odète prepare a lunch for us, which was a chunk of smoked ham and a length of beef sausage, a baguette, a piece of camembert and a jar of Sachs, Thouvignon Greek olives. She made sure that we had all the essentials: utensils, napkins, butter, mustard . . . A bottle of Sémillon completed our meal. We walked a few blocks to a park on the rue des Écoles where young people like us were wont to spend some time in a semi-secluded and permissive environment. The purple box was in my pocket. We found a place where the sunlight was half shaded by a large tree.

"Are you hungry," I asked

"No, I can wait a while. Are you?"

"I'm starving . . . ," I said and laid on my back, "for affection."

"I don't think that you suffer from a lack of it. In fact, I think you are an affection glutton. The more you get the more you want."

"And is that a bad thing?"

"As long as it is me who supplies it . . . no."

"Give me a kiss."

"Just one?"

"Well, you could make it a very long one . . . if it pleases you."

She smiled a very mischievous smile and darted her tongue in and out like a lizard. I had to laugh and she threw herself on me and slid it into my mouth. It was a very long kiss, long enough for my hand to gradually slide to her buttocks. She wiggled it under my touch and intensified her exploration of my mouth. For a moment I thought my plan had failed.

"What am I lying on," she said, pushing herself up. "Have you a rock in your pocket?"

"What? I have nothing."

"What is this," she said, putting her hand on my jacket.

"None of your business. Give me another kiss."

"No! I want to know what that is."

"Well, one can't always have what one wants. It's personal."

"I want to know," she said and tried to snatch it from my pocket.

"I'm not joking," I said and grabbed her hand. "This is very personal. If you saw it, it could change our whole relationship. Are you willing to risk that?"

Her surprise at my warning slowly changed to mischief.

"Yes. Let go!"

I released her hand and she withdrew the box from my jacket. She knew from the look of it that it was a gift. She opened it, looked at the contents for a minute and closed it again and lay down on my chest. A minute passed before she spoke.

"Is that for me?"

"Happy birthday."

She said nothing. After a while she took hold of my hand, not with our fingers entwined but holding it as an object with her thumb on my wrist. She began to sob and raised herself and kissed me, tears dripping on my face. She put her mouth to my ear.

"You sold your watch, didn't you?"

"I didn't need a watch."

"Édouard, Édouard, Édouard, what shall I do with you? And I gave you nothing for your last birthday. What can I give you?"

"Ah, your love is all that I need."

"But you already have that. I want to give you something special."

"Well, do you have any special love?"

"I have something that you might consider special."

She got up on her knees, pulled up her skirt a bit and sat straddling my hips.

"Ooh, Monsieur has another lump . . . another gift, perhaps?"

I pulled her down and rolled her on her back, pulling her skirt back to its proper place. I went to kiss her but she was laughing so hard that I could not.

"You're so naughty," I chided. "I'll wager that on our wedding night you will be as cold as a dead fish."

"I don't think so," she said and pulled my head to hers. As we kissed she slid her hand under me and took hold of the 'lump.' I acquiesced for the moment; big mistake!

"If you don't stop immediately I'll have to go home and change clothes."

She increased her attack. I had only seconds to avert disaster; stopping her was not the plan. I reached into our lunch sack and withdrew a napkin and shoved it into my trousers.

"Ooh, you little bitch," I moaned, as she continued to massage the 'lump' through the napkin. She was unrelenting and continued well past the climax. When she finally stopped we were lying face to face and she began to laugh uncontrollably. I could only smile; it was wonderful. We put our foreheads and noses together.

"Happy birthday, Édouard. A bit late but just as well appreciated, not so?"

Now it was my turn to laugh, both at what had just happened and what I was thinking.

"I have a similar gift for you. Let's see . . . yes, a Bastille Day gift. Will you be free that day?"

"I'm free right now!"

"Mmmm, no! Not here. All right?"

"Yes. I can wait. We're good at waiting, you and I."

We ate our lunch and Laure-Anne examined the necklace more closely.

"Did you notice the yellow patches on their bills?"

"Yes. I'm sure it was intentional . . . to indicate a specific species. Did you see the feathers?"

"Oh, yes ! How exquisite! *Deux oiseaux . . . joint ensemble à jamais.*"

"Yes, just like us," I said.

She turned her back to me and lifted her hair. I put the necklace around her neck and she turned to face me. The chain was of such a length that in order for one to see the birds she had to undo another button of her blouse, which she did when she realized that. I liked the setting, nestled between her breasts but it was not for the world to see, it was for her alone. I buttoned her blouse and kissed the space between the chain. She seemed to know my intent.

"I wonder what kind of birds they are."

"I'll look it up tomorrow. Feed me an olive."

She put an olive in my mouth but wouldn't take back her finger.

"I want that olive," she said.

"Come and get it."

She put her mouth to mine and we fought for it. In some things men are just superior to women; it was no contest.

Phillip Varady

We spent the greater part of the afternoon there and thought to get an aperitif before returning home. Laure-Anne's mother would serve a cold dinner on Sundays when the weather was warm so it didn't matter much at which hour we got back to the house. There was a fairly steep hill from the rue des Écoles to the rue Descartes and Laure-Anne walked backward the whole way just for fun. Our destination was my favorite café, which was in a small square at the top of the hill.

While we were still some distance away I noticed Laure-Anne's parents sitting at an outdoor table at our destination. I had been directing her, advising her when we approached a curb or telling her to bear to the left or right and now I aimed her directly at her parents. They noticed us as we came into the square, both of them quite amused at their daughter's action.

"Curb," I cautioned.

She slowed and found the edge with her foot and stepped up.

"Go left . . . more . . . just a little more . . . stop!"

Her father anticipated my intention and went one step further by turning a chair outward for her.

"Sit!"

Totally trusting me, she sat without ever seeing it.

"Say 'hello.' "

When she turned to see to whom she should say hello, three of us burst into laughter while Laure-Anne blushed in embarrassment. It was no time at all until she saw the humor of it and joined us. While we were enjoying our crème de menthe, her father asked about my plans for the summer.

"I doubt that I will be going home at all," I began to explain. "I will need to gather information for my treatise. I will have a mountain of notes that I must distill into some form that makes sense."

"What is the subject," Monsieur Thouvignon asked.

"France's Ascendancy Over Germany and Spain for Political Control of North Africa in the Twentieth Century."

"My God! I don't envy you a bit. Is there enough about that to make a treatise?"

"Oh yes! There is still conflict in some areas with Spain. Just months ago . . ."

As I rambled on, Laure-Anne and her mother were having a joyful conversation; I think that she was showing her the birds. I thought that my future father-in-law was already treating me as a son-in-law and I began to reciprocate. I liked the feeling knowing that he also noticed the change. I knew that I had gained his approval in spite of whatever it was that his daughter had threatened him with. As a reward of sorts he promised to give me driving lessons as the opportunity arose.

Monday evening as Laure-Anne and I were studying together I spoke to her softly across the table.

"I found out about the birds."

"So, what are they?" she whispered loudly.

"They're swans. They are called Whistling or Tundra Swans. The necklace shows them in their mating ritual."

Laure-Anne smiled at that.

"They are long lived birds and a pair will often spend a season together without mating, getting to know each other and the environment."

"That sounds like us," she said.

"There's more. They mate for life."

She reached across the table and held my hand. "That *definitely* sounds like us!"

She put a finger in her bodice and revealed the birds and a bit more.

When Eliane arrived for the summer I was totally involved in my research, which took my time six days a week until about three in the afternoon. She and Laure-Anne took to spending their days with Laure-Anne's classmates, some of whom I knew from meeting at the Thouvignons or on the streets in the neighborhood. Previously it had been all girls that she kept company with but now in their seventeenth year, nature was more and more beckoning them and I met quite a few young men when we gathered in the evening to pass the time.

Eliane had met a young man named Olivier who was from Nancy, a city in Lorraine, not very far from Saint Mihiel. His parents obviously had money because he was driving his own car. He had just completed his first year at the Sorbonne, although to the best of my recollection, I cannot say that I ever met him at school. He was an engineering student and typically, as I found out later, very precise about things, very analytical and totally unromantic. I do not mean that in the sense of being amorous, he displayed that quite a bit with my sister, but rather he could not see the poetic, the hidden and mysterious side of life.

We became good friends, partly because I wanted to keep watch on my sister, but beyond that he was interesting and intelligent . . . and very political. By August it was us four who went everywhere together. Olivier let me drive sometimes, me being a newly licensed motorist, much to everyone's horror, but without incidence. He had kept his apartment rather than return home for the summer, and we sometimes spent hours at a time there listening to American jazz and sultry French chanteuses sing about love and disappointment.

Olivier smoked cigarettes and got Eliane started on them. No amount of pleading or coercion on my part could dissuade her. At least she didn't do it at the Thouvignons. I seemed to have less and less influence over her, as it should be, I suppose, but I did not like it. One morning, when I should have been at school, while Madame Thouvignon and Odète had gone to the market, the three of us were sitting around the dining room table in our underwear, having coffee.

"So, is there something going on between you and Olivier," I asked my sister.

"Yes," she said without any further comment.

"Yes? Is that all?"

"Do you have a question, Édouard?" she asked playfully.

"Yes, I have a question. Are you fooling around?"

"Yes."

"Yes? What does that mean?"

"That means that I'm fooling around. Do you know what you meant by fooling around when you asked the question?"

"Of course I know what I meant but it may not be what you think."

"Then you had better be more precise, eh?"

"My God, you're becoming another Olivier. Before long you'll be standing up to piss. Well then, be precise, eh? Are you still a virgin?"

"No."

"No? When did that happen? *Where* did that happen? Why didn't you tell me?"

Elaine got up and came around the table to where I was sitting. She pulled my chair so that I was facing her, then with two fingertips, tugged at the top of her slip until her breasts were exposed for a brief second.

"Two years ago in Saint Mihiel," she said, "when I grew these. Olivier wasn't the first but may well be the last."

I was speechless; Laure-Anne was laughing so hard that I thought she would fall from her chair. I suppose my days as a big brother were over. Eliane sat on my lap and tried to console me; I didn't know how to react. Laure-Anne came up behind me and nestled my head between her breasts. The two of them were about to embarrass me in some way but I was saved by the sound of the front door opening downstairs. We all scattered. Later in the day, without Olivier present, we all had a good laugh.

As August ended, Eliane went back home to Saint Mihiel. She and Olivier had become very close, 'not just friends,' she had said. I was content with that, he was very attentive to her and I hoped for the best. She had not been home for more than a few days when we heard the news that Germany had invaded Poland from the west and although Russia also invaded that unfortunate country from the east later on, when all the declarations of war had been issued, it was only Germany that was the enemy. The expected invasion of France did not happen, much to my surprise, rather Denmark and Norway were taken.

My last year at the Sorbonne was intense. Not only was the work more concentrated but we students were all hoping and praying that we would make it through to the end without the Germans invading France or that the country would not be in such dire straits that we would be forced to leave school and join the Army. Anton seemed to be the one who had the best sources of information that could not be obtained in the Press or on the radio. Disturbing news was coming out of Denmark concerning the treatment of Jews and Shlomo advised fleeing to England now, having no confidence in the French army to defend the homeland.

Laure-Anne and I set our marriage date to Saturday 16 June but were reminded by Madame Thouvignon that Milan and his wife Lida, who had already notified her that they would not attend a church wedding, would also not break Sabbath to attend the following celebration. It was a small concession and we moved the day forward to Friday. I called home to inform my mother of the date and was assured by her that she and Eliane would arrive the day prior.

The Thouvignons placed their fullest trust in me and allowed Laure-Anne and me to come and go as we pleased. We did not abuse that trust, in that we went no further than we had already gone, but then the last year of school for us both did not give us much idle time. Monsieur Thouvignon confided in me one evening in private about a disappointment that he had since gotten over. Laure-Anne was the only Thouvignon that could carry on in the business from his side of the family. He had about the same feeling toward his brother-in-law Shlomo as I and thought to prepare Laure-Anne as best he could to take an active part in the firm, hence the need of a tutor and a university degree to prepare his daughter for that eventuality.

In mid December he offered me the use of the Citroën to drive to Saint Mihiel for Christmas. When I hesitated he added 'of course Laure-Anne may go with you if she so desires.' A phone call to my mother confirmed her willingness and I accepted the offer with much elation and anticipation. The trip took five hours and gave us a feeling of independence that we had not previously experienced. We stopped by the shop first and Laure-Anne met my Uncle Richard and Cousin Michel. My mother rode home with us and we surprised Eliane who had not been told of our coming.

The next day, the day before Christmas, we visited Grand-mère Jannot and Eliane's Uncle Jean-Pierre and Aunt Mathilde. That evening at Mass we met my Uncle Richard again and his wife, my Aunt Gèsele and eleven more Farinets. Once back in the house we sat around the fireplace drinking hot cider and rum mixed together and stayed up very late talking about our future and the threatening invasion. Christmas day it was my turn to be surprised when Olivier showed up, invited by my mother in advance of my phone call to her. We ate until we were in danger of bursting and could do little else than lay about for the rest of the day. Olivier left that evening.

In the morning my mother said good-bye to us and went to work. We left shortly afterward leaving Eliane very excited about coming to Paris for the wedding. On our trip back we saw many military vehicles going the other way and were a bit fearful that the expected invasion had finally occurred. It had not but the dark cloud of uncertainty that we were living under proved to be a true omen when the attack finally came in the second week of May when Luxembourg and Holland were invaded. Three days later they were on French soil.

The day before, a Sunday, Anton showed up at the Thouvignons and asked me to accompany him to Shlomo's house. On the way he explained.

"My son and his family left this morning with all that they could carry. They're going to Marseille and then to London. They've left much behind that will be claimed by his landlord if it is not removed from his apartment. Here, sign this."

He handed me a form and with only a glance I could see that it was a transfer of ownership for a motor vehicle—Shlomo's Peugeot Berline.

This was no time to protest someone's generosity, whether Shlomo's or Anton's; I signed.

"I'll bring it back to you after it's recorded. Do you know where you'll be sent?"

"Not yet, probably not until July."

"I'll pay his rent for that month and before you go you'll come by and take anything that suits you. He won't be back; trust me."

"I don't know what to say. This is so nice of you."

"Consider it a wedding present from Shlomo; it's costing me no more than his rent. Are you considering staying in Paris if you can?"

"I love Paris; it's fascinating to me especially since I was raised on a farm in the countryside but . . . we think we would rather be nearer to my sister. She and Laure-Anne are so close. The Peugeot will make it easier for us . . . if I can afford to put gas in it."

We arrived at Shlomo's house and Anton showed me what I needed to know about the car and handed me the keys. When I was seated behind the wheel he took my hand and put some money in it.

"Put that away," he said, "for gas."

Without looking, I put it in my jacket pocket.

"Édouard, you're a good man and it pleases me that Laure-Anne and you will marry but I'll tell you this. It's good that you can find work that you enjoy. You're not very aggressive . . . but then a schoolteacher doesn't need to be. Stay out of commerce; you'll get eaten alive. When you see an opportunity come your way . . . seize it. It may never happen again. Enjoy every day as it comes, do you know what I mean."

"Yes, but you sound a bit fatalistic . . . as though you'll never see me again."

"Oh, I'll be at your wedding; I guarantee that. Go on now; show your bride your new toy."

I thanked him and started off. This was so different than driving a borrowed car; this one was mine. I headed south toward the Seine, crossing it at Notre Dame. The thought occurred to me that God was rewarding me for my good behavior. It was just a thought. Laure-Anne was excited and delighted at our good fortune but in the coming weeks there was no joy in France.

Generals fought with generals, verbally; they were all French. The Germans swept through Belgium in days. Luxembourg and Holland had surrendered. We all wondered which would occur first, our wedding or the capture of Paris. I tried to call my mother to no avail. With so little information, we assumed that Saint Mihiel was in German hands and despaired that she and Eliane would be here. At both Laure-Anne's father's and grandfather's urgings, we did not postpone the marriage.

As the day approached more and more of the people that we invited called or wrote to say that they could not or would not attend, including Laure-Anne's two aunts. Most had joined the millions that had already fled Paris. The streets had very few people in them and fewer vehicles. The schools shut down, either from the lack of teachers or through the general confusion that seemed to pervade the city.

They say that all brides are beautiful but through my eyes it was easy for me to see that this was the most beautiful of them all. Although there was little emotion shown at the civil ceremony there was a look on her face that reflected what was in her heart as we stood at the altar, the look of fulfillment. A feeling of awe filled me knowing that this woman loved *me!* She had committed her life to *me!* My chest was tight; I wanted to grab her and hold her close. I answered the priest's questions softly but with conviction watching Laure-Anne's eyes. They were so full of life and joy; I felt something inside me slip away, something I had known all my life. It was like running in a race holding a large stone and someone suggests that you put it down and continue without it. When you begin again you wonder why you had not done that before. Your path and goal are the same but now it is so easy, so much more pleasant, a joy not a task.

Laure-Anne was answering the priest; tears flowed from my eyes. *I love her!* It was a revelation to me. I asked myself what then could I call my feeling for her up to this time. I was sure that *that* was love yet that could not compare to this. I was transported to another world where there was no sound and nothing existed beyond a meter from me. There was Laure-Anne and nothing else, perhaps some clouds. From the mist a pair of hands made a gesture for us to draw near to each other. I stepped forward and took her face into my hands, looking into her eyes until I could no long focus. Our lips touched briefly; they became slippery, salty. She embraced me and I held her firmly. Many hands were on my back, patting, rubbing; lips on my cheek, tender words in my ear, sobbing, joyful words. We stood there until I was conscious of the words . . . cajoling, congratulating, encouraging words.

We were ushered to the door of the church. The gloom of the interior of Saint Severin's gave way to the glorious daylight of Paris in June. People were rushing by us to line up at the curb on the boulevard

The Swans of Lorraine

Saint Germain as truck after truck of German soldiers drove by . . . in French trucks! They were standing, facing the crowd, weapons held across their chests, surveying their subjects. They were imperial, invincible, proud. Their faces showed, not contempt, but rather vindication. We had humiliated them at the end of the last war; how would they respond?

Some people were crying, others cursing, most just watching. One almost expected that if they had waved to the crowd that some would wave back. More than one comment was heard blaming our government and generals, others stating that the Germans could be no worse than what we were used to.

They stole the wind from our sails. How could we celebrate anything now? There we stood, the entire wedding party, two Sachs's, two Thouvignons and two Jannots, frozen in place.

"Come on, back to the house," Anton instructed. "In the midst of darkness there is light and the darkness cannot conquer it."

I looked at him thinking how Christian that sounded; maybe he was only pretending to be a Jew. He gave me a knowing nod and held an arm out to me. I approached him and he put his hand at the back of my neck.

"This day will never happen again . . . seize it! Don't let these" he waved at the trucks going by, "rob you of your treasure."

I smiled. He was right; this was the greatest day in my life. We climbed into the cars and drove back to the rue Descartes. Once inside the door, the aroma of Odète's cooking filled our senses. We gathered in the parlor and Monsieur Thouvignon got a camera; Madame Thouvignon came to me and embraced me casually.

"Édouard, will you do me a favor?"

"Certainly, Madame."

"My name is Nathalie and my husband is Jean-Marie. Will you call us by those names from now on?"

"Certainly . . . Nathalie."

She placed her hands on my face and kissed me on the lips, quite a long kiss for a mother-in-law. Then she embraced me again, this time strongly.

"I am so jealous of my daughter," she whispered.

She held me at arm's length and gave me the warmest smile.
Click

The afternoon sunlight streaming in from the parlor window was not wasted as the first of many pictures recorded this day for eternity.

Jean-Marie and Anton went to the cellar to choose some wine. It was a half hour before they came back up . . . unsmiling. Their mood changed instantly as they rejoined our company. Jean-Marie chipped some ice into a bucket to cool the champagne. The remainder of the day was memorable with all from the elder generation sharing anecdotes from their own marriages. I think that they thought that Laure-Anne and I were dying to go upstairs and be alone. We had waited two years; a few more minutes would not make a difference.

"Oh, I am so tired," Jean-Marie said.

Nathalie had just come to his side to refill his glass. He placed a hand low on her back, very low. I could not help but notice this first ever display of intimacy. She could not help but smile, a bit embarrassed.

"Well, perhaps we should all go our separate ways," she suggested.

We all stood immediately to acknowledge our agreement. Hugs and kisses were given and Laure-Anne and I were the first to leave.

When the door closed behind us we were in another world. We may just as well have been on Mars for all that we cared. The empty room between Odète and us suddenly became a kilometer wide. We took the two steps that brought us to the edge of the bed and faced each other.

"So, husband," she said with that mischievous look that she does so well, "what do we do now?"

"What? You're joking! I hope that you're joking; you are, aren't you?"

"I *know* . . . what to do. I meant . . . do we just take our clothes off and do it? Or did you have a plan?"

"A plan? No, that sounds too cold. Getting undressed is a good first step. Shall I leave the light on or do you prefer to be in darkness . . . like the last time?"

"The last time you were not entitled to see me . . . but you are now."

She kicked off her shoes and turned her back to me and I undid the clasps at the back of her gown. She pulled it forward off her shoulders and allowed it to fall to the floor. It went no further than her hips and together we pulled it down the rest of the way. She stepped out of it and kicked it to one side in a cinematic fashion and stood there with her hands on her hips. Then she unbuttoned my jacket.

I removed it and then my tie, shirt, shoes, socks and trousers. I had almost wished that it was winter and that we had no heat in the room; it would allow me to claim that as the reason for my slight quiver. I took hold of her and held her tightly. Her warmth felt good and I calmed down a bit. When I put my hand to her face she turned her head up, still smiling idiotically, and kissed me.

"I haven't got all night Monsieur Jannot. Can we move along?"

"I would think, Madame Jannot, that you would want to cherish every moment; to form memories of this very special time."

I know it was the little girl in her, being mischievous, doing the forbidden thing, that made her want to be playful, to act grown up, and to be the ultimate temptress that she knew from the cinema. I had done that with Fariza; Laure-Anne was different. I wanted to be tender, gentle, in awe of the commitment that we had made to each other. Suddenly the brightness of the electric light seemed obscene.

"What I want to do is what I have been waiting for," she said. "Two years is a long time to be denied; wouldn't you say?"

I said nothing. There was an old oil lamp on the shelf above my desk along with a box of long stemmed matches. The few centimeters of oil would last long enough for my purpose. I lit it, trimmed the wick and set it on my desk and went to the door to turn off the light. The mellow glow and soft shadows pleased me. I came up behind Laure-Anne who had not moved at all in some kind of protest to my romantic desires. I took hold of her slip at the waist and lifted it; she obligingly raised her arms. When I had it completely off I thought to fling it against the wall in the same fashion that she kicked away her gown but that would make me a party to her plan. I let it fall to the floor unnoticed.

"Your breasts are beautiful," I said as I turned her slightly toward the lamp.

My fingertips circled them, slowly drawing to the center. She stiffened a bit, leaning backward against me and put her hands on my thighs. I covered her with my palms thinking how wonderful it was to do this. I think that there is nothing in this world to compare with the shape and feel of a woman's breast. She allowed me to revel in this pleasure for several minutes before she turned to face me.

"Come out of these things," she said as she plucked at my undershirt.

I had no problem with the undershirt, which I pulled off immediately but I hesitated to remove my shorts. Laure-Anne sat on the bed and waited for me to overcome some inhibition. I delayed too long.

"Come here," she said quietly.

I stood before her as she put her fingers on the waistband. Her eyes were on my eyes as she pulled them down. When they were around my ankles I stepped out of them. She was still watching my eyes; the little girl was gone. She put her hands on my hips and tugged at me slightly; I moved forward a half step. She took hold of me and kissed what she held.

"Is that all right? Do you like that?"

"No. I think it's demeaning."

"Did Fariza do that?"

"No. She wanted to but I wouldn't let her."

"Why not; she was only a servant."

"I thought that if I allowed her I would be obliged to do the same."

"And would that have been demeaning also?"

"I didn't think of it that way. I just didn't want to do it to her."

"Would you do it to me?"

I dropped to my knees and took hold of her panties. She raised herself up from the bed slightly and I pulled them off.

"There is nothing I wouldn't do for you."

She clasped my head and kissed me so sweetly, so tenderly. No raging passion, no fierce emotion, only a deliberate show of affection that I came to expect from her. Still holding my head, she lay down and opened herself to me.

Morning brought us back to reality. France had been taken in only six weeks! Our generals tried to form a government that would salvage some pride but in the end we gave in to every demand of our conquerors. Thousands of German troops paraded past the Arc de Triomphe; Paris wept. Hitler had the surrender officiated in the same railway car in which the Germans were humiliated after the first war, and then had it blown up.

Remarkably, unless one saw German troops, one would not know that we had just lost the war. I was sure that many things had changed or would soon be changed but it was unseen by most of the public. The exception was that we all had to get up an hour earlier when they forced us to set our clocks to Germany's time; and of course the curfew at dark. People went to work, went to the cinema, sat in the parks on the warm summer evenings, sat at tables in their favorite cafés; it was disturbing. When we all got used to it they moved the curfew to midnight. The schools reopened and I immediately took my final exams.

In the middle of the third week in July I went to the Sorbonne to inquire about my assignment as a teacher, having no word at all since my graduation.

"Where were you last week," the clerk snapped. "All the posts in Paris have been filled so don't expect to stay here. It's off to the countryside for you."

"I never received a notice," I complained, "but that's fine with me. What choices do I have?"

He handed me three pages of assignments, most of which were penciled through with blue and red, reading either 'filled' or 'cancelled.' I slid my finger down the list, stopping at every entry that was still available, and was surprised at how many places there were which I had never known existed. There were four posts in Lorraine, two of which were cancelled: Sarrebourg and Forbach, which I supposed would become part of Germany again. The other two were Domrémy, whose location I knew, and Laxou, of which I had never heard.

"Can you tell me where Laxou is?"

"Never heard of it. Have you any idea at all?"

"It's in Lorraine."

"Lorraine, eh? You've heard about that, didn't you?"

I hadn't but could well imagine. Without me answering him, he told me about its partition. The western part was to remain French and the eastern part was to be annexed. He pulled down a roll-up map of France and began searching through Lorraine from north to south.

"Here it is, just west of Nancy. Do you want it?"

"Yes. Yes, that's fine."

The clerk flipped through a card index and found the posting.

"Copy everything on the card and sign it. Upstairs one flight you'll find the Bursar's office for your expenses and allowances."

I copied it all furiously and rushed upstairs to the Bursar's office. There were two others waiting before me. Another clerk motioned for me to come to her.

"Fill these out while you're waiting," she said and handed me some forms.

I sat at a table with the other two and began to fill out the forms.

"Where are you off to," one of them asked.

"Lorraine, a town named Laxou."

"You've heard about Lorraine, haven't you?"

"Yes, but Laxou is near Nancy . . . in our half."

He fell silent for a while until I started on the second form. He motioned to me to come closer and I leaned across the table to him.

"Not that it matters to me, but you're not a Jew, are you?"

"No, why?"

He tapped on the form half way down.

"Even if you were, I would lie. They'll probably never check."

I looked where he was pointing, an area requesting names and religion of applicant's spouse, parents and spouse's parents. It sounded ominous. I got through it without any problems. I was given my travel expenses (from my home of record to Laxou, 47 Km) and some money to tide me over until I received my first pay. Lastly I had to speak to another person who looked at all my papers and issued a travel permit.

"How will you and your wife be traveling?"

"By automobile."

"When are you leaving?"

"I don't know; I hadn't thought about it. In a week, I suppose."

"Don't delay. There will be severe restrictions on private ownership of automobiles . . . very soon."

"Then we had better go before that."

"All right, I'll make it out for this weekend, the 19th, 20th and 21st. That should give you enough time."

"I had planned to stop home for a few days to see my mother and sister."

"You must take the most direct route."

"It's on the way . . . where they live."

"Where's that?"

"Saint Mihiel."

He, also, consulted a map to insure that it was and then stamped the form and signed it with a notation.

"Three more days. Enjoy your trip."

Was this how it would be? How would the country function? What else would we have to bear? The thing that bothered me most was that all the people that I spoke to this morning were French. When I got home I called the director of the lycée in Laxou.

He was very pleased to hear that someone had taken the position and extended an offer made by another new teacher to share a furnished room. When I mentioned that I had a wife he at first tried to convince me to take it anyway but I would not. Then, after he had spoken to some person there, informed me of a cottage that one of their staff was seeking to rent but said that he thought that the rate would be a bit too high for a new teacher.

"I can give you the owner's phone number and perhaps it will work out."

"Yes, please. I think we can manage for a short time until we find something affordable. Has he other places to rent?"

"It's a woman, a widow. It's only this one place; she herself used to live there but now lives with her daughter a short distance away. Her name is Françoise Gaillard. You have a piece of paper? Here's her number."

"One moment."

I reached into my jacket looking for a scrap of paper to write on and came out with a hundred franc note—Anton's gas money.

"Go ahead," I told him and wrote the number right on the note. "Thank you, Sir. I'll come see you when we arrive . . . good-bye."

"Who was that?"

Laure-Anne greeted me with a polite kiss; Odète was in the room.

"My new director. I have a position in Lorraine, an hour away from Saint Mihiel."

"You've heard about Lorraine?"

"Yes. Let me tell you what happened today."

I recounted my experience at the Sorbonne and mentioned the cottage and the hundred francs. When I called Madame Gaillard I was astounded at how little she wanted for the rental and accepted the offer immediately.

I made another call to Jean-Marie at work and informed him of my schedule and destination. We planned the trip that evening. The following day, Thursday, Laure-Anne and I picked up Vlasta and we went to Shlomo's house.

"Anything you need, Laure-Anne," she said. "What stays will be lost."

Not having had the foresight to ask Madame Gaillard about what was in the cottage, we prepared for the worst. Linens and towels, dishes, cookware, utensils, blankets . . . we took all the necessities first then continued until the rear seat of the Peugeot was full. We were about to leave when Vlasta wanted to look around one last time. We waited outside for her and when she came out she handed Laure-Anne a small leather bag.

"Just some things my daughter-in-law left behind."

"Thank you, Grand-mère. You've been so nice to us. I hope it won't be too long until we see you again."

As they were embracing, Vlasta gave me a look of determination. It struck me that she was prepared for hard times. She said nothing on the way back to her house; Laure-Anne did most of the talking. When I walked her to her door she kissed my cheek.

"Do you have an address?"

"Yes, I should have thought of that. Of course we will write."

I wrote it down; she looked at it and put it in her pocket.

"Don't you worry about us," she said. "We will manage; we always have."

"God bless you," I said and we parted. I don't think that I have ever said those words to anyone in my life. It seemed appropriate; she and Anton made so much possible for Laure-Anne and me.

After dinner that night, we packed our things. In the morning Jean-Marie and I carried it all downstairs. Except for a box of books, which we managed to squeeze into the rear of the car, everything else was strapped to the roof, my two bags and just about everything that Laure-Anne owned. The Peugeot's small trunk was filled with cans of gasoline in case we had trouble finding any for sale. Jean-Marie had siphoned it out of one of the company trucks.

Surprisingly our departure was not an occasion for tears. We were all very calm, very optimistic. It was more than a month since Paris was taken and for the most part its citizens had resigned themselves to the fact that we were not our own masters. But we all had to go on, had to work, had to remain hopeful that some kind of arrangement would be made and they, the Germans, would all go home.

We had at least a five hour drive ahead of us and only a baguette to eat. We felt that we would survive on what money I had and the little that Laure-Anne said that she had although she did not say how much. We headed east, crossed the Seine and left Paris behind. We were finally on our own, ready to make our way in this world in spite of the present sad state of affairs our country was in. We were no more than ten kilometers outside of Paris when we came to a checkpoint manned by German troops.

"Oh, no," I moaned. "Look at that!"

Ahead of us were about ten cars and a truck. One car that had as much in it as ours was being emptied by its occupants; a soldier was looking through their things. One by one the vehicles in front of us were approached and either allowed to go on or were searched. A soldier carrying a rifle came to my window.

"Where is it are you going?" he asked in poor French.

"We are going to Laxou. It's a small town in Lorraine," I answered in German. "I have a travel permit."

"Are you Germans?" he asked in his own language with a smile as he took the permit from me.

"No. We are French; we both studied German in school."

He examined the permit and returned it to me.

"What is the purpose of your journey?"

"I'm a schoolteacher. I'm going to my first assignment."

"To teach German?"

"Yes, to teach German."

The lie flowed so easily, seeking to gain some favor so that we might be spared the inconvenience of unloading all our possessions. The soldier stooped a bit to look into the car.

"You certainly have a lot of stuff with you," he said to Laure-Anne.

"Yes, it's everything we own. We were just married."

The soldier walked around the car, looking into the rear seat, poking the bags on the roof. He stopped at Laure-Anne's window and looked at her closely, saying nothing and then came back to me.

"Have a nice trip," he said and waved to another soldier up ahead.

"Thank you," I said and slowly made my way through the checkpoint.

"Thank you? You thanked that bastard? For what? For letting us go where we want in our own country? And now you're a German teacher? Why didn't you shake his hand and compliment him for the fine job he's doing?"

"Would you rather that they made us unload all this stuff and look through it?"

Laure-Anne said nothing . . . for a whole hour. I knew what I had done; I tried to please the enemy in order to make our life a little easier. *Was that so wrong? They did not benefit from what I had done.* In retrospect I knew that that was not so. I had unknowingly taught that one soldier that we French would go along to avoid trouble. I was about to make a vow to never do that again but refrained, thinking that it might be rash of me to exclude all possibilities. I did not feel good about my decision but did not change my mind. I wondered how much of my thinking was affected by my German father.

"Do you want some bread?"

Laure-Anne's voice revealed neither anger nor concern. I wanted to say that I was sorry but that was not the truth. I was sad that we should be this way with each other. I was proud of her patriotism, if that's what it was, but would it cause us harm? I don't suppose that a patriot concerns himself with such matters . . . but *I* do.

"All right," I said without emotion.

"Don't think that you're doing me a favor. I don't care if you eat or not."

I pulled off the road and shut off the ignition.

"Tell me what to do to make you love me again."

We both knew that I had exaggerated the matter but I was hoping that she could not say that she still loved me while she was angry.

"That's not what it's all about and you know it."

"You mean that you love me?"

She turned her back to me and stared out the window. After a minute I put my hands on her shoulders; she didn't shrug them off. I slowly pulled her to me; she did not resist. I held her with my left arm while I caressed her face with my right hand. I bent to kiss her but stopped just a hair's-breadth away and waited. It took a few seconds but she raised her head slightly and gently put her lips to mine . . . but it was not a kiss. I puckered my lips for just an instant . . . but that was not a kiss either.

"Do you love me," I asked with our lips touching.

"Yes, I love you. Are you going to kiss me?"

"I thought that you would kiss me."

"No. You kiss me."

I puckered slightly.

"Not enough," she said.

"How much is enough?"

She puckered more than I had.

"A little more than that," she said.

"No, I think that qualified as a kiss."

"No it didn't. You're just trying to . . . ."

The Swans of Lorraine

I pulled her tightly to me and gave her as good a kiss as I knew how. She tried to outdo me and we spent quite a bit of time in the contest. By the time we arrived in Saint Mihiel, the matter was long forgotten.

The tears that were not present when we left Paris were abundant when we arrived at my mother's house. Joyous tears are not to be compared to sad ones. There is such power in that feeling that it gives one an insight as to the purpose of life: it is for this, for this very thing, to be so overwhelmed with love that nothing else matters.

For five days we experienced each other. My mother had gone to the shop on Monday morning to tell Uncle Richard that she was taking two days off. He was furious, she said, because she had her son to enjoy while Jacques-Henri was a prisoner of war. Laure-Anne and I discussed taking Eliane with us but decided that we could come back for her in two weeks. When we informed her of our plan she asked if it would be agreeable to us if Olivier could bring her instead of us making the trip to Saint Mihiel. It was.

Wednesday morning we drove off into the sunrise. Only an hour away lay our future. We were filled with expectation.

"Do you feel grown up now," I asked.

"Not yet but almost."

"What does it take, then?"

She thought about it for a while then put her chin on my shoulder and spoke.

"What it takes is that when we make love we don't have to close the door, because we're in our own place."

Chapter 4

We drove southeast from Saint Mihiel to Toul and took the main road toward Nancy. Madame Gaillard's instructions were simple: when we came to the outskirts of the town we would see a large white farmhouse whose ruined barn was no more than stone walls. We turned there and came to a circle, taking the second street until the end and then turn right. When we passed the last intersection the road would turn in to a lane and the cottage would be the only building on that lane and it bordered the Forêt de Haye.

We did all that and were about to go on a dirt road that disappeared into the woods. We saw no cottage, only trees.

"Maybe she didn't count this as an intersection," Laure-Anne offered.

"I think I'll go down there a bit."

"She said next to the woods, not in it."

The road curved to the right and would have hidden anything behind the trees. I put the car into gear and began to go forward.

"There! There's someone, ask her," Laure-Anne insisted.

The woman watched us from her window as we passed her house. We drove slowly around the curve and came upon the cottage on the right. It appeared to be square, about ten or twelve meters on a side and had stone walls on the lower half; upstairs was timber and stucco, gleaming white as though it had been newly whitewashed. A vehicle was parked in front of the entrance. We parked alongside it and got out. Laure-Anne came around to my side and took my hand; we smiled at each other. It looked wonderful.

"Hello," a woman called to us, coming outside. "Monsieur and Madame Jannot?"

"Yes, that's us," I said, extending my hand. "You must be Madame Gaillard."

The Swans of Lorraine

"No. She's my mother; she doesn't get around very well. I'm Virginie Denisart and we are colleagues, you and I. I teach at the school so you had better get used to calling me Virginie."

"Agreed! Then I shall be Édouard. This is my wife, Laure-Anne. We've been married all of a month now."

"A pleasure, Laure-Anne. Come inside and look around. We've made some improvements since my mother moved out."

As we entered, the smell of vinegar filled our senses. A young lady who had been cleaning the glass on the kitchen cabinets rinsed her hands and approached us, drying them on her apron.

"This is my daughter, Marie-Jeanne . . . Édouard and Laure-Anne Jannot."

We all began greeting one another at the same time. Laure-Anne was chuckling.

"It's just a funny coincidence . . . my father's name is Jean-Marie."

Marie-Jeanne smiled and invited us to see the place.

"We've put in a refrigerator . . . it isn't new but it works, and an electric water pump. There's cold water to the kitchen and bath. The septic and toilet were put in a year ago but Grand-mère never used it. We've arranged for someone to come for the outhouse."

The bathroom was tucked under the staircase and it was sparkling white, with tiles on the floor and half way up the walls. The worktable and counters were thick well-worn maple. Just to the left of the front door on the south side was a large oak table but no chairs. The staircase leading upstairs nearly divided the house in half along with a row of posts, which held a beam on which the upper floor rested. I would guess that the cottage was at least a hundred years old. The front door faced east toward the town and one could look right through the place to the rear door.

"All the windows, upstairs and down are new."

That amounted to nine windows. Upstairs were two very large bedrooms with two windows each, facing north and south on the gable ends of the house. Only the south room was furnished, with just a narrow bed and two chifforobes. Two windows framed the front door, one each in the kitchen and the dining area on the south side and one to the west in the bathroom. A stone fireplace dominated the north wall, the chimney coming up between the two windows upstairs.

"I see that you have brought much with you. I hope that you have what you need; my mother could not bear to part with her things."

"Oh, we'll do fine," Laure-Anne assured her. "All we lack is a parlor."

I couldn't imagine where everything could have gone. Certainly there was not two of everything at Virginie's place. Perhaps Virginie got rid of *her* things to make room for her mother's.

Marie-Jeanne took us out the rear door to see the garden. A low wall of stones separated it from the woods; it was that close. It was full of vegetables although it needed to be weeded and the large woodpile against the house looked to be sufficient for even the worst winter.

I hung back a bit to admire the trees as they walked ahead through the garden. I loved the woods that were here and there around Saint Mihiel and felt comfortable with the nearness of this one. Side by side the women were the same height; Marie-Jeanne's light brown hair was the same length that Laure-Anne's had been before she had it cut. She was beautiful; she reminded me a little of Eliane but her face was rounded gracefully.

"Sorry about the weeds; we just didn't have the time that Grand-mère did. The man who lives at the corner cut the wood for her, a very nice man."

"I think we saw his wife as we passed," I said.

"Yes, that's Nadine. We grew up together. She'll probably wander down here in a bit, wondering who you were. She and Vincent, their name is Vinchelin, are your closest neighbors; there's no one else down the *sentier*."

"Ah, so you don't even call this a street then; but it has an address."

"Your address is simply 'near' the Vinchelin's. When you get settled in it would be wise to go to the post office to let them know that you are living here . . . and of course to the town hall to let the Boche know."

"They are here in Laxou?" Laure-Anne asked, astonished.

"There is someone who comes to check on things but we are too small to worry about. Now and then a military vehicle comes through just to show us that they're around. They leave us alone for the most part."

When we walked around to the front, Virginie and the woman from the corner were putting things in Virginie's car. We approached them. The other woman had dark hair like Laure-Anne but it was very curly. It gave her a Spanish or Italian look. She was quite a bit shorter and slightly pregnant.

"Come meet your neighbor."

After we all shook hands, Laure-Anne inquired about Nadine's pregnancy.

"Before Christmas. We're hoping for a girl . . . Noëlle."

"How nice." Laure-Anne gave me a brief glance that I noticed the other women correctly interpreted . . . on second thought, misinterpreted, depending on whether they thought that she was pregnant or was trying her best to get that way.

"You must have left Paris in the middle of the night," Nadine said, "to be here so early in the day."

"Oh, no, we came from my mother's house in Saint Mihiel."

"Oh, so you are *Lorrains*!"

"Only me. Laure-Anne is pure Parisienne. I'm a bit worried about her, not being crowded on all sides with buildings and people."

"So, you met in Paris?" Nadine asked.

I hesitated. I didn't want them to think that I seduced a wealthy man's daughter whom I was only to tutor.

"He was my tutor," Laure-Anne declared, "and I fell in love with him. When he graduated from the Sorbonne we got married."

"The Sorbonne?" They all exclaimed together.

"Whom did you anger to be sent to Laxou?" Marie-Jeanne joked.

"Actually I chose to come here, to be in Lorraine. There was only one other choice and that was Domrémy."

"Ah, you've done well then," Virginie said. "Domrémy is so . . . so . . . you know; even Jeanne d'Arc couldn't wait to leave it. Well, you are the only one on the staff that went to the Sorbonne. Not even the director. Just imagine . . . we may be the only lycée in France that has had ten per cent of its staff graduate from the Sorbonne."

"You have only ten people on staff?" Laure-Anne asked, incredulously.

"All of Laxou is not much more than two thousand people. If you count Monsieur Leclerc, the Director, yes. I told you we were small."

We all laughed about the size of the town and compared it to Paris. The three younger women stayed outside and chatted while Virginie took me back inside. We sat at the kitchen table.

"You are not likely to see my mother, she's not well; in fact she should be put in an asylum. She is the cause of us having to replace every window in the house; she saw . . . things, trying to come into the room. She remains rational and pleasant when we give in to her wishes, so we go out of our way sometimes when we would rather not. The point is, Édouard, because you share the same name as my father, she has lowered the rent far below what it should be . . . and I will leave it as such as long as she lives, but I'll tell you this now . . . it will double when she dies."

I nodded to show that I understood.

"I know what your salary will be and I'm sure that you well appreciate the bargain she has given you . . . but business is business. Do you have the two months?"

I handed her the hundred-franc note. She smiled when she saw her phone number on it. She folded it twice and stuffed it in her bodice.

"I'm sure," she said almost laughing, "that you will pray daily for her good health. I'll see you again this afternoon or at most this evening with your change."

We rejoined the others and learned where everything in town was located. Marie-Jeanne took me aside to ask if I wanted to buy some gasoline because she had a very dependable friend who could always get some. We still had about a half tank and I told her that we were not planning to use our vehicle much. She and Virginie left and Nadine helped us unload the Peugeot, putting it all in the empty parlor. She said that she would come back this evening with her husband to see if we needed anything.

Finally we were alone in our own place, staring at a pile of our belongings.

"What do you want to do first," I asked.

She gave me that mischievous smile.

"I meant work," I said.

"I'll make you work, don't you worry."

"Out here in the countryside, decent people wait until the sun goes down then close the doors to their bedrooms."

"No they don't. You're just making that up. I'll wager that they do it right on the kitchen table in broad daylight. Come on!"

She sat on the edge of the table and began sliding her dress up over her legs. I watched her, very amused. When she had it all around her waist, I stood in front of her. She wrapped her legs around me and unhooked my belt. I put my fingers in the waistband of her panties and she wriggled out of them, lying back on the table.

The Swans of Lorraine

"Welcome to Laxou, Monsieur Jannot. I hope that you enjoy your stay."

Later, when we had put away everything that had a place to be put away in, we were about to go shopping for food. The small leather bag that Vlasta had given to Laure-Anne was on the kitchen table.

"What was in that," I asked.

"I haven't gotten to it yet. Let's see . . ."

She unsnapped it and removed several perfume bottles and a man's wristwatch.

"Does it work?" she asked, handing it to me.

It was not ticking and as I wound it up, Laure-Anne was trying each of the scents on the back of her hand.

"It works," I said.

"Ooh, I like this one."

She let me smell it; I liked it too. She continued, finding some souvenir medallions and two small silver picture frames and on the bottom, an envelope.

"Oh, my God," she whispered as she opened it.

She held it open to me and I removed the stack of banknotes. They were of different denominations and I sorted them out, putting them in piles. When we added them up we had four hundred seventy francs.

"We're almost rich."

She didn't answer but retrieved her handbag from the parlor floor and sat again at the table. She removed two hundred-franc notes and added them to the pile.

"From Uncle Milan. And two from Grand-père . . . and two from Papa."

We sat there amazed; we just stared at the money silently.

"We need to buy some furniture," Laure-Anne said.

And so we did. The following Saturday our neighbor Vincent, who was a plumber, borrowed his boss's truck with the promise to fill the tank with precious gasoline when we were done. A short walk to see Marie-Jeanne insured that her friend would bring twenty-five liters Saturday night. We went from place to place in Nancy and bought a truckload, mostly used. We put our new bed in the north room, both because we believed that in winter we would get some warmth from the chimney and also because of the squeaky floor in the south room. We put one chifforobe in each room and a dresser in ours. Two cushioned chairs,

Phillip Varady

two love seats, two tables and two floor lamps became our parlor. Four chairs turned the dining room table into a dining room. We listened to Shlomo's radio for a half hour that night before we proved the new bed.

Sunday morning was beautiful; a little warmer than the previous days but well appreciated. After breakfast we decided to investigate the *sentier* that continued past our cottage where it narrowed considerably so that it was impossible to enter except on foot. The further we went the fainter the path became but still it was easy to follow. There was not a trace of civilization in these woods, an idea that intrigued us. I knew a bit about trees and the fact that this forest was almost totally beech, oak and maple told me that it had been uncut for at least a few centuries.

At one point the trail seemed to split and the branch that we followed came to an abrupt end. We stood in a small clearing surrounded by willows. We looked beyond it for a continuation but saw none and so turned to retrace our steps back to the split. I was puzzled by this anomaly.

"We're surrounded by willows," I commented.

Laure-Anne said nothing. *What would a city girl know about it?*

"There must be a reason that there are willows here . . . only here."

I looked for a reason and thought that I found one.

"Look back to where we came from . . . how the ground slopes down . . . and there and there how it slopes up again? Willows like water. The ground water must be high here . . . maybe there's a spring. Look around."

The perimeter, which was shady, was covered with ferns and the clearing with some sort of grass. We walked around slowly, moving the grass aside with our feet.

"Oh, here it is," Laure-Anne said.

It was no more than a hands-breadth wide. We followed it upstream a few meters and found where it surged up from the ground.

"This is what's called an artesian spring. Take a drink!"

"There aren't any bugs or frogs in it, are there?"

I ignored her question and scooped some water to my mouth. It was cool and refreshing; I continued until she also dared to drink.

"Mmmm. That's nice," she said after her first mouthful.

When we were ready to leave we stood there, hand in hand, surveying this little idyllic island in the forest. We felt like children in their secret hiding place. Without saying it, we knew that this was 'our' place. The whole concept of having such a place when one is already grown seemed absurd; we had our privacy, our home, our bedroom . . . we didn't need 'our' place but we wanted it.

Monday morning I reported to the lycée and was assured that my position was secure. When I inquired why there was a need for such an assurance and if there was a problem, my Director, Monsieur Leclerc seemed almost amused at my ignorance.

"You haven't heard about what happened in Moselle?"

"No. What happened?"

"Any teacher that cannot teach his subject in German will be let go. We suddenly have an abundance of teachers and they have a critical lack of German speakers."

I was not about to make known my ability in that area. Moselle was further east, that part of Lorraine that was re-annexed by Germany. I did not want to move further away from my mother and sister . . . from the cottage and our new friends. The director beckoned for me to follow him as we went on a tour of the school. He was speaking but my mind was searching for my true feelings. All my life I had this desire . . . maybe curiosity is a better word . . . no, admiration . . . for things German, yet I didn't want to be German; I'm French. I could tell Jean-Marie about my real father but couldn't bring myself to tell him that he was German. Was I ashamed or prudent? I have never told anyone my inner feeling about this, not even my mother. She and I do not speak of it any longer.

"So, have you found a place, Édouard?"

"Yes Sir, I rented the cottage from Virginie."

"Look here, maybe you've gotten into that habit at the Sorbonne . . . yes sir, no sir. We don't do that here," he said, putting his hand on my shoulder. "You call me Jérôme like everyone else, understand?"

"Yes Sir." I laughed . . . we laughed. "Sure, Jérôme."

"Your family has money then, eh?"

"Ha! No, Virginie said that it was crazy to charge so little for the place. It seems that her mother has taken a liking to me."

"Well, yes. I've met Françoise and she is a bit different. Well, what good fortune then. Have you something to keep yourself busy until September?"

I smiled, thinking of Laure-Anne. Jérôme laughed.

"Yes, I'm sure that you will be quite busy. How long has it been?"

"Forty-six days."

"Why don't you and your wife come to diner this weekend? Corrine and I would love to get to know you."

"Thank you, that would be very nice but my sister and her boyfriend are coming to spend a little time with us."

"Hmmm, we'll be gone the first three weeks in August . . . how about," he looked at his calendar, "the 26th, a Monday?"

"Sure, we'll be there."

He gave me his address and even walked with me for a minute to show me the street. This was certainly different than the Sorbonne.

There was little for Laure-Anne and me to do around the cottage. Once the garden was weeded and I had cleared the north side of a thicket we began to invent work. If not for Marie-Jeanne and Nadine coming almost daily, the one or the other, sometimes both, I would have had some concern for Laure-Anne. I always had my books to pass the time. One day Marie-Jeanne showed up with her friend looking to make another sale of some stolen gasoline. We had not moved the Peugeot since we arrived and I declined.

Having our car brought to our attention, we spent the afternoon washing and waxing it. That's the way it went through Thursday, scarcely able to wait for Saturday when Eliane and Olivier would arrive. We walked through the town to see what there was to see and stopped at a café for a crème de menthe but I was not willing to do that often because of our limited means. Laure-Anne prepared salads every day, and they were good, but it was a way to hide her inexperience in the kitchen. Eliane could be of great assistance, having shared the responsibility of preparing meals with my mother since she was six.

Friday, when I was anticipating lunch, Laure-Anne told me to fetch a blanket because we would be having our meal in the woods. She had it all prepared and put a bottle of white with it from the refrigerator. In fifteen minutes we were sprawled out among the willows.

"Do you know," she asked, "who it was that painted that scene where some men were having a picnic with naked women?"

"I don't know. Manet or Monet . . . or maybe da Vinci," I joked.

Laure-Anne was not very good at hiding things. I knew what she was going to do.

"Did that kind of thing really go on?"

"No, not at all. That guy was painting his sexual fantasies. They ran him out of France for being a pervert and destroyed all his work."

"But I saw that one, in the Louvre, I think."

"Well, they should burn it. That kind of thing is sick . . . degenerate."

I tried to sound sincere but she saw through it.

"Do you know what?"

She had not the slightest trace of a smile but her eyes gave her away.

"Yes, I do."

"You do? You do what?"

"I know what."

"What do you know?"

"That you're a degenerate."

"Ah, you saw that coming, eh?"

"No. Your mother warned me about this. She said that all the women in her family would take off their clothes at the slightest provocation."

She laughed and took off all her things. I pulled her on her back and kissed and fondled her.

"Do you know what I want to do?" I asked.

"Hmmm."

She bent one leg and leaned it to the side. I reached behind me for the chilled bottle of wine and pressed it firmly between her legs.

"Oh, you bastard. You could stop my heart."

I fell back laughing, making sure to hold on to the wine lest she do something to me with it. When she recovered we ate lunch just like in the painting. As the afternoon passed, the sky darkened. We didn't hurry and I still had time when we got back to the cottage to bring some firewood inside before the rain came. I fired up the kitchen stove and filled the water box, about fifty liters. We spent an hour together in the bath making ourselves presentable for our guests. When the electricity failed during the storm, we had tomatoes and bread for dinner with a bottle of red and candlelight.

Eliane and Olivier arrived mid morning. The two women left almost immediately to buy some groceries, planning a feast for dinner. I was surprised when my sister got behind the wheel of Olivier's car, cigarette in mouth, and made her way carefully down the muddy lane. Olivier and I talked about school and then Eliane and then politics. He seemed to think that politics was only a means to legitimize unscrupulous business practices, that there was more to the war than nationalism. I knew that to be true but suspected that he was alluding to something that he did not want to express plainly.

Vincent and Nadine arrived only minutes after the return of Eliane and Laure-Anne, probably waiting until they saw the car again. Vincent invited Olivier and me to his place for a few beers while Nadine stayed behind. We were all back in our own places by lunch. Olivier didn't like Vincent much because of his vehement dislike of the Germans whom he constantly referred to as the Boche, or more precisely, the damned Boche or some even worse adjectives. I thought he was carrying it a bit far as he seemed to be directing it toward Olivier from the time I introduced him and he discovered that his surname was Mersch.

Dinner was roast leg of lamb and many glasses of red. We retired to our parlor and continued to drink until we were sitting on the floor a bit tipsy. I tried my first and last cigarette and suggested we all go to bed, which we did. Laure-Anne woke me from my sleep and together we opened our door to listen to the floor squeaking in the other bedroom. She began to giggle and finally laughed out loud. The squeaking stopped . . . for about a minute, and I dragged her back to bed. It wasn't until they left to go to Nancy on Tuesday that Laure-Anne told me that Olivier paid for all the groceries and wine that was bought for the weekend and that the lamb was already in the car when they went shopping.

We had our dinner with Jérôme and Corrine; they were very nice. They reflected very well the closeness of the staff at the lycée. Teaching was a joy for me once I got over my fear of the students. Eliane got a job with the phone company in Saint Mihiel, Olivier was back at the Sorbonne, and Laure-Anne spent most afternoons with Nadine learning how to cook. Jean-Yves Vinchelin was born on 10 December; although it was not the girl that Nadine wanted, she was very happy.

Marie-Jeanne was now a clerk in the town hall and it was she who first brought Laure-Anne and me to the Saturday night ball. It was held in a barn, more or less secretly because the French police didn't like it. The Germans didn't mind as long as we didn't stay out after the curfew. Many times we did and would make our way home on foot in the dark. We would bring a bottle of wine and dance to records. The farmer, of course, wanted a little something for the risk he took. After a few such evenings we became known to the others and could come without Marie-Jeanne. It was not open to the public, only to acquaintances. We became good friends with a newly married couple named Déaut, Jean-Michel and Martine. Jean-Michel was a good man to know, he was the one who offered me the stolen gasoline and generally could get some on only a one-day notice.

Christmas in Saint Mihiel was made possible through Jean-Michel's ability to supply the needed fuel. The eve of that day was very much a family affair with Uncle Richard bringing his whole family for a visit. Jacques-Henri was still interred in a prisoner of war camp even though the army had been disbanded and the word was that he might be shipped to Germany. Things seemed to be going smoother between my mother and uncle; she explained later that it was because Uncle Richard now had his two other sons working at the shop and wanted a bigger share and she would not give up more. We went to Mass on Christmas morning and I swear you could not tell from the spirit of the people that an enemy occupied their homeland. It brought a tear to my eye but I noticed that I was in the majority.

About noon Olivier arrived with his parents in a Mercedes. My parent and sibling and my spouse also, I discovered, have this diabolical joy in surprising people. The engagement of Eliane and Olivier was announced. I was the only one in the house who did not know. The Mersch's paid the bride-price in the form of a ham, which we devoured with gusto. Not to be outdone, my mother produced a bottle of Rémy Martin and we toasted the couple well. Just when I thought that this was the best Christmas ever, Laure-Anne announced that she had a gift for me. It took the form of a small card in a small red envelope. I was greatly intrigued as were all the others. I opened it to read the three words written on it, 'I am pregnant.'

"Shall I share this gift with everyone?"

"Are you pleased?"

"Do you know a word that means more than ecstatic?"

Laure-Anne hugged me and we stood there in front of everyone selfishly keeping it to ourselves for a moment.

"Édouard," my mother whined, "out with it!"

I think she guessed correctly but wanted to hear it spoken. I held out the open card to her and she snatched it from me when she saw what it said, parading it around for all to read. Laure-Anne and I felt something that we had not known before. I can't say that it was the thought of becoming a family; maybe that was a part of it. Maybe on some other level . . . if there were other levels, the love that we had for each other was about to be rewarded in the form of a child.

The evening had to come to an end sometime and the Mersch's departed, leaving Olivier for me to return to Nancy before he went back to Paris. Both Laure-Anne and I wrote letters to Jean-Marie and Nathalie, which Olivier would deliver. It was late when we dropped him off and on the short drive back to Laxou from Nancy, Laure-Anne asked a question that she knew was on my mind.

"Do you think that the Mersch's are collaborating?"

"They had money before the war; maybe they found a way to hold on to it. What did my sister think?"

"I didn't want to ask."

Neither did I.

One evening in January of 1941 Vincent paid us a visit along with a man named André Biston. It was a cold night and we would have sat by the fire but André pulled out a chair at the kitchen table where Laure-Anne had just finished cleaning up after dinner.

"You can stay," he told her.

We took seats. I know she resented being given permission to do something in her own house but she said nothing.

"You have an ashtray?"

Laure-Anne produced the one that Eliane had left behind. Vincent and André lit up and André took a few deliberate puffs before he spoke. I had a good idea who he was. Vincent had mentioned that some men were looking to form a committee. This man seemed to be trying to impress us with his own importance.

"How well do you know this Mersch guy?"

He spoke, with his head tilted back, to the cloud of smoke that he had just exhaled. I refused to answer because of his manner. When he received no response he turned to me and made a sign with his hand as if he were giving me permission to speak.

"Oh, were you speaking to *me*? I couldn't tell. How well do you know *me*?"

"You? I don't know you at all. What does that have to do with it?"

"Well, I don't know why you would take the word of a total stranger when it comes to the character of another total stranger?"

"Vincent has vouched for you."

"So, I am to be trusted then. Thank you, Vincent. And I vouch for Mersch."

André and Vincent looked at each other. This was not what they came to me to hear. I was making Vincent look bad in front of someone he wanted to impress.

"How well organized are you? How many people do you have? What are you trying to do?" I asked my question in rapid succession.

"Hey, I'm the one asking questions here," he shot back.

"Why?"

"What?"

"Why are you asking questions? What did Mersch do?"

"He didn't do anything; we just want to know more about him. If he's going to come in and out of Laxou we ought to know what he's up to."

"What he's up to? He's going to marry my sister; that's what he's up to. Do you think I'd let a collaborator marry my sister?" I stood up and jerked my chair as I spoke.

"No one's calling him a collaborator . . . ."

André got up and summoned Vincent with a nod of his head and they moved to the door. After a minute André left and Vincent came back to the table.

"Édouard, that's not a man to make an enemy."

"He's an idiot. I think he's spent too much time at the cinema. And you . . . the only reason he's here at all is because you said something to him about Olivier."

Vincent put up his hands in a gesture of innocence but then bowed his head.

"You're right, but it was more a matter of you getting to meet André than of causing Olivier any harm. I knew you'd vouch for him."

"And how about you looking like a good little soldier to André?"

I had hit the nail on the head. Vincent mumbled an apology of sorts and left. I did not see him again until spring but by then the 'committee' was pretty much a closed group. I was content not to be included; I have much experience at that. Olivier's open show of wealth bothered me but apparently he and his family were legitimate; Nancy no doubt had its own committee and, I hoped, more responsible leadership.

Nadine and Laure-Anne were constant companions. Not only did Laure-Anne learn cooking from her, now she was learning about being a mother also. Jean-Yves was six months old when Olivier and Eliane married in Nancy, a year and a day after our own marriage. Eliane planned to move to Paris with her husband for his final year but postponed their trip until Laure-Anne delivered. My mother, who had come for the wedding, remained at the cottage for the same reason.

Olivier and my mother seemed to be spending much time together and often went to Nancy to meet with his father. After two weeks she came to me to explain. The elder Mersch had contracted, verbally, to buy meat from her and Uncle Richard at a good price. There were shortages and many vendors were charging exorbitant prices but risked being denounced, which could mean heavy fines or even serving time in prison. By selling in Nancy to Olivier's father, none of the locals in Saint Mihiel were aware and just took their word that meat was scarce. Then she advised me to talk to my sister who informed me that Laure-Anne and I would never lack some meat in the house. Our cousin Michel would make a weekly trip to Monsieur Mersch and part of his payment would be in gasoline of which he had plenty. His construction company had contracted with the Germans for several building projects and his allocation for gasoline was huge. When I questioned the morality of working for the Germans my mother simply said, 'All their employees are French and they all need their jobs.' And also her oft repeated maxim, 'Business is business.'

In another deal my mother proved her business skills by having renegotiated the rental of her farmland to include a percentage of the crop grown. Cauliflower and green beans became the chief crops after wheat but we were always supplied with potatoes and onions too. Michel brought both the meat and vegetables to Laxou.

Four weeks after the wedding, on Bastille Day, when the night sky was just turning gray, Laure-Anne woke me and calmly advised that we leave immediately. I thought about waking my mother but decided against it and we drove to the hospital in Nancy. After waiting for three hours with no results I went back home to get her. On our return we were brought to the new mother and daughter.

Laure-Anne looked exhausted but content, proudly displaying the baby at her side. I walked to the bed and knelt, putting my face centimeters from my daughter's. To say that she was beautiful one would have to use that word in a poetic sense, in that all babies are beautiful. At the age of fifteen minutes, it was not readily apparent. Laure-Anne and I had each chosen names but had agreed on none, nor were we close to a compromise through the use of a hyphen. I leaned across the baby to kiss Laure-Anne and while she weakly held on to my neck she whispered a name that neither of us had taken into consideration.

The Swans of Lorraine

"Catherine?"

I stood up and nodded.

"Maman, come look at Catherine."

I left them alone to call the Mersch's house and spoke to Eliane. She came immediately but Olivier was off somewhere with his father. He came that evening. On the first of August they traveled to Paris, taking my mother home on the way. As soon as Laure-Anne thought it was suitable we brought Catherine to the willows and spent a good portion of the day there at least once a week. For several months it was Nadine who now walked down the lane to spend time with Laure-Anne.

Increasingly Vincent and I became good friends again to the point that he could ask stupid questions without angering me. He told me plainly that he was being depended upon to watch me. I had thought about offering him an opportunity to buy some of the Farinet's meat but still had just the merest of suspicion that he might turn us in. Happily my guilt for denying his family some meat was allayed when I caught him and Biston and two other men sneaking past my house one night with a poached deer.

With the beginning of the new school year the entire staff had to listen to some propaganda about the historic roots of Lorraine and about easing tensions by not inciting our students to rebellion. There was a veiled threat with unnamed consequences. For the most part we ignored it. Laure-Anne and I had gotten to know all the teachers and we visited each other, except for Virginie. Marie-Jeanne however would often stop by either to see Laure-Anne or Nadine who she knew she could find there if she was not at home. Having successfully completed my first year at the lycée, I received a salary increase.

Christmas that year was very different. First my mother was going to spend the holiday in Paris to await the arrival of Eliane's child. Simple mathematics told us that she was three months pregnant at the wedding. Elisabeth was born on 19 December. Then we received two crates of products, delivered by a rude man who was sent to make this one delivery all the way from Bar-le-Duc, a special gift from Anton. The crates contained most of the foods sold by Sachs, Thouvignon. A long letter from Vlasta was included and Laure-Anne read it aloud to me. Her grandmother indicated that despite rumors and threats, they were still optimistic. At the end she wrote, 'You may want to open the cloves today.'

We immediately searched through the crates until we found the tin of cloves. I popped the top and found a little white cloth bag, tied with a drawstring. I let Laure-Anne open it and out came a slip of paper with 'for Catherine,' on it and Vlasta's diamond wedding ring. Laure-Anne, with some difficulty, put it on her finger.

"What do you think?" she asked.

"It's beautiful. I think that Catherine will never have it," I teased.

"No, I wouldn't do that. I just wanted to wear it once."

"You'll have your own one day, I swear it. Right after I publish my first book."

We spent Christmas Eve with Jérôme and Corinne and went to Mass Christmas day with the Vinchelins. It was then that I discovered that Vincent was an atheist; he told me himself. Nadine said he became one so that he wouldn't have to buy anyone anything. Virginie invited all the teachers to her home for New Year's Eve. I would have thought that Marie-Jeanne would celebrate with her friends but she was there and volunteered to care for Catherine for a good portion of the evening. The news of the war was depressing, especially the advances made by the Japanese in the Far East. That was so far away . . . We had a good time.

Our daily life was being changed gradually by some new restriction or prohibition or shortage. We coped as best as we could; the 'committee' seemed better organized but more intrusive. Much whispering and many secret meetings did not necessarily mean more action; at least as far as could be known by me.

When warm weather returned we began again to spend time in the willows, usually on Sunday afternoon. Catherine was ten months old and wanted to explore all that she could see. We knew our little patch so well that we allowed her to roam about as she wanted . . . as far as the ferns. Sometimes, as naked as we may have been from time to time and when she sat in the spring, she was enthralled. All she needed was a towel.

More than once, each time on a Saturday, we would come across a small black car parked on the lane between the Vinchelins and us. Once, from the cottage, I saw a man walk past it going into the woods. It was curious.

Olivier had finished school and would go to work for his father in the construction business. In spite of the German occupation, Nancy was growing and there was quite a bit of work there. He and Eliane found a place to rent and visited us often.

Laure-Anne and I began to occasionally go to the Café Quatre Vents to be social. It was the nearest and we also discovered that it was the most popular one in the neighborhood. We could walk toward the center of Laxou and find many more but the people in this part of town all came here. If we left Catherine with Nadine we would have crème de menthe. If the Vinchelins came along I would have beer with them and Laure-Anne would have some red, she had lost her taste for beer. André Biston was a regular and acted like a nobleman in his court as he called out to people or gave them audience. All I ever got was a polite nod.

One morning in late July I was in the garden weeding the vegetables. I thought that I heard a vehicle but kept on working. Presently Laure-Anne came out to me; she was crying. As I held her she spoke through her tears.

"They've taken them away. Those bastards took them away."

When I would have asked her to explain, Jean-Marie appeared in the doorway.

"They're arresting all the Jews, the foreign born especially, but they will get them all sooner or later. They're going to send them to the camps."

We had heard rumors about the camps but knew of no one who had firsthand knowledge. At best they were called 'Labor' camps and at worst 'Death' camps.

"Laure-Anne," Jean-Marie was at the point of tears, "you didn't let me finish."

"Oh, no. No, no, no. Are they dead?"

"I don't know. No one can get to see them."

Laure-Anne was confused, as was I. Jean-Marie took her in his arms.

"They took your mother also."

Jean-Marie was crying; Laure-Anne was screaming, struggling to break free of her father. I felt helpless and put a hand on each of them. Her father embraced her until she stopped. He held her by the arms away from him to speak.

"Why? Why her?" Laure-Anne cried. "She's not a Jew. What's wrong with them?"

Laure-Anne began a tirade against the Germans, against Germany and even against things German. Jean-Marie let her go on, embracing her again. Finally she stopped long enough for him to explain.

"Vlasta's father was a Jew . . . and Anton's parents. Three Jewish grandparents make someone a Jew. You only have one."

"Where are they? Are they still in Paris?"

"No. They were taken to a detention facility in Drancy. At first they were taken to the Vélodrome d'Hiver and when I went there they told me that it would be a several days before all the processing could be done. Each time that I went in the next few days I was told the same thing. After a week I discover that everybody was sent to Drancy where the police refused to tell me anything, not even if they were there. There were thousands arrested; they can't relocate that many people without somebody noticing."

Laure-Anne had some reason to hope and seized upon it. Jean-Marie intended to stay overnight and Laure-Anne regained enough composure to be able to cook a meal for him. Later, while she was preparing it, Jean-Marie and I spoke outside. I asked questions to gain an historical point of view. The most disturbing thing that I heard was that they were all arrested by the Paris police; that they knew where every Jew lived.

Jean-Marie's business had suffered as a result of the British blockade of our country and many imported items were in short supply. To save overhead costs he took over the duties of keeping the books. He began coming to Bar-le-Duc on the first workday every month and would stop by to see us before going back to Paris. On his next visit he had no further word of his wife or in-laws but had strong suspicions. I think that he was resigned to the belief that they were gone.

Laure-Anne became bitter and hateful, seeking revenge against the enemy. Late one hot Saturday afternoon in August at the cottage when the Vinchelins were visiting we planned to go to the Quatre Vents. We were just leaving when Marie-Jeanne showed up so we invited her to come along but she declined and then volunteered to watch Catherine and Jean-Yves if we wanted to go without them. We accepted her offer and set off on foot. We were enjoying our first drink when André Biston strolled in and came to our table to greet Vincent.

"I want to help," Laure-Anne blurted out

He pulled another chair to the table and sat.

"Don't speak so loudly. You never know who's listening."

Laure-Anne nodded and looked around.

"Don't look around," Biston said.

The Swans of Lorraine

I have never seen a man speak as he did. He had a cigarette constantly in his mouth, never taking it out until it nearly burned his lips, which seemed to never open when he spoke. The cigarette would go this way and that and ashes would fall where they may.

"You want to help do what?" he continued.

"I want to get those German bastards out of France."

"And how do you think that you can help?"

"I don't know. You tell me and I'll do it."

Vincent seemed impressed, Nadine bewildered, I was concerned and Biston suspicious.

"Why is it that you suddenly want to help?"

"The Germans arrested my mother and grandparents and sent them to the camps."

"Are they Jews?"

"My grandfather is but not my mother or grandmother."

Biston pushed back from the table.

"We want to give France back to the French. This is not a campaign to save the Jews from a little hard work."

"What are you saying? You don't want my help?"

He looked at her then Vincent.

"Yeah, that's what I'm saying."

Then he smiled . . . then Laure-Anne spit on him . . . then he threw her wine in her face . . . then I punched him and he landed on his ass.

"You're in trouble Jannot. I didn't trust you when I met you. Now I know . . . now I know."

"You don't know anything, you idiot. How did you ever get to be in charge?"

"Collaborators and sympathizers and Communists. . . and Jews."

I grabbed him by his shirt and pulled upward, almost to the point of raising him off the ground and spoke very slowly and quietly.

"Don't you ever question my loyalty or patriotism . . . or my wife's. What happened to Liberté, Egalité, Fraternité, or did you forget about those things just like the Nazis?"

I turned him loose and took Laure-Anne by the hand and we started walking. It took about two seconds for Vincent to decide to follow. We passed the small black car parked on the lane as we made our way back home. Before we got there, a man who had been speaking to Marie-Jeanne in front of the cottage began walking toward us. We exchanged greetings as we passed; he drove away. Laure-Anne hurried inside to wash her dress before the wine stained it permanently. It was a white dress with a floral print that I particularly liked.

"Do you know that man?" I asked Marie-Jeanne.

"I see him at work occasionally."

"What did he want?"

"He likes to take walks down the *sentier*."

"Did he change his mind? We haven't been gone a half-hour."

"I suppose so."

There was more to this but I decided not to pursue it in front of everyone. Instead we spoke about what just happened at the café and had a good laugh. Laure-Anne returned to us pleased that she was able to wash out the stain. Aside, Vincent cautioned me to be wary of Biston. I would not be intimidated by him and we determined to continue going to the Quatre Vents.

Two weeks later as we were enjoying a beer at his house, Vincent informed me that he was still in Biston's good graces because he was needed to keep an eye on me. The small black car passed by and I excused myself and ran down the lane. The man was already out and walking toward the cottage.

"*Ho! Nicht so schnell. Ich möchte mit Ihnen sprechen.*" I called out.

He stopped and waited for me to approach him.

"Why do you speak to me in German?"

"You do speak German, don't you?"

"Obviously you do also. What of it?"

"*Verstehen Sie besser auf deutsch oder Französisch?*"

"I grew up speaking both."

He appeared to be an honest fellow, about the same age as me. I was pleased with myself that my guess about him was correct.

"Are you German or French?"

"I was born in France."

That didn't answer my question. I made another guess.

"In Alsace?"

"Yes. In Colmar."

"And now that is part of Germany. So are you German or French?"

"I'm German. Does that bother you?"

"Are you German because you want to be German . . . or is it more convenient?"

He didn't answer.

"What do you do here in Laxou?"

"I'm an administrative assistant, a liaison between local governments and the German civil authorities."

He was a man caught up in politics. I thought back to the time I told that German soldier that I was going to Laxou to teach German.

"I'm Édouard Jannot."

I extended my hand to him. We shook and he had a wry smile on his face.

"We share the same initials. I am Erich Jost."

A long conversation followed during which he glanced at his watch many times. I finally let him go and returned to Vincent's house. When he inquired as to who the man was I told him that I had only spoken to him briefly then went home to take care of something; that he just liked walking in the woods.

The next day Laure-Anne and I took our little trip to the willows and had an enjoyable afternoon. When we came back to the split in the *sentier* I directed her in the opposite direction. We came to another division, one at which we had been previously. Straight ahead one would come to a road that cut through the woods; the *sentier* continued for quite a way on the other side. We had taken that path before but this time we turned right on a barely discernable one. In no time we had come out of the woods and were on the rue de la Vôge, a street just two hundred meters or so from our lane. We saw Virginie, who lived in one of only three houses there and stopped to chat a while. Presently Marie-Jeanne came out of the house and joined us.

"I didn't know that the *sentier* connected to your street," Laure-Anne said.

"Oh, there are so many different ways to go. I don't think that anyone knows them all. It's been years since they've maintained them," Virginie said.

Marie-Jeanne was staring at me. She knew that I knew.

In the following months I spoke to Erich many times, usually when he passed the cottage. For all that Laure-Anne knew he was only a man that liked walking in the woods. When November came Erich didn't. They had obviously found another less convenient place to meet or more likely the cooler weather forced them to. I was in for a surprise one evening when I took my family to the Quatre Vents, this time for dinner, when Erich and Marie-Jeanne walked in.

"Oh, come sit with us," Laure-Anne called out.

I think that if I had had the chance I would have advised Laure-Anne against it but it was done and I acted as if it was no problem at all.

"I would like you all to meet my . . . to meet Eric," Marie-Jeanne said haltingly.

When I used his name in conversation I was careful to use the same pronunciation that Marie-Jeanne had used, making it sound as though he were French. We enjoyed dinner together. Of course Biston was there but he didn't seem to take much notice.

For the first time ever, the family celebrated Christmas at our house. Jean-Marie went to Bar-le-Duc on the 22nd, a Friday, to do the books. He had given his employees time off until the second day of January. Eliane drove by herself to Saint Mihiel to get our mother. Jean-Marie stayed at the cottage and Eliane got to show her mother her housekeeping skills. Both parents went home on the 26th.

January 1943, the year started well with the news that an entire Army group of the Wehrmacht had surrendered at Stalingrad. There was an excitement, spoken and unspoken, that the end was coming. Whether near or far, we knew in our hearts that we would soon be rid of these invaders. People were bolder to speak openly of resistance; there were more frequent acts of sabotage and occasional acts of violence against the Germans. None went unpunished but the punishment did not deter more action.

It was with such optimism that the Vinchelins decided to have another child and by March Nadine could announce that it was on its way. That same spring Virginie came into my classroom after school one day to inquire of her daughter.

"What do you know about Eric . . . or is it Erich?"

"I know what do *you* know?" I replied.

"I'm not sure I know anything about him but I suspect quite a bit. Probably the same as you do. Have you told anyone?"

"It's none of my business . . . not even Laure-Anne. What will you do?"

"What *can* I do? She won't stop seeing him. She walks around town like no one cares. Well, we'll see."

That summer Olivier and Eliane bought a house in Laxou. I didn't encourage them to do so and can only interpret it as a desire by my sister to be closer to me . . . or maybe my wife . . . unless, of course, they were moving to be less close to the Merschs. In any event we were within walking distance of each other and the women tended to meet at

Nadine's house because she was now five months pregnant. Marie-Jeanne was still her best friend although she did not spend as much time there as Laure-Anne or Eliane.

In October Eliane revealed that she was pregnant again and before the celebrating had died down, Marie-Jeanne declared her own pregnancy. It was one thing to be pregnant at one's wedding and make it proper but Marie-Jeanne said that she and Eric had made no such plans. Three days later Nadine delivered Jean-Jacques.

We were becoming very close knit, we three couples, and Marie-Jeanne also even if she never brought Erich around. I would run into him now and then in public but it was he himself who kept the conversations short. When I asked where he lived he wouldn't give a direct answer but said that his office was in Strassbourg. Marie-Jeanne tended to speak less and less of him.

Christmas that year was celebrated at Oliver's and Eliane's house. My mother stayed there although Jean-Marie did not come that year. Marie-Jeanne stayed the whole day and never mentioned Erich, even when my mother innocently inquired about the father. I felt secure and hopeful even in the midst of the occupation. We had decided to have a second child and by the first of March we able to tell the world that we expected *him* in mid October.

When the warmth of May came so did two little girls. Marie-Jeanne delivered Hélène on the 8th and Eliane had her second daughter, Joëlle, on the 12th.

In June the day that we had all been waiting for finally arrived. News of the landings at Normandy electrified us. Anything the resistance could do to draw away troops from the front or delay their supplies was put into motion. There were a few days when it looked as though the attempt might fail but the Germans were forced back and the beachhead was secure. The allies' steady advance forced the evacuation of Paris and it was the 25th of August when the cry went up, 'Paris est libré.'

In the midst of rejoicing there was anxiety. The farther the allies advanced, the closer the fighting was to us. There were no measures to take, no safe areas to flee to; no one knew where the main fighting would take place and which towns would be bypassed. As reports from the BBC came in we realized that we would be in the direct path of the advance. The first two Sundays in September saw the churches packed. We were ready . . . and frightened.

Phillip Varady

It was Tuesday morning and even though we knew that the fighting was getting closer, we opened school as usual. We had not been there an hour when Jérôme came into my classroom. He spoke quietly to me.

"The Americans are moving out of Gondreville and sweeping the Forêt de Haye. I'm going to send everyone home. When we're sure that the front has moved through Nancy we'll resume classes."

"Are they running or fighting?"

"From what I heard the fighting is brutal; they're making the Americans pay for every meter. There's no natural defense in Laxou. They'll probably fall back to Nancy and make a stand."

"Hmmm. Shall I send them home now?"

"Yes. Some are already gone; I've got three more to tell."

Jérôme left the room and I wondered what to say. I didn't want to simply dismiss them but I didn't want to frighten them either. They were waiting for me.

"Monsieur Leclerc has directed me to send you all home. We have received word that the Americans are moving through the forest and that there will be fighting here as the front advances. This is a day that we have all prayed for but it's not a day of celebration. There will be great danger as two armies come through our streets. Go now; you will be told when to return."

There was no movement at first; they all stared at me. I think they would have jumped up and cheered but for my admonition. When I gestured to them, they quickly left the building. I could hear their shouts once they were in the street. I put a few things in order and walked home. On the main road to Nancy I could hear sounds of unmuffled vehicles. I stopped at an intersection that afforded a view of the road and waited for them to appear. I watched as three Panzers slowly headed toward Nancy. I stopped at the Vinchelin's to tell Nadine but she wasn't there. Jean-Yves and Catherine were playing on the *sentier* and ran to me as I approached the cottage. A hug and a kiss apiece and they went back to play.

The front door was open; it was cool but the fire in the kitchen stove kept the cottage warm enough. Nadine was at the table with Jean-Jacques and I put a finger to my lips to keep her silent. I came up behind Laure-Anne at the stove and put my hands on her belly.

"How's the little one doing today?"

"Did you get sent home from school, bad boy?"

The Swans of Lorraine

"We *all* got sent home; the Americans are this side of Toul near Gondreville. It could be very soon; I saw three German tanks heading for Nancy. If they're pulling their armor back now it's to form a defensive position. I think Nancy will suffer."

Laure-Anne had turned to face me and Nadine came close to hear what I was saying. We hugged, the three of us. Nadine was crying; her parents lived in Nancy. Throughout the afternoon we could hear the Panzers, by ones or twos, unhurriedly making their way to the next battleground to the east.

Wednesday was sunless and we passed most of the day looking at the forest from our windows. *Where were they?* We saw nobody, heard nothing. Late in the afternoon I went outside to bring in some firewood and I could faintly hear artillery in the distance. Thursday we heard planes overhead and bombs exploding in the Forêt de Haye. When we went outside to look we saw the markings on the aircraft; they were American. A light rain and the cool temperature kept us indoors the rest of the day; we spent an anxious evening around the fireplace. Catherine slept in our bed but Laure-Anne and I were awake the whole time. In the middle of the night I got up to investigate some sound but could see nothing except a thin sliver of the moon. Morning was slow in coming; the sky was again overcast. We got up, leaving Catherine asleep and went to the kitchen. There were still some coals in the stove and I added some wood to make coffee.

"Édouard!" Laure-Anne gripped my arm.

Through the window we saw men running. They just suddenly appeared from the fog, German soldiers coming from the south, crossing the *sentier* heading for the main road to the north. We appeared to be in no danger; they were not stopping.

Suddenly there was a burst of gunfire. A bullet came through our rear door and we heard glass tinkling, the bathroom window. Bullets were hitting the wall of the cottage.

"Stay here, get down! I'll get Catherine."

As I wakened our daughter I could see the fleeing Germans from the window. Two of them had taken cover behind the stone wall twenty meters or so north of us. I could see the dark shapes of the Americans slowly coming through the fog in the woods from the northwest, trying to cut the Germans off before they could make it to the road. Laure-Anne was shouting.

"Over here! They're hiding behind the wall!"

Phillip Varady

My God! Is she crazy?

I left Catherine sitting on the bed and raced downstairs. Laure-Anne was standing in the doorway, out of sight of the two behind the wall, waving to the Americans who could be seen deep in the woods. Another burst of gunfire and Laure-Anne's belly turned red as she was thrown against the door and fell to the ground. I ran to her. A German soldier appeared pointing his weapon at me. He stared at me blankly for a second before he shouted to his comrades.

"Raus . . . raus. Schnell!"

The two behind the wall got up and started running. More gunfire and the head of one of them exploded in a hail of bullets.

Laure-Anne was trying to speak. I put my hand on her side and felt nothing solid. Her flesh moved away as I tried to stop the blood. I pulled her up to a sitting position and brushed her hair away from her face.

"Édouard . . ."

"Ssssh. Don't speak."

"Édouard . . ."

"Oh Laure-Anne, Laure-Anne, I love you so much."

It was a grievous wound. I had no false hope that she would survive. She tried to raise her hand but had no strength. I took it in mine and would have put it to my face but felt her pull on it. I held it, guiding it to where she wanted it. She extended a finger and slipped it under the chain around her neck.

"Édouard . . ." her voice was so faint, her eyes were closing.

I put my ear to her mouth.

"Don't die without me . . . please . . ."

Her hand lost all its strength and I let it down. The birds popped out from between her breasts as her finger lost its grip on the chain. Her eyes were almost shut . . . I put my ear to her chest and waited. There was nothing. Suddenly her head fell forward and I took it in my hands thinking that she was not gone . . . but I knew.

Can't we go back a minute or two? Can't this be some other way? Am I awake? Is this real? She's gone . . . this is real, forever. Forever, forever, forever . . . forever. No, no, no. It can't be. Not my Laure-Anne, no not my Laure-Anne.

"Aaaaaaugh . . . noooo . . . no, no, no."

My lungs forced out every last trace of breath in one enormous surge. My whole body was in pain. I wanted so desperately to do something but there was nothing to do. I sat alongside her and put my arm around her shoulder putting her head on my chest, holding it tenderly.

"Papa, what's wrong?"

My body hid Laure-Anne's bloody side but the evidence was flowing from between us. *Oh, God! Must the daughter go through the same horror as the father?*

"Come here, darling."

Catherine came around us and knelt at her mother's side . . . tears in her eyes. She knew something was terribly wrong; I could not hide that.

"Put your hand on Maman's face."

I raised Laure-Anne's head with my hand under her chin.

"She's beautiful, isn't she?"

Catherine stroked her mother's cheek then moved her fingertips to her lips.

"What's wrong with Maman?"

"Maman is asleep."

"Why doesn't she wake up?"

"Maman isn't going to wake up . . . ever again."

Catherine began to cry aloud.

"Give Maman a kiss . . . Catherine, give Maman a kiss."

Catherine put her lips to her mother's, pushing gently on her cheek with her hand as if she could awaken her. She sat next to her holding her arm with both her hands and rested her head against it. We sat there silently; I had no thought to do anything else.

An American soldier appeared in the doorway and spoke to me although I have no idea what he asked; I just shook my head. He moved on and suddenly there were soldiers everywhere, moving past the cottage. In a minute they were gone.

"Catherine, go out the front door and wait for me to come out. Catherine . . . go, go on . . . now."

She got up and slowly went to the door, pausing many times to look back. She stood there for a minute with her hand on the handle but finally went out. When I could no longer see her I got up and quickly followed her. My shirt was bloody, my trousers soaked. I could feel the blood running down my leg into my shoe. I closed the door behind me and picked her up, holding her on my left.

The sky was overcast; fog still drifted slowly as I walked to the Vinchelin's. I knocked and waited; Catherine was silent, looking back toward the unseen cottage. Nadine opened the door and a look of horror filled her face.

"My God! Édouard, are you all right? . . . Catherine?"

I put a finger to my lips to keep her from saying more. My hand was bloody, as was my arm . . . my whole right side.

"Could you watch over her for a while . . . maybe a day or two?"

"Yes, certainly . . ." she stared down the lane.

"I've got to take care of Laure-Anne."

"Is she . . .?"

I shook my head as she took Catherine from my arm. The walk back to the cottage took a while. I stood in the lane where one can first see it, remembering that day that we arrived in Laxou. What expectations we had. When I reentered the house I took a tablecloth from the cabinet under the stairs and draped it over Laure-Anne's shoulder, hiding the wound. I sat in the doorway where Catherine had been and cradled my wife's body. My hand rested on her belly . . . her beautiful belly that in a few weeks would have produced our second child.

I don't know how long I sat there. The sun never shined, even after the fog dissipated. My fingers moved across her face . . . repeatedly, running through her dark hair, over her lips. I kissed her . . . so many times . . . touched her belly . . . put her hand on my face . . . kissed her palm . . . I cried. A wave of uncontrollable sobbing drained me, I became calm, for a while . . . but it came back . . . again . . . and again.

"Édouard . . . I'll call someone."

It was Nadine, tears dripping from her face. I nodded.

"In a while . . . I need a little time."

She was gone and I was alone with my Laure-Anne again. Alone again. I pulled on her chain until the clasp was in front. I couldn't open it with one hand. It had sufficient length so I pulled it upward gently over her face and head and draped it over mine. I took the birds in my hand. What was it Laure-Anne said?

'*Deux oiseaux . . . joint ensemble à jamais* . . . two birds . . . joined together forever.' Two swans, mates for life.

Voices were around me, hands on me. Gentle voices, weeping, walking, warm water all over me, darkness . . . crying . . . crying in the darkness. Daylight . . . bright sunshine and I was crying. I was alone, amidst all my friends I was alone. Night . . . day, night, finally . . . I slept.

"Papa, wake up. I'm hungry."

Catherine was kneeling at the bed, her face a breath away from mine.

"Give me a kiss, darling."

She pecked at my lips.

"More?"

"Oh, yes. Now I want a hug too."

"You have to sit up, Papa."

The blanket was only laying on me and I sat up and put my feet on the floor. I was fully dressed . . . I remember walking home from Vincent's to put Catherine to bed.

"Come up here."

Catherine climbed up on the bed and plopped into my lap. She threw her arms around me and squeezed as hard as she could. I held her and carried her downstairs. Everything was as it should be . . . except for the bullet holes in the door no one would ever know. Someone had been here this morning; a fire in the stove and a pot of water for coffee. I sat Catherine at the table, sliced some bread and put it in the oven to warm.

The squeal of brakes and happy voices drew me to the front door. A small military vehicle pulled up with four American soldiers, my mother crowded between two of them in the back. One of them helped her to get out, his hands familiarly holding her hips as she stepped to the ground. She gave each of them kisses on both cheeks.

Catherine ran passed me to greet her. The soldiers waved and shouted silly things in French and left. My mother and Catherine exchanged hugs and kisses and came to the door.

"Where's Laure-Anne?"

"Maman is sleeping, Grand-mère."

"Let's get you some bread you hungry child," I said.

Catherine got back into her chair. I quickly buttered her bread and led my mother outside, closing the door behind me.

"Laure-Anne is dead. She was shot at the back door when the Germans were retreating."

At first my mother was speechless and then when she noticed, she put her fingertips on the chain and pulled on it until the birds were visible and then fell into my arms weeping. I held her and let her cry. I could not console her; I didn't know how. I waited until she regained her composure.

"Maman, I won't let you near Catherine if you're going to fall apart."

Rather than protest, she acknowledged understanding of my restriction.

"Did she see it?"

"No. She was spared the horror; she came minutes later. We sat together . . . the three of us . . . for a while. She kissed her mother good-bye."

Now I was in tears, forced to remember that time. I suppose that I will have to endure this one more time whenever Jean-Marie contacts me.

"Let's go inside. I'll be all right. What does Catherine think of all this?"

"For now she accepts that her mother is sleeping. Sooner or later that will be unacceptable to her and she will know the loss. I won't lie to her . . . neither will you."

"All right, go. I want to see her."

As I reached for the handle, the door opened.

"There you are! May I have more bread Papa?"

"Sure. You know what? I think we have some plum jam. Would you like that?"

We had breakfast as if nothing had happened. There was a knock at the door.

"Édouard, how are you doing?"

"Jérôme! It's nice of you to come by. Are we going to start classes again on Monday?"

"Today is Monday, Édouard. I came by to remind you of what I said yesterday at the funeral. I didn't think you heard me and I didn't want to intrude with talk about work. Come in when you want. Take a few days . . . I am so sorry . . ."

"Thank you. My mother just arrived . . . maybe tomorrow . . . or Wednesday."

"Sure. Whatever you want."

I returned to the table. The funeral . . .?

One by one during the day they came to see me. Eliane first, Olivier went to work, then Marie-Jeanne with a pot of stew, then Nadine; Vincent also went to work. That afternoon when school was out they all came . . . my colleagues. In the evening the Mersch and Vinchelin families came. We tried not talking about it but it was pervasive. I was glad when they all went home. We put Catherine to bed and I made a small fire to overcome the chill. My mother and I sat in a love seat which

I had placed directly in front of the fireplace. She was holding me as if it were twenty years earlier.

"What now . . . my son?"

"If it were not for Catherine . . . I suppose I could ask Nadine to care for her while I'm at work."

"Do you have gasoline in your car?"

"Yes, it's full. We hardly ever use it."

"Take me home tomorrow to get my things. I'm moving in!"

The idea was startling but on second thought very practical. I don't know of any reason why she stayed in Saint Mihiel other than to not give in to Uncle Richard. The three of us left after breakfast. When we were finished loading everything, she had as much as Laure-Anne and I when we first left Paris. We went to the shop and she had me wait outside while she told them about Laure-Anne.

When I came in they offered their sympathies and my mother and Uncle Richard left to see someone. Michel and Daniel seemed very different, no longer as unfriendly as I remembered. They made a fuss over Catherine and we chatted about things for a half-hour until Uncle Richard returned . . . alone.

"She'll be another minute or two. She had some other business to take care of. So, let me see that little girl."

He picked up Catherine and spoke in a jolly fashion to her. She liked him. He found some candy and offered her a piece. She took two and offered one to me.

"I'm ready," my mother exclaimed as she returned five minutes later.

Uncle Richard delayed us long enough to wrap some meat for dinner that night. My mother had obviously made some arrangement with him but she still had some secret. She managed to avoid whatever it was and spoke of other things on the way back to Laxou. When we were just outside town she asked me to take her to my landlady's house. I did and Marie-Jeanne invited us in; Virginie was at school.

"It's your grandmother, isn't it, that is the owner of the cottage?" my mother asked.

"Yes, her name is Françoise . . . Françoise Gaillard."

"Is she here? May I speak to her?"

"She's here but she doesn't see anyone."

"Tell her that Édouard's mother would like to see her."

I had told her about the low rent and the reason for it . . . and what would happen at her death. Marie-Jeanne didn't think that it would do any good but went to ask. In a minute she was back followed by a plump white haired woman in a black dress.

"What's your name?" she barked.

"I am Claudine Jannot."

"I had an Aunt Claudine . . . didn't like her one bit. What do you want?"

"My son . . . Édouard, says that you were very nice to him for charging him the rent that you do. He also said that your daughter was going to double it when you died."

"She said that?" Françoise asked Marie-Jeanne and repeated it to me. I nodded. "That bitch! Bitch!," she screamed at the door.

"I would like to buy the place before she gets her hands on it."

Françoise walked right up to my mother and put her face to hers for a few seconds then turned to Marie-Jeanne.

"Get my stick; we're going to see Favier."

"Grand-mère, you haven't been out of the house in four years."

"Don't give me any of your mouth or I'll beat you with that damned stick. Don't you think I can walk to the next street?"

Marie-Jeanne got her cane and was helping her to the door.

"Not you," she told Marie-Jeanne. "You stay here. You, Claudine, bring the little girl, I like her."

When they left, Marie-Jeanne shook her head at me.

"I'm glad that it's you and not me that has to work with my mother. Do you know who Favier is?"

"No."

"An attorney."

When they came back after a while, Françoise had only half a cane. She came to me and patted my cheek then left the room. My mother waited at the door with Catherine, expecting to leave immediately. I waved them on but stopped at the door.

"Marie-Jeanne . . . could you . . . I'm going to get rid of Laure-Anne's things. Would you like some of her dresses and skirts and . . . You were both the same size. Eliane is a little heavier and Nadine is too short."

"Yes, that's so nice of you; she had some very nice things."

"I'll come by with them later."

"Maybe you should wait until the morning when my mother will be in school."

"Yes, all right. It's probably worse than we think. See you then."

"And Édouard . . . that's very sweet," she said, pointing to my neck.

She pulled up on my chain, guessing that it was the same chain that Laure-Anne had worn for years. She kissed my cheeks. I could not wait to hear what my mother had to say . . . which turned out to be nothing. After bringing all her belongings in the house we had some salad for lunch. Nadine came with Jean-Yves and the baby and I took the opportunity to ask them to help me sort out Laure-Anne's things. When they agreed to do it I decided that I didn't want to help and took Catherine and Jean-Yves into the woods.

"Are we going to the willows, Papa?"

"Yes. Is that all right?"

"*He* can't go! That's *our* place!"

"Can he take a walk with us then?"

"Oh, sure. He's my best friend."

After a nice dinner my mother read a story to Catherine and put her to bed. I was sitting by the fire sipping some of her Rémy-Martin when she came back down.

"Nadine took a few things, the shoes will fit Eliane but not the dresses and skirts. The little bit of jewelry we'll save for Catherine . . . and that diamond ring."

"Oh, that. It was a gift from her grandmother."

"Hmmm. Well, if you can manage to make another trip to Saint Mihiel we could bring back my bed. That narrow piece of junk you have upstairs is not big enough for the two of us."

"I'll ask Vincent. If I put some gas in it, his boss may let us use his truck."

"Oh, that would be wonderful. There's so much I could bring."

"Tell me about Françoise's broken cane."

"Do you remember Claude Abbas?"

"Isn't he the man who rents your farmland?"

"Yes. He made an offer to buy it years ago, before the war. I turned him down but he said the offer would still be good and left papers with Denoyelle, the attorney. When your uncle and I finished our business with him I asked if Claude's offer was still good. It was and I took his promissory note. I put the house up for sale. I gave the note to

Françoise as a down payment, she signed a contract and I gave her my note for the balance. I have to give her a little interest until I pay it off."

"Where does the broken cane come in?"

"Favier, her attorney, said he wanted to speak to her daughter before he went ahead with the transfer. She convinced him by smashing his telephone with her cane, that it would be better if he did it now. He thought so too."

That was amusing; I wished that I had seen it

"How much was the cottage?"

"If it was your cottage, you would know."

"If it was mine . . .? Shall I pay *you* rent now?"

"That won't be necessary. Family is always welcome."

"What did you and Uncle Richard decide."

"He bought me out."

"I don't suppose that you'll tell me what that was worth either."

"You're so smart. That's why you went to the Sorbonne. Do you want more cognac?"

"Yes. That's all I can get out of you."

"Oh, I have something for you. Do you know why there are no houses between here and Nadine's?"

"No, I never really thought about it."

"Well, it's because it's all one property . . . mine."

The Swans of Lorraine

Chapter 5

Wednesday morning it was raining. I had thought about going to work but when I smelled warm bread I decided to take one more day. Laure-Anne and I had always come downstairs together so there was never breakfast waiting. My mother and Catherine were at the table waiting for me. Catherine came to give me a hug.

"Papa," she whispered, "Doesn't Grand-mère have a bed?"

"Yes but it isn't here."

"Is she going to bring it here?"

"Yes, in a few days. Can you wait a few days?"

"Oh, I don't know . . . she's pretty loud."

"Ssssh. Come get your bread."

After breakfast the grandmother showed the granddaughter a box full of trinkets collected over a lifetime in Saint Mihiel. The rain gradually stopped and sunlight occasionally broke through the clouds.

"I'm going for a walk," I declared.

"Can I come, Papa?'

"No, not this time. I'm not going to the willows; I just want to look at something."

Catherine came running and stood in front of me with her arms spread. It was a little game that we played. I held her hands and she put a foot on my knee. I knelt on the other one and she climbed up, using my hands to steady herself. She walked across my thigh to fall across my shoulder. I carried her to the front window looking at the woods in front of the cottage.

"How would you like it if Grand-mère stayed here all the time."

"It's all right if she stays in your room."

"Well, she's going to stay in your room, she not allowed in my room."

"Well . . . if she has her own bed."

"She will have her own bed."

"Can she cook?"

I walked into the woods in front of the cottage. It was so near but I have never been in them, thinking that it was someone else's property. Everything was still wet from the rain and my shoes and the bottoms of my trouser legs were soon soaked. There was nothing special here, not that I was looking *for* anything, but rather looking *at* everything.

How selfish I had been. When I had retreated into my own special sanctum, letting grief, pity and despair remove me from the world of the living, Catherine was out there on her own. *Who tended to her needs? Eliane? Nadine? Oh, Laure-Anne, I miss you so much! Is Catherine all that I have left of you? I want more . . . but she is all that I have. So precious, so pragmatic . . . at three years old. She made me smile . . . I didn't want to smile . . . ever again. The memory of you is painful . . . I don't want to forget you but I don't want the pain. Catherine is a constant reminder of you but she is a joy. I cannot sort it out; I cannot choose a path that my life must take. I will be a leaf in the wind, going where fate takes me until . . . what? Will I know when I have arrived? Will I know when the path is of my own choosing and not the wind?*

"Papa, look!"

Catherine came running with something to show me when I came back to the cottage. I knelt to receive her.

"Papa, are you crying?"

"No, I walked into some wet leaves."

She looked at me as if she knew.

"Hey, I see something in your eye," I told her.

She moved her face close to mine and turned it up for me to investigate.

"No, you're too close . . . there, that's better. Do you know what I see?"

"No, What?"

"I see Maman."

She smiled at me instantly, then tilted her head slightly and smiled harder.

"Hey," she said, "give me a kiss."

I gave her a peck.

"More?" I asked.

"Lots more."

We both stuck our faces out and pressed our lips together without embracing.

"You know," she said, "I think I want a hug too."

I scooped her up and brought her into the kitchen.

"I have lots of hugs. If I don't give you enough, you just ask when you want one."

"Catherine, when your papa lets you go, get dressed. You and I have some shopping to do."

I put her down and she hurried upstairs. I poured a cup of coffee.

"It's so easy for a child, isn't it?" I mused.

I put my cup on the table. My mother was standing at my side.

"Hey," she said, "give me a kiss."

I kissed her . . . more than a peck.

"More?"

"Yes, I think I want a hug too."

We all got ready to go out.

"Where are you off to, Édouard?"

"I thought I'd stop by the school and tell them to expect me tomorrow."

"Will you pass Marie-Jeanne's place?"

"I could go that way . . . yes, the dresses."

A few stray clouds persisted and there was a coolness that indicated that we had seen the last warm day this year. We all walked past the Vinchelin's to the circle; the markets were to the right and the Denisarts to the left. I was thinking that since my mother didn't ask for grocery money and being as business minded as she was that I could expect that she will propose some plan to share expenses. I knocked on Marie-Jeanne's door.

"Hello, I thought perhaps you weren't coming."

"Oh, first it was the rain and then I had a few things to do. I'm on my way to school to tell them I'll be back tomorrow."

"Well, you've got all day then. Come in, can I get you something?"

"No, I'm fine."

"Coffee is already made, come in the kitchen and let me see what you've brought."

The kitchen was cozy with a small coal stove in one corner. Hélène was sleeping in a wicker crib in just a diaper. Marie-Jeanne poured two cups.

"Is it any better today?" she asked.

"Yes. I think the human mind and heart cannot continue long at the intensity that I experienced. I didn't want to admit that I would ever feel less but . . ."

I did not want to talk about it; it made me remember. We sat in silence for a minute as Marie-Jeanne went through the things that I had brought.

"The blouses and skirts will be all right but the dresses may be a bit snug; I'm a little bigger on top than she was. Let me try one on; there's no sense in taking them if they won't fit."

I agreed and was surprised when she took off her blouse and skirt right there in front of me. I could see that she wore only a slip and wondered at her lack of modesty. She chose the white floral print that I liked so much and pulled it over her head, wiggling as she slipped into it. She smoothed it over her hips and buttocks and pulled the bodice tight, turning her back to me.

"It looks like it fits well. Button me up."

When I had finished I sat in my chair as she turned this way and that. She mesmerized me; she must have known it.

"It's the dress, Édouard."

"Yes, I know. I didn't mean to stare."

"I don't mind, Édouard. I don't mind at all."

The front door burst open and men came pouring into the house led by André Biston. André was brandishing a pair of scissors and the man behind him, wearing a black beret and black shirt, had a pistol.

I leaped out of my chair but they were quickly on me. One man grabbed me by the shirt, popping off most of the buttons, and then many hands pushed me back down.

"We're going to give you a haircut, slut!" Biston said loudly, waving the scissors in front of her face.

"Get out of my house! You have no business with me," Marie-Jeanne screamed.

"We have business with all you collaborators."

"You're crazy. I'm no collaborator."

"You may only have had your ass on the sheets but you were still collaborating."

"Biston," I yelled, "you're going too far. You have no right to judge or to punish."

"Watch it, Jannot. You might be next."

"Are you going to invent charges against me also? She's not guilty of anything."

André stood in front of me waving the scissors slowly back and forth. Then he spread his arms and moved backward, forcing the men to make room for him. He was putting us on a stage so that all could see what was about to happen.

"We have collaborators . . . and we have sympathizers. We have Communists . . . and we have Jews . . . and then we have this type. What is this, citizen?" he asked with a smile as he tapped on my birds with the scissors. "Do you like to wear women's jewelry? Maybe he likes to wear women's clothes too. Who knows?"

The men began to chuckle and make suggestive noises. I looked at them, from one side to the other. They didn't turn from my gaze . . . only one, Vincent. He was in the back, probably hoping that I wouldn't see him. André put the scissors under the chain my birds were on and lifted it. He took them in his hand; I did nothing. I knew that if he pulled it from my neck, I would be on his, scissors or not.

"Very pretty. You like birds . . . eh? You like pretty things?"

I knew what he was doing. He had nothing to accuse me of so he set out to discredit me. I wondered which way he would go, make me out as a deviant or as Marie-Jeanne's lover. His eyes went from me to her to his audience. He let go the birds.

"Jannot the bird! *Coin coin, coin coin*. Nothing to say, Bird?"

I was about to tell him that they were swans not ducks but saw no point in correcting him.

"You think this whore did nothing wrong? You think maybe we should have just let our women make the Boche feel at home? What was to be next? Invite them to dinner? She's going to be punished for what she did, to be an example."

"Why are you picking on *me*?" Marie-Jeanne shot at him angrily. "You think that I was the only one?"

"Oh, we know there were others but you're one of the first."

"Others? You think there were others? I'll tell you how many others there were. How many Germans were in France . . . that's how many others."

"Shut your mouth, you whore. You're going to get what you deserve."

André made a motion to the men to take her outside.

"You miserable excuse for a man. What did you want me to do? Crawl into bed with *you*? I'd rather eat shit than let *you* touch me."

As the two men were reaching for her, André swung the scissors at her face, striking her in the cheek. I saw a flash of blood as the man closest to André backed away and ducked. Marie-Jeanne fell to the floor being held by the other man. I leapt from my chair and grabbed André from behind before he could do more. Someone punched me in the back of my head and another pulled at my arm. I was dragged backward and the man with the pistol stood over me.

I could hear Marie-Jeanne crying in pain; they pulled her to her feet.

"Get up," the man in the black shirt said and kicked me.

The baby started crying but one of the men stood between Marie-Jeanne and the crib and would not move. She was holding her cheek, covering the wound; blood was streaming down her neck.

"No one will be kissing those lips for a while, eh?" André chuckled and looked around at the men. "Everyone will know that this whore slept with the Boche."

Marie-Jeanne was terrified; she pushed on her cheek with her fingers. André took the place of the man that stood by the crib and opened and closed the scissors many times. He was enjoying her terror. He opened the scissors again and took one of the blades in his hand; Hélène was screaming.

"And everyone will know that this is a *fille de Boche.*"

I lunged at Biston but his hand was already in the crib. When I hit him we both fell to the floor face first with me on his back. He was reaching for a poker by the stove, having lost the scissors when we fell. I picked them up and as the men grabbed at me I drove them through his hand. I was punched, kicked and dragged but I held on to the scissors, still through Biston's hand. He was shrieking and someone kicked me in the stomach and I let go.

Biston was screaming and cursing. I managed to sit up against a wall and *black shirt* put his pistol to my forehead. He looked as though he would kill me with the slightest provocation. I was dazed and had blood running into one eye. Just then a hand holding a carving knife appeared, coming toward my face but came to rest on *black shirt's* neck.

"Enough, enough!" Vincent screamed.

Everyone shut up except Biston and Marie-Jeanne who was trying to get to the crib but was restrained by the two men.

"You're a dead man, Vincent," black shirt growled.

"Are you all crazy?" Vincent yelled. "Did you come here to kill? To mutilate babies? André's gone crazy and you do what he tells you like idiots."

No one said a word.

"Get her out of here," Biston snapped.

No one moved.

"Get her out of here," he screamed this time.

Black shirt lowered his pistol and stood up. Men started shuffling toward the door, the two holding Marie-Jeanne were pulling her as she cried for her daughter. Vincent stood there until black shirt moved away then rushed to the crib. He picked up the baby who was screaming in pain. I felt sick; on Hélène's chest, Biston had carved half a swastika. He had dragged the tip of the blade and it created a tear rather than a deep cut but it was bleeding. It started at her clavicle, turned on her left nipple, again on her stomach and ended at her belly button.

"Let's get her to a doctor," I said.

"We'll have to go to Nancy; our doctor was in that bunch."

"We've got to stop the bleeding."

I picked up her blanket and wrapped it around her then took a diaper and gently pressed it against her chest. Vincent covered my hand with the blanket and we started for the door. Françoise was standing at the foot of the stairs and just watched as we hurried into the street. We walked quickly to Vincent's house and went inside to look at the wound first before we left.

"What happened to you?" Nadine asked when I walked in the door. "Were you in a fight? Oh, dear God," she exclaimed when we put Hélène on the kitchen table and showed her the wound. "What happened? Whose child is this?"

"It's Hélène. André went berserk; he broke into Marie-Jeanne's house with a gang of thugs. They dragged her off to shave her head."

"Come on, let go," I said.

Vincent knew just where to go; we were only five minutes away. The doctor took almost an hour to treat her using more than a hundred stitches. When he brought her back to us she was sleeping.

"I had to give her morphine," the doctor said. She'll sleep for a good while . . . by then she shouldn't have any pain. Nasty wound, wasn't a clean cut, more like a tear. What did that madman use, a screwdriver?"

"Scissors," we both said.

"What have we come to," the doctor said, shaking his head, "when the ones we want to take revenge on are gone? Innocent children . . . lonely women . . . so sad."

The doctor cleaned my face and head where there was blood but found nothing serious. Other than being sore from kicks and punches, I was all right.

We left with instructions to return in ten days to have the stitches removed. On the drive home I questioned Vincent.

"I haven't thanked you yet for coming to my aid but why were you there at all?"

"I didn't care if Marie-Jeanne slept around but when André told us who the father was I was sick. How could someone who we knew so well do something like that? She was Nadine's best friend; didn't she know how we all felt about the Germans?"

"Thank you for bringing us to the doctor."

Vincent didn't respond.

"Vincent, do you have regrets?"

"I didn't want the child to bleed to death but . . ."

"But? Are you going to justify this?"

"No. It was brutal . . . insane. André is a mental case. But the child will grow up in Laxou, just like our children. She'll do all the same things as if she was one of us . . . but she's half German. How can she ever be one of us?"

Vincent's question cut me deeply. I was one of 'us' and I was no different on the outside than any of them. Was being half German so terrible? The doctor was right; they were taking revenge on the wrong people. What was it that they were avenging? What hurt . . . what loss did they think they were repaying?

The loss of Laure-Anne was greater than what Marie-Jeanne and Hélène suffered but I knew the greater evil was Biston. That German soldier was being expedient; Biston was hateful. If I had had the power of God to strike down one or the other . . . it would not have been Biston. Was I being selfish? I didn't care. Was there anyone in the world whose life I would not trade for Laure-Anne's? No . . . maybe Catherine. How miserable all this makes me feel . . . that I do not know if I would trade my daughter for my wife.

We arrived at the Denisarts but no one answered our knock. We drove back to Vincent's but I did not want to be there and I had him drop me off at the cottage. Françoise had seen me and would let Marie-Jeanne know who had her child. When I related the whole episode to my mother she was distraught, partly, I think, because she was spared the reprisals that Marie-Jeanne suffered. When I uncovered Hélène's chest she was in tears.

We had just begun preparing dinner, the sun was only a glow on the horizon and it was drizzling outside. I answered a knock on our rear door.

"Marie-Jeanne! Come in, are you all right?"

She was wearing an overcoat and a scarf; her right cheek covered by a bandage. She came in and scanned the room; Hélène was in Catherine's old crib near the fireplace in the parlor.

"Do you have her?" Her voice was different, as though she had a mouthful of food.

"Yes, she's sleeping in the parlor."

The small fire was only to take off the chill and did not give off much light. By the time I had turned on a floor lamp, Marie-Jeanne had already opened the undershirt that we had put on the baby.

"Oh, no. Oh, no, no, no."

She let out such a mournful cry, which turned into uncontrollable sobbing. I knelt beside her and took her in my arms. I could not tell which weighed more heavily on her at this moment, her daughter's wound or the thought that she was the cause of it (which she was not, Biston was responsible) but whatever it was, I could not console her. After many gentle words by my mother and me she came to the table as Catherine sat by the crib.

"She'll be all right, Marie-Jeanne. Look how nice she sleeps."

She put her face in her hands and seemed about to start crying again.

"How about you, dear? Édouard said that the same man cut your face but that he couldn't tell how bad it was. Was it bad?"

She touched the bandage with her fingertips and nodded.

"Did you see a doctor?"

"No. The doctor was one of *them*."

"Let me see it."

"I'll be all right. Believe me, Claudine, it will heal."

"That's not the point. I want to see it or are you a doctor?"

"It's been taken care of; it will be all right."

"Without a doctor? I want to see it, Marie-Jeanne."

When she saw that my mother would not be denied she stood and removed her overcoat. Her long scarf was thrown over both shoulders; she pulled the ends to the front and let it slide backwards off her head. She was completely bald.

Marie-Jeanne looked at each of us fiercely, almost daring us to join all the others in condemnation.

"You've done nothing wrong, Marie-Jeanne," my mother said. "We do not choose who we love . . . it is a gift from God and every gift from God is perfect."

Marie-Jeanne's confrontation melted away and she and my mother embraced.

"Thank you, Claudine, thank you so much."

My mother was watching me over Marie-Jeanne's shoulder, in a way explaining her own relationship with my father.

"And you, Édouard," Marie-Jeanne said, now embracing me, " you were the only one who . . . thank you."

"So, let us see the cut."

She peeled the bandage downward slowly; some of the gauze was caked in the dried blood. A slight tug on it did not free it. I fetched what medical supplies I had and we cut off the bandage and soaked the gauze with peroxide. When it released we saw a jagged gash from mid-cheek to just above the corner of her mouth. It was stitched with a double strand of black thread in a running pattern with perhaps eight stitches. There was only a knot holding the first stitch and a tied loop on the other end.

"How deep is the cut?" my mother asked.

"The last part of it went all the way through. He broke two teeth."

"Who stitched it?"

"I did. I just pushed the needle in and pushed the needle out."

My mother shuddered at the thought.

"You didn't do too good a job; it seems pulled somehow, maybe not lined up correctly. You should go to a doctor, the one Édouard took Hélène to."

"No," she snapped. "Enough people have seen me already; I don't need anyone else to gloat or pity me."

"He's not like that," I protested.

"I'm not going."

"Suppose it doesn't heal correctly . . . the scar could be terrible."

"I don't care."

We sat there through an awkward silence; Marie-Jeanne let us put some iodine on the wound and replace the bandage and then she put the scarf back on her head.

"How are things at home?" my mother asked.

"My mother doesn't know. I spoke to her through the door; she thinks that Hélène is at Nadine's. I don't want to be there; she warned me so many times."

"Have you eaten anything?"

"I didn't think that I should eat."

"Are you hungry?"

When she refused to answer, my mother got up and set the table . . . for four. Catherine came to tell Marie-Jeanne that Hélène was beginning to make some sounds and while dinner was cooking Marie-Jeanne nursed her. Catherine stayed with her; we could not hear the conversation but it was continuous. At dinner there was little talk; Marie-Jeanne had difficulty chewing without pain and took much longer than us to finish. After I put Catherine to bed, my mother convinced Marie-Jeanne to have a little cognac, 'as an antiseptic' she said.

"Do you want to tell us about that," I said, pointing to her head.

I didn't think she was eager to talk about it but we all knew that I would hear of it from someone sooner or later.

"They brought us to the Quatre Vents and put two chairs in the middle of the street so everyone would get a good look."

"Us?"

"There was another woman, I didn't know her. First they cut our hair very close with the scissors. Biston was walking through the crowd calling us names and saying how we were paying for our betrayal of France. Every now and then he would take our chin in his hand and make us look up at the faces of the people. He'd say something like 'Can't you look at your neighbors?' or 'Let them see what a whore looks like.' Then they used razors on us. Not Biston or that thug, Elie Pilot, the one with the gun; they walked around like a pair of peacocks, so proud that they caught us . . . their contribution to the war effort."

Marie-Jeanne finished the cognac, wincing with pain from the sting.

"What did you do about the cut on your cheek?"

"Some woman had brought me a napkin from the café. They started calling her names and she called them some and left. Most of the women there left. I thought that they would let us go when they were finished with the razor but Biston wasn't satisfied yet. He stuck the scissors down the front of my dress and snipped twice. He cut through my slip too; I think he meant to. Then he and Pilot tore my dress off. I was holding my slip with one hand and the napkin with the other. I stood there like that . . . in my slip with two sleeves of my dress 0.on my arms . . . and my shoes . . . and they told me to go home. They followed me all the way to the circle, shouting insults, calling out to the people we passed, saying things like 'look at your neighbor who was a whore for the Boche.' Some of them laughed . . . some spit on me."

We didn't know what to say. Marie-Jeanne seemed composed after recounting the event, more composed than I was. I poured another cognac and held the bottle over her glass; she nodded and I poured another for her also.

"Do you know how many people I met on my way home that knew me? Do you know how many offered to help . . . had a kind word?"

Marie-Jeanne put the cognac in her mouth and tilted her head to the right to soak the wound from the inside.

"It doesn't hurt so badly anymore."

I didn't know which pain she was referring to and didn't want to ask.

"Marie-Jeanne, stay here tonight. It's raining, the baby is sleeping . . ."

My offer didn't seem to interest her.

". . . and you'll have all day tomorrow to think about how to deal with your mother."

She agreed. I brought Marie-Jeanne and Hélène upstairs to my room, got a blanket for myself and we all went to bed, except mine was in front of the fireplace. A few more pieces of wood gave off some heat to compensate for the hardness of the floor. I had not been there a half hour when a hand touched my shoulder.

"Édouard . . . . how selfish of me. You must be so sore from the beating you took. Come upstairs. The bed is large enough for both of us."

In the soft light of the fire her bald head didn't seem so disconcerting. She wore only a slip . . . which hid very little. I *was* sore, I didn't think that she had other thoughts and I needed some sleep. I left the blanket and followed her back upstairs in my underwear, in the dark. We went to sleep back to back and I awoke with her nestled behind me with an arm over me. I slipped out of bed and went downstairs to get dressed. I made a fire in the kitchen stove and brewed some coffee. After eating a bit I left for school.

It turned out to be a good day. I was not smothered with sympathy; they welcomed me back with a smile and let me go about teaching. Except Virginie, she greeted me with a scowl but was not so insensitive as to berate me for my mother's actions concerning the house so soon after Laure-Anne's death. All the good things about teaching and school life reappeared as class after class brought me closer to my former state.

Marie-Jeanne was still at the cottage when I returned. My mother wanted to look at her wound again and had just now put new bandages her cheek. She wanted me to escort her home, I agreed and she put on her scarf and overcoat.

"This way," she said, moving toward the rear door. "The way I came."

We walked along the *sentier* in silence. The colors of autumn made the woods beautiful, as did the summer foliage and the spring blossoms in their season. In fact only the bare branches of winter made it look desolate . . . unless we had snow. This route was longer but I knew she preferred it because we would encounter no one. It was only when we came out of the woods and stopped near her house that she spoke.

"Édouard, you are the finest person I know. I want to repay you somehow."

"There's no need. I'm glad that I was there to help."

"I know that so soon after Laure-Anne's . . . your life is so unsettled. Sometime in the future when you feel the need for companionship . . ."

I put my arm on her shoulder and gently forced her to approach her door. I didn't want her to finish her offer. Inside Virginie finally let me know her thoughts about the sale of the cottage but stopped abruptly when Marie-Jeanne took off her scarf. Now it was her turn, Virginie being harsher with her daughter, even telling her that she got what she deserved. She was still ranting when Marie-Jeanne, completely composed, took off Hélène's undershirt.

"Oh, dear God. What happened?"

"The same good citizens that thought I deserved *this* also thought that this *fille de Boche* deserved *that*. What do you think of their judgment now, Maman?"

"Who did this?"

"André Biston and Elie Pilot were the leaders but before you think that you will have them punished . . . Doctor Lemoine and that policeman, Gazin, were part of it. How many more wanted to be there . . . the Mayor, the Judge . . . the Chief of Police?"

Virginie was frustrated; she changed her mood and picked up Hélène.

"Why are you here?" she asked me.

Marie-Jeanne recounted the events of the last two days and when she was done Virginie put her hand on my arm.

"The Denisarts are lucky to have friends like the Jannots."

Virginie kissed me, Marie-Jeanne offered her left cheek and I kissed her and went home.

Vincent drove my mother and me to Saint Mihiel on Saturday and we came home with a truckload of furniture. We now had two sofas in the parlor besides the china cabinet and a low boy and a rug in front of the fireplace. My mother had her bed and dresser. Her refrigerator was better than ours and we brought that along. Vincent and I spent the afternoon putting it all in order. My mother offered to buy dinner at the Quatre Vents and we were in good spirits when we arrived.

Pilot was there along with a few friends but I couldn't remember if they were also at Marie-Jeanne's house. He gave us only a cursory glance and we ordered some wine. We were about to order dinner when Biston, his hand in a splint, came in with another man. He spotted us at once and came to our table.

"Did you see the plucked chicken, Bird?"

We ignored him in silence.

"What's the matter Bird? You have nothing to say?" He turned to his cronies. "The Bird has not a quack in him. Come on, Bird . . . quack for us."

He wanted a confrontation and he would have one. I got up to face him; Pilot also got up and opened his jacket to reveal his pistol. I had no fear that he would shoot me in public. I was thinking of a way that I could provoke Biston so that he would give me justification to punch him in the mouth.

"How's the hand, Biston?"

"Just a scratch, Bird."

"You know, Biston, I like that name. I think that I'll tell all my friends to call me that from now on."

Biston was confused; he looked to his friends who offered nothing. I could not imagine what those behind me thought.

"Oiseau! That's me!" I shouted so that everyone in the café would hear. "When they ask me why I am called that I will tell them it's because when the rodents were running wild I put my talon into one named André Biston. The man that saved France by shaving women's heads and mutilating babies. I hope that your hand shrivels into a claw then when people ask about it you can tell them Oiseau did it. Is that a deal?"

I extended my hand to him; he put his wounded right hand behind his back. There was not a sound in the café. From another table we heard a man say 'By God, I will!' and watched as he came to me and took my outstretched hand.

"It's an honor to shake your hand Oiseau. You're the real patriot, not this moron."

I thanked him and we all took our seats. Vincent patted my back and my mother gave me a kiss. From behind me I heard a man calling a name in a loud angry whisper.

"Yvonne . . . Yvonne . . . get back here."

"Oiseau . . ."

I turned to face the woman.

"I would like to shake your hand also. I tried to help that poor woman and received nothing but insults."

I stood up and shook her hand. She waited a few seconds and then decided to kiss my cheeks. She whispered in my ear.

"You should run for mayor. You would get the vote of every woman in Laxou."

Yvonne went back to her husband; Biston, Pilot and company went out into the street. I signaled to the waiter that we were ready to order. He arrived with the proprietor.

"I think," he said, "that if you continue to come here I will lose one of my best customers."

With that he put another bottle of wine on the table and extended his hand to me.

Later when we were back home and I had put Catherine in her unshared bed, I found my mother at the kitchen table with a calendar making notes. She waved away my inquiries.

"Is there any more cognac?"

She pointed to a cabinet and I fetched it. There was only a spoonful left. When I made a disappointing noise she looked up then got up and brought out a new bottle and placed it in front of me. She stood behind me and placed her hands on my chest.

"Well done, Oiseau. I am very proud of you."

She gave me a kiss and went to bed.

So, I will be Oiseau now . . . the protector of women and children . . . the avenger. They will call me Oiseau for the wrong reason. I am Oiseau . . . a single bird, when I should be one of a pair of Oiseaux, two who mate for life.

I drank the little bit of cognac that was in the glass but did not open the other bottle. I went to bed; there was nothing to celebrate.

Monday morning at school a few of my colleagues greeted me calling me Oiseau. By afternoon, all but one was calling me that. At first it was a novelty and many, outside of school also, used that name but then many went back to Édouard. For many the change was permanent and their persistence gradually brought the others back to Oiseau.

The following Saturday Hélène was to have her stitches removed and I went to the Denisarts to insure that transportation was available. Virginie had a car but walked to school as I did. I discovered that her vehicle had not run for months and volunteered to drive Marie-Jeanne and the baby. Marie-Jeanne refused to go, demanding that her mother go instead. Virginie refused and walked down the street.

"Could your mother go with you?" Marie-Jeanne asked.

"She's gone shopping. Why won't you go?"

"I don't want anyone to see me."

"So, wear your scarf. What's the problem?"

"Just take her by yourself then."

"No, I won't drive with her just lying on the seat."

"Then I'll take them out myself."

"No you won't! Get your daughter and get in the car."

I was angry and she knew it. I did not think that she would jeopardize the friendship we had because of her pride. She put on her scarf and got into the car. At the doctor's office she would not get out and I went in alone. Although the doctor assured me that the wound would heal perfectly, the look of it disturbed me. It would be an ugly scar. I thought to lecture Marie-Jeanne on the way home about her avoidance of notice but reckoned that when her hair grew back she would get over it.

Phillip Varady

As I drove down the lane to the cottage I saw Jean-Marie's Citroën. I did not relish this meeting. His loss equaled mine, his only child, placed in my care. At least I was spared seeing his anguish; I had enough of my own. We embraced, we cried, we felt each other's loss, we both focused on Catherine, the last remnant of her beloved and beautiful mother. Just when I thought that I couldn't bear another minute of reliving the grief, Jean-Marie announced that he was leaving. I was glad to see him go.

Jean-Marie's visit was a prerequisite for me to get on with a new part of my life. My recovery depended on my not having direct reminders of my grief like my father-in-law. He would suffer through another reminder; it would be a while before he received official notification of the death of Anton, Vlasta and Nathalie in Auschwitz. We all have to bear our own burdens and I was growing tired of bearing Marie-Jeanne's. I saw her less and less frequently. A burden that I would have gladly borne was hidden from me by my mother. She informed me after the difficulty had passed that Catherine cried every night for her mother.

In January 1946, Françoise died. Marie-Jeanne attended the funeral wearing a black mourning veil. I would not have guessed that it was her but for the little girl holding her hand. When it was over, I went to talk to her but she left immediately, leaving Virginie alone to accept the condolences of the mourners. I know that she saw me and that I was coming to speak to her. I put it from my mind; if she wanted no contact with me, I wouldn't force it on her.

In March I was accepted as an assistant professor at the University of Nancy, to begin with the fall semester. June brought Nadine's long awaited daughter, Michèle. Two days into the new year, 1947, Eliane had her long awaited son, Philippe. My mother found work when our local butcher expanded his shop to serve our growing population. When she heard of the proposed expansion she inquired about work. He knew she was a butcher because of the way she would criticize a poor piece of meat and the way she knew where the best cuts were. I also think she said more than once that she could do better than he.

Nadine and Jean-Yves were wonderful in that they were substitutes for my mother and me when we were working and could not care for Catherine ourselves. It was in the summer of that year that Catherine no longer wanted to spend a day in the willows. I no longer went there myself after that. Jean-Marie would come for a few days every August and for a day sometime around Christmas every year. He had remarried but his new wife never accompanied him.

In the early fifties there was a new American presence in the area as the increasing Soviet threat made necessary an increased preparedness on the part of France and the United States. American military installations were constructed in Nancy, Toul, Metz, Verdun and a few other smaller villages. Dollars boosted the economy, not only those that were spent on beer and prostitutes, but many clerical and warehouse positions were filled by Frenchmen.

On a warm Sunday morning in May of 1952, just minutes after my mother had left to go to Mass with Catherine, I received two visitors at my back door. It was Marie-Jeanne and Hélène. The daughter was wearing what could be called her Sunday best and the mother had on one of Laure-Anne's dresses under a light sweater. On her head she wore an oversized kerchief that covered even her shoulders. It did not cover her cheek and the scar was plainly visible. It was not horrendous but on a beautiful woman's face it was a tragedy. The way the wound had healed caused a dimple just above the right corner of her mouth and perhaps altered her speech slightly.

"Well, what a surprise. Come in, come in. What brings you to my door?"

"Hello, Édouard. It's been a while. You wouldn't recognize Hélène would you?"

"No, I certainly wouldn't."

She was a beautiful child, a bit shy holding on to her mother's hand, standing just a little behind her for protection. When she would not turn her face up to me I crouched, forcing her to look at me.

"Hello, Hélène. How are you today?"

When she didn't answer I took her free hand.

"Are you afraid of me, Hélène?"

"No."

"Good. Maybe you'll tell me why you're dressed up so pretty, eh?"

"First communion."

"Wonderful. You're a very pretty young lady, Hélène."

She withdrew her hand and retreated a bit behind her mother. Marie-Jeanne was making hand gestures as she began to explain why her daughter had to wait until she was eight years old to receive her first communion.

"Well, you know . . . sometimes . . . well, anyway, we were walking in the woods and I thought it would be nice to see you. She needs to be at the church before the eight o'clock Mass."

"You look well, Marie-Jeanne, in spite of . . ."

"I try not to let it bother me and for the most part I don't even think about it."

I closed the door behind them and they moved to the kitchen table, the sunlight from the front window just reaching their feet.

"Hélène, would you like some hot cocoa?"

She nodded and I prepared it for her. Marie-Jeanne had gone to the front of the house and was looking up the lane. I left her daughter at the table thinking that she wanted to speak privately to me. When I approached her she removed the kerchief and gave her head a shake and her long light brown hair fell gracefully over her shoulders. I could not resist putting my fingers through it. I smiled.

"It's beautiful . . . and so are you."

"Thank you. How have you been?"

"I've been busy . . . I'm writing a book . . . should be finished this summer."

"I wasn't talking about your work, Édouard."

"I've learned how to live again . . . I have Catherine."

"Catherine is not enough."

"No, no she isn't but she is all that I have."

"It doesn't need to be that way."

I looked at Marie-Jeanne and saw a beautiful woman. I was comfortable with her; we were old friends who had feelings for each other as friends do. I had been too long without a woman in my life and she was giving me an opportunity to correct that. She could easily be my lover but never my wife. She wasn't asking any more from me other than to be a companion; I thought for a moment that I could allow myself to do that. There would never be another woman that could replace my Laure-Anne. The thought of being passionate with Marie-Jeanne was exciting but a sense of guilt prevented me from considering it further. I put my hands on her face, both hands, deliberately, to show that her scar had no part of my decision.

"I wish it wasn't that way but . . . for now, it is."

I kissed her lips gently, briefly. She put her hands on my wrists and when we lowered our arms we held hands.

"I am so jealous of Laure-Anne."

The Swans of Lorraine

I wanted to end this conversation and turned toward the kitchen; we both noticed that Hélène had changed seats so that she could observe us. I poured two cups of coffee and we all had a pleasant chat for a while. When they were leaving Marie-Jeanne kissed my cheeks and when I extended my hand to Hélène she extended her arms. I thought it was cute and we kissed cheeks also. I had the feeling that Marie-Jeanne and I would meet again in the not too distant future and she would again inquire about my emotional needs.

As I watched them walk away down the *sentier* I fingered my birds. I wished that she had been more persistent or that she had given some indication of her intention to see me again. *I wonder what a tundra swan would do in my case.*

I was wrong about Marie-Jeanne. The years rolled by and I saw no more of her. In 1959 Catherine was out of school. I wanted her to go to the University but she said that she had enough of an education. She had taken two years of English, which gave her some advantage when she applied with the service that provided manpower to the American bases in the area. She got a job as a clerk, working in the office of a warehouse that supplied vehicle parts at the American base in Toul. A bus brought her back and forth to work.

That Christmas at the cottage, with Jean-Marie present, she presented us with the man that she said she wanted to marry. He was a twenty-year-old American soldier with whom she had worked these last six months. He had studied French in his lycée and they had equal mediocrity in each other's language. Jean-Marie and I were saddened and apprehensive that she would go to the United States and we would never see her again. We did not withhold our blessing however, and they married on 2 February 1960.

His name is Robert Karl Gustavson and his home is in what must have been originally a French town in Wisconsin named Fond du Lac. His tour of duty would be over in October. They moved into a rented house in the small village of Vaucoleurs, which is southwest of Toul and is about as close to Bar-le-Duc as it is to Laxou; Jean-Marie visited every month; my mother and I tried to come every weekend, sometimes with Eliane and occasionally with some of Catherine's cousins. In all honesty, I could find no fault in her choice of husband; he was intelligent and courteous, and displayed unfeigned respect and affection for my daughter. All the family was there to say good-bye to them on the day they left and Jean-Marie was to pick them up at the Gare de l'Est in Paris to take them to the airport.

That same year in June, my niece Elisabeth had married and after Catherine's departure my mother announced to me that she was moving into that recently vacated room to live with Eliane. 'It is too depressing to live with you,' she said. She was gone in a week and then I was truly alone.

The Swans of Lorraine

Phillip Varady

Chapter 6

I was fifty-two; we were in the first year of a new decade. The
University of Nancy has grown to such an extent that it is now
two separate schools. Laxou is almost swallowed up in the ever-growing
urban expansion of Nancy, which is now an area with more than two
hundred fifty thousand people. Some say that the seventies will be super
this and super that. In fact many of my students are borrowing that prefix
from English and are using it as a proper word in French to indicate a
new version of something that is superior to the older one or as an
exclamation when they like a thing. My life certainly didn't qualify for
that usage, not in the farthest stretch of meaning although bits and pieces
here and there kept me sane and alive. The alternative at times seemed
very attractive and I am likely to credit Eliane for keeping me away from
the edge of that abyss.

    She has thoughts of moving to Villers lès Nancy, just south of
Laxou, into an apartment, to be nearer to work. After a series of low-
paying clerical jobs she finally found a decent employment last spring as
a secretary at the Laboratory of Physical Chemistry and Microbiology for
the Environment which is a division of the University of Nancy I. She is
happier now than she has ever been these last seven years since she and
Olivier divorced. Mother refuses to move with her, threatening to move
back with me, which is the only reason Eliane is still in Laxou. Neither
one of them really wants that, in fact neither do I. I teach at the
University of Nancy II, a few kilometers away but our usual Sunday
diner and unannounced visits, either hers or mine, keep us as close as we
ever were.

    It is the middle of July, I have just begun my vacation, and the
weather is agreeable so far; it won't be really hot until August. I am
writing my third book, this one about the diminishing role of France in
North Africa. I plan on writing in the morning, take lunch until about two

in the afternoon then stroll around the neighborhood to see what might turn up. Sometimes it may be nothing if all my friends are busy in which case I'll hang out with a book at the Quatre Vents in a shady spot, sipping some Moselle until someone shows up with a plan. Today is Saturday and I had no trouble finding a way to pass the afternoon. Coming to the corner where my lane meets the street, I saw my best friend and neighbor, Doub, who was formally known as Vincent Vinchelin. We all call him Doub, short for 'Double V.' He waved to me to come into his yard. He was now a sanitary engineer in Nancy.

"Hey, Oiseau, come on in. You want something? I'm having a beer."

"Sure. What's up?"

"I was just going to call you. I'll be right back."

I took a seat at a large wooden table, which served every purpose imaginable. I have seen an automobile engine in parts on it and one year Mother butchered a deer there. He returned quickly with two half-liters and set one before me.

"Up," he said as I took hold of it. "We're going to beat those two card cheats so bad, they'll go home weeping."

We gulped down about half before stopping. The two he referred to were my old friend Jean-Michel Déaut, whom we called Jeami, who sold farm equipment. He and his wife Martine were the ones who Laure-Anne and I used to go dancing with. The other was René Cardelli, a dentist and a bachelor. We would tease him about being unmarried saying that the only female that could live with him was his cat. We were all in our early fifties except for René who was only thirty-eight. Doub began telling me about what was going on in Laxou and continued for a half hour without stopping. When we spotted our friends approaching he finally quit.

"So, how's the book coming?"

"So-so. Sometimes I bore myself with it. I need to make it more exciting."

"Hey, guys," Doub called out. "I hope you brought plenty of money. You'll be lucky to get home with a bed sheet to cover your asses."

René and Jeami shook hands all around and took seats opposite one another.

"Nadine!" Doub called out loudly.

Phillip Varady

When he received no response he called again even louder. A muffled reply came from within the house. Presently she came out carrying a tray with four glasses of beer, which she served to us.

"Ah, Nadine," he whined, "these tiny glasses!"

"You'd do well to get off your fat ass now and then. I'm not going to wait on you all afternoon; I have plenty to do before I go to work."

She cooked at the Café Deux Hémisphères in downtown Nancy. Happily, I am invited to the Vinchelin's every Monday, Nadine's day off. As she turned to go she removed a deck of cards from her pocket and threw them on the table with a slap. We all knew that she wasn't angry; it was just a warning she gave him whenever we played belote.

Our version of the game is called 'Coinchée' which allows for a bit of cheating but it must be done in the correct manner. Cleverness and boldness are the essence of a good cheat. If one is caught the hand may be thrown in or the bet could be doubled. It is possible to make your opponent think you are cheating when you are not just to raise the stakes. We got right into it, two evenly matched teams, who as luck would have it, sometimes played all afternoon only to come away with no gain or loss.

As the afternoon wore on, Doub and I were ahead by about twenty francs apiece but were behind in the current game. Jeami had brought along a half-liter of Mirabelle, which he dispensed at irregular intervals in thimble-sized glasses as he saw fit, usually when he and René won an exciting round. They had just won a hand and we enjoyed another taste as Doub went in for another four beers. All that alcohol emboldened Doub and he began making offers to increase the bet, cards unseen. We were behind by four hundred points in a 2000-point game; René and Jeami had 1920. I questioned Doub's wisdom but that's what made the game exciting.

We all agreed; the stakes were doubled. René dealt; Doub bid first.

"I have a little ninety," he said.

A good bid and high enough to make it hard for our opponents to exchange too much information about their holdings. Just then Doub slammed his cards face down on the table and began to claw at his nose, making some vile noises. He pulled a handkerchief from his pocket and wiped and poked for a minute as we all wondered what had happened.

"A damned fly went up my nose," he explained.

"Bullshit!" Jeami exclaimed. "That's a damned signal!"

"No, it's not," Doub protested. "You want to see the little son of a bitch?"

Doub opened his handkerchief and pointed to some dark matter.

"There! There's the little bastard. Do you believe me now?"

"Ah, please. You think I'm going to examine your snot to see if it's a fly? That was a signal and everyone knows it. I'm going to throw the hand in."

"Wait a minute! What do you think I have?"

"I'll bet you have the twenty and the fourteen of spades."

"Well, I don't and . . ." He reached into his pocket and put ten francs on the table. "And that says you're wrong."

The two men stared at each other for a minute. This type of thing was not uncommon but Doub had a way of raising it to a new level.

"You have a bet," Jeami said, matching the ten-franc note. "Let's see them."

"I'm not showing you my hand; I'm going to play these cards." He turned towards the house and shouted. "Nadine, come out here."

Nadine came out and Doub held his cards above his head facing the rear.

"Either one of them." Jeami said.

Doub agreed.

"Jack or nine of spades, Nadine?"

"No, neither one," she said. "I've got to get ready for work."

"Damn!"

"Ooh, that hurt," Doub said as he picked up the money. He gave me a wink.

Hurt? Hurt feelings! A signal! He's got them in hearts. Son of a bitch! I didn't have a heart in my hand. I had the ace, ten, king, seven of spades and also an ace of clubs. I should bid a hundred and ten but this could be big.

Jeami passed. Everyone was staring at me.

"A hundred and . . . twenty."

"Ah! You'll be sitting in your shorts in a minute," René said. "Double," he added confidently.

All eyes turned to Doub. He was smiling at me, a cigarette dangling from the corner of his mouth, but he was very carefully scrutinizing my face for a clue. They turned to me to insure that I didn't give one. He stared at me and waited for me to do something, anything. I had already overbid the hand and he wanted me to confirm it. With Jeami and René watching me so closely, there was little that I could do. I stared back at him until he reckoned that it was up to him and his cards to say more.

"Come on, Doub . . . not all day, eh?" Jeami complained.

"Redouble," he croaked. "Redouble," he repeated loudly. "You guys are going to be naked in a minute."

Nadine came out of the house to go to work and kissed him on the cheek.

"Nadine, before you go, get these guys some bed sheets," he cackled.

Doub jumped up and slammed the jack of hearts on the table.

"It's all over. Get your money," he exclaimed.

When I didn't follow suit he looked worried but followed it with the nine. The ace and the queen fell and he shouted as he slammed the ten to the table, taking out the last trump. Now he was in trouble. He had to lead to one of my aces but had to guess which one or we would lose. I wriggled my nose, as if I had a fly on it and he slammed the eight of spades to the table.

"I'm master!" I shouted and laid my hand on the table.

René and Jeami couldn't believe it. Not a point for them and we won the game. As I came around the table to hug Doub I noticed Nadine and a young woman standing nearby. They were probably waiting for us to finish. Nadine approached me and motioned for me to follow her.

"This young lady is looking for you. I have to leave."

Nadine drove off. I shook the woman's extended hand. She was a beauty, mid twenties, very light brown hair, almost blond. Reminded me of Jackie Kennedy the way she had it. Dressed as though she just came from work.

"Hello, Professor Jannot. I was just at your house looking for you but you weren't there. I was on my way home when I heard your friend shouting and I recognized you."

"So, you know me?"

"Yes, we've met before."

"On my life I don't know how I would have forgotten that. What was the occasion?"

"It was a long time ago; you made hot cocoa for me. I'm Hélène Denisart."

"Denisart? Marie-Jeanne's little girl?"

"Yes but not so little anymore," she chuckled. "In fact we are colleagues of a sort. I work for the University Henri Poincaré."

"Well, that's wonderful. I can see that you've grown into a beautiful young lady, I'm very happy to say. What can I do for you?"

"Could we talk sometime . . . soon. Not right now. It's about my mother."

"Sure. Where do you want to meet?"

"I was hoping to talk to you at your place . . . if that's not an inconvenience."

"No, not at all. The housekeeper came by today so the place is decent again."

"Is tomorrow morning all right?"

"Yes, that's fine. What time shall I expect you?"

"I'll come right after Mass, about quarter past eight."

"Good. We can have breakfast together."

"That will be nice. Thank you, see you then."

"Yes, till then."

I watched her walk away thinking how her movement reminded me of Laure-Anne. That was the only thing that did; the rest of her was so different. As I walked back to the table I wondered what she could want concerning her mother. I hadn't even seen her in close to fifteen years . . . no, eighteen. The guys were on their feet holding their little shots of Mirabelle. I think we were done for the day.

"Oiseau, you and Doub are a pair of lucky bastards," Jeami said. "You put one over on us. Come on, drink up."

We threw down the shots and Jeami refilled them.

"So, who was that?" he asked.

"Her name's Hélène. She works at the University."

"I know her . . . Denisart. She's a patient of mine," René said.

"Denisart?" Doub murmured. "So that's her. I see her all the time. They live two blocks away. What'd she want from you?"

"She made an appointment to see me. Didn't say about what."

Doub made a face and was about to say something but I gave him a look and he remained quiet. We finished our shots and René and Jeami left. Of course Doub would remember; he was there.

"I haven't seen the bitch in years and now her pup walks around as if she owns the place. What does she want from you?"

"I told you . . . she didn't say. I don't know why you're so hard on the girl; she didn't do anything."

"Aaah, just the thought of it makes me sick."

"Come on, let's go down to the Quatre Vents and get something to drink. I could eat a bit too. How about you?"

"Yeah, come on."

Sunday morning the dark sky began to release its contents just as I got back from the baker's where I bought some brioches and croissants for this morning and some bread for a few days. That was good timing; in ten minutes it was raining hard. Quarter past eight came and went and I assumed that the weather had kept her from coming. About eight thirty there was a knock at my rear door. There was Hélène complete with umbrella, raincoat and high rubber boots.

"I didn't expect that you would come through the *sentier*. Come in, come in."

I spread some newspaper for her to place her boots on and helped her out of her raincoat. She was wearing a sleeveless top and jeans.

"Thank you for taking the time to see me. I'm sorry that I'm late but I was offered a ride home from the church and thought to get an umbrella but then I decided to change also."

She walked into the kitchen, turning slowly in a complete circle, looking at everything.

"I'd like to say that it was just as I remembered it but it was so long ago. I *do* have the feeling that nothing has changed."

"You're right, I suppose. Why did you come by the *sentier* in this weather; it would have been faster on the street?"

"Why would an environmentalist walk through the Forêt de Haye when she could look at a bunch of old houses? My mother used to take me there all the time when I was a child, even in winter. She rarely came out of the house for anything else. The last time publicly was when my grandmother died and then no one knew it was her in that veil."

"I would have come but I was in Épinal for a lecture series and didn't hear of her death until the day after."

"It was a small group, mostly teachers and two cousins."

I poured the coffee and put some bread in the oven. Years ago Eliane had tried to talk us into buying a gas oven to replace the old wood burner but neither Mother nor I wanted to part with it. I put the brioches and croissants on the table with some butter.

"You didn't have to go through all this bother, Professor. I usually just have a piece of bread and an apple."

"All my friends call me 'Oiseau'. Please, sit."

"Sure. Thank you."

"You look very modern . . . very American."

"Ha, no. The look is international, very 'cool.' At work in a lab coat, no one knows what you're wearing anyway."

"Ah, so I suppose it's 'super,' eh?"

"Yes, there you go."

We had our breakfast and talked about school, my books, her car, pollution and so much else until there was nothing left to eat. I was surprised to discover that she worked at the same lab as Eliane and was a hydrobiologist. The look on my face gave me away.

"Are you surprised because I'm a woman?"

"No, not at all. It's because . . . I'm sorry. Perhaps it is . . ."

We sat quietly for a moment; she finished her coffee. I couldn't tell if I had offended her but then she smiled.

"I don't believe we ate all that," she said.

"More coffee?"

"Yes, please. Oiseau . . . how strange. I wouldn't think that you chose that name for yourself . . . was it given to you?"

Thinking back to why Biston first used it, I murmured 'given' and pulled the birds from inside my shirt.

"May I see them?"

I slipped them off and gave the necklace to her and poured the coffee.

"They're beautiful. They're Tundra Swans . . . from the size of the yellow spots on their bills I would say they were *Cygnus bewickii*. You knew that didn't you. I guess I was showing off. They're becoming an endangered species. The loss of their summer habitat to population growth is . . ."

I just smiled. I kept up to date on my beloved birds.

"You knew that too, didn't you? Where was this made?"

"*That,* I don't know. I bought them in Paris before the war in a Far Eastern gift shop. There's not a clue on it anywhere."

She gave it back to me and I slipped it over my head.

"It was a birthday gift to my wife. She and your mother were friends."

We blew and sipped the hot coffee.

"About my mother . . . she and my grandmother often spoke about you and you are the only one that I can remember that she has ever spoken kindly of or praised for their character."

"Well, that was very nice of her."

"And . . ." she paused to sip some coffee.

I looked at her, waiting for the rest of the sentence. She continued, with the cup at her lips, watching me over the rim as she blew into it.

". . . I remember you kissed her."

I sipped my coffee, waiting for her to make that observation relevant.

"If I ask the next question will I be prying?"

"There was never anything between your mother and me. I kissed her to show her that she was still a beautiful woman and that the scar on her face was not a reason to avoid people."

"I don't think the scar bothers her all that much; she's a bit irrational about her hair. She has never cut it for as long as I can remember."

"Is that a problem?"

"For me, no, but you don't know the effort that she puts into keeping it clean and well groomed. She spends at least an hour a day on it."

"Is this related to what you wanted to speak to me about?"

"No. I got off track with curiosity. Actually, there was a bulletin circulated in our lab about staffing an expedition to French Polynesia in '71 to assess the effects of tourism and nuclear testing. I would dearly like to go but since my mother refuses to go out of the house, she would simply starve to death. I would like . . . and she certainly needs . . . that she re-integrates herself into society."

"And this is where I come in, eh?"

"Yes. My grandmother was content to allow her to become a recluse but when she died I began to badger her to end her isolation . . . to no avail."

"And you think that she will listen to *me* . . . someone she hasn't seen in eighteen years?"

"You're my only hope . . . her only hope. She needs to do this, don't you agree?"

"Yes, I suppose . . . but then I don't know her thinking."

"Will you at least talk to her?"

I wasn't eager to do this but because she was an old friend, I considered it.

"If I do, how will it be arranged?"

"Does it need to be arranged? You could just stop by one evening."

"I would prefer that she knows that I'm coming and agrees to see me."

"Hmmm, I don't think that I can just tell her that I asked you to come over . . . she would know why. Are you working or on vacation?'

"I just began my vacation yesterday. Why?"

"I was going to tell her that I met you at some University function or meeting."

"There is very little happening anywhere right now."

"She won't know that. I could tell her that we both had problems with our paychecks and when I heard some clerk in accounting call out your name, I invited you to the house."

"Better that you should say that you *would* invite me if she is agreeable."

"Yes, all right. If you give me your number, I'll call you tomorrow afternoon and if it's agreeable you could come in the evening."

"Not tomorrow evening; I'm having dinner with my neighbors . . . and I doubt if I'll be home in the afternoon. What time do you get home?"

"Between four and five usually."

"Ah, if you can't reach me by phone, I'll be at the Quatre Vents until about five-thirty. I'll buy you a drink."

"Well, perhaps I won't bother to call then."

She had a peculiar smile on her face when she said that, a bit mischievous, just like Laure-Anne used to do, but I knew she was only joking. I gave her my home number and my number at the University. We finished our coffee and she got up to leave.

"Hélène . . . where would you be going in French Polynesia?"

"The first stop is a small island called Mangareva and then Papeete in Tahiti."

"Do you think that there is a position for an historian who has never been out of France in his whole life?"

"No, I don't think so but I could bring along the bulletin and maybe you could find something that you could qualify for."

"Not very likely but bring it anyway; I'm curious."

Phillip Varady

I stood with her at the door as she put on her boots and raincoat. It was still raining although not as hard as earlier and I fully expected her to go home through the woods the way she came.

"Thank you so much . . . Oiseau, and for breakfast too."

I would have extended my hand but fantasy gripped me and I stood there with my arms at my side. My gamble was rewarded when she leaned forward and we exchanged *les bises*. I watched as she disappeared down the *sentier*. When she was out of sight I poured some Rémy in a glass . . . then doubled it. Two gulps and my chest felt warm . . . but then it already felt warm before the cognac.

Édouard, have you lost your mind? She's half your age! Something inside me stirred. I had not felt this in so long a time . . . *What did Mother tell Marie-Jeanne?* 'We do not choose who we love' . . . *Ah, dream on, Édouard . . . love?* I didn't know! It felt wonderful but then reality hit me. *Don't play the fool, you fool. Why in the world would a beautiful young lady like Hélène ever think of you in the way that you are thinking of her?* I was suddenly depressed with the obvious answer; she wouldn't. I would settle for her friendship; to be in her company; to share a little of our lives with each other. That would be nice.

I was at a loss as to what to do to occupy myself until evening. I tried to work on my book but could not concentrate; television was boring, even preparing lunch did not interest me. When the rain had almost stopped, but not quite, I put on a rain jacket with a hood and went into the woods. I knew where I would wind up. I paused when I thought that I was at the right place but didn't see the other path. There was a large maple tree where the other *sentier* began and I didn't see it. As I walked up and down I found the remains of the stump of that tree, long fallen and rotted away. As I moved to the left I could see the clearing in the willows, almost reluctant to go farther. I had done nothing; I was a perfect gentleman who had only shared a breakfast with the daughter of an old friend.

As I entered the clearing, the memories of how it used to look seemed to be exactly what I was seeing. I found the spot where we used to sit . . . or recline . . . or make love. It was where the ground gently sloped downward facing south just where the ferns ended and the grass began. One could stretch out there with one's head and shoulders slightly elevated giving one a view of the derrière of the one on top.

"Laure-Anne, Laure-Anne, what am I doing here?" I murmured. "This is not a place of solitude . . ." *This was always a place full of joy and excitement . . . a place that was made just for us . . . and Catherine. Is your soul here . . . if that kind of thing is possible? Are you watching . . . do you know? Does the Tundra swan pine away for the rest of its life? I think that nature is not so cruel as to allow that; he either dies or finds a new mate. I did not die. I did not die!*

"Laure-Anne, I did not die," I whispered.

At first the words seemed to be a sort of justification but as I repeated them over and over a fire ignited in my memory. I was consumed with a thought, an idea, a hope; I suddenly needed to know. It became imperative for me to know. I rushed home to shower and shave, to change into dry clothes. I drove rather than walked and showed up eight hours early at Eliane's house for dinner. My nephew Philippe answered the door.

"Hello, Uncle Édouard. Did you come for lunch? We just sat down."

"No, I came to speak with your mother."

We went into the dining room and without any formalities I got Eliane out to speak privately with me. I must have seemed desperate because she came without a word of protest.

"What's wrong?" she asked.

"With her last breath Laure-Anne said to me, 'Don't die without me.' What did she mean?"

Eliane was at first puzzled that I should ask her so intimate a question, something that perhaps only my wife and I would, or should, know. But then I could see the light in her eyes as she made sense of it.

"Do you remember that afternoon in a café on the rue Descartes when you got mad because neither Laure-Anne nor I would tell you what she threatened her parents with?"

"Yes, she promised to tell me but she never did."

"The previous summer, just before I left to come home, Jean-Marie came into her room, first to apologize to me, telling me how wonderful I was and how he was so happy that Laure-Anne and I were such great friends . . . but that he was going to end your stay and find another tutor. He was convinced that you and Laure-Anne had a relationship that went beyond teacher and pupil and wanted you out of there before it became intimate. Laure-Anne protested saying . . . lying, that there was nothing to it, that it was unfair of him to think that her demand to replace Fariza had anything to do with feelings for you."

"Her father didn't believe a word of it and was adamant; you were to go immediately. Finally Laure-Anne told the truth, that she loved you. He took her by the hand and practically dragged her downstairs to her mother and repeated what she had said. Nathalie agreed . . . you had to go. Laure-Anne said, 'I'll die without him.' And her father said something like, 'Nonsense, you're young, you'll get over it.' And she said . . . you had to be there to see her, to hear just the way she said it. She said, 'I'll die without him. I'll see to it.' It was scary . . . we all believed her."

Now I was puzzled. I don't think Laure-Anne would expect that I would have committed suicide at her death. I didn't think the two statements were related and I told Eliane so.

"You're being too specific," Eliane said. "She was willing to give up everything for you, including her life. She was asking you not to give up everything for her."

That interpretation was agreeable to me; it made me feel less guilty. I nodded slightly and perhaps showed the beginning of a smile.

"Ah, yes . . . not give up everything. That's good, Eliane."

"Well, you've given up everything except working and breathing; don't tell me that you want to do something else after all these years?"

"Oh, yes, I want to be alive again."

Eliane suddenly showed surprise at my reaction.

"You've found someone! After twenty-six years, you've found someone."

"Well, I *met* someone . . . I wouldn't say that I found her . . . and certainly she hasn't *found* me . . . and . . . well . . . I'd like to think that there would be . . ."

"Who is she? Someone I know?"

"It's a little too early to say anything."

"Édouard, I shall pester you until you tell me. I'm telling Maman."

"No, wait. Please don't say anything. There may be nothing at all to say."

"All right; you can buy my silence for a few details."

"Sure. She's beautiful . . . intelligent . . ."

"Édouard! You know what I mean."

"She works at the University."

"Do I know her?"

"You've probably met her somewhere, sometime."

"Why would you think that? Oh, a conference, or a staff meeting . . . or lunch. Am I close?

"Speaking of lunch, what do you have?"

"Come on, tell me when."

"No, that's all you get. I'm hungry."

I took a seat at the table; Eliane got me a plate. I know that it was going to be torture for her to go the entire afternoon without telling anyone or without me giving her enough information to determine who it was. Philippe and I had a good long talk; he was working for his father, as was his sister Joëlle. He had an apartment in Nancy, which he shared with a girlfriend that I as yet had not met; they were planning to be wed next June. Olivier's father had left the business but not before securing new contracts from the army, the French army. In the past they had also done work for both the German and American armies. Philippe left before dinner and the three of us retired to the garden for an aperitif.

"So, Édouard, anything new happening in your life," Mother asked.

"Yes, as a matter of fact, maybe something very exciting, very different."

Eliane was just pouring me some crème de menthe and patted my cheek.

"Could you put some ice in this please," I asked her.

"The water is cold; I had the pitcher in the refrigerator."

"Just two or three cubes . . . please?" I handed her the glass.

"All right but don't you say a word until I get back."

She hurried off thinking that I was about to name the woman that I was interested in. It amused me how eager she was to hear about my love life. She should know that I would tell her before I told our mother. I waited a moment but then saw no sense in it.

"I may take a journey to the South Pacific . . . maybe on a ship named Calypso."

"Calypso? Isn't that . . ." Mother began to ask just as Eliane returned.

"Calypso Xenakis? The Chemistry professor who works in my lab? That's who it is!" she exclaimed triumphantly.

We both stared at her in bewilderment.

"That's her . . . she's the one."

"She who? One what?"

I put my fingertip on my nose and smiled. *A once in a lifetime opportunity!*

"Nothing . . . go ahead, I'm sorry . . . that name . . . you were saying?"

"Well it might not be Jacques Cousteau on the Calypso but an expedition is being put together to study the environment in Tahiti and another island and I'm trying to find out if there is some way I can get on it; if not perhaps I may take a sabbatical and go there anyway."

"Well, that is exciting. When would you go?"

"I have no details at all. I think I'll go to my office tomorrow and see what I can find out."

"Is there someone special you could ask?" Eliane winked at me.

"Hmmm, maybe I'll ask Calypso Xenakis."

I arrived at mid morning, not to find out about the expedition but in reality to research some minor points in my book that I could have delayed researching for a while. After only a half hour I decided to risk a trip to Villers lès Nancy. I was more certain than ever that Eliane and Hélène had met some time or other in the last three months. There couldn't be more than sixty people working at that lab. I got in my car and was there in ten minute. I parked as far away from Eliane's car as I could and went in through a rear door instead of the main entrance where her office was. I began peeping from door to door.

"Excuse me, Sir. Are you going in?"

A technician with a handcart loaded with Styrofoam boxes was beside me.

"Oh, no . . . sorry. I was just curious."

Embarrassed, I started down the hallway when I noticed a sign which read 'Analytical Chemistry'. There was a clerk sitting at a desk inside a small office. Feeling a bit mischievous, I approached her.

"Excuse me, is there a Professor Xenakis here?"

"Professor Xenakis's office is right through there. She may be here but I haven't seen her today. She may be on vacation in Crete."

I entered the hallway and at the desk in the first office was a shapely woman in her early forties, not slim but not overweight, with dark eyes and so much hair . . . black and curly, over her shoulders and half way down her back. She was on the phone and when she saw me she gave me a nice smile and held up a finger. A nice looking woman for forty or so. As I waited she motioned for me to take a seat. I felt devilish.

"So sorry to keep you waiting. How can I help you?"

"Are you Professor Xenakis?"

"Yes, and you?"

"I'm Professor Jannot from History at Nancy II and I was wondering if you had a bit of devilishness in you."

"Ha, you've come to the right place. What are you up to?"

"Well, I wouldn't want to get you involved if you are a married woman."

"Never had time."

"Good. Here's what I'd like to do."

When I explained it we had a good laugh; she even had a few excellent suggestions herself. She informed me that she would be gone the first two weeks of August, to take vacation in Greece, so I only had a limited amount of time.

"I like you Jannot," she said. "What's your given name?"

"Édouard but all my friends call me Oiseau. Calypso is such a beautiful and strange name; shall I call you that?"

"Only my mother calls me that. Everyone immediately thinks of Jacques Cousteau. No, call me Kaly; like that it means beautiful. Do you think so?"

"Yes, yes I do. A very appropriate name. Till later, Kaly."

"Ciao, Oiseau."

I returned to the campus of Nancy II and finished my research a little past noon and ate in the cafeteria. I saw a few people I knew but spoke to no one. I returned home and corrected the text that pertained to today's research and went on for a page or two. I spent an hour in the garden pulling weeds and harvesting radishes, scallions and snow peas. Most days when I was home my lunch consisted of a garden salad and a cup of yogurt. When I was done washing the harvest it was almost four o'clock. I didn't realize how late it was and hurriedly washed and shaved and walked to the Quatre Vents.

I took my usual place where I knew the shade would be in about a half hour. Large maples trees were at either side of the property, one giving shade in the morning, the other in the afternoon. André Biston was there but we ignored each other; those times were history. I almost got my wish; the two small fingers on his right hand never worked the same after I put the scissors through it; they were in a constant half-curl. He sold real estate and as an indicator of how we had forgotten those bitter times during the war, he once approached me making an offer for the wooded property in front of the cottage. I told him that it was not for sale but did not tell him that Mother owned it. Her 'business is business' outlook might have her selling it out from under me. I liked my isolation, such as it was.

"How's it going, Professor? A little Moselle?"

"Hello, Bernard. I'm a little dry today. I'll have a half-liter of Kronenbourg."

When the waiter returned I drank half of it immediately and placed the glass on the only spot of shade on the table. I felt heady, not from the beer but from expectation. I smiled to myself and let my thoughts wander. *What would it be like? To hold her in my arms . . . to put my hands on her body and have her respond to my touch . . . to wake up in the morning with her lying next to me?. . . Ahhh.*

When I returned from my reverie shade covered the table. I took hold of my glass and watched the derrière of a young lady as she reached into her red Renault across the street. Nice! I drained the glass; it was warm. She was heading this way. It was Hélène, smiling broadly as she approached. She was wearing a short bright red skirt to match her car, and a white blouse with a bit of red ribbon like a necktie at her collar.

"Hello, Oiseau. I hope I haven't kept you waiting long."

She extended her hand and I rose to greet her.

"No, no. I've just finished my first drink. Please . . . have a seat. Your car looks brand new; is it?"

"Yes, it's only three months old."

"Hmmm, I have a Renault too but *mine* is five years old."

"They all look so much alike. I wanted to get a Mustang but they were too expensive."

"You're better off with the Renault."

"Maybe. Well, first off, here's the posting for the expedition."

I scanned it, passing quickly over the scientific positions to what was left. There it was 'Documentarian – to chronicle and assemble in a comprehensive form all data other than findings included in technical reports. Applicant must possess . . .' I was in!

"You have to submit your application by the end of July and notices will be sent out in the beginning of September. Did you find anything?"

I put my finger on the line.

"That's only a clerical position. It doesn't pay much."

"So, you think that I would be overqualified?"

"I don't know. Can you assemble data comprehensively?"

"Have you read either of my books?"

"No, I didn't know that you had written any until you mentioned them."

"The second one was titled 'France and Great Britain and the Partition of the Ottoman Empire.' If ever someone wanted to see an exercise in the compilation of data, truly Byzantine data, this was a *tour de force.*"

That didn't impress her. I suppose one would have to read it to see the great difficulty that was overcome. Bernard was coming.

"You would like . . . ?

"Another, Bernard but a demi this time. Hélène . . . ?"

"I'd like some crème de menthe . . . with ice, please."

"Forget the beer. I'll have the same . . . with ice."

Bernard left and I turned my attention again to the posting, looking for the purpose and sponsor of the expedition. It was funded by the Sorbonne and the ANS.

"So, the government is paying for all this. Why?"

"They had some very disastrous results from nuclear tests at Mururoa and the island of Mangareva suffered terribly. My job would be to see if the fallout was chelating and if so how long it would be until the flora and fauna had removed it from the ecosystem. The inhabitants rely heavily on seafood and some species could be extremely harmful."

"Hmmm. And on Tahiti? What would you do there?

"Determine the extent that ground water pollution from industrial chemicals and inadequate sanitation has entered the food chain . . . and go swimming."

Bernard brought our drinks and I filled the glasses with water. We took a few refreshing sips.

"All right, tell me how it went with your mother."

"Ah, not exactly as planned . . . I must apologize."

"What went wrong?"

"Well, I told her that I had to go to the main campus to get something and we shared a table in the cafeteria and that when I found out who you were I mention her name saying that she spoke often of you. Then I said that I asked you how long it had been since you two had seen each other . . . and it was at this point that I thought she was becoming suspicious because of the way she said 'Yes . . . and?' So, I said that you said 'too long, I should stop by sometime.'"

Just what I did not want!

"And she said . . . ?"

"She said that I should have invited you and I told her that I did but that you were having dinner at a friend's house . . . then she asked if I got your phone number and I said that I did . . . and she said to call you and tell you to come after dinner tonight."

"It would be too late."

"She said to tell you that if you said that, that you and Vincent could skip a few beers for once."

"Ha, she said that? All right, I'll come but I still don't know what time that will be. How late is too late for her?"

"She stays up late every night and sleeps in every morning."

We sipped our drinks and inquired about each other's interests. She had many; the things that young people do, scuba diving, rock climbing, skiing, dancing on the weekends. My interests were all academic; I felt old. We were getting ready to go and I mentioned that I would call her to tell her about the results of the impending meeting with her mother, when she came up with a better idea.

"I have an early day on Thursday. Why don't I come by your place with a half kilo of shrimp and we could have lunch . . . and you could tell me all the things my mother will certainly omit when she tells me about it."

"That sounds great. Should I get anything?"

"Some Soave. My neighbor, her name is Josette Mazzani, gave me a recipe for Scampi . . . mmmm. I'll bring everything we need."

We parted with a handshake and I went straight to the Vinchelin's for dinner. Of course Doub and I had to have a few beers first but when the aroma of the roast came our way we made sure that we did not fill up on liquid. I could say nothing at all about either Marie-Jeanne or Hélène seeing how he never got over that time so long ago. We always had plenty to talk about so conversation never suffered. About an hour after dinner I claimed fatigue and went home, just long enough to get a flashlight and come right back out to take the *sentier* to Marie-Jeanne's house. When I got there only one light was on in the kitchen; I knocked.

I didn't know what to expect. Hélène gave me no warnings so I supposed that her mother was not some wild haired hermit living in filth. The door opened a crack for an instant and then fully. With only the light of a television giving illuminating from behind, I could not see her features very well. She was wearing a shiny bathrobe; her hair was in a single braid, which she had draped over her right shoulder, ending at her fingertips.

"Hello, Marie-Jeanne."

"Come in, Édouard. It's nice to see you."

She closed the door behind me and placed her hands on my face and kissed me on the lips. I had just got my arms around her when she ended it.

"I've waited a long time to return that kiss," she said, smiling and put her palms on my chest. I held her loosely at the waist.

"You're still beautiful; that much has not changed. How have you been?"

"Oh, I manage to keep busy . . . and fit. Come . . . have a seat."

She led me by the hand to a sofa. As I got comfortable she lit an oil lamp, which she placed on the table in front of me and turned off the television.

"I don't like the house brightly lit in the evening. Did you know that or did Hélène tell you that? I see you've brought a flashlight."

"Ha! No, I came by the *sentier*. I thought it would be nicer."

Actually I didn't want Doub to see me walking past his house.

"In the dark? Well, would you like some Moselle or maybe some cognac?"

"Cognac would be nice."

"Good. I'll only be a minute."

I watched as she went into the kitchen. She was barefoot and the bathrobe was red satin. I assumed that Hélène had retired; she would certainly have come out to greet me if she was up. Facing me was a wall full of books, which I could not remember seeing years ago on the few occasions that I was in this house. The room seemed cozy . . . very neat . . . the furniture was not Virginie's, and she was only dead four months. It was more than a few minutes before Marie-Jeanne returned. She was cradling two glasses in one hand as she exited the kitchen, turning out the light. She had undone her braid and her hair was now loosely hanging down her back. She placed the glasses on the table but stood where she was.

"How are you doing financially," I asked.

"That's not a problem. My grandmother invested her money very well and left it all to me. She may have been crazy but she received good advice. My mother was not very happy with that and left all hers to

Hélène, including this house. We just replaced all the furniture in this room two months ago; some of it was ancient."

"And the books?"

"Mostly mine. It took a while to get that many."

"Are you going to sit down?"

"Sure. Do you like my hair?"

She turned her back to me and leaned her head backward and shook it. Her hair shimmered in the glow of the lamp where it highlighted the slight curl in the long waves.

"It's beautiful. I can't remember ever seeing hair that long. It must take quite a bit of your time to keep it looking so nice."

"I have plenty of time to take care of it . . . and my body."

She turned to face me. She had loosened the sash of her robe and stood there with it half-open to her waist. I was surprised . . . but pleasantly. Her near nakedness was not offensive nor did I feel intimidated. She wanted me to look and I did so . . . with a smile.

"You have an amazing body for a fifty-year old."

"Forty-nine," she corrected. "Am I tempting you?"

"Ah, Marie-Jeanne, I didn't come here for that. We are old friends not old lovers. Come on, cover yourself and sit by me."

"So, I have waited all these years for nothing, eh?"

"We each did what we thought best for ourselves. We weren't waiting for each other. Come on, sit."

She closed her robe and tightened the sash, giving me a childish pout. She plopped herself next to me with her hands folded on her lap and her face downward. I put an arm around her and gave her a friendly hug. She nestled against me, pulling on my hand until it rested inside her robe on her breast.

"Marie-Jeanne . . ."

"I know, I know . . . but it feels nice to have a man's hand on me again."

I let her move my hand over her breast for a moment but then removed it and forced her to sit upright.

"It wouldn't be so hard for you to find a man who would be glad to do that for you, but I think you need to put a little effort into it."

"You think there are men out there who would find me desirable?"

As a jest, and to suggest that even *I* could find her desirable, I put my hand on her breast again and gave it a little squeeze.

"Oh, yes. I think you would be irresistible to many men."

"But not you, eh?"

"No, not me."

"Then you shall not enjoy my treasures," she said like a spoiled child and pulled my hand away, "but . . ."

She was in good spirits, not at all distressed as I feared she might be if I rejected her. She had a lilt in her voice, almost a giggle.

"Come on, let's drink. This is Rémy just like your mother gave me. I've grown to like it."

We raised our glasses and while I had my head back she slid her hand up my leg.

"Oh, Édouard, what have you got there?"

I almost choked.

"Well, what did you expect? You're not exactly ugly, you know."

"Ah, you're good for me, Édouard. We could easily be more than friends."

"I agree, but we won't."

"Give me a kiss."

I kissed her, not too passionately but not like I would kiss my sister. When it was over she murmured sweetly.

"More?" I asked.

"Hmmm, lots more."

"No, only one more then it's down to business."

"Well, come on then."

She set out to overwhelm me with passion in the intensity of her kiss and I allowed her to do her best. I could not say that I did not enjoy every second of it but I could not jeopardize my fantasy with Hélène by being intimate with her mother.

"Oh, Édouard, you excite me. Are you going to leave me like this?"

"Maybe you should take a cold shower."

"You're a heartless bastard, you know."

"Yes, I've often been told that and I won't change now."

"Do I have any hope?"

I thought about Hélène and how unlikely it would be that anything would come of it. I thought that I could be very happy with Marie-Jeanne, even as my wife.

"I'm not made of stone, you know. Who knows?"

"Ah, just enough to keep me from throwing myself off a cliff. You're such a charmer, you know?"

"Well, I try."

"Sure. You'll probably go home and masturbate. What a waste! Here I am, a willing, voluptuous, damn near nymphomaniac, passionate, voluptuous . . . did I say voluptuous?"

"Yes, and I'll agree . . . you're voluptuous. It's not easy for a forty-nine year old to be voluptuous but you've done a fine job of it."

"But you're going to keep your trousers on, aren't you?"

"Yes. Now let's stop all this; I want to talk to you seriously."

"About what?"

"About you not coming out of the house."

"I come out of the house all the time."

"Well, you must sneak out in the middle of the night then; your daughter thinks that you're a recluse."

"I *do* go out at night a lot but sometimes I spend the whole day outside."

"Why is it that Hélène thinks otherwise?"

She wouldn't answer but brought her feet up on the sofa and curled up against me, laying her head on my chest. I put one arm around her and caressed her face. I had hit on the problem. I waited patiently; knowing that if she would tell me at all it would only be if she wanted to . . . if she wanted help.

"You know I was hurt . . . that I needed someone to love me, to comfort me. My grandmother went catatonic afterward; she used to enjoy being violent . . . it was amusement for her, but after she saw real violence she withdrew from the world. My mother was sympathetic but she had that 'I told you so' attitude and only tolerated me. Then there was you but Laure-Anne had just died and I couldn't ask for much . . . you had your own grief to get through."

"I did try to comfort you afterward but you seemed so distant . . . so bitter, as though you didn't want my help."

"I know . . . I was wrong. I was taking it out on everyone."

"So you stayed in the house to deprive them of your company? That must have really taught them a lesson."

"At first I didn't want to go out until my hair grew back but by that time I didn't want to go out at all. You had stopped coming by and there was no one else I wanted to see. I might have welcomed Nadine but she would have been uncomfortable knowing how Vincent felt. I had Hélène. We would go for walks in the woods, spend all day there, leave at sunrise and come back after sunset. We did it for years . . . no matter what the weather, even in winter."

"And when you came to my house . . . ?"

"I could no longer stand being alone. Hélène was eight and she wasn't my baby any more. She didn't want to take walks with me anymore. She had suffered some cruelty by some girls in school but that passed and now she would rather be with her friends. I brought her along just so that I wouldn't make a fool of myself . . . but I did, didn't I? I threw myself at you."

"No, you didn't. You were very dignified and you presented me an offer. *Today* you threw yourself at me . . . and still very dignified."

Marie-Jeanne was laughing quietly.

"I wonder how far I would have to go before you called it undignified."

"You're wandering from my question. Why does Hélène think that you never go out of the house?"

"Because I make sure she never sees me when I do. I would leave in the morning before my neighbors were up and come back through the garden in the afternoon before they got home."

"Why? What was the point?"

"To be thought of as being still a victim . . . so Hélène wouldn't blame me for her suffering."

"Surely she wouldn't blame you when it was Biston who did it."

"What Biston did was only I part of it; I did the other part . . . I chose her father. I couldn't tell her one part without telling her the other so I told her nothing. Not a single thing. My mother stayed out of it even when Hélène asked her; she would tell her nothing. All she ever learned was that her father was German and it was someone at school who told her that."

"After all these years what would be the harm?"

"You don't see it. She has a miserable social life. She has a few good friends . . . all female, no boyfriends. The few that she had didn't last very long and she always cried when they broke up. It's the scar; you remember where it is. When her breasts developed the scar tissue didn't grow at the same rate; the nipple is a mess. After she was fifteen she wouldn't let me see it any more, her own mother. I don't know if you noticed but everything she wears has a high collar or is buttoned all the way up. Shall I tell her that a madman did it because he thought I was a whore?"

Phillip Varady

"If she knew the whole story, I don't think she'd blame you. It's a shame about the scar though; she's such a beautiful girl."

"We both have learned to live with it; there's no sense in upsetting things now. I think she's given up hope of finding a good man. Maybe that's why she's so reckless . . . jumping out of airplanes, climbing rocks and who knows what else."

The conversation gradually changed to *my* family and how they all were doing and for the most part I was glad to talk about something else. Marie-Jeanne tried, not too subtly, to weaken my resolve with cognac. I did have more but she had much more, arriving at a state in which she was both amused and amusing. It was late and I got up to go; she walked with me to the door without trying to delay my departure. When I expected that she would kiss me good night, she turned her back to me.

"Do me a favor?"

"Sure, what?"

"Put your hands on me again."

"Ah, Marie-Jeanne, why do you torture yourself?"

"Come on, would it hurt? Let me have a sweet dream, eh?"

She had opened her robe and I put my hands on her belly and slowly brought them up to her breasts. She moaned and shuddered a bit; I kissed her neck. In all, it did not last a half-minute. She turned around and kissed me briefly.

"Good night, Édouard. Thank you for stopping by."

"Thank you for an interesting evening. Are you going to come out of your isolation?"

She smiled and appeared not to have understood me; maybe she was in deep thought or maybe it was the cognac.

"Are you free tomorrow morning?"

"I can be; what do you need?"

"Could you drive me to Nancy . . . to a salon."

"To get your hair done."

"No. To have it cut off! Do you know how much trouble it is to keep it this long?"

I didn't know whether to talk her out of it or not. I liked it as it was but I didn't want her to do it 'for me.'

"All right, I'll be here around nine."

"Better make that around ten, for coffee. I'm not going to bed yet; I want to reread a chapter in a book on relationships. I think it was titled

'How To Let A Man Know You Are Interested In Him.' I think there was one part that I didn't understand."

I was halfway out the door but took her in my arms again.

"I'm glad you still have a sense of humor. I'll see you at ten."

"Édouard, I'll behave from now on. I don't want to scare you away."

I reassured her and left. I felt strange, physically aroused by the mother and emotionally aroused by the daughter. I thought that I must be assertive toward Hélène but how to do that eluded me. I didn't want to offend her or look like some old fool who should remember his age. Maybe in some subtle way I could let her know how I feel and see if she responds . . . make it ambiguous so I could say that she took it the wrong way if she reacts badly.

Tuesday was enjoyable. I dropped Marie-Jeanne off at a salon and walked around downtown Nancy for an hour and a half. I bought a bottle of cologne for myself and found an interesting second hand book in German about the behind the scenes political intrigue in Egypt during the war. When I got back to the salon, Marie-Jeanne was not there. I looked directly at everyone there and did not see her. When she spoke my name I realized that she had been standing outside the whole time and I did not recognize her. Her hair was now shoulder length and very curly and very blond.

"Do you like it?" she asked, grinning like a schoolgirl.

"God in heaven, if you looked like that last night I would have . . ."

"Really?"

"That and maybe a few more cognacs . . . and . . ."

"Don't spoil it. Just say you like it."

"I like it. You look fabulous. Let's have lunch."

We had lunch and then Marie-Jeanne wanted to buy some new clothes. I dropped her off at her house about four in the afternoon and drove to the Quatre Vents where I met René. We had a few beers and something to eat and I got home about nine and immediately began reading my new book. I could not stay awake past ten and retired.

I read another chapter at breakfast and decided to go to the University library to learn something about the author. It was published in Dresden in 1956 which made it suspect but if it was accurate it made British diplomats in Egypt look foolish and the French, both Vichy and Free look petty and conniving. I discovered that the author was Swiss but that the work was never published in the West. He had often lectured abroad and had a mailing address. I went to my office and typed a letter to him requesting a copy of the original work unless he knew that this East German edition was the same.

I called Hélène at her laboratory to confirm our lunch tomorrow, which she did after gushing about the change in her mother. I couldn't resist putting my mischief into motion and drove to Villers lès Nancy to see Professor Xenakis to put my scheme into action. I would have stopped in to see Hélène but thought better of it. Rather than go straight home I stopped at a large wine shop in Nancy that was more likely to carry Italian wines. We had a strong Italian minority in Lorraine that was invited here by the Germans after the Franco Prussian War to work in the mines, replacing Frenchmen that refused to live under German rule, like my great grandfather Farinet. After a hundred years they were assimilated, like Nadine and René, but we *Lorrains* adopted much of their culture. I found Soave from six different vineyards represented in the store's selection; I chose a familiar one that I often bought, which I considered the best.

It was late afternoon before I got home and I was torn between going to the Quatre Vents and reading more of the book. I chose to read until hunger got the best of me. I ate alone but spoke to Biston a bit; he was there more often than I, it seemed. If Marie-Jeanne was going to live a more normal life, certain possibilities might arise.

"Hey, André, whatever happened to your friend Elie? I haven't seen him in years."

"He had a bit of bad luck . . . he's away."

"Away? Did he move away or is he away working?"

"He's away sitting on his ass in a cell for eight years. He'll be out in four if he behaves himself. The man couldn't control his temper and picked on the wrong guy at the wrong place and the wrong time. Got his head split open in the deal, almost died."

"Hmmm, I remember that he liked to carry a gun."

The reference was not lost on Biston. He stared at me for a moment.

"It wasn't like that; things were different then . . . things . . . he changed. We've all changed, eh?"

"Yes, I suppose. Those were not good times; we had to change to something more normal, something more tolerable."

"Yeah, sure. Nothing ever stays the same."

There you go, Biston! Words of wisdom from the likes of you.

The Swans of Lorraine

I thought about that as I walked home. I had ended Marie-Jeanne's isolation but never considered that Hélène had ended mine. Even if nothing comes of it, she had permanently ended my self-imposed exile from the world of the heart. I did not feel guilt for it; too much time had passed. No one, not Eliane or Mother, not even Jean-Marie would have objected if I remarried, especially Jean-Marie; he waited only five years after Nathalie's death to remarry. It was becoming a priority; Jean-Marie was younger than I am now when he started over and he has two grown sons.

Did I want to start over? I am a grandfather of three. Do I want more children of my own? Would Hélène want children? I'm sure that she would. Marie-Jeanne wouldn't; I'm also sure of that. Hélène's response tomorrow will decide much.

I put the two bottles of Soave in the refrigerator and went to bed.

Chapter 7

After breakfast the next morning I reviewed my text covering the war years and looked to see how I could integrate the information from my newly purchased book. Its title was 'Codename: Sphinx.' The new data created some inconsistencies and I decided to wait until I received some word from the author before making changes. I spent the rest of the morning finishing the book.

About noon I showered and shaved. I used my new cologne for the first time; its advertisement promised exciting results. I chose a sporty looking shirt and a pair of loafers to give myself a more youthful appearance. I debated whether or not to wear my birds and decided that their absence would be more noticed than their presence. I renewed the fire in the stove and spread a red-checkered tablecloth on the table in the garden. It was placed to take advantage of the late afternoon shade but I didn't think it was worth the effort to move it for one luncheon.

Just before one o'clock I heard the gravel crunching in the driveway and went to the door to greet her. She was wearing a dark green skirt and a pale yellow blouse; one button at the neck was open. She had bags in both hands and greeted me as she rushed to the kitchen table to deposit them. When she had her hands free we exchanged *les bises* but then she gave me a peck on the lips.

"You're wonderful," she exclaimed. "You're amazing! I couldn't believe it when I got home that afternoon. What did you do to her? What did you tell her?"

"I put her under my spell. She thought that I was a real charmer. I never thought that about me; do you think there's any basis for that?"

"Oiseau, for my mother to think that you're a good man, seeing that she hates almost everyone, you must be a very exceptional man and I'll be a witness to that to anyone."

"Ha! That's nice. What did you think of her new hair style?"

"Oh, I love it. It's so 'now', you know. It's like she stepped out of the dark ages. I don't know where she got the inspiration to go in that direction but it says something about her. I think she's going to begin living again where she left off . . . in her twenties."

"Yes, maybe so. So you think now that you can go to Tahiti?"

"Absolutely! You know, she went to the grocer's today. What you did was nothing less than a miracle."

Suddenly she became very serious, very calm.

"Oh my God! I've been praying for months for this . . . and it happened. And you're the one who made it happen . . . you're an instrument of God."

"Hélène, if I went to church more than once a year . . . that would be a miracle!"

"Oh, I couldn't believe it; I walked in the house and called her. She answered from the kitchen and when I went in, there was this strange woman and I thought my mother had finally invited someone to visit. I looked passed her but she was alone and then I realized . . . Oh, how funny it was. We were jumping around and laughing and hugging."

We talked about it while Hélène started preparing lunch. We peeled the shrimp together and she put some vermicelli on to cook. She was still talking about it as I brought out a bottle of Soave.

"Oh, Bolla. You got the good stuff; it's my favorite. Could you put some ice cubes in mine, please?"

"It's chilled. It was in the refrigerator."

"I know but a like it on the rocks."

I got a bigger glass and put some ice cubes in it poured the wine.

"On the rocks . . . like it was Scotch or something."

"You've got to modernize, Oiseau. You should tell your card-playing buddies that you're going to get away from it all for a few weeks and then go off somewhere and do something totally different. You'll be a different person."

"To your health." We tasted the wine. "Like jumping out of an airplane?"

"Only once and once was enough . . . but it was thrilling. This year we're going to Corsica to go scuba diving. We've rented a villa for two weeks in a town named Calvi. We'll fly to Ajaccio and take a two-hour drive up the coast; the scenery is supposed to be breathtaking. My friend Alicia and her boyfriend were there four years ago."

"Is that who you're going with?"

"No, they're married now with a kid. I'll be going with three other girls who work with me at the Center. It's all arranged; we're going the first two weeks in August. I'm so relieved that I don't have to buy two weeks of groceries for my mother. Are you ready to eat? The shrimp won't take but a few minutes to cook."

"Absolutely. I'll set the table."

A delicious lunch in a garden with a beautiful young lady who talked incessantly with such excitement about her future plans, both recreational and vocational, and I just sat there and enjoyed the food and the stories she told. When I poured the last drop of wine I could see disappointment on her face. I fetched the second bottle and more ice cubes and she lit up again.

"Were you praying for a second bottle?" I teased.

"I was hoping for one. I guess that I wasn't desperate enough yet to pray."

We finished the little bit left in our glasses and I poured us each another full glass. I didn't want this afternoon to end. I was so content; I looked at Hélène and smiled.

"Oiseau, why is it you don't go to church?"

"Hmmm. I suppose we treated God like a doctor. You didn't go unless you needed him. When I was a child I needed him often; I saw . . . I saw a man kill himself. It left me in an awful state; I was very unhappy for many years. My friends never thought of me as one of them so my sister became my best friend. As I got older and more self sufficient I was less dependent on God until things got to the point where everything was perfect and we only went on Christmas and Easter . . . and then only because my mother wanted to go. When my wife was dying in my arms I didn't even think of him . . . didn't pray . . . didn't . . . ."

"And now?"

"Now? I suppose I've grown used to being alone. I don't think about God anymore."

"I know how you felt as a child; I went through the same thing although not for the same reason. On my second day of school the other children began calling me 'tite Boche' and I didn't even know what it meant. My mother said that they were wrong, that my father was French and to ignore them. Well, they wouldn't be ignored and I suffered terribly for it. It was my grandmother who began taking me to church and taught me to ask God for the things I needed. I prayed often and gradually got most of what I wanted and needed out of life."

"Most? What are you lacking?"

"Ha! A man that loves me, that's all"

"If I thought that God could find me a woman, I'd be on my knees every day."

Just like that, all the clever little lines that I had rehearsed became unnecessary. I didn't say that with any intention of provoking a response from Hélène but respond she did. The awareness in her eyes was an acknowledgement of that remote possibility.

"Hélène, I didn't mean to . . . it wasn't . . .

"No, no. That's all right."

An awkward silence followed. If I don't say something she'll think that I'm enjoying the idea . . . but she's not saying anything either. What could she be thinking?

"If God is in the match-making business I'm sure he'll find a man for you that is your age."

"The trouble is that the men my age begin their thinking in their pants. Even so, the moment I let them get a little intimate, they lose interest."

"Yes, the scar," I muttered.

"You know about the scar? My mother told you about *that*?"

She was furious.

"No, no, no. I was the one who took you to the doctor when it happened."

She had gotten up from her chair but sat down again and put her hand on mine.

"You know what happened then . . . don't you?"

"Yes, I was there."

"Tell me."

"I don't know if I should. Your mother and grandmother kept it from you all these years for some reason. Do you want me to defy your mother?"

"I want to know what happened. I don't want you to suffer for it but you're my only source of information."

"I'm not. Your mother knows. When was the last time you asked her?"

"Years ago but it was always a waste of time. In fact she wouldn't even tell me the time of day it happened."

"Things have changed, she's changed. Maybe now she would give you some details. Ask her again."

Phillip Varady

That was not a satisfying answer but the thought held promise. I could see from the faces she was making that she was debating within herself and finally she broke out in a big smile.

"All right, I give that a try. If she doesn't tell me then I will badger you until *you* do. You're too nice a guy to torture me with silence."

"I can be resolute if I have to."

"No, I don't think so. Come on let's drink this wine before it warms up."

"Is that a tactic? Do you think you can out-drink me?"

She just laughed and held out her glass. We finished it all at once and she poured a refill. She held out her glass again.

"Come on, Oiseau. Up!"

"Slow down. There's not enough wine here for either of us to get drunk, just enough to make us feel good."

"All right. I already feel good. I like being around you. *You* make me feel good."

"You make me feel wonderful, Hélène, but that shouldn't be."

"Who's to say what should and should not be? Only God . . . or are we masters of our own destiny . . . or do we work hand in hand, eh?"

"Sometimes I think we're just leaves in the wind."

"No. We can make things happen. Did you turn in your application for the expedition yet?"

"I'm going to the University tomorrow morning to do it. I may have an advantage. In the list of directors I saw the names of two men I went to school with. It's not as though we were the greatest of friends but we were friends nevertheless."

"Well, good. I hope they pick you. I hope they pick *me!* Hey, why don't you come up to the lab and I'll show you around."

"Sure thing! I'll be there about mid-morning."

We drank and chatted about Tahiti and Corsica and Abruzzo where she had gone rock climbing, until the wine was gone. When she was at the door, ready to go, I cautioned her.

"You're a little tipsy, you know. Wait a while before you ask your mother about that time and don't say you were here or that you even spoke to me. If she thinks I said anything at all you'll get nothing from her."

"All right and thank you so much. I'll talk to you in the morning."

She leaned toward me, hesitatingly, unsure. I put my hand behind her head and kissed her, she responded. It was not intense but it lasted long enough for both of us to understand that something had begun. When she was gone I thought I would just sink to the floor and die. I was overwhelmed; my knees were actually shaking. I made it to the kitchen and poured a good amount of cognac and collapsed in a chair. I took many small sips and thought about shouting with all my might.

It was about fifteen minutes later when my front door opened and Eliane came strutting in, sniffing. She went right by me, out the back door and was back in seconds. She sat down opposite me and took the glass out of my hand and drank my cognac.

"Calypso Xenakis! Or should I say Kaly Xenakis, as her friends call her. You had me so confused the other day that I believed I had jumped to a false conclusion. You are so clever, Édouard, so clever but your girlfriend talks too much."

"What are you talking about, Eliane?"

"She was in our office today just before lunch trying to get some paperwork processed. We tried to get her to come back later but she practically begged us saying that she had the afternoon off and she was going to make some shrimp Scampi for her new boyfriend and could we please, please, please do it now. One of the clerks who knew her asked who it was but she would only say that he was a professor."

The thought that she and Hélène had missed seeing each other by only a few minutes was sobering. It was fun fooling Eliane but I didn't want anyone to know about Hélène right now, at least not until our relationship had a more solid foundation.

"And you drew a conclusion?"

"You're damn right I drew a conclusion. What is that out there? Yogurt and salad? There's a pile of little shrimp tails. Two empty bottles of wine. Let me guess; Maman came over for lunch."

"Yes, that's right. If you don't believe me, call her."

"You're joking, right?"

"No, I'm serious; call her."

"You're bluffing! You're such a liar."

"Call her. Why aggravate yourself. I'm telling you the truth; I just brought her home. Call her."

Eliane stared at me with fierce eyes but she blinked.

"Damn it! I thought I had you."

When she admitted defeat so easily I could not help but laugh out loud.

"You bastard . . . it was her."

"Was who?"

"Kaly Xenakis, you moron."

"Don't know the lady. Wait a minute . . . yes I do. I think I met her twice in the last twenty-four years. Didn't speak to her for more than ten minutes total, both times. Tall brunette, rather skinny as I remember. Is that her?"

"Don't try that with me. It was her and you know it."

"Give me a kiss."

"No. Tell the truth and stop lying."

"If you give me a kiss I'll get serious."

"If you give me a glass I'll give you a kiss."

I got up, a bit shaky, and got another glass. I poured two shots of cognac and set one in front of her. She turned her face toward me but I motioned for her to get up.

"I want a hug too."

"Are you drunk?"

"Not yet. Give me a few minutes. Come on."

She got up and hugged me and gave me a kiss. I embraced her tightly and spoke in her ear; my eyes were full of tears.

"I think I'm in love. Can you believe that; after all these years?"

"Wait a minute." She separated herself from me and swallowed her cognac. "Say that again."

I was laughing in spite of my tears; the alcohol was catching up to me. I had to keep my wits.

"Sit down, sit down. You're wrong; it's not Kaly Xenakis . . . but if it was . . . what are you so mad about?

She couldn't answer right away. I think she was mad because I tricked her, not because I had a girlfriend.

"You're right. What am I mad about? My brother has managed to enchant a lady who is at least ten years younger than him, maybe fifteen years, who is attractive, intelligent, makes good money, is exotic . . ."

"It isn't Kaly Xenakis."

"Give up, brother. I won't believe a word of it."

"As you wish but she kissed me."

"Well, that's not much to go on."

"You don't understand. It was one of *those* kisses."

"An invitation?"

"Exactly! An invitation. Did you ever give one of those?"

"Give me a kiss and I'll tell you about it . . . and another cognac."

"Are you cooking tonight?"
"I don't think I'll make it home in time."

It wasn't pleasant getting up the next morning. I was all the way downstairs before I realized that my poor vision and the noise in my head were due to a thunderstorm. Two glasses of orange juice and two cups of coffee did little to ameliorate the hangover. I didn't dare eat anything although by then I was feeling a bit better.

The drive to the University was slow; beside water on the road, visibility was poor. Just at the entrance to my parking there was a three car accident; someone appeared to be injured and was being helped into an ambulance. I managed to back out and go around to the other side and found a spot. The paperwork for the expedition took only ten minutes and a few more for the clerk to look up two phone numbers for me. I left immediately and drove to Villers lès Nancy.

Hélène spotted me through the door and greeted me in the hallway with a handshake.

"What did your mother say?"

"She agreed that maybe it was time to tell me some of it but told me not to expect everything. She said that she would think about it for a few days."

"Well, there you go. I'll bet once she starts she'll tell it all."

"I'll still badger you for whatever she leaves out. This doesn't let you off the hook. You know, you don't look so good. Didn't you sleep well?"

"My sister came over and we stayed up late. So, what do you do here?"

She showed me what she was working on and some of the larger projects the University was involved in. She wanted me to meet the three others that were going to Corsica with her and I met Christiane, the first one who worked here in the same lab. I was introduced as 'my friend, Professor Jannot.' The second, Isabelle, worked in the soils lab next door and the third in Chemistry.

"Good morning, Kaly," Hélène said as we walked past her desk. "This is my friend, Professor Jannot. He's from History; I'm looking for Hoa. Professor . . . Professor Xenakis."

"Good morning, Professor, nice to meet you again," I said.

"Always a pleasure, Professor. She's in the next office, Hélène."

"Oh, I didn't know you two knew each other."

"We've met a time or two," I said.

When we met her friend I asked about her name and she told me that it was Vietnamese. We chatted briefly and left after only a few minutes. Kaly watched me over the tops of her glasses as we passed her. I could see on returning to Hélène's lab that I was keeping her from her work. She said that she was going dancing Saturday night with her friends and asked about having breakfast at my place on Sunday. I agreed and we said good-bye. I thought that I had better see Kaly. I suppose it was very obvious to her.

"She's the one, isn't she?"

"Is my secret safe with you? I haven't told Hélène how I feel about her."

"I don't know whether to scold you for getting involved with a child or commend you for having whatever it is that she finds interesting."

She looked me over like a judge might look at a convicted felon trying to determine his punishment. I wasn't going to defend my actions, at least not to her.

"Sit down, Oiseau. You seem like a nice guy and Hélène's not stupid. Tell me what your sister did."

I recounted Eliane's action and when I got to the part where I had her convinced that she had made another false assumption we burst out laughing. Kaly suddenly stopped and was pointing behind me. I turned to see.

"Did he like the shrimp, Professor?"

"Eliane, what are you doing here."

"Playing a hunch. When I saw your car in the parking I could think of only one reason why you would be here. So, did he like the shrimp?"

"He *loved* the shrimp! I told him that now he has to come to *my* place for some Greek cooking. What are you doing tonight, Oiseau?"

What in the world is she doing? Is this the punishment?

"Tonight? Well, I don't know . . . "

"You've got nothing to do. Go ahead, Édouard. What's the problem?"

"Well . . ."

"Eliane, you can come too if your brother is afraid of being alone with me."

"Oh, no. I wouldn't want to intrude in your evening."

"Well, Oiseau?"

I was trapped. I thought briefly that Kaly and Eliane had planned the whole thing from the start just to teach me a lesson. She could have called her when I left with Hélène. Eliane loves that sort of game.

"Sure! As long as we don't get drunk on Ouzo and wind up dancing on the table to bouzouki music."

"Oh, no! That was exactly what I planned. All right, we'll just have dinner and sip a little Metaxa."

"Sounds nice, Édouard. I've got to run. Give me a kiss."

She had a look of triumph on her face. I gave her a peck and she left.

"Why did you do that," I asked Kaly.

"Because I could. Would it be so terrible?"

"You're complicating things. It was just supposed to be a ruse to throw Eliane off the track. Now she thinks . . . I don't know what she thinks. I don't know what *you're* thinking. What *are* you thinking?"

"I'm thinking that I have an opportunity to get to know an interesting gentleman who has a mysterious power to attract younger women, myself included."

"You're not serious, are you? We hardly know each other."

"Well, this evening may correct that . . . or I may throw you out. Where do you live? I'll give you directions."

"In Laxou."

"Oh, we're practically neighbors; I live right here in Villers lès Nancy. Go past the lab and . . . here."

She drew a rough map to her apartment.

"About six," she said.

I left wondering if I was sane or not; I could not decide. It was still raining so I had lunch in their cafeteria. It slackened a bit in the afternoon as I headed home. I picked up my mail and another bottle of Rémy. As soon as I got in the house I called the two men that I knew at the Sorbonne but could only reach one of them. I explained to him what I was attempting and although he thought it was unusual he knew of no reason why I should not be considered. Most importantly he said that he would recommend me. I showered and shaved and dressed casually. I would have had an aperitif but I thought to give my body a reprieve. I sat at the kitchen table to sort my mail; the first was an official document from the Probate Court in Paris. I couldn't imagine what they could be sending me. I opened it to find a decision of the Court entitled:

Phillip Varady

Disposition of the Remainder of the Estate of Anton Sachs and Vlasta Sachs, his wife.

Two pages of places, dates, actions filed and dismissed and much legal wordage that I didn't understand led to a conclusion on page three.

IT APPEARS to this Court that Nathalie Sachs Thouvignon, the child of Anton Sachs, predeceased her father;

AND FURTHER, that the only issue of Nathalie Sachs Thouvignon surviving at the time of Anton Sachs' death was Laure-Anne Thouvignon Jannot;

AND FURTHER, that Laure-Anne Thouvignon Jannot died intestate on 15 September 1944;

NOW, THEREFORE, it is hereby ADJUDGED, ORDERED and DECREED as follows:

1.   *That Nathalie Sachs Thouvignon is found to have predeceased her father Anton Sachs, pursuant to the terms of Article V, paragraph A of his Last Will and Testament;*

2.   *That, pursuant to Article II of the aforesaid Last Will and Testament, as the only surviving issue of Nathalie Sachs Thouvignon, Laure-Anne Thouvignon Jannot became the sole residuary beneficiary of that portion of the estate of Anton Sachs bequeathed to Nathalie Sachs Thouvignon, said residuary estate including real estate and all business property of Anton Sachs, according to Article V, paragraph D of the Will.*

3.   *That, Laure-Anne Thouvignon Jannot's heir at law is her husband, Édouard Jannot, and thus all of the real estate and business property formerly belonging to Anton Sachs, and bequeathed to Nathalie Sachs Thouvignon, passes to him.*

AND there being nothing further to be done in this matter, it is ORDERED stricken from the docket and filed among the ended causes.

The will was not included with the disposition. I found it in a separate envelope and tore into it. Anton made numerous bequests to many people and charities; on the second page I found what I was looking for.

To my daughter Nathalie Sachs Thouvignon, I leave all that property contained in a deed to Anton Sachs, and Vlasta Sachs, his wife and known as 10 rue de Vaugirard, Paris and all its contents unless otherwise specified or bequeathed, and Twenty shares of Sachs, Thouvignon et Compagnie.

A little farther down the page I saw Laure-Anne's name.

The unspecified remainder of my assets held by Credit Lyonnais shall be divided equally by my three grandchildren: Charles Sachs, Louise Sachs and Laure-Anne Thouvignon Jannot

Twenty shares did not seem worth much but Anton's house did. I had no idea how much Anton had left in his account, certainly not a fortune but just as certainly more than a sou. I couldn't understand how it took so long to settle his estate and who the petitioners were. It must be Jean-Marie and Shlomo, unless some association with Uncle Milan had a part in this. I wondered what I would do with Anton's house. I might have enjoyed living in Paris again but not now. I suppose that I will sell it; that should amount to a small fortune at today's prices. *Ha, more than enough to finance a trip to Tahiti.*

I daydreamed for a while, opened the rest of my mail and got ready to leave. I was at the door when the phone rang. I almost didn't want to answer it, thinking it was Eliane but I was a bit early.

"Hello?"

"Édouard, Jean-Marie here. Did you receive the notice?"

"Yes, I just got done reading it, and Anton's will."

"I want to buy your shares. Is that agreeable to you? I'll show you the books so you'll know that what I'm offering is the true value."

"Anton once warned me to stay out of commerce and I think that was good advice. I have no desire to be a part of your business . . . yes, I'll sell them."

"I need to have some papers drawn up. Suppose I come to see you Monday afternoon? Is that all right?"

"Sure. I'll be home. How's the family?"

"Great! Geneviève wants to come with me so you'll finally meet her. The boys are taking a larger share of the business and I think I will retire this year."

"Well, it's about time. How old are you now, seventy-two?"

"Seventy-four. We just bought a house in Saint Martin and are planning to spend our winters there."

"Saint Martin in the Caribbean?"

"That's the one. You must come visit us this winter if you can get away."

"I will if I can. Actually I was planning a trip to Tahiti . . . to work, but I'd like to come anyway."

"Wonderful. See you Monday."

"Till then."

I hung up and left the cottage. What a week this has been; three women in my life and an inheritance. I felt very optimistic, very powerful . . . I felt like *somebody*. The rain had ended and the sun came out just in time to set. I felt mischievous; I now looked forward to my dinner date. Kaly's directions were good and I found her place without trouble. She was renting an apartment in a newly built complex, very modern looking, very 'super.' Her apartment was on the third floor, the top floor.

She opened the door wearing a pair of jeans and a white low cut fuzzy pullover that plainly revealed that she wore nothing under it. Her eyes looked beautiful, so large, so expressive. The red on her lips was the only color on her face. The aroma that filled my senses was delicious and I paused to inhale it the moment I stepped into her apartment.

"Mmmm, this promises to be a memorable evening," I said.

She just laughed and took me by the hand into her kitchen.

"I don't know how much you know about Greek cooking but there's no souvlaki or dolmas in this house. First there is *aginares*, then *mythia saganaki* and then *octopodi krasato*. How does that sound?"

"It's all Greek to me."

"Oh, isn't that original . . . but you're right. All right . . . those are artichokes with dill and then mussels with feta cheese and then octopus in red wine with a little fennel and of course *psomi sta karvourna* because you're French."

"Which is . . .?"

"Bread . . . just plain toasted bread.

"When do we eat?"

"I could put the stove on low; that would give us an hour."

"An hour for . . .?"

"A little Metaxa and whatever."

"Well, let's have a little."

"The Metaxa or the whatever?"

"Let's start with some Metaxa and talk about the whatever."

Kaly put the stove on low and brought out the bottle and two small brandy glasses. We sampled it, savoring its special character.

"I keep secrets well, Oiseau. Do you know what I mean?"

I took the glass from her hand and set both of ours on the table. I tugged at the bottom of her pullover. She was watching my eyes and smiling. I slid my hand under it, forcing it upward slowly. She raised her arms and let me remove it then pushed me down on the sofa, her long black hair falling around my head. She put her hands on my face and brushed my lips with hers, briefly at first. My hands found her buttocks and she writhed under my touch. She was deliberately unhurried, kissing me for only a few seconds at a time but longer and longer, more and more sensuously, expertly.

"Would you like some whatever," she asked.

"I would love some whatever."

She moved upward, placing her breasts at my face. They were large and soft; not firm like Marie-Jeanne's but smooth and fragrant. My lips almost ached to again find a place that they were so welcome. She allowed me to revel in my delicious pastime for a few minutes but then conducted me to her bedroom. How wonderful it was. Dinner was a tasty intermission. I think that the taste of Metaxa and the taste of Kaly will be forever inseparable.

"I'll be busy over the weekend," she said. "Call me Monday."

"I'll be busy Monday."

"Oh, isn't that just like a man. You get what you want and then you're busy."

"It seems to me that you also got what you wanted."

"I did but I want more."

"You can have more on Tuesday."

"Good . . . and you can buy dinner. I'm not your cook, you know."

"Hmmm, yes, that's too bad. What are you then?"

She held me around the waist and rubbed her pelvis against mine.

"We're each other's toy and like all children we'll grow tired of playing with the same toy all the time and go look for a new one."

"Right now I'm very happy with the one I have," I said.

"Well, you'd better get all you can by next Saturday because I'll be in Crete for two weeks."

"Well, I suppose that I could come on . . .Tuesday and . . . Wednesday, Thursday, Friday . . . and Saturday or are you leaving on Saturday?"

"No, Sunday morning. You would really come every night?"

"Yes, is that too often?"

"So, you like your toy, eh?"

I slid my hands inside her robe around her hips to her cheeks and pulled her toward me, massaging them gently.

"It's the only toy I have."

"Do you want to play with it some more?"

"I have all night."

"*Theé mou,* I picked a good one. Come on."

Anne-Marie, my housekeeper was already at work when I arrived home Saturday morning. My dirty laundry basket was outside the front door and when I went inside I could hear her upstairs vacuuming the carpet. She had made a fire to brew some coffee for herself; something I usually did. It was ready so I poured two cups. The vacuum stopped.

"Madame Cossin," I shouted, "Coffee is ready."

She came down immediately, dragging and bumping the vacuum behind her.

"That machine would last longer if you took more care in handling it."

"That's just the point. It's about time you replaced this relic."

"It works perfectly."

"It's too heavy."

There was no point arguing with her; she would always have the last word. She was a very hard worker and took pride in what she did. She was in her mid-thirties with streaks of gray in her brown hair and looked a bit undernourished. I don't believe that I ever saw her smile.

"Your sister has been here."

She said it as a fact, not inquiring if she was correct or as to the reason for her visit. I said nothing, knowing that she wanted me to ask how she knew. She sat at the table to drink her coffee.

"The fireplace is full of butts. Why don't you get an ashtray or a new sister?"

"She's not the only person who comes here that smokes."

"You stayed out all night." Another fact.

"Yes, I stayed at a friend's house."

She came to me and unashamedly put her nose on my chest and sniffed.

"A lady of means. That wasn't pisswater she was wearing."

"Why did you smell my chest?"

"Why do you think women put perfume on their tits? It's so the scent will be there, right up front, when the next woman comes along. Just like a cat marking its territory. Did she rub them on you?"

"Do you put perfume on your tits, Madame Cossin?"

"How can you ask me a question like that, you dirty old man?"

"Ah, I'll wager that there's a lucky young man somewhere that you rub your tits on, eh? Come on, out with it."

"Professor! What's gotten into you? Why are you talking to me like this?"

"You're blushing! It's true!"

She turned her back to me. I walked around her and held her by the shoulders.

"A woman sniffs my chest to see if I'm fooling around and won't admit it when she herself is caught."

She just blushed all the more.

"If I didn't already have someone I might look for another pair to rub against."

I put a finger in the front of her dress and pulled slightly, leaning to get a look. She slapped my arm and laughed.

"Get out of here you crazy man."

"You laughed. By God, I thought that was impossible. Ah, maybe you only laugh when someone looks at your tits."

"There's nothing wrong with my tits," she said, raising her voice. "Hello?"

Eliane was standing in the doorway. Anne-Marie almost choked from laughter and retreated with her cleaning gear into the bathroom.

"I don't think I want to know what that was all about."

"I was just teasing her. Give me a kiss"

Eliane kissed me then put her nose on my chest then sniffed at my neck. She smiled at me.

"Don't you believe in washing up after you make love?"

"I washed!"

"Ah-ha!" She pointed her finger at me. "Got you!"

I could say nothing. I would not have told her but now I rather enjoyed that she knew. It was like it was in Paris when we shared secret things.

"Just so you know, Kaly is not the one. We're just seeing each other for the sex."

I explained how this all came about by accident, mostly, to play a joke on her.

"Why should I believe any of that?"

"Well, since you found out about Kaly and me I could have simply acknowledged your good detective work and you would have been pleased with yourself. Why in the world would I insist that there was someone else?"

"So you're in love with someone else but in bed with Kaly."

"I don't know if . . . I don't have any . . . I don't know if *she* loves *me*. If I did I wouldn't fool around. All right?"

"Let's see . . . a beautiful woman . . . who comes from a faraway place . . . with dark hair, dark eyes . . . just in it for the sex. Am I talking about Kaly . . . or Fariza? A history professor who learns nothing from his own history."

She was right but I was in such a good mood and I didn't want to be reminded what the consequences might be. I began sniffing the air aimlessly each time coming closer and closer to Elaine's chest. She looked confused and I put my nose right on her. I stood erect and looked confused myself.

"What?" she asked.

"I don't smell anything. You must have washed better than I did."

"I didn't have sex, you idiot!"

Anne-Marie had just come out of the bathroom and turned right around and went back in.

"Why not?"

"What? A man who lived like a monk is asking me why I didn't have sex. While you were sleeping alone I was wearing my man out every chance I had."

"Shall I come back later, Professor?"

"Have you had any lately?"

"No, I haven't had any lately."

"Professor . . .?"

"Ah, maybe that's why you're so irritable."

"I'm irritable because I'm talking to an idiot."

"Give me a kiss."

"No!"

"Give me a kiss or I'll pinch your butt.

"You can't pinch my butt; I'm your sister."

I made a weak attempt to pinch her but she kept her distance.

"Professor, I'm leaving."

As Anne-Marie started passed me I put my arm around her shoulder and brought her to Eliane.

"I'm going to start calling you Anne-Marie. Madame Cossin is too old-womanish and you're not old-womanish. Do you know how I know that you're not old-womanish?"

She turned her face to the floor and would not answer.

"If my sister asked would you tell her?"

Anne-Marie looked at Eliane and then at me and nodded.

"All right," Eliane said a bit desperately, "How does he know that you're not old-womanish."

"In context, Anne-Marie. Use the same vocabulary you used when it came up."

She started to speak but then burst into laughter. She tried again but had the same result. Finally she worked up the necessary composure and blurted it out.

"Because I have a man to rub my tits on."

We all laughed. I got my kiss and Anne-Marie set about cleaning the kitchen. Eliane steered me out the back door into the garden so she could have a cigarette.

"Last night while Kaly was rubbing her tits on you, Maman and I had a visitor."

"Who was that?"

"Marie-Jeanne.

"Really?"

"Oh, you don't know anything about that?"

"I know plenty about that. I just didn't tell anyone. I wanted her to do something, to be the one who initiated things instead of everyone running to her. I told her she would have to put some effort into it."

"Whose idea was the new look?"

"Entirely hers. I liked what she had; her hair was down to mid-thigh. How did things go?"

"Very well. She came to thank Maman for her kindness back then, for not letting her wallow in guilt for loving a German. She had us both crying."

"Does she have any plans?"

"She wants to work with Hélène in the Ecology Laboratory. She's gone through every textbook that her daughter used both in the lycée and the University. She said that she's been sampling soil and water in the

Forêt de Haye for years and knows it better than anyone. If she doesn't qualify for a job in the lab she said she would enroll to get the required degree."

"That's amazing. She never said a word to me about it. Can she get some kind of honorary degree based on her knowledge in the field?"

"I was wondering that myself, so I made a few phone calls and found out that it's been done before. What they said was that she needs to draw up a petition stating why she would merit a degree and if they accepted it, then she would have sit for a board of review. I told her I would try to set it up if they could find a quorum; so many people are about to leave for vacation."

"When would you know?"

"I'll know Monday; we could work on the petition together and I'll submit it but I don't when they could do the review if they accept it."

"Hey, *I'm* going to have a visitor on Monday. Jean-Marie called to say that he wants to come to Laxou to do some business with me. Can you believe it; Anton's will has only now made it through Probate Court. I inherited his house in Paris, some cash and some shares of the company. Jean-Marie wants to buy them."

"How much cash?"

"It didn't say."

"Do you know what that house is worth? I'll bet you could get a million francs for it. You're going to sell it, aren't you?"

"Yes, I wouldn't leave you and Maman, you know."

"Or Kaly . . . or the other one, eh?"

"You want some coffee?"

"No, I've got to get going. Philippe and Sylvie invited me for the day. He said that Olivier would stop in for a minute but wouldn't stay."

"Why don't you rub your tits on him for old time's sake?"

"Why don't you take a cold shower? Has Kaly done this to you or is it the other one? But you know . . . I think it's good for you. Will you be over tomorrow night?"

"Absolutely. And I'll consider what you said before."

"You're so good. Give me a kiss."

Eliane left and Anne-Marie asked about my plans for the rest of the morning. I told her that I would be upstairs working and she said that in that case she would wax the floors. I got another two pages written but grew tired of it. The thought came to me that boredom was my motivation to write.

"Professor?" Anne-Marie called from the stairs.

"It's all right; I'm decent, the door's open."

"I'm done. If you need to go out within the hour use the rear door; it's dry there."

She came to my door to get her money, which I was counting out.

"Thank you, Professor."

"Thank you Anne-Marie. You don't mind if I call you by your name, do you?"

"No. Now that *you've* stopped being such an old fart, I suppose we need not be so formal although I'm not sure if your change was for the better."

"And thank you for not being embarrassed in front of my sister."

She smiled and took the money from my hand and then smacked it.

"There's nothing wrong with my tits. I would show you but I don't want to get you excited. You're an unstable man, no telling how you'd react. See you next week."

I finished what I was doing and went to the garden for two ripe tomatoes and a small onion, which I sliced up. A little vinegar, some olive oil, a touch of basil and I had my lunch salad with a piece of bread. A cup of yogurt with plum preserves and I was done. I didn't know if we had a card game this afternoon; René said he'd be busy taking care of patients before he took off on vacation next week. A call to Doub confirmed René's absence but he said that Jeami was bringing his younger brother and it was my turn to buy the beer.

As I prepared to shower I smelled my shirt. I could not discern Kaly's perfume and I wondered if women's noses were more sensitive to that sort of thing. I had better learn a lesson from this before the wrong nose smells me. When I had myself properly de-scented I went to the grocer's for the beer and brought it into Nadine's kitchen. She was ironing.

"How's it going, Nadine?"

"Can't complain. The restaurant is going to close the week of the ninth; half of us will have off the first two weeks in August and the other half the second and third. I'm in the first group. It didn't matter; Vincent didn't make any plans . . . except to lay around."

I put some beer in the refrigerator and opened one, pouring a glass full. Nadine got another glass and finished the bottle. We clicked glasses and took a gulp.

"How about you, Oiseau. Anything new?"

"Yes," I said, lowering my voice. "Marie-Jeanne has come out of hiding. She visited my mother yesterday. Do you think you would visit with her? She won't come here . . . unless Doub is at work or something."

"Oh, I'd love to see her. Have you seen her? How does she look? Why are you smiling like that? What?"

"I've seen her twice. I took her to a salon to have her hair done and I couldn't recognize her afterward. She's a blond, a curly blond; she hasn't gained a kilo and she wants to get a job at the University."

"Really? Doing what?"

"She wants to work with her daughter in a lab."

"Hélène works in a lab there?"

"Yes, you met her last week. She was the one looking for me at the card game."

"Oh, my God. She was beautiful. What does she do at the lab?"

"She has a degree in Biology and works as a researcher. Marie-Jeanne might get the same; she's been studying all these years."

"When do you think . . .?"

"Hey, Oiseau, how's it going?"

"Hey, Doub. You ready?"

"Yeah, but it won't be the same without René. Alain can't think past three cards. By the way he's bringing a case of beer."

"I just brought one."

"He thought because he was the new player that he had to buy. That's all right; it won't go to waste."

"No, *you'll* go to waste if you drink it all," Nadine chided.

"They're here. I'll take four bottles out and put the rest in the basement."

I let Doub go out alone so I could speak to Nadine in private.

"Can you call me before eight in the morning?"

"Sure, I'm up at seven; I go to the eight o'clock Mass. Vincent will be lucky to get up before ten."

The afternoon was boring; Doub was right. Alain was a terrible player and Jeami got abusive when they lost. We had already quit when Nadine left for work. Doub and I went to the Quatre Vents to get something to munch on; Nadine had put a light diner away for us. Sitting there quietly I wanted to be with Kaly.

"Oiseau, telephone."

"Who knows I'm here?"

"I think it's your mother. Who else calls you Édouard?"

I went inside fearing bad news.

"Hello?"

"Hello, Édouard. I want to take you to the cinema tonight. Are you willing?"

"Marie-Jeanne? Where are you?"

"I'm home; come pick me up."

"All right. I'll be there in five minutes."

"Oh, well . . . all right. Come on."

As I walked back to Doub I wondered what to tell him. Let him think it was my mother or something closer to the truth.

"Everything all right?"

"Yeah, it wasn't my mother, it was a lady friend. She wants me to take her to the cinema."

"You? Lady friend? Who is this? Someone's grandmother?"

"Hey, I'm not that bad. There are probably hundreds of women who would like someone as handsome as me to take them out."

"Sure, and I'm going to be the next President of the Republic. Who's this one?"

"Oh no you don't. If I gave you her name, you'd start a rumor that would have us about to elope or something. See you later."

I walked back to the cottage to pick up my car then drove to Marie-Jeanne's. She answered the door in her slip.

"Now there's a change. For years you wouldn't even answer the door and now you do it half naked."

"Hello, Édouard. I wasn't planning on you being ready immediately. Do I get a kiss or are we going to shake hands?"

I opened my arms and she put her arms around me; I put my hands around her waist . . . lower waist . . . very low. We kissed.

"Ooooh, something came up. Did I excite you?"

I slapped her rump.

"Go get dressed."

"Look at the newspaper on the table. I've circled some possibilities; you can pick one if you'd like."

Marie-Jeanne went upstairs and I looked at her choices. 'Elise ou la Vraie Vie' about a girl in an automobile factory, 'Z' about Greek politics, 'Macadam Cowboy' about life on the streets in New York City. I looked at what she didn't consider. She was back in a few minutes.

"Have you picked one?"

"Yes, 'The Garden of the Finzi-Continis.' Is that all right?"

"That didn't look very interesting; I thought you would certainly pick 'Z.'"

"Why is that?"

"Because it's an historic film about Greek politics."

"And the other is an historic film about Italian politics."

"Well . . . all right, but you buy dinner."

"You're taking me out and I have to buy dinner?"

"I have a limited income."

"And I'm fabulously wealthy? Ah, maybe I am. I didn't tell you about that."

I explained about Anton's will on the way to the cinema, explaining that I had no idea how much my inheritance was worth. We went directly to the cinema and I became engrossed in the film, thinking of Anton and Vlasta, Nathalie and Milan and Lida as the victims instead of the Finzi-Continis. Shlomo was no fool; he got out while he still could. Afterward Marie-Jeanne was aware of the reason for my selection.

I told her about my conversation with Nadine and she expressed a desire to meet with her. So, we had dinner at the Café Deux Hémisphères but did not see her. It was busy and Marie-Jeanne didn't want to go into the kitchen. We talked about the movie over some wine while waiting for our meal.

"Marie-Jeanne, I've been watching . . . I don't know if you have but did you notice men looking at you?"

"Yes. Does it make you feel good that they perhaps envy you?"

"Yes it does. Does it make you feel good to know that your scar takes nothing away from your beauty?"

She put her fingertips on my cheek and moved them across my lips then kissed me. When she sat back I put my fingertips on her scar and moved them across her lips and kissed *her*.

"I'm glad it doesn't bother you," I said.

"It doesn't bother you. I don't give a damn about the rest of them."

I ordered more wine. I was glad she was able to overcome all that.

"Why didn't you tell me about your work, about applying for a job in the lab?"

"I read that some men are put off by an intelligent woman."

"You don't believe that, do you?"

"Not any more . . ."

"Why?"

"You must have been very sweet to get someone with a university degree to cook Scampi for you."

Oh God. Hélène told her about that. Did she mention her feelings? She must have for Marie-Jeanne to even bring it up.

I was thinking of a defense.

"Or do you just want a younger woman?"

"Marie-Jeanne, it's not what you think."

"What do you think that I think?"

"That I'm robbing the cradle."

"Oh, I wouldn't go that far. Eliane says she's at least forty."

Kaly! Oh, God, thank you.

"You look surprised. How old did you think she was? How old did she *say* she was?"

"Give me a kiss."

"What? What are you up to?"

"Give me a kiss and I'll tell you."

"The truth?"

I had to think for a minute. Suppose Eliane told her about the joke and the 'other woman.' There was no way around that; I had to risk it.

"Sure."

"Well, it took long enough to decide."

"Are you going to kiss me?"

She gave me a nice kiss.

"Is she pretty?"

"Yes but you're prettier."

"Nice figure?"

"Yes but yours is nicer.

"Good in bed?"

"Yes but . . .

Marie-Jeanne burst out laughing.

"But I *could be* better. Why don't you find out?"

"Anything else you want to know?"

"Édouard, I have no claim on you. Don't think that you need to defend your actions to me. I understand now why you turned me down. You're such a gentleman; you could have had us both."

"I don't think you could do that; share me with another woman."

"I am sharing you but not the bed part. I haven't given up on you."

"Anything else?"

"Yes . . . do you love her?"

"No."

The waiter came with our food and we remained silent for a while and then talked as we ate, about her work and the studying that she had been doing. We had our coffee and then strolled around hand in hand through Place Stanislaus and then back to the car. We said little on the way home until I pulled up to her house.

"Do you want to come in for a while?"

"No, it's been a long day; I'm tired."

"There's something I need to ask you . . . a favor."

"What's that?"

"Hélène has been asking about her past. I've steadfastly refused to give her the slightest detail but when she asked why after all these years it made a difference, I didn't want to say. There are still some things I don't want her to know and if I start giving *some* answers . . . well, you know."

"What is it you want from me?"

"You tell her! The things I don't *want* her to know, you *don't* know. You can tell her everything you know and that would be it. I'll tell her that I won't discuss it further. And also, she'll believe you because you're not hiding anything. Will you do it?"

"Yes, I suppose I could. Shall I mention Biston by name? I still see him and don't want to kill him anymore. How would I justify that?"

"Some of it won't be easy. Use your judgment."

"Where and when?"

"If I don't see her tonight I'll leave a note."

"Sure. Well, I'll get on home then."

"One more thing . . . you don't have to tell me if you think it's none of my business but why don't you love the Greek?"

"We have an agreement . . . it was her idea but I agreed. This is just for a while. She says we're like children with toys, that we'll get bored with each other and look for a new toy to replace the old."

"That sounds very adult. So, after you two children have played with each other a certain number of times it's time to move on, eh?"

"Something like that."

"Give me a kiss; I had a wonderful evening."

"Yes, me too."

We kissed. Sometimes one can tell many things from a kiss and sometimes nothing. Marie-Jeanne was telling me that she loved me and I think I was telling her the same . . . a little.

"Hey, one more favor."

"Sure."

"Can you please get bored with her in a hurry?"

Chapter 8

I was up early Sunday morning in anticipation. As I started a fire to make coffee I decided to modernize my kitchen a bit. I think that with some money coming I could easily afford a new stove, one that wouldn't require that I heat the house just to make coffee, or maybe that and an electric coffee maker, or maybe just a coffee maker and I'll keep the wood stove. The phone rang.

"Hello."

"Good morning, Oiseau. It's me, Nadine."

"Ah, Nadine, how are you? Marie-Jeanne had me take her to the cinema last night and we stopped at your place to eat but it was so busy; she didn't want to bother you but wants to see you."

"Can you come up with something?"

"This doesn't need to be a top secret operation. Just tell Doub that you have to go to work an hour early and drive to her house. I'll let her know to expect you."

"But suppose . . ."

"No, Nadine, don't suppose. Just do it. Are you going to let him pick your friends?"

"But you know how he feels."

"Yes . . . maybe I'll have to test his friendship too. You owe her that much."

"All right, I'll do it. See you later."

"Good girl, ciao."

On my way out of the house to go to the baker's, a small white mini-truck was coming down the lane through a light fog. A young lady in a blue uniform got out and approached me.

"Monsieur Jannot?"

"Yes, that's me."

She handed me a small manila envelope and a clipboard.

"Sign here please."

I signed and saw that the sender was Credit Lyonnais.

"Did you come all the way from Paris?" I asked.

"No, Sir." She smiled. "From the airport in Nancy. The letter was here yesterday but I couldn't find your house. When a clerk in the town hall told me where it was I came back but no one was home. Sorry for the delay."

"That's all right. I should do something about getting this lane named. Well, thank you, it was prompt in any case."

I opened it to find a bank check for 142,032 francs. The accompanying document explained how that figure was arrived at including twenty-seven years of interest. I put it in my pocket and went to the baker's where I bought some very expensive pastries and some bread. Another stop for a newspaper and I headed home. The water was hot when I got there and I brewed a pot of coffee; a few more pieces of wood on the fire would supply enough heat for a second pot. The fog had lifted and I opened both front and rear doors to allow the cool morning air to dissipate the heat although the stone walls helped keep the ground floor cool all summer.

Hélène arrived wearing jeans and a bright yellow blouse; obviously she went home after Mass to change. We exchanged *les bises* and I brought her to the table to look at the pastries I'd bought.

"Oh, damn you. They look so good and I avoid all that. I'll only have one . . . maybe. Are we going to sit in the garden?"

"Sure. Take all that out and I'll bring the coffee. Take a towel; everything is wet out there. Do you want some bread?"

"Hmmm . . . no. I'll just have these."

She looked so beautiful. I had pleased her in some small way; it made me happy. I felt very domestic; it felt so natural to sit in the garden with her and enjoy breakfast together. I poured the coffee and thought, *should I sit opposite her so that I can look at her or next to her to be close.* When I got to the garden I found that the choice had been made for me as she dried two adjacent chairs.

We each devoured a cherry tart covered with chocolate and commented on the sweetness of it and the charm of breakfast outdoors with a warming sun and the stillness of the forest.

"My mother said that you would tell me about what happened years ago. Why didn't she tell me herself?"

"I'll tell you if you answer a question for me."

"All right."

"You wanted to come here even before you knew that I would tell you these things. Why was that?"

"Because I like your company . . . I like your house, this garden."

"Do you know how I feel about you, Hélène?"

"I think that you would like me to be more than a friend."

"Did you know that I was falling in love with you?"

"Yes, I knew."

"Do you think it's possible that I could fall in love with you in so short a time?"

"I don't know. I've never been in love."

"Knowing how I felt, why did you come?"

"That wasn't enough reason for me to stay away. You're different, not just older; you have a heart, a very good heart. I wondered if I got to know you better if I would feel something . . . if I would love you . . . if it would just happen."

"But you don't know anything about me."

"I do now. Last night when my mother agreed to this I asked about you. She spoke for a half-hour . . . I think she wishes that she were having breakfast with you instead of me. Am I wrong?"

"No. She's told me how she feels. I can't respond to the mother when I long for the daughter."

"What do you feel for her?"

"When she brought you here when you were small we spoke about a relationship and I thought that we could very easily have been lovers but the thought made me feel guilty and nothing ever came of it. After eighteen years she wants to stir those embers but my mind is on you. We're friends, maybe a bit more; I enjoy her company. We'll hold hands in public, kiss good night but it won't go any further than that."

"Would it go further if I wasn't in your life?"

"Yes. I don't know when that might happen . . . how long it would take me to get over you. I wouldn't take your mother as a consolation prize; she would have to be the most important person in my life."

"That's so sweet . . . so honest. It puts me in an unwelcome position. You've put the happiness of all three of us in my hands."

"My mother told your mother on the day you both were attacked that we do not chose who we love. It was a great comfort to her. She also said that love was a gift from God and every one of God's gifts was perfect. Love is not to be regretted even in this case where one's happiness is the other's sorrow. I don't envy you."

"I'm not ready to make that decision yet. I hope I will never have to."

We both ate another pastry and I poured two more cups of coffee and waited.

"So, why did my mother want you to tell me instead of telling me herself?"

"There are some things she will absolutely not tell you. She knows that I don't have any knowledge of these things so I can't be tricked into revealing them and that you couldn't infer anything from the way I responded or refused to respond as you might if she was telling you about them. But I won't refuse to respond; she said to tell all that I knew."

"Tell me about the attack."

I did, starting with my visit to Marie-Jeanne with Laure-Anne's clothes and ending with Virginie's gratitude the next day. I left out no detail that I could remember except the names of Elie and André. I let her know how Doub still feels and what Nadine feels toward her mother.

"Did you know these men?"

"Some of them."

"Are any of them still around?"

"Some have died, like the doctor, the man with the gun is in prison, and there are two that I know that are still around including the man who attacked you both."

"Who is he?"

"I'll tell you his name if you really want to know but I'm hoping that you don't. Think about why you want to know and what you want to do about it after all these years. They escaped punishment back then and nothing will be done now. Do you want revenge . . . a focus for your anger . . . will it be a benefit to know? Ask me again if you want when you come back from Corsica and I'll tell you."

"All right. Did my mother lie to me when she said my father was French or was that mob wrong and all this was a horrible mistake?"

"He was an Alsatian, born in France when Alsace was a part of France. That would make him slightly younger than me; when I was born it was still in Germany. When it was re-annexed he accepted German citizenship willingly and worked for the Third Reich as an administrator in Lorraine."

"You knew him?"

"Quite well. I liked him but I think he went along with the Germans because it was the easier road to travel."

"What's his name?"

"Erich Jost."

"Where is his home?"

"He was born in Colmar but the office that he worked out of was in Strasbourg. Are you going to try to find him?"

"I don't know; he's a total stranger. It's not as though I would have any feelings for him. He would only be a curiosity . . . but I'm curious. What do you know about him?"

"He was a very honest man; he would refuse to answer a question rather than tell a lie. He loved your mother very much although he was a bit reckless about her safety, which is probably why the Resistance found out that they were seeing each other. He brought her to the Quatre Vents one night and sat with my wife and me. He spoke French as easily as he spoke German and sometimes we would converse in either language."

"I didn't know you spoke German."

"Not only German but a smattering of Latin that Eliane and I learned as children and a few phrases in English that my son-in-law taught me."

"Mother said you had a daughter. Where is she; how old is she?"

The conversation for the next two hours went back and forth between that part of my life that Hélène knew nothing of and Hélène's father, of which *she* knew nothing. I think that I made him a more real person by describing him and presenting him as a man who collected stamps and butterflies, who liked listening to Wagner and Liszt, and as a man who dreamed of being a pilot one day.

"Ah, Oiseau, put the bread in the oven. I don't dare eat any more of this pastry."

We went into the kitchen; I heated the bread while she brewed the second pot of coffee. I was standing at the table buttering the bread when she came behind me and put her arms around me, resting her head on my shoulder. I continued until I had finished then turned within her arms. She rested her head on my chest; I put my arms around her. We stood there like that for a long time until she raised her head to speak.

"I've got to go to the bathroom."

"Me too; you first."

After my turn when I retook my place at the garden table, Hélène had put our two chairs together. When I sat she snuggled against me and I put my arm around her.

"Oiseau, I have a yearning and you are fulfilling it. I want to be loved but I want to love in return also. So far that has escaped me. It is not something that one can learn to do but I take every new feeling that I experience as a move in that direction. Is there a point that one knows that one has arrived?"

"Oh, yes. Hundreds of them. Just when you think that it couldn't be any better, it gets better. A good indicator would be when you stop thinking 'how good he makes me feel' and think 'how good can I make *him* feel.'"

"Hmmm, that has never happened. Oiseau . . . are you hinting at something?"

There was no emotion in her voice and I couldn't tell what she had on her mind. I didn't mean that as a proposition, still . . . *no, don't think that!* There was no mischief in her voice. I didn't want to offend her yet there was no annoyance or anger in it either. I would do well to be cautious.

"No, no, I meant in general. I hope you didn't take that to mean . . ."

"I was just teasing. No, I didn't take it the wrong way although I would like very much to arrive at that point."

She took my hand and smiled. *Was that to say that she wanted to arrive there with me?* I must take it that way otherwise all this is futility. I must not do anything precipitous. *Patience, Édouard, look for those little signs, a touch, a word, the fire in her eyes.*

"Then I should help you find a young man your age and forget about the love I have for you."

"Are you always so principled?"

"No."

"No? So, when do you break your own rules?"

"That's none of your business, mademoiselle." I smiled at her.

Hélène sat upright in her chair and gave me a wry smile in return.

"So, you have secrets, eh?"

"Everyone has secrets."

"Sexual secrets?"

"Yes, sometimes."

"You had an affair?"

"Everyone has an affair."

"Did you love her?"

"No."

"So, you slept with someone you didn't love?"

"Yes, everyone does."

She studied my face in deep thought.

"Do you like long hair on a woman?"

"Yes."

"Dark hair?"

"Yes, my wife had long dark hair . . . once."

"Dark eyes?"

"Yes."

"Your wife had dark eyes?"

"Yes."

"Like Kaly's?"

"Yes, like Kaly's. What are you getting at?"

"You slept with her."

"Why would you think that?"

"I was surprised that you knew her and asked myself why a history professor would know a chemistry professor. Certainly not professionally, and then she didn't greet you like an old friend it was more like . . . I don't know. I've seen her flirt with a lot of guys. And then your answer . . . you didn't say 'no.' Instead you asked why I would think that. That was a 'yes' answer, even if you didn't know it."

"That doesn't prove anything."

"You slept with her. Come on, tell the truth."

I didn't answer.

"What did you say about my father; he would rather not answer a question than tell a lie? Come on, tell me. I'm going to tease her and find out anyway."

"Don't do that."

"Why? You don't want her to know that I know?"

"Exactly. Part of the deal was that she wouldn't let you know; how would it look if she found out that I told you?"

"So, she knows about me? Did you tell her?"

"No, she guessed. You didn't help, parading me in there to show me off as some kind of trophy to your girlfriend."

"Is that what you thought I did?"

"That's what *she* thought you did and that's how she guessed."

"What kind of deal do you have with her?"

I first explained how I met her and how my sister was to blame for it getting so involved and then how it became what it is now.

"It stays purely physical; if I start getting emotional, she'll throw me out."

Hélène closed her eyes for a minute; I guessed what she was doing.

"I just can't picture Kaly doing it; she's always so businesslike and efficient."

I flashed a big smile.

"Oh, there too? Did you have fun?"

"Yes, I had fun. Does that bother you at all?"

"Nooo . . . it just seems peculiar. You two don't go together. She's analytical and you're philosophical. It won't last."

"It wasn't planned to. What are you doing the rest of the day?"

"Hoa just got engaged and we're having a little party at her place at four."

"Where does she live?"

"In Maxéville, only a few minutes away."

"Do you want to stay for lunch?"

"Sure. What do you have?"

"You can pick it from the garden or find it in the cabinet. We can make it together but I've got to make a telephone call first."

"Go ahead; I'll see what you have."

I had to look up the number, having called so infrequently.

"Hello" a sleepy voice answered.

"Good morning, Catherine. It's Papa."

"Papa, it's six in the morning . . . oh, is everything all right?"

"Yes, wonderful, perfect. Everyone is well. How's everyone there?"

"Good. The kids are having a great summer. Bobby got the promotion to assistant manager; that's an extra eighty dollars a week."

"Are you taking vacation this year?"

"We thought we'd go camping on the lake for a week."

"Come to France."

"We want to Papa. I think next year we'll be able to afford it."

"When is Bobby's vacation?"

"The last two weeks in August."

"Damn, I'll be in school . . . but never mind. Will you come if I send you the tickets, the kids too?"

"Can you afford it?"

"Yes, no problem. I just inherited some money from your great grandfather. Will you come?"

"Wait a minute, I'll ask Bobby."

I watched as Hélène brought in four tomatoes and went back outside.

"Beau-père, how are you. Yes, we'll come. It can only be for a week; I have work I need to do here."

"Can you leave on a Saturday and go back on the following Sunday; you'll be home on Monday."

"Hmmm, okay. Where will we be staying?"

"I thought that you and Catherine would stay with me and the children with Aunt Eliane. I'll be working that week but I can get off early every day. I've got a little bit of *clout*."

"You remembered that word."

"Yes and it seems that your French has improved somewhat."

"We decided to have the kids grow up bi-lingual. We speak nothing but French at home one week and only English the next. Do you want to hear Michael? I'll get him up."

"No, no, let him sleep. I'll hear plenty from him when you get here. Is the third week of August better than the fourth?"

"Yes, that's better. That's why I can come home on Monday; I'll still have the rest of that week."

"Good. What airport will you leave from?"

"Madison is just as close, but we'll get better service from Milwaukee. We can stay at my brother's house there on Friday night."

"Good. Check the tickets when they come and call if there's a problem. Give my love to the kids."

"Sure. See you soon."

I went out to the garden to see how Hélène was doing. She had harvested some scallions, lettuce, cucumbers, and sprigs of basil, chervil and dill and was pulling on yet one more crop.

"What have you there?"

"Carrots. They're not mature but they're tastier like this."

As we prepared lunch we talked about the similarities in our diet and then in our lives and found many more, much more than the dissimilarities. We spent the afternoon probing each other in many areas; the questions were sometimes personal but were always answered. We found no reason to be embarrassed at any of our responses.

The Swans of Lorraine

I lied to her but once when she asked about my father; I said that he died when I was young and I never knew him. I had two reasons for my answer, the first and long standing one was that I never wanted to distance Eliane from myself by making her my half sister although after all these years I think it might not have made a difference. The second was that I didn't want the fact that both our fathers were German, when that was socially unacceptable, to be a bond between us. If a relationship developed it had to be on better grounds than that and I felt that Hélène would find that coincidence very comfortable and make more of it than was relevant.

When it came time for her to leave we stood at the door.

"It took a bit of courage for me today, to express my feelings for you," I said. "I was afraid you would find my love unwanted and distance yourself from me."

"I find absolutely nothing about you that I would distance myself from. Oiseau . . . if I said that your age doesn't make any difference . . . that would be a lie. But I think that there's a point where nothing makes any difference; at least I have this romantic notion that true love is like that. Is it?"

"There is a point where nothing in this world has any value when compared to the love received from the one you love. When both have reached that point then only God is greater."

"I told you that you were philosophical, but that was a beautiful way to put it, especially from a man who never goes to church."

"You'll experience it for yourself one day."

"I hope so. I've got to go. Can I give you a real kiss?"

"And what would that be?"

"When we kissed without knowing each other's feeling, we held back. I know *I* did. This would be more . . . honest."

I put my arms around her waist and she put hers around my neck and our lips met. That kiss was no mere physical sensation; its meaning transcended the physical. Here was a woman who willingly and agreeably wanted to be in my arms and have me kiss her. She knew exactly how I felt and thought it possible that she might arrive where I am. I wanted to tell her over and over how much I loved her but would not pressure her like that.

"Mmmm, that was a real kiss," I said

"Good. I'm glad you liked it, I did."

"Hélène, the joke I played on Eliane to keep this secret from her . . . do you think I was wrong? Should you mention anything to your mother?"

"Oh, that's difficult to answer. If I say let's keep it a secret, it would mean that perhaps nothing will come of it and there is no need to cause my mother anxiety for no reason but if we tell her I'm sure that she will react badly. Just how, I could not say."

"Well, we should choose a course of action now."

"Yes, I suppose. Why don't I invite you to dinner tomorrow and we can give a little hint and see what happens?"

"I have dinner with my neighbors on Mondays."

"All right, Tuesday then."

"I promised Kaly that I would take her out to dinner that night."

"Dinner, eh?" She smiled knowingly. "And Wednesday?"

"Wednesday is good."

"Good!"

We kissed both cheeks and a peck.

I cleaned the table and the dishes and then myself and decided to walk to Eliane's house. I felt full of energy . . . younger. I took a longer route than necessary just so that I could look down the street that Marie-Jeanne house was on. What I hoped to see, I did: Nadine's car parked in front. Going to Eliane's from there I had to pass the church and it made me think that it was more than coincidence. It was early, the door was open, and so I went in. It was empty, which suited me just fine.

I was not sure what I hoped to accomplish but I felt that somehow my separation from God could be narrowed a bit. He certainly took his time to make up for the loss of Laure-Anne. Regardless of what the Church may teach, I didn't know for sure one way or the other, but I believed that bad things happen to good people because of the evil in the world. I didn't blame God for Laure-Anne's death and I didn't know if I should thank him for Hélène but it seemed like a good idea for me to get a bit closer to him, to be in his good graces so that things would move ahead with his blessings . . . and his protection.

I walked down the aisle a few pews and took a seat. I didn't pray; it was more like I explained the situation to God and told him what it was that would make me happy. I didn't make any promises; I had the notion that one only makes bargains with the Devil but seeing that Hélène went to Mass every Sunday, if our relationship reached the point where it was no longer a secret, I would certainly accompany her. Having done all that I got up to leave.

"Is there something I can help you with?"

A priest stood at the last pew. He smiled, exuding confidence in his own ability to improve my life.

"Thank you, Father, no. I just needed to do a little catching up. I'm fine."

"Would you like to make your confession?"

"No, I didn't come here for that."

"How long has it been since your last confession?"

"Father, please believe me. Everything is good."

"If you don't confess your sins they won't be forgiven."

"I don't have any sins to confess. Please leave me be."

"That kind of attitude will imprison you in your guilt."

"I felt good coming in here and you're trying to make me feel guilty. What the hell kind of priest are you? Is that supposed to help me?" I snapped at him.

"My son, you are in great need of help. Don't let your pride and your anger . . ."

"Get out of my way, you idiot. You've made this a wasted trip."

He was still imploring me as I walked out the door. Once I had put some distance between him and me, I paused under a tree.

God, I know he was only doing his job but really, my life has been moral and ethical. I have nothing to confess of any importance. Except Kaly, if that's a sin. We're two unmarried people who are only . . . am I making excuses? I'm sorry; I'll try to do better.

I arrived at Eliane's house feeling guilty. *Damn that priest!* Eliane will get me out of this, just like she always has. I walked into the house and took her by the arm and pulled her back outside.

"This thing with Kaly has me torn apart. The more I think about it the guiltier I feel. I should end it but I don't want to hurt her feelings. What should I do?"

"I thought you two were having a good time? What's wrong?"

"There's someone else to consider."

"Oh, are you going to bring up the other woman again?"

"Well, she's a part of it too but she wasn't too disturbed by it."

"She wasn't too disturbed? So, who *was* disturbed?"

"Is what Kaly and I are doing a sin?"

"Has somebody else been talking to you about this?"

"It doesn't matter. Is it a sin?"

"I don't know. If it makes you feel guilty it would be the logical thing to do to stop doing it. Tell her it's over and don't worry about her feelings."

"Just like that?"

"Yes, just like that. How long have you known her?"

"Not till you shouted her name. What? A week?"

"Édouard, it's not as though you were breaking up a longstanding relationship. Dump her! There's nothing to get over."

"Just like that?"

"Yes, just like that."

I embraced her and spoke softly to her.

"You're so good for me. You've always kept me from doing stupid things."

"Yes, you're damned lucky to have a sister like me. Give me a kiss."

I kissed her and felt very much better. I held her tightly.

"I'm going to pinch your butt."

She tried to get away but I had her.

"If you do, you pervert, I'm telling Maman."

I pinched her butt.

"That's it. You're in trouble now. I'm telling her."

"Go ahead. She'll like what I'm going to say a whole lot better."

"What could you possibly say to get out of this?"

"Catherine is coming home."

"Oh, you bastard! You're taking advantage of me."

She pinched my butt maliciously.

"Ow, that hurt."

"Go tell Maman, you sissy."

We went back inside to tell Mother. She was overjoyed, as were we all. I gave them all the details and the lodging arrangements that I had proposed and everyone was happy with it, especially Eliane whose vacation coincided with the visit. We drifted out to the back yard seeing that dinner was still a long time off. Eliane asked if I wanted an aperitif.

"Yeah, some crème de menthe would be nice . . . with ice."

"What is this 'with ice' thing? Why do you need it so cold?"

"Ah, my true love likes it that way."

The moment I said that I regretted it. The occasion could occur . . .

"You have a true love, Édouard?" Mother asked.

"I do but *she* doesn't. I'm waiting to see if she responds to my affection."

"Well, I hope she does. You look a lot better than you normally do. Who is this person? Someone we know?"

"I told Eliane that she's met her and you have too but I won't say any more."

"Why the need for secrecy?"

"Ah, that's a secret too."

"Well, does she have a brother?"

"Maman! Don't you even suggest that," Eliane said indignantly.

"Darling, you need something. A man in your bed is a good start."

"Maman, please. Not you too."

"What? Your brother suggested the same thing?"

I laughed and got Mother started too. Eliane was embarrassed.

"Well," Mother continued, "everyone should have their heart's desire even if they deny that that desire exists."

"What about you, Maman. What's your heart's desire? Now you can't deny that you have one or you'll make yourself a liar."

"No, I have one . . . more than one. Your sweetheart and Catherine coming home are two and your sister in a loving relationship again is another."

"I meant for yourself, something just for you."

Mother stared off into space for a moment then smiled then looked at me and gave me the briefest of indications that what she had in her mind also concerned me. Eliane got just a glance.

"I always wanted to go to Munich . . . to spend some time there, maybe a month or two . . . to get to know the place."

"Munich?" Eliane protested. "Why would anyone want to go to Munich? And how would you get by? You don't speak the language."

"Yes, I do. I've never lost it. There are more people around here that speak it than are willing to admit it. Your brother and I often converse in it just to keep it up. And why Munich? I don't know, I've always been fascinated by it. Strange, isn't it?"

Mother never took her eyes off me. She knew that I knew and it made her happy.

"Well, when would you like to go? In time for Oktober Fest?"

"Ah, that would be nice. If I could get to see Catherine again and go to Munich too. And how would this dream be financed?"

"You could sell the cottage."

"Oh no. You love the place. I'd never do that to you."

"Then sell it to *me*."

"Oh, you have that kind of money on a professor's salary?"

I took the check out of my pocket and held it in front of her face. "Is that enough?"

"Oh, my God, yes. I didn't pay half that much, not even a third."

"So you'll do it then . . . I mean go to Munich?"

I was on my knees in front of her and she hugged me and began crying. Between sobs she managed to communicate her answer in the affirmative. Eliane, realizing that this was more than she understood, joined us and we cried together. After a while we regained our composure and dried our eyes.

"The cottage would have been yours anyway; you didn't have to buy it."

"Maman, you can have all of this . . . except whatever Catherine's tickets cost."

"No, just give me what I paid . . . plus thirty per cent . . . business is business you know."

We had a wonderful evening making plans for Catherine's visit and Mother's trip to Munich. When I was about to leave, Mother came outside with me.

"It would be nice if he were still alive . . . and single."

I hugged her for a long time. Hope has the quality of making one an optimist even in the face of incredible odds.

"Yes, it would be very nice," I said.

I wiped away her tears with my thumbs and kissed her.

"You've given me something to pray for."

"No, Maman. I think you've given it to me."

Monday morning I went to the bank to deposit the check and then to a travel agency. There was some difficulty getting from Milwaukee to Nancy quickly. Their first flight left Milwaukee at seven Saturday morning and they would arrive at Nancy at ten Sunday morning. I enclosed a short note with the tickets and mailed them out immediately. I wandered around Nancy looking at things that I might buy when I knew how much Jean-Marie was going to give me for the shares. I realized that Anton wanted to give the shares to his daughter, which would mean giving them to Jean-Marie. If Nathalie had lived, all of his holdings in the company would have eventually passed to Laure-Anne. Now it will all go to his sons. I had no problem taking the money *and* it was legal. I saw a few things I really wanted but came home with only an electric coffee maker with a box of filters and a twelve bottle wine rack.

I had my lunch and worked in the garden until the Thouvignons arrived at two o'clock. Jean-Marie was driving a new white Mercedes 280SL, a very impressive automobile. Geneviève was also impressive, a bit younger than me and very attractive. She was nicely dressed and removed her kerchief and sunglasses when she got out of the car. Her hair was as long and as blond as Marie-Jeanne except that Geneviève's hairdresser made her look like a socialite instead of a cinema star. Jean-Marie and I hugged and slapped each other's backs.

"How are you, Édouard? It's been too long."

"Things are good. It's been a good year. You look well, Jean-Marie."

"Geneviève, come meet my old friend . . . my son-in-law, Édouard Jannot."

"Jean-Marie has been talking about you for years. It's a pleasure to finally meet you. I read your book about the Ottoman Empire."

"Really? The pleasure is all mine then. Jean-Marie has done well . . . intelligent, beautiful . . . and I'll wager a great cook too."

"Ah, not quite. But I make good coffee."

"Good. I just bought a new coffee maker. You can show me how much to use if you'd like some or I have some chilled white."

We slowly moved through the house chatting about our families. We stayed in the kitchen while the coffee brewed and then went to sit in the shade at the garden table. I informed Jean-Marie that his granddaughter would be visiting in three weeks. He said that he would try to come again to see her. Geneviève seemed to have no interest in Catherine and I took that to mean that she saw her as a potential heir. Only then did I realize it myself; surely he would leave her something. When I poured the second round of coffee, Jean-Marie opened his attaché case.

"Well, Édouard, let me tell you about the twenty shares," he said.

"The long version or the short version, dear?" Geneviève said. I could sense that she preferred the short one.

"The whole story," he replied with a bit of warning in his tone.

He shot a glance at her while digging out some papers. Well, he has not changed a bit; I had seen him do the same to Nathalie many times.

"My father built this business from nothing. I joined him when the first war ended and we were finding new markets almost every week. The trouble was that supply often was lacking or of poor quality. Anton moved to Paris after the war and split the business that he and Milan had in Prague. Their markets were all in the Austrian Empire and Anton thought that they would lose most of it to local entrepreneurs in the new nations. Milan thought otherwise. They agreed not to compete with each other and to share the same suppliers equally. Anton needed markets; Thouvignon and Company needed suppliers."

"I knew the reasons for the merger but not the details. Anton proved to be a shrewder businessman than Milan. I know what Central Europe went through."

"Yes, that's so. He also talked my father into a shrewd deal. My father thought that they should be equal partners. Anton had a warehouse full of goods and my father had a growing business with customers screaming for those goods. Anton proposed a 60/40 split with a written contract that he would leave twenty shares of his sixty to Nathalie at his death. Of course I would marry Nathalie, which neither she nor I had any objection to. We might have done it in any case; we were seeing each other for months when the deal was made. She was nineteen and I was twenty-four."

"So, the twenty shares represent twenty per cent of the company?"

"Yes, it's not like a public company with millions of shares. There were only two shareholders, now there are three, including you. Shlomo inherited his father's forty shares. It was Anton's intention that the Thouvignons would control the company after his death. His thinking, and he told me this, was that all would stay in the hands of his children or grand children . . . after I was gone of course. My father and mother died in an automobile accident in thirty-two. I have two sisters but my father left them only cash and me only shares."

"I see more clearly why you were desperate to get Laure-Anne into the business. Would it have all gone to Charles then?"

"Laure-Anne would have been an absentee owner; Shlomo, then Charles would have run the business; the profits would still go to the shareholders but salary could eat up quite a bit of profit. So, now we get to the purpose of my visit. I want the control that my father and Anton agreed on and I need Laure-Anne's . . . excuse me, *your* twenty shares."

I didn't think for a second that the mention of Laure-Anne was a slip of the tongue. He wanted me to know that he considered me a fortunate legal impediment to taking control of the company.

"Well, I told you that I would sell them to you and I will."

"Good. Here are our profit statements for the last three years. You can see here, here, and here what the net income was per share for each year."

Jean-Marie handed me a pencil and a pad.

"I'm prepared to offer you seven times the average of the last three years."

I made a quick calculation and arrived at nearly four million francs.

"I'll round it up to four million. Are you surprised?"

"Yes, I'm in shock. I think I need a brandy. Would you like some?"

"Sure. Bring three glasses and we'll toast the deal."

When I went back into the cottage I saw a man getting out of a taxi in front of my door. I went to see who it was. He was paying the driver and when he stood up I recognized him: Shlomo. He saw me, looked at Jean-Marie's Mercedes and came to the door with a briefcase in his hand.

"Édouard, good to see you again."

He extended his hand to me and we shook.

"Hello, Shlomo. How are you?"

"You didn't sign anything yet did you?"

"No, Jean-Marie made me an offer and I was about to accept."

"Oh, then I am not too late. They said at the office that he and his wife were going to Bar le Duc for the day. I didn't believe that for an instant. I caught the shuttle flight to Nancy and here I am."

"What do you want, you leech?" Jean-Marie said from behind me.

"You? . . . calling *me* names? I'll bet you offered him half of what those shares are worth. What was his offer?" Shlomo asked me.

"Four million."

"Ha! A crook would offer you more. Did he tell you about the supermarkets?"

"Did you know he tried to sell the house and keep the money?" Jean-Marie asked.

"Bullshit! It's under a court order. I couldn't sell it even if I wanted to."

"He almost went to prison for trying to bribe a judge."

"If that old fool was wearing his hearing aid none of that would ever have happened. He even admitted later that he wasn't sure what I said."

"He said that after you offered the second bribe and he took it."

"You don't know anything."

I left them standing at my door and got the bottle of Rémy and four glasses and went back to the garden.

"Would you like a brandy, Geneviève?"

She was absolutely annoyed, fortunately not at me. She had to be nice to *me*.

"Yes, thank you. I see that you had enough sense to walk away from those idiots. Every time they are together this happens. They have even made an agreement that Jean-Marie will be at the office on even days and Shlomo on the odd ones."

"What made you read my book?"

"Well, since you are a part of the family and no one else in it has ever had a book published I thought I should read it. I spent my teens in Lebanon so it was of some interest to me."

"It was written for the history student and as a reference to the politics of the times. Did you like it?"

"Yes. It mentioned so many places I'd been to and you mentioned my grandfather twice."

"To our health . . . and a pleasant afternoon."

We sampled our cognac and looked through the house at Jean-Marie and Shlomo still arguing at the front door.

"And who was your grandfather?"

"Gilbert-Guy de Montclauvent."

"Ah, that Syria-Lebanon debacle. Then your father is Henri."

"No. My mother is Henri's sister, Patricia, who married Paul Rochefort."

"Of *the* Rocheforts?"

She didn't answer but smiled in acknowledgement. Then my original assessment of her was wrong. She didn't marry Jean-Marie for his money, her family had so much more than he could ever hope to have.

"In all honesty, Geneviève, you know what I originally thought of you?"

"Yes, that happens all the time. Actually, I married him because I loved him. The Rocheforts have invested a bit of money in Sachs, Thouvignon and would like Jean-Marie to be able to control the company . . . as part of a larger organization."

The Rocheforts were mercantile giants and outspoken anti-Semites. I never liked Shlomo much but that had nothing to do with his being a Jew; he was too picky, too self-centered. Jean-Marie, it seems, had misrepresented the shares' true value; he also tried to foist Fariza's child on me. Anton gave me very good advice when he said they would eat someone like me in the world of commerce.

I saw Jean-Marie coming through the house alone.

"Did Shlomo leave?"

Just as Jean-Marie was coming out the rear door, Shlomo came around the corner of the cottage.

"His kind of Jew can't enter the home of a gentile," Geneviève said quietly.

"All right, let's get this settled," Jean-Marie said.

The two of them sat and began bringing papers out to complete and compete in this sale. I poured two more glasses of cognac.

"Not for me, thank you." Shlomo said.

I wondered if this was also forbidden to him, to accept food and drink from a gentile. It irritated me.

"Are you refusing my hospitality, Shlomo?"

Shlomo was sweating; he thought I favored Jean-Marie. Jean-Marie had a twinkle in his eye; he thought he had won. I believed that Shlomo was more honest but I did favor Jean-Marie for several reasons. While we all waited to see if Shlomo would compromise his faith, a plan . . . a beautiful plan formulated in my mind.

"No," he finally said, "it's just a bit early in the day."

He took a sip . . . or maybe he only made it look like he took a sip.

"Ah, today is not a day for sips. Let's drink to a satisfactory conclusion of this matter. Come on everyone, up"

We touched glasses and swallowed it all, Shlomo a few seconds behind us. He pushed his glass away and I could see his lips moving as if he were speaking to himself. A prayer of forgiveness, perhaps.

"First," Shlomo said, "let me settle some outstanding matters. Here is a check for seventy thousand francs for the contents of the house . . . including interest. This was a court-ordered account in my trust. The artwork was all bequeathed."

"He had already sold the stuff when I had the court order forced on him," Jean-Marie gladly explained.

"And here is a check for eight hundred seventy-two thousand francs for the rental of the house, including interest, also a court-ordered account in my name. Maintenance and taxes and fees by the rental agent were deducted."

"Oh, yes, the rental agent," Jean-Marie sighed sarcastically. "Louise Gerber, the former Louise Sachs. Have you met her, Édouard?"

Shlomo valiantly resisted Jean-Marie's provocations, which were nonetheless enlightening to me. This was a far cry from Mother's 'Business is business' mentality. He then proffered a stack of papers to me.

"And this is an offer that I am authorized to present to you to buy the property for one million five hundred thousand francs."

"A developer wants to demolish the house and put up a luxury hotel in its place. He'll probably sell it for twice that," Jean-Marie offered.

"You can hold on to this and consider the offer. It's a good offer, a fair offer and if someone goes higher . . . I'll match it. Shall we get down to business now?"

Jean-Marie did not answer for a moment then smiled at Shlomo and nodded his head slightly as if he were pleased with him; Shlomo smiled back at him.

"So then, you are done, Shlomo?"

"Yes," he answered after a few seconds. "Did I forget something?"

I began to think that they both were sharing a secret . . . something that I should know.

"No, let's get on with it," Jean-Marie said.

He had been sitting opposite Shlomo and motioned to Geneviève to switch chairs with him. They both brought out notepads and began to write. When they were done and looked at each other's figures, Jean-Marie began again. Then it was Shlomo's turn to recalculate. This went back and forth a few times until Jean-Marie snatched Shlomo's pad and showed it to Geneviève. She wrote something on it and returned it to Shlomo. He stared at it and stroked his chin.

"Édouard, may I use your phone?"

"Certainly. It's on the little table by the stairs."

Just before he went into the house he stopped and looked back at us then at his notepad. It took a few seconds for him to decide what he was going to do but then he went inside. When he was gone the Thouvignons looked very smug.

"Having broken one taboo, I suppose two won't send him to hell any sooner," Geneviève commented about his entry in the house. We sat silently for a moment.

"Édouard," Geneviève said, "you must come and stay with us in Saint Martin this winter. Bring a friend; it's a very romantic place."

"I'd like to, I really would. And there *is* a friend I would like to bring but I don't know when we could get away."

"Is it serious, Édouard?" Jean-Marie grinned.

"Yes, it took a while, didn't it?"

Jean-Marie mumbled some sort of answer. As I thought about it, it seemed to me that the age difference between him and Geneviève was about the same as between Hélène and me. She appeared content with Jean-Marie at age seventy-four, which was one of my concerns thinking of my own future. We waited for Shlomo's return; apparently he had backers whose approval he needed. When he came out we could see defeat on his face.

"I cannot match that figure," he said dejectedly to Jean-Marie. "It's yours."

It occurred to me that never once did Jean-Marie appeal to any sense of loyalty to the family . . . and Shlomo, telling him that it was his seemed a bit arrogant. It will be his when *I* say it is. Jean-Marie handed me his notepad with a new page showing and only the sum revealed, not the path that led to it. It read: 8250000 total, 412500/share.

"May I see your figures, Shlomo?" I asked.

Shlomo turned back that page and wrote them again on a new page. It was odd that even the losing bidder did not want me to see how he arrived at his offer. He handed me his pad and it read: 8100000 total 405000/share.

"Gentlemen, here is what I will do. Jean-Marie, I will sell you ten shares at your price and Shlomo, I will sell you nine shares at *your* price. I intend to keep one share for myself."

There was not a smile in the lot of them. I had given neither of them a controlling majority.

"Well, is my offer acceptable?"

No one said a word; they had not planned on this.

"Why are you keeping one share, Édouard?" Geneviève asked.

"This one share is for my daughter as a legacy from her mother and her grandmother. I'll keep it in my name but she'll receive the income from it. I will not exercise my right to vote my one share so you two will have to work out whatever differences you have and learn to get along. Sometime in the future, either when I die or decide to turn it over to her, my daughter will do with it as she pleases."

Geneviève and Jean-Marie were whispering back and forth while Shlomo was nervously looking into the cottage as if to make another phone call.

"We accept," Jean-Marie said.

"I accept also," Shlomo muttered.

"So, let's have another drink," I said, much too cheerfully for this gathering.

"There is one more piece of business first." Jean-Marie announced. "The income from the twenty shares was placed in a joint trust account until settlement."

Shlomo produced a check and he and Jean-Marie signed it. I wondered why they had not done this first and when I saw the amount I realized that they thought that I would not sell a single share if I had known. It was almost twenty million Francs. This was staggering. I could not spend this in a lifetime.

We had our drink, we all signed papers, I received my two additional checks and called a taxi for Shlomo to get to our little airport for the shuttle back to Paris. I wrote out Catherine's name and address for both of them.

"If she wants to sell it when it's hers, I suppose she'll favor the one who was most generous to her through the years. It won't be either of you two, you'll both be dead and gone but your sons might want to keep in touch."

Jean-Marie and Geneviève left shortly after Shlomo so as not to arrive back in Paris too late. I added up the five checks plus the one I received yesterday and it totaled roughly twenty-eight million eight hundred fifty-four thousand francs. I walked down the lane for one of Nadine's priceless home cooked meals.

It was still early and I knew that Doub wouldn't be home yet, which was good. I wanted to talk to Nadine. She was chopping ingredients for dinner when I came in.

"Hey, Nadine, how'd it go with Marie-Jeanne?"

"Oh, Oiseau, I'm so glad I went. She's so different and she hasn't changed a bit. You know what I mean. That hair! And she hasn't gained a gram. I told her that I saw Hélène and didn't even know it was her."

"Did she ask where?"

"Here. I told her here."

"What did she say to that?"

"She asked why she came to my place and I told her that she was looking for you. Was I not supposed to say that?"

"Hélène was afraid that if Marie-Jeanne knew that her daughter had talked me into visiting her that she would resist any persuasion I might exert on her."

"So, did I ruin it?"

"No. Marie-Jeanne is glad she changed her life. Sort of like the end justifying the means. I'm having dinner there on Wednesday so we'll confess to the lie and that'll be the end of it."

"She seems sure that she'll get a job at the University. Does she have a chance?"

"Eliane was going to check into that today; I'll call her later. Yes, it's possible; she may have to take some courses but she's competent in her field. She's been taking soil and water samples from the forest for years and has built up quite a volume of data."

"I thought she didn't go out."

"She was secretive about it; even Hélène didn't know. She told her that the samples were from her garden."

"I hope things work out for her. She suffered too long."

"She's someone who gets what she wants. You'll see. What's for dinner?"

"This is going to be chicken and creamed onion soup and then we'll have dilled trout with asparagus."

"Mmmm. Champagne would go well with that."

"You'll be lucky to get more than a beer."

"No, I think I'll go get two bottles."

"Did you win the lottery?"

"Laure-Anne's grandfather left her some money and the will was only settled a few days ago."

"Should I ask how much?"

"I don't mind; it wasn't much. A hundred forty-two thousand francs."

"Jesus, Mary and Joseph, not much? Go get your champagne."

I went and was on my way back when Doub passed me without knowing it. It struck me that I what said of Marie-Jeanne was the same thing that Eliane said of Laure-Anne; she gets what she wants. I wondered about that. It was obvious when I got back to the Vinchelin's that Doub knew about the inheritance. I wanted people to know that I had come into some money but not how much. It would explain how I was able to spend more than I was making . . . for a time at least. I didn't want to be treated like a millionaire.

"Hey, Oiseau, don't expect any beer tonight. Come on, I'll get some glasses."

"No you don't," Nadine chided. "That's for dinner. You have your beer till then."

Doub grumbled a bit but got two bottles of beer out of the basement and we sat outside at the table.

"Doub, do you know why Marie-Jeanne's daughter came looking for me last week?"

"No. What did she want?"

"She wanted me to talk to her mother; to get her to end her isolation."

"Did you do it?"

"Sure. She wanted to live a normal life again; she just needed someone to hold her hand for a little while."

"And you're holding her hand?"

"Yeah, do you think she's suffered enough?"

Doub didn't answer right away, instead he made gestures with his face and hands, supposedly giving thought to the question but I knew he was looking for a way to say 'no' without antagonizing me. When he delayed too long I asked another question.

"Why did you jump in to help me?"

"That idiot Biston was going too far."

"*Was going?* I'd say he already *went* too far both with Hélène *and* Marie-Jeanne."

"With the baby, yes; that was just cruelty but with Marie-Jeanne . . . I don't know."

"Do you remember the other woman they shaved with Marie-Jeanne?"

"Yeah, we all knew her."

"Did anyone disfigure her face?"

"No, they just shaved her head."

"Did they tear her dress off?"

"No."

"So what did Marie-Jeanne do to deserve the extra punishment?"

"I don't know . . . nothing, I suppose. We didn't plan any bloodshed and that thing with the baby, like I said, Biston went too far; that was all his own idea."

"All right then, you agree that they got more than they deserved."

"Yeah, I suppose."

"You suppose? Come on, Doub, give me a straight yes or no."

"Yes, all right? They got more than they deserved."

"So, how do think that we should make it up to them."

"You're kidding? I'm not making anything up to them."

"So, do you want to punish them more instead?"

"All right, Oiseau, you've made your point. You think I'm being stupid, don't you? What do you want me to do?"

"You're not being stupid, you're being unforgiving . . . but then you're an atheist, what would you know about forgiveness. And I don't want you to do anything; if you don't want to associate with her, that's fine but remember that she was Nadine's best friend. Do you choose your wife's friends? Would you forbid Nadine from seeing her?"

Doub just looked at me. He respected my intelligence and because I had laid out the matter in a logical fashion, he knew that my assessment was the right one.

"Come on, let's talk to Nadine," he said.

In the kitchen he put a hand on her arm to stop her . . . to get her undivided attention. She was puzzled, I was hopeful and Doub was tongue-tied.

"Oiseau told you about Marie-Jeanne, eh?" he finally managed to say.

"Yes, he told me," she replied nervously.

"Do you want to see her?"

"Yes."

"Yeah, it'll be all right. Go see her if you want."

Nadine threw her arms around Doub's neck and gave him a loving kiss. She had tears in her eyes and hugged him tightly, whispering in his ear.

"All right, Nadine. Save it for later; we've got company."

Dinner was superb, deserving of the champagne. We talked, mostly about my money and what I planned to do with it. I gave nothing but vague answers. The subject of Marie-Jeanne never came up. When Doub said that he was ready to go to bed I asked a favor from him.

"How much trouble would it be to put an electric hot water heater in my place?"

"If you only want it for the bathroom, it could be done in a few hours. If you want it for the kitchen too, we'll have to dig under the house or pull up some floor."

"Just the bathroom for now. I'll call someone in the morning."

"What do you mean, call someone? What's the matter with me? I'll get what we need and put it in tomorrow."

"That would be great, Doub. You're a good friend."

"I know . . . wait until you get the bill," he joked. "I'm going to bed."

That was good, now Nadine and I had another chance to talk.

"How did you do it?" she asked.

"He's got a good heart; you just have to remind him of it now and then."

"Did you confront him?"

"No, it never came to that. I just made him see that it was time to end it."

"Well, this is for a good job."

Nadine gave me a kiss and a hug. I thanked her for her wonderful meal and said good night. On my short walk home I thought about what a memorable day it had been. A whole series of events seemed to follow one event, not that that event was the cause of everything that followed but it stood out as a singular experience. That event was my meeting Hélène at Doub's house.

I have been nothing but . . . I wanted to say lucky . . . but I don't believe in it; the concept is flawed. It's like gambling; for every franc lost there's a franc won. If one player wins and credits it to *good* luck then the players that lost must credit it to *bad* luck. The one must equal the other, so then in other things there is as much good as bad luck in the world. Was all my good luck then a result of Laure-Anne's bad luck? The idea was sickening and abhorrent.

I was rejoicing because of the things that happened to me. If it was at the expense of Laure-Anne's life I would be miserable and guilt-ridden and I refused to be that and needed another explanation. I didn't have one but I didn't allow that lack to worry me. In due time I would know and I thought of myself as a patient man, a rich patient man.

The Swans of Lorraine

Chapter 9

The first thing I did Tuesday morning was to call Eliane and have her pick me up on her way to work.

"Did your car break down?" she asked when I got in.

"No, but I can't use it; I need to leave it home. It's complicated; I'll explain it later. I have a ride home so you won't have to come get me."

"Couldn't the same person have picked you up? Your campus is not exactly on my way to Villers lès Nancy."

"There wasn't time to make other arrangements; this was a sudden idea."

"Is Kaly spending the night?"

"No, Kaly is not spending the night. We *are* having dinner tonight but that will be the end of it. I don't feel right having a mistress."

"How are you getting home from Kaly's place?"

"I'll have my own car by then.

"The sex was no good, eh?"

"How can you possibly come up with a conclusion like that with so little to go on? You do that all the time. What did I ever say that could make you think that?"

"All right; so, it was good then?"

"Are you manipulating me?"

"If you're embarrassed to talk about it . . . you're not doing strange things with her, are you? Oh, my God! Does she wear black leather and tie you up? Is that it?"

"Not very clever, Eliane. But if you think it's all right for siblings to share intimate details of their sexual lives . . ."

"Sure. We're grown-ups. What could be the harm?"

"I agree. You first."

"Very funny."

"Well, when you have something to share we can continue this discussion."

"Also very funny. Do you have any suggestions?"

"Eliane! Are you saying that you're looking? Has boredom and sexual frustration finally motivated you to spread your legs for some guy?"

"You're so crude. Do you know that?"

"Well, what would you call it?"

"I'd say that I was bestowing my affections on a worthy gentleman."

"Sure. I can just hear Kaly using that phrase. The minute her ass hits the sheets she goes into high gear and doesn't stop until she runs out of gas."

"Now that's what I want to hear."

"All right. Let's change the subject. What did you find out about Marie-Jeanne?"

"She'll have to wait for a few weeks; too many staff are on vacation. Also, she'll have to submit written proof of her expertise in the field in which she seeks a degree."

"I think she may be able to do that. I'll talk to her about putting her notes in order. I suppose Hélène can check them over first."

"I called her last night to tell her; that's just what she said."

"Oh."

"She also said that you were coming to dinner tomorrow. Is Marie-Jeanne the other woman?"

"Don't you ever give up? Just drive."

"Well, it has to be someone."

"Maybe it's you," I said and put my hand on her thigh and blew in her ear.

"You pervert; you're going to make me have an accident."

Eliane dropped me off at my campus and left for Villers lès Nancy. I hurried to my office and called Hélène. She was surprised.

"Good morning Oiseau, is everything all right?"

"Yes. How are you?"

"Good. What's on your mind?"

"Nadine told your mother about the day that you came looking for me at her house."

"She didn't say anything to me."

"Well, maybe it doesn't make a difference but it gave me an excuse to talk to you."

"How sweet. This is not a good time to talk; I've got to get to my station. See you tomorrow night."

"Sure. Till then."

"Oiseau, have fun tonight," she teased.

"Hey, about that. We're going out for dinner and I'm going to tell her that this is over. I just don't feel right about it."

"Are you doing that for me?"

"Yes," I said after a moment.

She was silent and I wondered what it meant to her.

"Thank you," she said softly.

We said our good-byes and I immediately called Kaly.

"Hello, Oiseau. Nice to hear from you . . . finally."

"How was your weekend?

"Busy, but I got my curriculum finished. What about yours?"

"I haven't started yet. I come back to work on the seventeenth. History doesn't change much; it won't take too long."

"Is that an oxy-moron?"

"Not unless you're a revisionist. What time shall I pick you up tonight?"

"Seven is good. Come up for a drink before we go out. And don't plan on staying past midnight; I have to be at work in the morning."

"Sure. See you later."

I walked from the University to the bank where I deposited my fortune. Twenty-eight million in a market account and the balance in my checking except for two cashier's checks that I had drawn, one to Claudine Jannot in the amount of sixty thousand francs and the other to the local Mercedes dealer and stamped 'Not valid for more than ***100000francs.'

A few streets away was a well-known men's clothing store, which was my next stop. There were not so many customers this early and I easily found a salesman to assist me.

"I want a whole new wardrobe. I want to look like a successful thirty year old businessman, not a fifty-two year old professor."

"We have all the latest styles, Sir. I'm sure you will find just what you want."

"Young man, pay attention. I don't want the latest styles; I don't want to look like some fool in his fifties who think he's in his twenties. I want my wardrobe to say that the wearer can afford finer clothes, has good taste, is conservative . . . is self confidant. Can you manage that or do I need an older more experience person?"

The young man smiled in a way that gave me confidence. I'd wager that he was going to select for me his dream wardrobe, one that he would like all his friends to see him in, especially his lady friends. It took all of an hour and a half to equip me with everything. Suits, jackets, trousers, shirts, sweaters, socks, shoes, belts . . . and a dozen items that I would never have thought of. He was very good, very thorough, and I very happy with my purchases.

"Have you an automobile, Sir, or shall I call a taxi for you?"

"Yes, call a taxi but I want to leave all this here for a while. I've got to pick up my new Mercedes first; no sense loading all that twice."

Fifteen minutes later as I walked into the showroom I saw exactly what I wanted: a deep blue Mercedes 280SL with tan leather upholstery. I walked around it looking at every feature, feeling the texture of the leather. Just as I opened the door, a salesman approached.

"A very beautiful automobile, Sir."

"Yes. I'll take it."

"We have a wide variety of colors . . ."

"This one, just as it is . . . how much?"

"Ah, this one is 95,000 francs, Sir."

"I don't think so; my father-in-law has one just like it and he didn't pay that much. If you treat me right I may bring my girlfriend here and buy one for her too."

I pulled out the check with their company's name on it and held it up to the salesman's face.

"For only a few francs I could get another with the Citroën dealer's name on it."

"Please, Sir, let me verify the price. I'll be back in a moment."

I got in and put my hands on everything, adjusted the seat and the mirrors, looked into the map compartment, began pulling knobs . . . and the salesman came back.

"So sorry, Sir, I was in error. My manager informed me that that price was for the fully equipped model. This one has some features missing and is only 81,500 francs."

"Good. Let me have your pen. How soon before I can drive it out of here?"

"We can start on the paperwork while they prepare it for the road . . . within a half hour, I would say."

"Very good. What's your name?"

"I'm Jean-Luc Colnot."

"Well, Jean-Luc, I appreciate good service; I don't like waiting. The next time I'm here I will expect the same."

"You can depend on it, Sir. If you could step into my office and fill out the papers."

I went back to the clothing store and loaded up. It took all the space behind the seats and the front passenger seat too. It was too early for lunch, so I decided to go home when a thought struck me. I found a public telephone and called Jean-Marie at work. A secretary informed me that he was in a conference.

"Would you like to speak to Madame Thouvignon?"

That was a surprise . . . that she had an active part in the business. In fact she would probably be a better source of the kind of information that I was looking for.

"Yes, please. Tell her it's Édouard Jannot."

Only a few seconds passed before she was there.

"Hello, Édouard. How strange that you should call me. I was going to call you tonight with some news."

"What news?"

"You first; what can I do for you?"

"Well, I put all that money in the bank and I know that it should be somewhere else. Can you help me?"

"Sure. Hold on while I make a call."

A minute later she was back.

"There is an investment counselor in Nancy on avenue Anatole France. Do you know where that is?"

"I'm on it now. I was just going home after buying my 280SL."

"Oh, good for you. An excellent choice. What color?"

"Deep blue, like your eyes."

"Édouard . . ."

"I always notice a lady's eyes. I would never . . . you know."

"Well then, that was very nice of you. The man's name is Patrick Ulrich. He is an associate of a company that does business with Rochefort. I'll give his manager a call and tell him to expect you in . . . what?"

"I could be there in five minutes."

"All right, hold on again."

I had fallen into a whole new world. Money is power . . . at any level. Beggars without a sou will make a king out of a man with only one franc. The way I treated those salesmen was totally unlike me . . . but they were willing to put up with my behavior in order to make the sale.

"All right, Édouard; he's making the call. Do you have something to write on? Here's the address . . ."

All I had to write on was a deposit slip and all I had to write with was Jean-Luc's pen. I didn't even know I took it but I'm sure that he did.

"Go ahead."

She gave me the address and the man's manager's name and told me to mention it as though I knew him.

"And now for my news," Geneviève gushed. "Shlomo blundered. His backers were not happy with forty-nine per cent and pulled out. He was not willing to come up with four million francs and so he sold out, all forty-nine shares."

"Really! Jean-Marie bought him out?"

"No . . . not exactly. Jean-Marie was straining his resources at four million; he would have had to rely on *his* backers if he bought all twenty shares. That was one of the reasons we agreed to the deal; that we could do it without them and still deny anyone else controlling interest. We certainly could not have bought all forty-nine shares by ourselves. No, the buyer was Rochefort."

"Oh."

"You don't sound so happy, Édouard."

"I was counting on Jean-Marie and Shlomo competing for Catherine's one share by being generous to her."

"She won't be forgotten. I'll come up with something; trust me. There will still be a competition between Thouvignon and Rochefort for the share. What kind of work does her husband do?"

"He's an assistant manager of a supermarket."

"That's of some value. How about schooling?"

"He's got a two year degree in business management. What are you up to?"

"Oh, I don't know. Just finding out a few facts . . . looking for some possibilities. Where does he live in the United States?"

"A place called Fond du Lac in Wisconsin."

"Oh, my cousin mentioned something about Wisconsin a few weeks ago, something Rochefort was planning. It had to do with the Dutch cheese business. When did you say they were coming for a visit?"

"Third week of August."

"We'll be there. Catherine's his only grandchild . . . so far."

"That's nice. She'll be glad to see her grandfather again. I'd better get going to meet that guy."

"Édouard, Jean-Marie mentioned that all your friends have a name for you. What was it?"

"They call me Oiseau."

"Well then, Oiseau, I'll see you soon."

"Until then."

I went to see this Patrick Ulrich who jumped when I introduced myself and the man practically fell over himself trying to please me when I mentioned his manager's name. After noontime had come and gone and we had still not finished our business, he closed his office he took me to lunch. We sat in the restaurant for hours as he explained his investment strategy. He was very knowledgeable about finances and put me at ease. At his request I telephoned the bank when we returned and was a bit apologetic about transferring the twenty-eight million after only a few hours. I was shocked when they said that it would take two days before they could release the money. Patrick said that he would stop by the cottage when he had completed my portfolio. Imagine that . . . a portfolio. Me, with a portfolio. I made sure that he understood exactly where the cottage was.

When I got home Doub was throwing things in a truck.

"All ready to go. You'll have hot water in about an hour. Is that yours?" he said as he walked over to the Mercedes.

"Just bought it."

"Oh, now you're really going to get a bill."

"Doub, you're amazing. I thought you would come tonight."

"On my time?"

Just then another man came out of the cottage and greeted me.

"Electrician," Doub explained. "That's another bill. Come on, Mimi; it's almost quitting time."

They drove off just like that. I'll see him later and settle up.

I brought all my new clothes upstairs and emptied all the bags on the bed and filled them with all my old clothes, including what I was wearing. I had nothing left except underwear. I was getting rid of it all including those things I liked, that I was comfortable wearing. That was a symptom of my past, being comfortable with things. No more.

I put away all my new things, took my first hot shower and shaved, put all my old clothes in my Renault and drove them to the church where I left them at the poor box. From there I went to Marie-Jeanne's house. Hélène answered the door.

"Oh, you look nice but aren't you a day early?"

"I've come on an errand. How was your day?"

"Not very busy, and you?"

"Very busy. Got some new clothes . . . a few other things."

"For your dinner date?"

"Not particularly . . . just a coincidence. Is your mother home?"

"Yes, I'll get her."

"Come back out with her."

When they came to the door both of them were curious.

"Put out your hand," I told Marie-Jeanne.

When she did I placed the car keys in them.

"It's yours. If you've forgotten how to drive . . . take some lessons; maybe Hélène will teach you. Get yourself a license. I'll bring the paperwork tomorrow. See you then."

I walked off toward the end of the street to take the *sentier* home. Once in the woods I slowed to a stroll. I still loved it here but it was so full of reminders. I indulged myself by taking my time. *You still want to hold on, don't you Édouard?* Yes, a little bit; there is a fear of letting go completely. I do not yet see the anchor that I can grasp to pull myself into the future.

I arrived at Kaly's apartment on time. The woman who opened the door was *super*-Kaly. She looked fabulous in a tight fitting black dress, lacy on top and short on the bottom. It was her eyes that my eyes finally came to rest on; they were so expressive, so easily read. There was such a welcome in them, such warmth.

"Are you just going to look or do I get a kiss?"

"Can I look a bit longer; you're beautiful."

"And you don't look like a professor any more. Come on, give me a kiss."

We enjoyed a long kiss, a very long kiss. I could learn something from her. We sat for a while and had some Metaxa, slowly sipping it. She had made reservations in my name at an Italian restaurant in Nancy and it was more convenient for her to drive being more familiar with the route. I never mentioned the Mercedes. On the way she asked me what I knew about Italian wines and I replied 'not much if you want red.' So, she set up a little game for me to act out when ordering the wine to make me look more sophisticated; I liked the way she did things. They knew her at the restaurant and made a fuss to please us. The sommelier came to *me* to ask our choice of wine. I ordered the Valpolicella as Kaly had instructed me.

"Would you like Ripasso, Sir?"

"Do you have Le Canne?"

"Yes Sir, we have a good selection."

"*De grand cru*, please," I added beyond Kaly's instructions.

"Oh, how nice," Kaly said. "Am I worth it?"

"Do you want me to make a comparison between good wine and good women?"

"Not if it's something about improving with age."

"Oh, no, how gauche. I was going to say that once one has found that his taste is drawn to a certain vintage, one will always return to it to relive that delicious time."

"Ah, seeing that you don't have to win me over, that's a beautiful complement."

Dinner was delightful; Kaly was attentive and interested in me and my past. She spoke of growing up in Crete and where fate had taken her. It was ten thirty when we got back to her apartment.

"Kaly there is nothing about you that does not please me."

"Oh, Oiseau, you have that look. The next word is 'but' isn't it?"

"I'm sorry. I should have declined the first invitation."

"No, no, no. To have missed that night would have been a tragedy . . . for both of us. I knew better than to make love with a man in love with someone else. You're a real gentleman, Oiseau. Most men would have told me good-bye in the bedroom . . . but only afterward. You have honor and honesty."

"So, you will let me go without violence?" I joked.

"Sadly, yes but only if you will let me show you something first."

"Sure, what is it?"

She took my hand and led me to her bedroom.

"Kaly . . ."

"You will not regret this, Oiseau. Believe me, I will show you some things that you have never known. Are you so comfortable with the way you make love that you will not experience something new?"

"Like chains and whips?"

"I'm serious. Come on, do this for me. I want to leave you with something you will never forget. It isn't just for you, it will be for Hélène too. Come."

True to her word I was out of there by midnight . . . barely. I was truly amazed . . . truly amazed.

Wednesday morning I considered how unable I was to resist Kaly's charms in light of my resolve to leave unsatisfied by her. It was a matter of principle . . . or maybe it wasn't, maybe it was a matter of having an extraordinary evening or having nothing at all. In any case what she taught me was worth any feelings of guilt or self-condemnation that arose from my weakness. I couldn't wait to try it out on my own.

I felt good. With a good pot of coffee ready I set about completing a difficult section of my book. It seemed that my mind was exceptionally clear and I went through the text wondering why there had been a difficulty. When the coffee was gone I thought about what I wanted to do today. I had a few very good ideas. First I called Eliane at work and told her to meet me at her car for lunch. Then I went to the town hall and asked how I could get my lane named.

"It's a dirt road, Sir and you're the only one living on it. No name, sorry."

"Well what does it take?"

"I'll have to look at the land records for something. Be right back."

She was back in a few minutes with some papers.

"It's all one property . . . on your side of the road. There is some dispute between the town of Laxou and the Department of Meurthe and Moselle as to the jurisdiction of the other side. The town would favor naming the road but there would have to be multiple owners and a consensus to name it."

"So, what do I have to do, put more names on the deed?"

"No, Sir. That would still be one property owner. You need to subdivide the property and sell it to multiple owners and then vote on a name; we allow the local residents to do that."

"All right, I'll be back."

Next stop was Mother's house.

"Come on, Maman. We're going to the bank. Bring your deed.

"How much are you giving me?"

"As much as you want."

"Fifty thousand?"

"Sorry. It's sixty or the deal is off. The check is already made out and I'm not paying another five francs to have a new one drawn."

"Édouard, am I being foolish?"

"No, Maman. If after all these years you still want to know him . . . to see him, you should do it, stopping at nothing."

"What if I find him?"

"Then God will have answered your prayer. Are you then going to curse God for granting you the thing that you prayed for? Don't be afraid."

We went to the bank and then to Favier, the son, for the legal work. After transferring the cottage to me I asked for another transfer.

"What is it you want, Professor?"

"I want my road to have a name. The town clerk gave me the prerequisites and here is a list of people to transfer the property to. I want a power of attorney from each of them; I have no intention of letting my place get crowded in. I'll need a survey and the property subdivided into four minimum sized lots starting behind the Vinchelin's property and the rest in my name. What designation will the road have?"

"I don't think it could qualify as an *avenue,* maybe a *rue* or *allée* or a *chemin.*

"Or *sentier*?"

"Yes, there are already many so named."

"Good. Then it will be known as *sentier des Cygnes.*"

"Are there swans there?"

"There were two . . . once. There will be two again."

"All this will take a while but I'll call you when it's done."

Mother invited me to stay for lunch but I told her I was meeting Eliane. She thought that was nice of me. I promised her a surprise this evening. After arriving at Villers lès Nancy I waited only ten minutes for Eliane.

"I'm taking you to lunch. You drive." I explained.

"Where's your car? It *is* broke down, isn't it?"

"No. It's in Laxou. We need to make a stop. I inadvertently stole something yesterday and want to return it first. I told the man where to meet me. Turn right here and go straight ahead. It isn't far."

We parked across the street from the Mercedes dealer and waited.

"What did you steal?"

"An instrument; it was used in an expensive deal. Look at those cars over there. That blue one with the top down . . . now, that's a beautiful car. That white one . . . it looks just like Jean-Marie's. I wouldn't mind having one of those."

"Hmmm, yes. I like that red one with the top down."

"That looks like a 280SL. Jean-Marie's is a 280SL."

"It must be nice to have money like that."

"Let's go over there and take a look. You don't mind do you? I'll still be able to see the man when he comes."

I could see Jean-Luc inside the showroom. It didn't take long for him to spot me and he quickly came outside.

"Oh, here comes a salesman."

"Hello, Jean-Luc. I'm sorry about the pen. I didn't realize it until after I had left."

"It's nothing, Professor. We give them away."

"You dragged me here to return a cheap pen?"

"No, not at all. Jean-Luc, have that red 280SL over there ready to go in an hour. My sister is trading in that car across the street. Come on, Eliane, let's get the paperwork done so we can go to lunch."

One would think that the human nervous system would short circuit if too much input arrived at the brain in too short a time but Eliane proved that to be incorrect. By the time her reactions slowed to that of a normal person, Jean-Luc had backed away a few steps and I was again able to breathe having forced her arms from around my body. Buying her lunch was a waste of money; she never kept quiet long enough to eat. When we went to pick up the car her hands were shaking. I offered to drive and got a nasty look for my concern. Being overcautious can be equally as risky as being reckless when driving and I feared that she would have an accident on the way back to Villers lès Nancy but we arrived unscathed.

"Park over there by that other 280SL," I told her.

"Édouard, how much was it?"

"You know, one time Maman told me 'if you bought it you would know how much it cost.' It's a gift, Eliane."

"Did you give Maman money for the cottage?"

"I gave her sixty thousand."

"You've spent it all then, including Catherine's tickets."

"I got another seventy thousand for Anton's furnishings."

"What are you going to do with that?"

"You're parked next to it."

"Oh, Édouard. Good for you. Give me a kiss."

"All right but don't get carried away. I'm your brother, you know."

She kissed me and tried to hug me sitting there but wound up sniffing me.

"She did it again! *You* did it again."

"It's over Eliane. We said good-bye."

"Did she take her clothes off to say it?"

"Enjoy your day, Eliane, and please . . . drive a little faster. I think this model can do 200 kilometers per hour.

I took a leisurely drive back to the cottage thinking that I should get on the open road and see if it could really do that much. *Ah, to be young and reckless again. Can you be fifty-two and reckless? I am, I am.*

Patrick called and said he could be there in a half hour. I told him to come. I got in the shower to de-scent myself before going to the Denisarts. It was amusing trying to choose what to wear; it all looked so unlike me but I'll get used to it. It was put in perspective when Patrick arrived; we were similarly dressed.

He explained the laws concerning inheritance to me and what he had done to lessen my tax liability, although the government would still get a large amount. At my insistence he had investigated Rochefort's history and having found no compelling reason not to invest in it, twenty per cent of my funds would be put into their stock. The rest would be spread broadly in investments that over time had proven to return an average of ten per cent. It was hard for me to believe that from now on I could expect an annual income of 2,200,000 francs. All that was needed was for the bank to release my money.

I thought about walking to Marie-Jeanne's but finally decided to show off my new car. I parked it in front of their house and pretended to be busy with something until they came out. When their excitement abated I gave the keys to Hélène and let her try it out. Marie-Jeanne and I went through the house to the garden.

"So, you have a new toy," Marie-Jeanne said.

"Yes, I got rid of one toy and bought another."

"The Greek?"

"Yes, that's over."

Marie-Jeanne kissed me both as a greeting and to show her appreciation. Her garden was bordered by tall hedges except at the rear where the woods began and it was a perfect place if one wanted privacy.

I felt in a good mood and my hand slid down her back a bit to rest almost on her derrière. She kissed me again.

"Do I sense some need arising?" she asked.

"I was just being friendly."

"Why don't you decide to be friendly some night when my daughter isn't home?"

I let my hand slide a bit lower and squeezed her gently.

"Why don't you get me some crème de menthe . . . with ice?"

She wiggled in my hand and then went inside. I knew that I could be familiar with her . . . she allowed me, she enjoyed it but I felt as though I were exercising a right. I had the same attitude when I treated those sales people impolitely. I had something they wanted; therefore I could take liberties that were less than proper. I got comfortable and put the thought from my mind.

Hélène came out of the house with three glasses of crème de menthe and a pitcher of water. As she stood by my chair filling my glass, I put my hand on her in exactly the same place as I had done to her mother; she smiled.

"Where's your mother?"

"She went upstairs to change."

Hélène squatted next to my chair and leaned toward me. I put my hand behind her head and kissed her. She took a seat next to me.

"Are we going to let something slip tonight?" she asked.

"It would be better to test her reaction to a future event rather than a past one."

"Like you and I making plans to do something together?"

"Exactly. Do you have any ideas?"

"Not yet but I'll think of something before the evening is over."

Presently Marie-Jeanne returned wearing a bright yellow cotton dress that Hélène had to zip up for her. She looked very youthful and I told her so. That started the both of them commenting on my fashionable attire and the 280SL. That reminded me of the paperwork for transferring ownership of my old car. Marie-Jeanne signed it and Hélène took it saying that she could get it recorded on her lunch hour tomorrow. Then they inquired about my wealth and I revealed the source but not the extent.

We moved inside for dinner and the conversation wandered to many subjects.

"Can I come over Thursday afternoon, Oiseau?" Hélène asked. "I get out of work early."

"Haven't you heard it all yet?" Marie-Jeanne asked dryly.

"I suppose but I want to hear more about my father."

"I don't think Édouard can tell you much more."

I realized that Hélène's request was part of the plan; it seemed too innocent but maybe it was better to go slowly.

"You're welcome to come over any time, Hélène. I might remember a few more things."

Marie-Jeanne seemed a bit annoyed but didn't raise any objection and we continued to eat in silence.

"Maman, did you ever try to find him . . . afterward?"

"No."

I knew from the brevity of her answer that she didn't want to talk about it. I wondered why she had no interest in finding him.

"Would you mind if I tried to find him?"

"Ha! With the little you know it would be a waste of time and effort."

"It might not be so hard if he moved back to Colmar. Even if he stayed in Strasbourg, how many Erich Josts can there be?"

"What?" Marie-Jeanne exploded. "You told her that?" she fired at me. "How did you know that?" she screamed.

"He told me," I answered, totally confused at her anger.

"I sat next to you the whole time and he never mentioned any of that."

"At the Quatre Vents?"

"Of course at the Quatre Vents. You never spoke to him anywhere else."

"Yes I did. We spoke almost every Saturday afternoon at my place before he went down the *sentier* to meet you."

"Damn! . . . Damn! Damn! Damn!"

Marie-Jeanne pounded her fist on the table. One blow caught the edge of her plate and sent her meal flying across the table.

"Damn you, Édouard. Why didn't you tell me before I let her go to you?"

I didn't like being made the villain for something I did in total innocence.

"Why didn't Erich ever tell you that we met?"

"Get out. Get out of my house!"

Marie-Jeanne rushed into the kitchen and came immediately back.

"And take your car with you," she screamed as she hurled the keys at me. "I don't need your charity."

The three of us stood there and looked at each other. There was no point in trying to reason with her so I picked up the keys and walked out. I could hear Marie-Jeanne and Hélène arguing even with the door closed. I couldn't drive two cars and I wasn't going to leave my new Mercedes there, so . . . When I got home I poured a good shot of cognac and sat at the kitchen table and sipped.

What was the problem? I began a process of elimination to determine why she was so adamantly against Hélène having any knowledge of her father. I had thought that Marie-Jeanne loved the man. *Erich must be a terrible person or Marie-Jeanne was so lonely that she didn't want to share Hélène's affection.* The latter made more sense; Virginie only tolerated Marie-Jeanne; Hélène was the only person who loved her.

Headlights illuminated my front windows and I went outside. It was Hélène. She came to me and threw her arms around me.

"She turned on *me*," she sobbed. "She accused me of not loving her if I wanted to find my father. She called him all kinds of names."

It took a while to calm her down and have her tell me in more detail what had happened. It seemed that my guess about Marie-Jeanne not wanting to share her was correct. We stood there holding each other in the doorway, Hélène crying on my shoulder.

"Hélène, your mother is coming down the lane."

Hélène raised her head and kissed me. I tried to push her away but she had her arms around my neck. Finally she released me.

"Did she see us?" she asked quietly.

"Oh, yes, I'm sure she did."

Hélène wasn't going to pretend that she didn't see her mother and turned to face her as she neared the cottage. Marie-Jeanne came right up to us.

"Go home, Hélène. I want to talk to Édouard privately."

"If it's about my father, I'm not going."

"It's not about your father. It's about me. Go home . . . please."

Hélène's gaze shifted from Marie-Jeanne to me, looking, no doubt, for support or some indication of my love for her. This was not a prudent time for that . . . but then . . .

"Hélène, let your mother and me settle our differences. Come for dinner tomorrow. I promise that my cooking won't kill you."

My little pleasantry broke the tension; they both smiled for a second. Hélène took it as a show of support and Marie-Jeanne as mediation. Hélène surprised me when she gave me a brief kiss on the lips.

"I'll go, Oiseau, but only because it was you that asked. I know that you will look after my interests. Good night."

Once she was gone Marie-Jeanne shook her head and smiled.

"What's so funny?"

"That kiss she gave you when she saw me coming. Was that supposed to hurt me? She knows how I feel about you."

"I tried to stop her but she had a good hold on me."

"I'm sure you hated every second of it. She was acting like a little schoolgirl. She thinks that she's going to compete with me for your attention and affection the same way she thinks that I have successfully competed with Erich for *her* attention and affection."

"It's more than that. You hate Erich . . . why? I thought you loved him."

I had the feeling that Marie-Jeanne was going to tell me all about the reasons that she was so against Hélène finding her father. With only a little persuasion on my part we made our way to the kitchen table.

"I could use one of those," Marie-Jeanne said, pointing to my cognac.

I got another glass and poured a shot for her. She swallowed it and I poured another and she sat.

"I can't believe that you didn't realize that it was information about Erich that I didn't want her to know. What were you thinking . . . that I didn't want to share her affection with that bastard?"

"Marie-Jeanne, you told me to tell her . . ."

"I know what I told you, damn you. Why couldn't you figure it out?"

"Did you come here just to accuse me of being thick headed?"

"No, I'm sorry. I came here to ask you not to help her look for him and maybe talk her out of it altogether."

"I might if I had a good reason. Is there one?"

"Yes, two good reasons, either one by itself would be enough."

She drank the second cognac and held the empty glass out to me. I refilled it.

"Did you come here to tell me what those reasons are?"
She nodded her head.
"Do I have to swear not to reveal them to Hélène?"
"I was going to make you do that but it doesn't matter. You have to know; I can only count on your wisdom not to reveal anything."
"Well, let's hear it then."
"You've got to promise me one thing . . . that you won't hate me."
She began to cry.
"Please don't hate me."
I knelt beside her chair and held her.
"Marie-Jeanne, I promise I won't hate you."
When she calmed down she picked up her glass but put it down again and pushed it away. I took my seat and she reached across the table and clutched my hands.
"When Erich first came to the town office and we all knew he was working for the Germans. We disliked him but had to do business with him. He was very polite, never treated any of us badly and told us one time that if it wasn't him, a Frenchman, doing this work, it would be a German; and who did we think would look after our interests better? Well, that made sense and I began being more cordial to him. Remember the train that was derailed?"
I nodded.
"The Germans threatened reprisals. They took five hostages and were going to kill them if no one came forward with the names of the men who did this. One of the hostages was my mother's friend, yours too, Monsieur Leclerc, the director of the lycée. We all thought it was barbarous, killing innocent people because they couldn't find the guilty ones. It was the next day that I overheard two men in the town hall talking and one said 'Poor Chipot, what bad luck to be taken as a hostage. The only guilty one in the lot.' Well, I thought it was stupid to derail that train when you knew that innocent people would die for it. After all, what did they accomplish? The next day they put all the cars back on the tracks and they had gained nothing.
I wasn't going to let four innocent people die for the act of one guilty one. I told Erich the man's name and the same day they shot him but they released the other four saying that they were being generous, only killing one instead of five. Erich warned me never to reveal what I had done, even to people who agreed with me because one day they might be on the other side. We started to see each other after that; only

on Saturdays because that was the only day he was in the area. When I got to know him I fell in love with him and that was after, and in spite of the fact that he told me that he was a Nazi. Not just sympathetic to their cause but a party member."

"And that didn't bother you?"

"All that meant to me was that he didn't like Jews. I didn't know any Jews, so it didn't matter all that much. I was in love; nothing else mattered. Saturdays were heaven for us. We met in the woods, made love in the woods until it was time for him to go back to Strasbourg. In the winter it was different; we would find some isolated café in the countryside to eat where no one knew us and then find some farm road and make love in his car."

"What made you come to the Quatre Vents that night?"

"We were drunk. Couldn't you tell?"

"No, it never occurred to me. Did you two ever plan to marry?"

"Ha! Right from the beginning he told me that he had no intentions in that area but I thought that I could win him over. Ha! I'm doing the same thing with you. So, am I stupid? Well, anyway, when the Allies landed at Normandy Hélène was only a month old but he said that he was ordered to evacuate immediately. I begged him to stay but he said that he would be shot as a collaborator. I suggested moving to another part of France where they wouldn't know him and he said that it was too risky. Then I was desperate and said that I would go to Germany with him. He tried to talk me out of it saying that I might suffer for it and I told him that I didn't care as long as I could be with him. He refused to allow me to go with him and I told him that he couldn't stop me, that I would go no matter what."

Marie-Jeanne paused for quite a long time, drank her third cognac and motioned for me to refill her glass. I didn't put in quite as much as the previous three. I waited; she would continue when she was ready.

"That was when he said . . . I'll never forget his words . . . even the tone of his voice . . . he said . . . 'You stupid bitch, I've got a wife and children in Strasbourg.' He walked away and I have never heard from him since nor do I ever want to . . . or have my daughter ever speak to him. What would that bastard tell her? How I collaborated with the Germans? How I got a man killed?"

"You did what you thought was right and you saved four lives. Those four innocent people should not have been asked to sacrifice their lives when so many men that we trained for war ran from the enemy.

Would those four condemn you? Would their wives and children say that you should have let them die and not turned that other man in?"

"There were many that would have said that no sacrifice was too great and if I had been caught, instead of shaving my head they would have put a bullet in it."

"Well, that didn't happen. Let the past stay in the past."

"So, you won't tell her?"

"No, she doesn't need to know any of that but if she asks me to help her find Erich, how shall I dissuade her unless I tell her something."

"You obviously have some influence over her; think of something."

"All right, I'll do what I can."

"Good. I'm going home; will you drive me?"

"Sure. Come on."

She got up and then decided to have her last drink. We walked outside to the passenger side of the car.

"Édouard, Hélène has never known a father but she came to you for help. If she got closer to you, if you were the one she came to for advice . . . perhaps she may not feel the necessity of looking for Erich."

"She said that Erich was only a curiosity but also that she was curious. I don't think she will seriously look for him unless you forbid her to. You realize that you have created a competition and she will defy you for no other purpose than to show you that you do not control her life. Don't push her; let me handle it."

"All right. I know you'll do what's best. Édouard, am I making another stupid mistake with you?"

"About Hélène?"

"No. About me."

"What are you talking about?"

"We go out, you kiss me, you touch me. I like it when we are intimate but will it ever go beyond that? Do I have any future with you? Am I being *your* stupid bitch who is there when you want me but who will never share your life?"

I took her in my arms. She was right; I was using her because I could. She would put up with my behavior because I had something she wanted. It wasn't fair of me to do this. I should either stop seeing her or give her what she was hoping for from me.

"What do you want from me?"

"Marriage would be wonderful but I have no delusions about that. Even to be your lover would be wonderful, to know that you are there when I needed you, to be there when I wanted you. To feel wanted, to be loved, to share my heart with someone. To end my loneliness."

"Marie-Jeanne, I stopped seeing Kaly because I felt guilty. How would this be any different?"

"You didn't love her and she didn't love you; that's what is different."

She was right; I had affection toward her not lust. I was still unwilling to jeopardize my chances with Hélène by sleeping with her mother yet I could not be so cruel as to tell her that there was nothing between us and that she should give up all hope of being anything more to me than a friend with whom I might be a bit intimate from time to time.

"Listen, this thing with Kaly, from start to finish we knew that it wasn't serious. We neither asked nor promised each other anything. It wouldn't be the same with you and me."

"Because you have feelings for me?"

"Yes, you know that I do. I didn't just meet you; you're not a stranger."

"So, someone you just met, someone you have no feelings for . . . who wanted you in her bed . . . you could make love to but me who you've known for years, who you have feelings for, who asks for the same thing . . . you deny. Then, if I am correct, you won't make love with me because you care for me too much. Is that correct?"

"You're twisting things around. It's because I care for you that I don't want to start something that is going nowhere."

"All right, I'll give up all my expectations . . . now there is nowhere to go. Will you make love to me?"

She was tearing apart my opposition to her proposal. She could destroy, one by one, every reason that I put forward but one; the one that I dare not reveal. I don't see any way out of this except to plainly say 'no.'

"Will you at least answer me? Do I not deserve at least that?"

"Marie-Jeanne . . . there are things . . . it isn't only . . ."

"Damn you, Édouard Jannot! I want a man in bed with me. I want a man inside me. You are the only man on this planet that I would ask. Can't you just do it? Can't you find some reason to make me happy for one night? What would it take?"

I took her in my arms; she was crying. Now I am causing her pain and I feel more sinful by refusing her than I did by agreeing to make love to Kaly. Yet, I can't just agree and say 'all right, let's do it and be done with it.' She wants some affection also and I am capable of showing her real affection . . . but where will this lead?

"Marie-Jeanne, if I agree . . . I couldn't be cold to you; I have genuine feelings for you. What would you think if I expressed them?"

"I would think that you were being honest. We can make it plain from the start what we expect from each other in this relationship no matter how short it is."

"Relationship? Is that what you want to call it?"

"Would you rather leave some money on the night table and call it something else? I wouldn't mind if that's the only way to get you there."

"How private would this relationship be?"

"If you don't want your family to know, we will be discrete."

"Not just my family . . . everyone."

"Are you agreeing to something?"

"Yes."

"Me too. Will you make love with me?"

"Yes."

"Now?"

"Yes."

"May I stay all night? Hélène won't know if I am home or not."

"Yes."

"Are we going to stand here all night or do you think we should go to your bedroom?"

"Did you ever make love in a Mercedes?"

"You're not serious . . . are you?"

"No. Let's go upstairs."

She sent me to my room by myself saying that she would be only a minute. I undressed and got in bed, sitting there with the sheet covering me from the hips down. Marie-Jeanne came in and sat on the bed with her back to me; I unzipped her dress. She stood facing me as she removed it and then removed her panties, her only other garment. She came to the edge of the bed and waited, allowing me the opportunity to look at her. She really had taken good care of her body and she knew it. She had such an air of confidence; I liked that.

"Well, Denisart, what are you waiting for?"

"Nothing, Jannot. I am done with waiting."

Chapter 10

In the morning I was the first to awake. Putting on a pair of shorts, I went downstairs and started filling the tub with hot water. With some difficulty I awoke Marie-Jeanne and with more difficulty convinced her to come downstairs and get in the tub with me.

"I don't have a robe," she protested.

"You don't need a robe; I have no neighbors."

So, we went downstairs near naked, both of us. Being a gentleman I gave Marie-Jeanne the sloping end and just as I was about to get in, the phone rang.

"Damn. Couldn't they have waited? I'll be right back."

I stood naked in the kitchen to answer the call.

"Hello," I said in a less than friendly voice.

"Oiseau, it's me, René. Sorry if I woke you; I thought you'd be up by now."

"It's all right; I was awake. What's up?"

"I was wondering if you could feed my cat while I'm on vacation. I asked Nadine first but she said that she and Doub were going to take a trip to the mountains for a week. It would only be until she got back."

"Sure, René. Just write out instructions for me. I'll be glad to do it."

"Super! I'll drop off my key when I get the chance. I leave Saturday morning."

"Where are you off to?"

"Where the women are . . . to the beach. They put on quite a show, you know. Most of them don't wear tops when they sun bathe."

"Well, good luck, René. I've got to go. See you later."

"Thanks, Oiseau."

I hurried back to the tub and had one foot in it when the phone rang again.

"Damn! I should have left it off the hook."

I hurried back to the kitchen.

"Hello, what is it?" I snapped.

"Oiseau, it's Hélène. Is something wrong?"

"I'm sorry," I said, lowering my voice, "no, everything is good. I was just getting the tub and ... well, never mind. What's up?"

"I found a service in Nancy that finds people. I called them and told them that I wanted them to find a man for me. I gave them all the information that I could remember and they said if I had more it would be easier but that they could do a search on what I had and would send a report."

"I thought that we would talk about it before you did something like this."

"Finding him is not the same as meeting with him. I still haven't decided if I want to do that but then if I can't find him there is no problem."

"Yes, I suppose. Did they say how long it might take?"

"They said sometimes it's just a matter of looking up the name in a telephone directory and they would know in days but then it could take months if there are many people with the same name. Oh, I gave him your address and phone number. I can't have him send anything to my house; my mother would tear it up. And I also said that you knew more about him than I did, so he may ask you some questions."

"All right, I'll do what I can. We can talk about it later. Let me get back to my tub while the water's still hot."

"Sure, what time shall I come over?"

"Is this an early day for you?"

"No, not this Thursday. I can get off about four-thirty."

"Come right over then."

"Good. I'll stop home and change first."

"No, come right here."

"All right, see you later."

"Till later, then."

I hurried back to the tub and this time I was all the way in it when the phone rang again. I ignored it.

"Aren't you going to answer it," Marie-Jeanne said, laughing.

"To hell with the damned phone. Turn around and sit in front of me so I can wash you."

"I'm already washed. *You* turn around and I'll wash *you*."

"All right but take it easy; I'm a little sore."

"*I* didn't make you sore; it must have been the Greek, eh?"

"No, it was you. You were as tight as a virgin."

"Well, maybe if we did it more often you wouldn't be so sore."

"Oh, I don't know. The cure may be worse than the ailment. Hey, stop that! That part is clean enough"

"Who was on the phone?"

"The first one was a friend of mine who wants me to feed his cat while he's on vacation and the second was someone from the University who couldn't find something. And the third one will call back if it's important enough."

"Are we going to have breakfast first?"

"First? What's second? Oh, will you stop that! All right, that first."

"I don't want to make you sore, you know."

"I'll go slow; it'll be all right."

"Good. I like slow."

It was eleven o'clock before I got Marie-Jeanne home. She agreed to take back the keys to my old Renault. I went in with her for just a minute.

"Oh, good. She cleaned up the mess when she came home. I guess she wasn't that mad at me after all. Do you want to stay a while? I could make lunch."

"No, I need to talk to my mother about something and then I need to talk to Nadine about cooking dinner and then go shopping."

"Édouard, you will try to talk her out of this, won't you?"

"I agree with you that she shouldn't have any contact with him. Don't worry."

"I won't. You've made me very happy. Did you enjoy it? Was I all right?"

"Hmmm, it's a little too early to tell. Maybe we need to do it again before I'm sure."

"Are you still sore?"

"I think that I'll be in good shape by tomorrow."

"Call me in the morning."

"I will. Till later."

I was at Mother's house two minutes later. She was working in the kitchen.

"Hey, beautiful lady. How's everything?"

"Édouard! What a surprise to see you at this time of day. Will you stay for lunch?"

"I was going to take *you* to lunch. What are you making?"

"Pickled herring and potato salad."

"Sure, I'll stay. Listen . . . about your trip to Munich, have you made plans or are you still only thinking about it?"

"It sounded like such a good idea but then I thought about it and . . ."

"No, no, no. You've got to go. You will never forgive yourself. Even if you don't find him you will have seen where he lived. Go, have people wait on you, have them do your laundry. Spend some money. Maman, don't worry about the money; I've got eight hundred thousand francs in my checking account."

"Really? Really! Son, I won't worry a bit about spending *your* money."

"Good. Have Eliane take you to a travel agent. If she can't do it . . . call me."

"I will. Put a bottle of Moselle in the refrigerator and tell me about the money."

Lunch was delightful. Mother wanted to practice her German and spoke a bit about those things that she once told me were none of my business including news of two gentlemen friends.

"What do you mean by gentleman friend?" I asked.

"It could mean anything you want it to mean," she replied with a smile.

"Well, I never met either of them. When did this happen?"

"I met one when you and Eliane were children, you were about twelve then. The other when I was working at the butcher shop here in Laxou."

"The butcher?"

"No, not the butcher; he was married. Don't ask any more questions because you know what I'll say, don't you?"

I didn't want to leave but I had another errand to run. I went to see Nadine to ask her what to buy to duplicate the meal she had prepared last Monday. 'Buy it at the fish store, not the supermarket,' she cautioned me. And then, not trusting me to even boil water she told me to come back to her house and she would prepare it for me and if I could tell time, I could cook it. She confirmed what René said about taking a vacation and I told her that I would call Doub later. I came into the house just in time to answer my telephone.

"Hello."

"Monsieur Jannot, this is Marc Szabo from the investigation agency."

"Oh, yes. Mademoiselle Denisart said that you would call. How can I help you?"

"Well, first, I explained the options to Mademoiselle Denisart but she never chose the extent that she wished to pursue this."

"What options are there?"

"The least expensive service is merely reporting if such a name is listed in the local telephone directory but if it is a common name that is not much help. For a more thorough search we can look into public documents and records such as a driver's license and . . ."

As he ran through his options I was in conflict with my feeling. I don't know if I should do as Hélène wished or as Marie-Jeanne wished. I was finally persuaded by my own feelings as if it was me, and by what Hélène said about 'finding is not meeting.'

"Monsieur Szabo," I interrupted, "do everything you can. Make sure you bill *me* for your service and everything, absolutely everything is sent to *my* address. Is there any other information that I can give you?"

"Yes, we have only an approximation of his age, height and weight. Do you know the day and year of his birth? Color of his hair and eyes? Any distinguishing characteristics?"

"I would guess that he was born about 1920; the date, I don't know. Light brown hair, brown eyes. He had a tattoo of a butterfly on his right forearm. Oh, come to think of it he once mentioned going home for Christmas for his birthday. Whether he meant the very day or only near Christmas, I don't know. Anything else?"

"Did he have a profession or trade?"

"He was a civil servant; other than that I don't recall that he had any other skill."

"A wife or family?

"Yes but I know nothing about them. They lived in Strasbourg in 1944; after that I have no further information."

"Very well, Monsieur Jannot, this will be a great help. We will send periodic reports as we increase the depth of our investigation. I'll be in touch."

"One minute, Monsieur Szabo. I have another name for you. I want this billed separately and carried to the same level as the other. The man's name is Rheinhold with an 'h' Popp, p, o, p, p. He was born 11 December 1895 in Munich. He was in the German Army in the first war, a captain in the artillery. His description matches Jost's but a bit taller. He has a scar on his neck on the right side that ends on his chin. He speaks French . . . if I think of anything else, I'll call you."

"Very well, Monsieur Jannot. We will begin the search today. Is that all?"

"Yes, thank you . . . Marc? Was that your name?"

"Yes, Sir. Good day."

I put the trout in the refrigerator and went to the garden to pick a salad. I had no hope to duplicate Nadine's chicken and onion soup. I took a bottle of Moselle and a bottle of Chablis from my near empty wine rack and put them with the trout. *Why don't I have a wine cellar?* Obviously because I don't have a cellar.

I thought about taking another bath but I had washed afterward and Marie-Jeanne didn't have on any perfume . . . and then Hélène didn't go sniffing on me . . . and then, also, there wasn't enough time.

I washed and shaved and changed my shirt, poured a crème de menthe and sat in the garden and went through my mail. Only one letter interested me; it was from the author of my second hand book. He said in it that he was paid for the rights and thought no more about it until he received my letter. After careful scrutiny he found seven places where the tense of the verb was changed, three omissions and one outright contradiction. It made the work useless.

Hélène arrived while I was reading the letter and I only noticed her when she came out the rear door. She was wearing a floral blouse like Laure-Anne used to wear and a short black skirt. I rose to greet her and she put her arms around my neck.

"How are you?" she asked.

"I've had a wonderful day . . . and you?"

"I've been waiting for this moment."

She kissed me with intensity. I put my hands on her hips and slowly slid them behind and downward. The length of the kiss would determine how far I would go. She knew it and made it last quite a while. I had no desire to exercise restraint. If she had not quit just then I'm sure that I would have had mother and daughter in the same day. The thought was both pleasant and frightening.

"Did the man from the investigation service call?"

"Yes and he jogged my memory about your father's birthday, somewhere near or on Christmas. He'll send reports as they go through different levels of searching."

"You're wonderful. I knew that you wouldn't refuse to help me. My mother is so . . . well, you know. I don't know why she's so against it. Did she say anything about that?"

"Yes, she did. To tell you the truth, your father was not so nice a character."

"I thought you said that you liked him."

"I did but I wasn't his lover. Your mother knew him more intimately. Don't ask questions because I won't answer them. The truth of the matter is that it would hurt your mother if you knew. She feels that if you spoke with your father that he would tell you exactly what she has been hiding all these years. Let me just say that I agree with her in this. You should leave it alone but since I love you, it is hard to deny you anything. I'm hoping that he can't be found and that that will be the end of it."

"You don't want me to know him?"

"No I don't. But I won't stop you if you want to continue in this search. I'll even help you but my heart isn't in it."

"I've got to know. Can you understand what it means to me? He's my father."

"Yes, I understand more than you could imagine; that's why I'm helping you. Go get us a crème de menthe."

We finally took our hands off each other. Oh, how I would like to have my hands on her without her clothes being in the way. I sat at the table thinking about how I would resolve my affair with Marie-Jeanne. She would be hurt, I'm sure, but we had no commitment. It's just that I thought that it might be traumatic to her. *What could I do?* Hélène had just returned with the aperitifs when I noticed a vehicle pull in front of the house. It was René.

"Come here," I told Hélène.

"What?" she said, but came near.

I opened a button of her blouse and then not thinking it sufficient, opened another.

"What are you doing?" she asked, quite amused at my actions.

"Hey, Oiseau," René called out.

"Watch his eyes," I said quietly to Hélène.

"Hey, René. You remember your patient, don't you?"

"Yes, Mademoiselle Denisart. How are you?"

"Oh, hello Doctor. I know, I know, I should have made an appointment months ago. I promise that I will see to it . . . soon."

"Well, good. We can never be too careful about our teeth. Uh, here's the key, Oiseau. I left the instructions on the kitchen table, so there won't be a problem."

"All right then, don't worry about it. Have a good vacation."

I was purposely being reticent, hoping that he would leave quickly. He seemed to get the message.

"Sure. Well, don't let me keep you. Good-bye."

"Good-bye, René."

"Good-bye, Doctor."

René left with a wonderful expression on his face.

"What was that all about?" Hélène asked.

"First, what do you think he thought?"

"That you rushed him out of here so that the two of us could be alone . . . ah, you wanted him to think that we wanted to . . . ah!"

"No. But you're right, that's what he thought. Did you watch his eyes?"

"Yes."

"And . . . ?"

"When we shook hands, I thought he was a bit close and then his eyes dropped for a second; he was looking down my blouse."

"Did he see the scar?"

"Of course! He didn't need to look down my blouse to see it. With two buttons open the whole world could see it."

"Did it matter to him?"

"It didn't seem to . . . oh, you, why are you wasting your time teaching history?"

She stood in front of me and put her hand on my cheek, looking into my eyes.

"So you think I should show it to the world."

I looked down at the scar and traced the visible part of it from her clavicle to the roundness of her breast with the tip of my finger.

"You could start with one button and let everyone get used to that and ask their questions. After a while you won't even think about it. Look how well your mother has done; she almost wears her scar as a badge."

"All right, I'll do it for you . . . and your friends. You *were* showing me off, weren't you? Come on, tell the truth."

"It was just coincidental . . . part of your lesson."

"Hmmm. I think you are guilty of the same thing that you accused me of when I introduced you to *my* friends."

I think she was right. I didn't plan it but I liked the way René smiled when he left. It made me feel . . . younger, a part of life again. We sat in the garden and enjoyed the warmth of the sun and the cold of crème de menthe with ice. The sun had dropped behind the trees and we moved inside. I had put one of Mother's lace tablecloths on the dining room table along with two candles. While I was making a garden salad, Hélène lit them and poured us two glasses of Chablis. We talked, we had the salad, and a little more wine and she came with me again to the kitchen while I cooked the trout and asparagus.

This felt so right. We harmonized, we worked together so well, we knew what the other wanted and we were happy to do it. Nadine had done a magnificent job in preparing the trout. All I did was look at my watch and flip it over at the right time. I took all the credit for the meal.

When we were finished we both cleaned up and put everything away. We sat at the far end of the parlor on the most comfortable sofa and opened the bottle of Moselle. We talked . . . and we talked, never running out of subjects, never at a loss for words. As the evening wore on we changed our positions; she lay in my lap then I lay in hers. She would caress me and I would seek to go a bit farther. I opened one more button of her blouse; she did not stop me. I kissed her scar and would have kissed her breast but I was afraid. *Little steps, Édouard. Patience.*

It was late; we both were exuberant. At the door I buttoned her blouse to its original state and she laughed.

"Are you afraid of my mother?"

"Yes. Am I wise to fear her?"

"Hmmm, yes. You'd better be careful, Oiseau. You know what a mother will do to protect her child from a dangerous person."

"The only danger is that I will go mad with the love that I have for you."

"I think that the cure may be coming. Each day I think of you in a different way; each day you are closer to my heart. You'll see, Oiseau, I am not so far away."

We kissed good night . . . very tenderly. My whole body ached . . . I had to bear it. She would be leaving for Corsica on Saturday; I had to see her one more time. Sleep was impossible; my thoughts were racing through my head. I needed her so much. I got up weary on Friday morning and mechanically made my breakfast. I thought to wait until eight o'clock when Hélène got to work and give her a call. As that hour approached, the phone rang.

"Hello."

"Good morning, Édouard. I thought you were going to call me."

"Oh, Marie-Jeanne, I didn't think that you were up this early."

"I sleep more restfully now; perhaps I don't need as much sleep. You don't sound well; what's wrong?"

"Just tired . . . got up too early."

"Did you want to come to dinner later? Hélène said that she was going out with some friends tonight in Nancy."

"Uh, no, I'll be busy tonight myself. Doub and Nadine are leaving for vacation tomorrow and I told him I'd buy him dinner at the Quatre Vents while she was working."

There was a short silence.

"You're not meeting Hélène, are you?"

"No, what are you talking about?"

"It just sounds so contrived, so well planned."

"Marie-Jeanne, do you want to explain?"

"We talked last night. She said some things that led me to believe that you two were . . . well, you know . . ."

"No, I don't know. Say it!"

"Are you sleeping with her?"

"No, I'm not sleeping with her," I said calmly, evenly.

"You swear?"

"I swear."

Another short silence. *She doesn't believe me!*

"Come for lunch, and then you can give me a driving lesson."

"Sure. I've got a little work to do on my book and then I'll be there."

"All right. See you later."

I immediately called Doub at work. He wasn't there yet but I left word for him to call as soon as he got in. Next I called Hélène. When someone got her to the phone she sounded very happy.

"Hello, it's Hélène."

"Hello, it's Oiseau. You sound cheerful."

"Yes, we almost got the day off. The whole lab is going on vacation and no one wants to work but we've got to finish up things and clean up."

"What did you tell your mother last night?"

"About what?"

"About us."

"Nothing that I can think of."

"Why did she think that we were sleeping together?"

"What? She said that? I never gave her that idea."

"She asked me and of course I said no. Why would she even think that?"

"I don't know. I'm trying to think of what we were talking about that could have led to that assumption."

"Well, you must have been talking about me at some point."

"Oh . . . ooooh. She said that she would do everything she could to keep me from finding out about my father and I said that I would do whatever it took. Then she asked if that included being nice to you. You told me about holding hands and kissing, so I said that I wasn't doing anything that she wasn't doing. She had nothing more to say after that. But she's doing something that *I'm* not doing, isn't that so, Oiseau?"

Oh, God! I am my own worst enemy.

"That's why the mess from dinner was still on the table the morning after our fight . . . because she didn't come home that night."

What did you tell yourself that night, Édouard? I'm only doing this for Marie-Jeanne?

"Answer me, Oiseau. She's sleeping with you, isn't she?"

The anger in her voice was obvious. There was no point in denying it now.

"Yes. Hélène, I . . ."

"That bitch! I didn't think that she'd go that far."

"Hélène, I'm sorry, it's just that . . ."

"No! It's not you. It's her. This doesn't change anything between us. That's what she wants to happen. Ooooh, that makes me so mad."

I couldn't believe what I was hearing.

"Oiseau," her tone turned tender, "I'm not mad at you. It makes no difference if it was my mother or Kaly or anyone else; I never asked you to give that up for me. How could I unless I was willing to take their place?"

"But it's your mother. Don't you think that that's a little different, a little strange?"

"You're always so nice, such a gentleman. She was counting on that. It won't work this time. Don't you dare distance yourself from me! Do you hear me, Oiseau?"

"You're incredible, do you know that?"

"Hmmm, wait until I come back from Corsica."

"What about tonight, tomorrow morning?"

"We're all going to a club after work and tomorrow morning I have to pick up Hoa. We're riding together to the airport."

"I'll be lost without you."

"It's only for two weeks; you'll survive."

"I suppose I'll have to. Hurry back."

"I will. Be good, Oiseau, wait for me. Ciao."

And she hung up.

I felt like shouting and jumping up and down; I thought that my heart would explode. I have snatched victory from the jaws of defeat. It didn't last long when the thought of what her motivation was: a competition with her mother. But that didn't preclude her loving me. It may only have been the catalyst. The phone rang.

"Hello, Doub?"

"No, Monsieur Jannot. It's Marc from the investigation service."

"Oh, excuse me Marc. I was expecting another call. What is it?"

"Well, I have good news for you. We found one of them . . . with just one telephone call."

"Which one?" I asked with some foreboding.

"Popp! It wasn't very hard at all. When I mentioned his name to our contact in Munich he said that he knew the man. It turns out that he is a member of the town council. A very well known and respected man. My contact is mailing me a copy of the page on him from Munich's *Jahrbuch*. We're quite sure that this is the man; former military, born in 1895, speaks French . . . There aren't that many families named Popp, you know."

"Is there a photograph?"

"Yes, it's on the page. It should be in your hands in a few days."

"Wonderful. What about Jost?"

"Nothing yet; it's still too soon."

"Keep me informed, Marc, and thank you."

"Absolutely!"

My first thought was to rush to Mother's house and tell her the news but then I would have to tell her to wait in suspense for the details. That didn't sound like a good idea. I poured another cup of coffee and the phone rang again.

"Doub?"

"Yeah, what's up?"

"I'm going to buy you dinner tonight. Shall I meet you at the Quatre Vents?"

"I'm not even going to ask why; you can afford it. Maybe I should pick you up when I get home. There's a lot to do before I can leave all this work in some idiot's hands. I don't think I'll be later than six."

"All right, pick me up at my place."

I finished my coffee and decided to work on my book. Once I began a new page I felt totally bored with it. I came close to throwing the whole thing away. I was writing for the extra income it provided, which I no longer needed and to enlighten those people who wanted an in-depth history of those times and events, which were few. My first book sold about a thousand copies, the second, about eight thousand. As boring as this one seemed, I doubt that it would sell even a thousand. I put it away and wandered about the house looking for something to occupy myself with. Finding nothing, I did ten minutes of gardening and was again at a loss for something to do.

My mind kept coming back to the news of my father and I realized that I wanted to tell Mother so badly that I would overlook the agony of waiting. I drove to her house and found her cutting some meat for stew when I came into the kitchen. I took the knife from her hand and embraced her.

"So, for what do I get a visit and a hug?"

With my mouth by her ear I whispered as I held her tightly.

"He's alive, Maman, he's alive in Munich."

I felt her chest expand suddenly and just as suddenly she was sobbing into my shoulder. It took a few minutes until she calmed down. She turned her head to me.

"How do you know?"

"I had someone find him. I spoke to the man today and he said that within a few days we would have some information and a picture."

"Are they sure that it's him?"

"Well, there could be thousands of guys named Popp, who were born in 1895, who speak French and were in the army . . . but I think that there is only one."

"What about you, Édouard? Are you thrilled? Do you want to meet him?"

"I'm thrilled for you . . . I don't know if I want to meet him. I *am* curious."

We spent time sharing those things that we were positive about of our feelings and those things of which we seemed to be afraid. Mother was resolved to go no matter what. We decided on a departure date of 7 September and I would arrange everything tomorrow in Nancy. I declined lunch explaining about Marie-Jeanne and her driving lesson.

Marie-Jeanne was not in the house when I got there. There was nothing on the stove and nothing in the refrigerator that looked like lunch. I found I bottle of Riesling and poured a glass and went outside to explore her garden.

"Hello," Marie-Jeanne called from a shed. "Is it lunch time already?"

"What are you doing out here?"

"I collected water samples this morning and I'm testing the pH."

"From the forest?"

"Yes, the farthest one was about five kilometers away. For those that are outside the normal range I'll have to do a qualitative analysis to find out what's in the water."

The shed was large enough to park a car. It was a miniature laboratory; it was amazing. I gave her my glass and went inside to fill another.

"How long has this been here?" I asked.

"Since Hélène was in the lycée."

"So you got her started on hydrobiology."

"No. It was more like this was something we could do together. It started out as her class assignment, testing the soil in the garden. We just kept at it. Are you hungry?"

"Yes, I'm starving."

"Fill the blue enameled pot about two-thirds full of water and put it on the stove. I'll be done in five minutes."

I became the assistant cook and did as I was told. Marie-Jeanne came in and was washing her hands when I came behind her. I put my hands on her hips waiting for her to turn around. When she did she gently pushed me away.

"No funny business. I don't have time. I give you lunch; you give me a driving lesson. I've still got lots of work to do."

Obviously she still did not believe my denial. I didn't care to bring it up lest I get caught in a trap, having to admit to something or being condemned for my silence. Lunch turned out to be spaghetti and meatballs and some Chianti, which I suffered through. The driving lesson went well; she had not forgotten how to drive and was ready to take her test. I think that I was dismissed with only a 'thank you' when we got back to her house. All I could do was to wait and hope that she gets over it. I stopped by the wine shop on the way home and got a mixed case of white and one bottle of red. I read my own book while waiting for Doub.

He picked me up about six and it wasn't until our second beer that we were able to sit at our favorite table. Biston was there, of course, but I only nodded at him when we arrived. Doub and Biston were less friendly, having parted company after the attack on Marie-Jeanne and Hélène. Biston looked on him as a traitor while Doub referred to him as 'that French Hitler.'

"René said that you changed your mind about going somewhere."

"Ah, it was Nadine. All the time with 'Are you going to sit on your fat ass for two weeks?' I told her if she wanted to go somewhere to go. So, she calls Jean-Yves and tells him that we're going with him and Sonia and the kids to some lake near Dieuze. So, Sonia calls me to say how happy she was that I could spend some time camping with the grandchildren. What could I do?"

"So, you're going to sit on your fat ass by a lake with a glass of beer in your hand and yell at your grandchildren."

"You're right, that's it exactly. Hey, isn't that your car?"

It was and Marie-Jeanne was driving it. So, she came to see if I was really taking Doub to dinner. She parked across the street and stared at us for a moment then got out and crossed over. She wasn't smiling.

"Who the hell is that?" Doub asked.

"Marie-Jeanne."

"Really? What's she doing here?" Doub said a bit too loud.

"I came to see you, Vincent. I never thanked you for the help you gave to me and my daughter."

That sounded like a good excuse to come here.

"Uh, yeah, sure . . . you're welcome."

"Are you going to invite me to join you?"

"Oiseau, did you arrange this? You know how I feel."

"No, Vincent? That's all right. I'll sit with this guy over here."

Marie-Jeanne walked to Biston's table and sat down. Biston, not accustomed to ever having a pretty woman in his company, true to form, opened his mouth predictably.

"Who the hell are you?"

"Do you remember this?" Marie-Jeanne said and turned her scarred cheek for him to see.

"Denisart, the whore! Still fucking the Boche?"

Marie-Jeanne smiled and stood up, turning as if to go and in a flash punched his grinning mouth. His beer flew over his head when he fell out of his chair.

"You're going to pay for that, you bitch. I'm calling the cops."

"You want cops? I'll get you some. Police, help Police." Marie-Jeanne was screaming at the top of her voice. "Get this child molester. Police, Police!"

Every patron in the café could hear her and some got out of their seats to see to whom she was referring. Biston was getting up from the sidewalk, muttering curses when Marie-Jeanne kicked him in the groin and he went down again. By then I had my arms around her to stop her from doing more harm. She might really be arrested. Some of the other patrons helped him up and tried to get him to sit but he wanted to get away from here. Marie-Jeanne watched him until he was out of sight then went limp in my arms, sobbing. As I held her I could sense a difference in her movements. I held her away from me to discover that she was laughing . . . holding her stomach and laughing. She got me laughing just as much. Doub came to us and joined in.

"Marie-Jeanne," Doub said as best he could, "I'm sorry, really. Please join us."

It took only a second for her to throw her arms around him. We brought Marie-Jeanne back to our table and called Bernard for another round of drinks.

"Would Madame like a beer and a cigar?"

We were all in a good mood. Marie-Jeanne held her hand toward the waiter.

"I would like some band-aids for that and some Rémy," she said.

"Yes, me too; this calls for a toast. You too, Doub?"

"No, I'll stick to beer . . . oh, what the hell. Sure, you're paying."

"Three Rémys, two band-aids and . . . I'll have to add André's broken glass to your bill."

We joked about Marie-Jeanne and then about Biston. I tended to her cut knuckles and we toasted 'old friends' with Doub proposing it. No police came to arrest Marie-Jeanne and we joked about that too. Doub wanted to go after the meal and I had a stop I wanted to make, so we left early. I asked Marie-Jeanne to drive where I directed.

"Who lives here," she asked.

"Someone who would love to meet you . . . but don't worry, he won't."

"Do you want me to wait in the car or are you going to deposit me on the doorstep?"

"No, come with me. You'll see."

Corrine Leclerc answered the door.

"Oiseau, how nice to see you. Come in, come in."

"How are you Corrine? Do you remember Virginie's daughter?"

"Of course! Hélène isn't it?"

"No, she's the granddaughter; I'm Marie-Jeanne."

"Oh, yes. How silly of me. Come in; Jérôme will be so happy to see you."

I had heard that he was convalescing from cancer treatments and was not responding well. We found him in a sitting position with his feet stretched out on the sofa watching television. He brightened up when we came into the room.

"Oiseau! Come over here; let me get a good look at you."

I squatted next to the sofa and we clasped hands. He was squeezing with all that he had but that wasn't much. We spoke briefly about his condition and I introduced Marie-Jeanne using her full name lest Jérôme would make the same mistake as Corrine.

"Ah, Virginie's daughter. You look lovely, nice to see you again. Sorry I couldn't make it to the funeral."

"That's all right. There were only a few who came. How are you feeling?"

"Well, they said that my days were numbered and I reminded them that ten thousand was a number too but they just smiled politely. Six month . . . a year. Only God knows and he hasn't told us yet."

"Well, Jérôme, we will certainly pray for you," I said.

"Now that's something from a man who would shock the priest if he showed up more than twice a year. Thank you, Oiseau, and I'll thank God for you."

"This won't be the first time, you know. Back in '42 when you were a hostage . . . I prayed for you then. What worked once can work again."

"Ha! What a time that was. Every once in a while I think about poor Chipot. You know they said one of his own informed on him. You play with fire and you get burnt. To this day I thank God for that informer, whoever he was and whatever his reason; four time a year I light candles for him."

Jérôme was a good teacher even when he wasn't aware of it. I let the conversation move on to other things. He reminisced about Virginie while Corrine made coffee. We stayed about an hour and I had Marie-Jeanne bring me home. We sat in the car.

"I thought everything was going to turn to shit today," Marie-Jeanne said quietly, "but it didn't end up so bad. Our little visit to Jérôme was very clever but very nice; it was the best part of the day and I want to thank you for it."

"I'm glad you learned something from it. Do you want to come in?"

"No, not tonight. I just want to sleep; it was a very emotional day. I don't think there was one emotion that I missed."

"Give me a kiss."

"One kiss and out you go, understand?"

"I promise."

I leaned toward her and gave her a brief kiss.

"Well, maybe two."

We kissed again for a much longer time but I kept my promise. I was exhausted too not having slept well the night before. It didn't appear that tonight would be any better.

I awoke the next morning with a feeling of guilt for actions that I had as yet not taken. I prayed for Jérôme and for myself and felt better. I got dressed and dragged myself downstairs and made some coffee. I could find no bread, no pastry, no brioche, nothing. I made two soft-boiled eggs and drank my coffee.

"So, you're home this time," Anne-Marie said as she charged into the kitchen. "And you have coffee made. God bless you. Did you steal that car?"

"Good morning, Anne-Marie. Why don't you sit down and have some? Yes, I stole that car and if you turn me in you'll be out of a job."

"You haven't got her upstairs, have you? You're not trying to keep me from going up . . . she's not dressed yet, is that it. Well, it's all the same to me; I'll have my coffee."

"Where do you get these ideas from?"

"You've got a dirty lace tablecloth on a table you never use. So, someone special came to dinner. The candles are burned halfway . . . a *romantic* dinner. I'll probably have to wax the table."

"Are you a character created by Arthur Conan Doyle?"

"Who's he?"

"Never mind. Hey, let me ask you a question. I know that I can count on you for an honest answer."

"As long as it isn't personal."

"Well, it's hypothetical, a 'what if' kind of question."

"Go ahead."

"How old are you, thirty-four?"

"What happened to the 'what if'?"

"All right, let's *suppose* you're thirty-four . . . all right, thirty-three and you have two good looking men after you. They both love you."

"I like this question already."

"One of them is forty-three and the other is twenty-three. The older guy has a good income and the younger one is still trying to make ends meet. Which one would you choose as a husband?"

"The younger one."

"That didn't take long to decide."

"Professor, you got to look out for yourself. It doesn't bother me if people think that I'm selfish but I don't mind giving when I'm getting. You know what I mean?"

"No, you're confusing me."

"I would work to help the younger guy get somewhere as long as he takes care of business in the bedroom. The older guy could give me things but he's going to be all used up when I'm still looking to wet the sheets."

"Anne-Marie, you have a marvelous way of expressing things. I'm going to raise your pay by ten francs."

"Well, it's about time. Just for that answer?"

"No, so that you don't turn me in for stealing that car."

I counted out her money and just to tease her, I watched very closely as she stuffed it in her bra.

"Hey, don't you be getting any ideas, old man."

"I've got an errand to run. If that young lady doesn't come down soon, you go up there and chase her out. And don't forget to wax the table."

I drove to Marie-Jeanne's place looking for bread. She had plenty and a cup of coffee too.

"You like Italian food?" I asked.

"Sure. Are you taking me to dinner?"

"Yeah, but this is a fancy place. We'll have to get you some clothes first."

"Ooooh, I like that, shoes too?"

"Whatever you need. Get your hair done too."

"What's wrong with my hair?"

"I don't know. I thought women always got their hair done before a big date."

"Well, I could do something to it, something expensive."

"Don't cut it."

"All right, I'm ready."

"Can I finish my coffee first?"

"You could let me drive and take it with you."

We left as soon as I finished my coffee. Our first stop was a ladies apparel store. I told the clerk what I wanted: a black evening dress, lacy on top, short on the bottom. The third one Marie-Jeanne tried on I liked but she had to take off her white bra and I could see her breasts through the lace. The clerk made some suggestions and I let her and Marie-Jeanne pick out what was needed, shoes included. Next stop was the hairdresser's where she told me that I had an hour to run my errand. I stopped at the bank to get some cash and then the travel agent. A round trip rail ticket to Munich and one month's rental at a hotel near the town hall.

All that took only a half hour so I wandered around window-shopping. Having no need to buy anything I reckoned that if something caught my eye that I would get it. As I was looking in a jeweler's window something *did* catch my eye: a pair of onyx earrings. There were two stones on each earring, the one at the top was round and the other was a teardrop pendant. A bargain at three hundred francs the clerk said;

I thought so too. I put them in the map compartment of the car before returning to the salon.

Marie-Jeanne was sitting under a dryer and held up her hands with all her fingers spread. She may have had her nails done too but I think she meant ten minutes more. I got the car and parked outside waiting for her. I was surprised when she came out. Her hair seemed blonder than before; she twirled around at the car to let me see it all. The ends seemed almost white and there was a band of slightly reddish hair above that. Whereas her hair before had been startling, this was flamboyant. I liked it.

"I got my nails done too, see?"

I smiled and motioned for her to get in. First, she got a shawl she just bought out of the trunk to keep her hair from getting wind-blown. We made another stop to buy some cosmetics and we left Nancy. We stopped again for lunch in Laxou, at a café near Champs le Bœuf; Marie-Jeanne said that her hand was too sore to eat at the Quatre Vents. I dropped her at her place and went to see Mother whom I found sitting in her neighbor's yard. I was greeted in German by the neighbor who was happy that Mother also spoke it so that they would not forget it all. I gave her the tickets and the three of us continued in German for a while. I stopped at the Quatre Vents to ask about last night and was told that nothing ever came of it but they might hear something latter if and when Biston showed up. I made one more stop at the baker's and stocked up for a few days; I didn't want to get up early to do it.

There was not much to do at the cottage. Anne-Marie had brought back my clean laundry and I put it away. I read my mail sitting in the garden with a crème de menthe and when I couldn't stand it any longer I got ready for the evening. I had thought to wear a jacket and casual shirt but considering how Marie-Jeanne was going to look I decided to wear a suit. I got into a happy mood while I was in the shower thinking as though I was courting her. If I could jump out of an airplane or go downhill skiing I might impress Hélène, but getting dressed for dinner at a fancy restaurant was what Marie-Jeanne would enjoy and it made me happy that I was making her happy.

As I was shaving I began discussing this with my reflection. My reflection started singing an old song that I liked. *'Oh, Valentino, oh, Valentino, tout le bal n'attend que toi.'* Poor Valentino didn't know what he had until his love made the first move. The Valentino singing to me had it happen twice at the same time; perhaps the other was luckier. I stepped out of the cottage in my new black suit and was ready to get behind the wheel of my new Mercedes but the sky looked threatening so I put the top up then drove to Marie-Jeanne's house. The front door was locked but the rear was open. I called out her name when I didn't see her.

"I'll be out in a minute; I'm in the tub."

I made my way through the kitchen; the door to the bathroom was wide open.

"Oh, don't you look nice."

"Hmmm, you look nicer," I said.

"You're going to get all wet and soapy if you start. Give me a towel."

She stood up and stepped out of the tub into the towel that I was holding open for her. She kissed me as my hands explored her lower curves.

"You're early. Have a little crème de menthe while I dress."

"I just had one."

"Well, have another one."

"I want to watch."

"You want to watch me dress," she laughed.

"Why not? I watched you undress."

"All right. Make two drinks and come upstairs.

When I got upstairs she was sitting in front of her mirror putting on her make-up wearing only her panties. I stood over her and watched everything she did. She was amused but continued undeterred. When she had that done she put on her new bra. It was brief and black and lacy and it forced her breasts upward.

"Aren't you going to put a little perfume on them?"

"On *them?* . . . if you like. Pick one."

While she put on her stockings I sniffed at four different bottles.

"This one . . . it smells a little like peaches. Can I put it on?"

"Don't overdo it and don't put your hands in the bra . . . just a finger."

I did it properly and she turned her back to me and pulled her panties down a bit and I put more on her cheeks. We drank our aperitifs and joked about that.

"One kiss before I put on my lipstick."

I made it a good one and helped her slip into her dress and zipped her up. Lipstick, hair and shoes and she was ready. She was beautiful.

"Do you have a camera?"

"Hélène might have one in her room if she didn't take it with her."

She was back in a minute with it. I thought it would be better in natural light and we went outside and took one of each other.

"I can take one of both of you," Marie-Jeanne's neighbor called out.

"Oh, Josette, yes. Do you know my friend Édouard Jannot?"

"Only by reputation. You're Oiseau, aren't you?"

"By reputation? And what did you hear of that."

"That you put your talon in a crazy man that was brutalizing some poor woman."

Marie-Jeanne and I smiled; I was glad that the story had not been corrupted over time, except that the crazy man was not named. Marie-Jeanne turned her cheek to Josette and put a finger on the scar.

"I was that poor woman."

"Oh, and now you're . . . shall I take it in front of the car?"

Josette took two more pictures, which finished the roll. We finished our drinks, Marie-Jeanne got her shawl and we were on our way. When we were parked at the restaurant I brushed her hair back with my fingers to expose her ear.

"Your ears are naked," I said, almost as a complaint.

"I didn't have anything that would go with this outfit," she apologized.

I reached into the map compartment for my gift and handed the box to her.

"Well, then you'd better put these on."

She smiled; I hoped that she wouldn't cry and mess up her make-up. The smile turned to a giggle as she removed her shawl and put them on. She was like a little child. When she had both of them on she faced me holding her hair back so that I could see them well.

"Do you like them?"

"They're beautiful. Why are you so nice to me?"

"Because . . . it makes me feel good."

I had almost said 'because I love you.' I wondered at that. She gave me a near kiss and we went inside. The place was nearly full and I noticed the heads of many men turn as we went to our table. I'm sure Marie-Jeanne did also. When we were seated she looked around and made a face to show that she was impressed.

"This is very different from the Quatre Vents. How did you find this place?"

"Kaly brought me here. You don't deserve any less."

"Ah, that was a very good answer. So, you like it here?"

"They have some very good Italian whites on their wine list that are hard to find anywhere. I was going to talk you into a picatta or scaloppini so I could order one that would go well with it. It is a wine that I have never tried before."

"That's all right. Chicken or veal?"

"Either one would go well with it. It's a Trebbiano blend."

"You're speaking to an amateur. Go ahead, I'll have chicken."

A waiter came with a candle for the table and I asked him to send for the sommelier. It was the same man I had fooled when I was here a few days ago. He seemed to remember me but wouldn't acknowledge it seeing that I was here with a different woman.

"I noticed when I was here a few days ago that you listed Verdicchio. I've never tried it; what can you tell me about it?"

"It has a strong flavor, a bit of citrus and a bit fruity. Its strength would go well with a more highly seasoned dish. I would recommend our Vincisgrassi, a very robust lasagna. Would you like to sample some?

"Hmmm, we were going to order some picatta or scaloppini. Is there something comparable in a French wine?"

"If you like Sémillon you will like Verdicchio."

Sémillon . . . that was what Laure-Anne and I had when I gave her the birds.

"How good a selection do you have?"

"We have several years, Sir. We have the more popular Verdicchio dei Castelli di Jesi but I think you will enjoy the Verdicchio di Matelica; it's from a very good year and it has a slightly greenish color. You won't be disappointed."

He was right; I loved it. Marie-Jeanne said it tasted just like Soave. I beckoned her to lean over the table and whispered loudly to her.

"I should have ordered a beer for you. You're a barbarian."

She was amused and sipped more of her wine. While we were eating our mussels she beckoned *me* to lean over the table.

"Don't turn around. There a woman a few tables away that keeps staring at me."

"She's probably jealous. Forget it."

"No, no. Every time I look up, she's staring over here."

"Are you sure she's looking at you?"

"Well, if it isn't me, she's staring at the back of your head and that's not worth staring at, believe me."

"Eat your mussels."

I had the veal picatta and Marie-Jeanne the chicken scaloppini. They were both good; we sampled each other's. The sommelier came back when we were done.

"How did you like the Verdicchio?"

"Excellent choice; it went well with the picatta. What do you recommend for dessert?"

"If you are in the mood for new tastes perhaps you will want to try a new appellation although strictly speaking it has not yet been officially granted."

"I put myself in your hands. What is it?"

"A Tokay Pinot Gris."

"How can France grant an appellation to a Tokay?"

"The same way the Hungarians can grant an appellation to a Médoc."

"I'm intrigued. Bring it."

We were in no hurry; I planned to enjoy myself here. We could hear rain outside and strong winds. No one would want to go out in that.

"I've got to go to the lady's room," Marie-Jeanne said and got up suddenly.

I waited until she was gone then got up myself both because I needed to go but more because I wanted to get a look at the woman behind me who was staring. I hoped it wasn't Kaly; after all she was to be on a plane in the morning. When I turned around I did not see anyone remotely looking like her. *What a relief!* I came back from the men's room before Marie-Jeanne returned and thought no more of it.

We had some ice cream and were enjoying our desert wine when I heard a familiar voice from behind me. Kaly and the man she was with stopped at our table.

"Marie-Jeanne, how nice to see you. I thought it was you but your hair is so different. I like it; it's beautiful."

"Hello, Kaly. I waved to you once but I guess you didn't see me."

The two women introduced us two men to everyone and continued their conversation.

"So, what have you been up to?" Marie-Jeanne asked.

"Getting ready for my vacation. I leave in the morning for two weeks in Crete."

"Oh, I envy you. I need to study and put a report together. I have to face a board of review to get my degree in Environmental Sciences at the University. I'm trying to get a job in the Environmental Lab where my daughter works."

"That's right down the hall from me. Who's your daughter?"

"Hélène Denisart."

"Really! I didn't know that. I'll be sure to mention that I ran into you. She's such a sweet girl. Well, you two, enjoy the rest of the evening. I have to get up early."

I was in a sweat. What could I say; I didn't know what that was all about. How is it that I am continually a victim of female intrigue? When they left I sat down and smiled at Marie-Jeanne. She was almost laughing at her little act. I poured more wine, grateful that she didn't know what Kaly knew. I said nothing more about it until we were on our way home.

"Are you going to tell me what that was all about?"

"I thought it might be her and when you weren't curious enough turn around the whole night because you didn't want her to see you . . . I was sure. When she went to the ladies' room, so did I. I just said 'Kaly?' and she said 'So, you know who I am. Who are you?' I said 'I'm Marie-Jeanne and I have this friend named Eliane who said that you were seeing her brother . . .' and that when I confronted you, you confessed. I said that I wasn't bothered by it, seeing we had nothing between us at the time. Then she asked what was going on between us *now* and I told her that it was a little different. I complimented her on her hair and mentioned that mine was even longer but that I cut it when I started seeing you. That's all. Everything that happened after that was her idea but I enjoyed it too, didn't you?"

"Yes, you noticed how I couldn't stop laughing."

"Ooooh, are you embarrassed to have your ex-lover meeting your present one?"

"She's not my ex-lover; she was never my lover."

"Why are you so sensitive?"

We were at the circle in Laxou. I pulled off the road; it was still raining hard.

"Where am I taking you?"

I was not happy that Kaly knew that I was involved with both mother and daughter. My displeasure must have shown on my face but I could not admit it to Marie-Jeanne without explaining why it displeased me.

"Take me home," she said after a moment's hesitation.

I drove to her house without comment. I didn't care what she wanted to do.

"Wait for me; I've got to get a change of clothes."

That woman loves to keep me off guard. I mellowed a bit. She came out minutes later under an umbrella, clutching a plastic bag with her things. When we got out at my place the driving rain and the water running off the roof got both of us soaked before we could make it through the door.

"Would you like something?" I asked.

"A fire would be nice."

"Yes, all right. I'm having a little cognac, do you want one?"

"No, I had enough wine. I've got to go again."

I busied myself lighting the fire and when Marie-Jeanne came out of the bathroom she went upstairs and returned with a quilt, which she spread out in front of the fireplace. I poured my drink and joined her on the quilt, waiting for the fire to grow and give off some heat.

"So," Marie-Jeanne said, "I want to ask you a question that could not be answered the last time it came up and I must ask you to be honest or there is no sense asking it. Will you promise to be truthful?"

"You should get out of those wet clothes."

"Do you promise?"

"At least get out of that dress."

I pulled down her zipper.

"Will you answer me?"

"Yes."

"Yes, what? Yes you'll answer me or yes you'll tell the truth?"

"Both."

"Good. Well, you told me that I was prettier than she was and had a better figure than hers but you couldn't say who was better in bed . . . not then, but now you can. So, tell me . . . and be honest."

"A gentleman doesn't discuss one partner's performance with another."

"Then don't be a gentleman; you promised to answer truthfully."

"Hmmmm, truthfully . . . hmmmm, I guess I would have to say . . . hmmmm, I'd say that she was much better than you."

"You didn't have to be *that* honest."

"Why didn't you tell me that before I answered?"
"Am I terrible?"
"No, you're not terrible; you're just not creative enough."
"What am I doing wrong?"
"I could show you if you came out of those clothes."
"All right."

Chapter 11

We had Sunday morning breakfast, the mother and I, out in the garden, just like the daughter and I had been doing. It took a while to dry everything; the storm had ended about sunrise. It was cool, unusually cool for the second day in August. We sat around with sweaters on until noon when it warmed somewhat. We stopped by René's place to feed his cat then had lunch at Marie-Jeanne's.

"Do you want to spend a day in the woods tomorrow?" she asked.

"Doing what?"

"Well, primarily, you'd be the water bearer. I want to take samples of this storm's run-off. Some of my collection sites are quite a distance."

"All right . . . how far is 'quite a distance?'"

"Well, the forest is about ten thousand hectares; we might walk twelve kilometers there and back."

"No wonder that you're in such good shape. How often do you do this?"

"At least once a week but this time I want to collect both rainwater and runoff. I can tell lots of things from the difference."

"Do you take lunch along?"

"No. We should find enough to eat. Berries, grubs, worms, snails . . . you know."

"You're joking . . . I hope."

We spent a while talking about the trip. I had no idea that she was so professional in gathering data . . . or how serious and dedicated she was. Hélène had given her guidelines on how to prepare a report and how to use accepted parameters to draw conclusions. I was anxious to see her at work.

Late in the afternoon I left to go to Mother's house. No one had told me that my niece, Elisabeth, would be there with her husband Pierre and their two kids. As yet I had more grandchildren than Eliane but it was only a matter of time. Joëlle and her husband, Jean-Claude had no children yet and Philippe would be married next year. Something that I had thought about before came back into my mind, the thought of having more children with Hélène. It was pleasant to think about; almost amusing. *Imagine that . . . at my age.*

We spoke mainly about Mother's trip to Munich. Everyone thought it was a great idea for her to get away on a vacation without one of us with her but no one could see the logic of going to Munich. It seemed to me to be amazing that we could keep this secret for fifty-two years. I dearly hoped that she would get to meet the man no matter what the circumstances because she had kept alive this romantic notion all these years. Like Hélène, I had a curiosity to know but it was only when she had finally done something about it that I felt motivated to do the same. I think that I will eventually tell her that we had this thing in common . . . but not yet; I still didn't want Eliane to know. How could I tell Hélène and then ask her to keep it secret from her sister-in-law?

I went home after dinner and watched television. I was lonely.

Monday I did as Marie-Jeanne instructed and wore old clothes. Luckily I had not given away the old pair of pants that I wore when I planted the garden which I retrieved from the tool shed. She gave me a canvas protector to wear over them to keep me from tearing them to shreds when we had to go through briars. The weather warmed nicely and the walk was not so rapid as to wear me out. We found an abundance of berries and to my astonishment Marie-Jeanne ate grubs, which she found without any trouble. She would bite off the heads and just pop them in her mouth. A few chews later she would spit out the exoskeleton and do it again. 'Give me a kiss,' she said and I replied, 'maybe tomorrow.'

I wore a knapsack containing Styrofoam boxes to hold sample bottles. As we filled the bottles the load became heavier and heavier. She acknowledged that this was not normal but because the heavy rainfall afforded the opportunity, she had to double the load to sample both rainfall and run-off. She drove me home and we had dinner at my place. I went to bed early. Laying there I thought *'I forgot to feed the cat! Poor thing, but it won't die.'* I thought that for the next two weeks that we would fall into some sort of routine, seeing each other every day.

Tuesday, after I fed the cat and had breakfast, we went to the markets together do our weekly grocery shopping; we also stopped off to make an appointment for her driving test. She needed time to do her lab work and I to work on my book, so we decided to meet every day for lunch at one house or the other then go to the other's for dinner. Whether we shared a bed or not, we would both sleep in our own.

Thursday I received the copy of the *Jahrbuch* page from Munich and I went to Mother's house to let her be the first to know.

"I have something of interest for you."

I gave her the envelope but she just stared at it.

"Well, open it. You've been waiting so long."

She nervously tore the envelope open and unfolded the page.

"It's him! Oh, dear God, it's him!"

She showed the picture to me and even I could tell that after all these years that it was the same man in the only photograph that we had. She read it all slowly, asking me to translate a word or two that she wasn't familiar with, then gave it to me. The *Jahrbuch* was published in 1969 so I assumed that all the information was current. I read through it and looked for those things that might affect Mother's desire to see him again. It mentioned that his first wife had died during the war and that he remarried in 1950. His military record showed that after the first war he remained active and when the second war began he was a major, rising to the rank of general by its conclusion. He served in Holland, Belgium and France at the beginning and then in Greece and Italy. He returned to France in December 1944 for the Ardennes Offensive, which was, in effect, the beginning of the final retreat. He was elected to the town council in 1964 and has served there to date.

"Well, Maman, what will you do?"

"I will go to see him. It doesn't matter if he's married; I want to tell him about you. How do you feel about that?"

"What do you hope to accomplish?"

"Édouard, your whole life you have been longing to meet him. Do you deny that?"

"No, but it was never the most important thing in my life." *Especially not now!*

"Well, do you want me to tell him about you? There's no point in me going otherwise. I'm not going to intrude in a married man's life to reminisce about old times when we were lovers."

I wanted her to go, to meet him, for herself and not for me. Of course I was curious and had always fantasized about one day meeting him but this was the wrong time. I could not tell her anything that would dissuade her. Perhaps by the time she took the trip my life would be settled. I would know when I saw Hélène again.

"All right, Maman. Tell him about me. And tell me, is this going to be a one day visit then?"

"No, of course not. I'm not going to pop into his office and say that his son wants to meet him and then just disappear."

"Oh? So, how long do you expect to stay?"

"You rented the room for a month . . . I will stay a month. I still want to see Munich. Maybe he will give me a tour."

"Ah ha! Very good! Well then, I wish you a very enjoyable time."

Again, I could see hope in her. Circumstances did not have a chance when one has hope. *Ah, was I speaking of her or me?*

I was counting the days until Hélène returned, which I realized was the same day that Catherine would arrive, unless Hélène was coming back on Saturday. There would not be enough hours in the day; I could not ignore my daughter who has not seen her family in ten years. It will work out.

I wanted to go back to the Italian restaurant again but Marie-Jeanne said that she could not possibly wear the same dress to the same restaurant twice in succession, so on Friday we made another trip to the dress shop where she picked out another outfit in white. I was spared the expense of more jewelry because she said that her pearl earrings would go well with the dress. The good food and good wine made me decide to come here at least once a week. It was a bit expensive but after all, I was rich.

Sunday morning, having breakfast alone was depressing. Just when I thought someone was visiting it turned out to be only Nadine picking up René's key. I longed for Hélène and the joy of her company. She was always surprising me with something she did or knew, which kept adding to her character, her *persona*, her intellect and mystique. After so many years of living alone I now found that to be intolerable. I wanted to be with somebody . . . almost desperately. I went to Marie-Jeanne's place a bit early for lunch.

Even though it was Sunday she was still doing her tests and trying to complete her report. She asked me to prepare lunch, telling me what she had chosen and how to prepare it. Chicken salad and cucumbers wasn't much of a challenge and I had it done before she had finished her lab work. An idea struck me and I called Catherine.

"Hello," a young voice answered in English.

Phillip Varady

« Michel, c'est toi ? »

« Grand-père ? »

« Oui, c'est moi, ton grand-père. Ça fait longtemps depuis que je t'ai parlé. Tu me comprends bien ? »

« Oh, bien sûr ! Maman dit que je sois un bon étudiant. Nous te verrons après seulement une semaine »

« Oui, et cela me fait très heureux. Je te promets que toi et ton frère et ta sœur passeront un temps merveilleux ici en France ».

« Je suis sûr, Grand-père, je peux attendre à peine »

« Bon, maintenant va chercher ta mère. »

"Hello, Papa."

"Hello, darling. I see that I didn't wake you today. How's everything?"

"Good. We're so excited. We're going to spend the day at the lake so we all got up early. Michael said he spoke to you in French. How did he do?"

"Perfect! So much better than the last time."

"He's so pleased. What's happening with you?"

"I called to tell you that I was renting a car for you. It'll be at the airport; this way makes it so much easier when we need to travel. None of our vehicles can hold all of you. Do you still remember how to get home from Nancy?"

"Of course, some things you never forget."

"Good, then you understand that no one will be at the airport to welcome you?"

"Okay, sure. We'll just come to your house then."

"Yes, and I think that I will have someone special here to meet you?"

"Who?"

"A lady friend."

"Oh, Papa. Really? How wonderful. Tell me about her."

"No, no, no. When you get here you'll meet her."

"Oh, you're terrible. Do you want to talk to Bobby?"

"No. Bring Jennifer and Bryan to the phone."

I spoke to my other two grandchildren for a few minutes. Jennifer was nearly as proficient as Michael but Bryan's vocabulary was lacking, but then he was only four years old. Marie-Jeanne came in while I was on the phone and served lunch. I was in a very good mood when I sat at the table.

"Your grandchildren?"

"Yes, they'll be here in a week from today."

"Just when you go back to work."

"I know but Eliane goes on vacation and I can manage to get away early every day. It won't be so bad. Eliane is planning things to do."

"So, I guess I won't see you for the whole week, eh?"

"Oh, I don't know. We'll see how thing work out."

For Marie-Jeanne, the most important thing was for her to get her paperwork in order to present it to a board of review, probably in the next few weeks. A whole week away from me would help. She showed me what she had prepared so far but I could not help her much being outside of that type of thing. She had to rely on Hélène to make it presentable in the right format.

That evening at Mother's, Eliane and I went over what she had planned. There were day trips to Nancy on Monday and Verdun on Tuesday, a carnival in Épinal on Wednesday, a rock concert in the Exposition Park in Nancy on Friday night and I insisted on dinner at the Italian restaurant on Saturday. There were still many hours to fill but we thought that enough ideas would be brought up to keep everyone busy. Eliane asked me for some grocery money because she and Mother had volunteered to prepare lunch and dinner at my house next Sunday, not trusting my cooking or menu planning.

Time began to drag on Monday as things slipped back into a routine. I worked on my book but accomplished little, then went to lunch at Marie-Jeanne's but that was short because she wanted to get back to her work. She informed me that she would take another trip into the forest on Tuesday but did not ask me to accompany her. I didn't want to anyway; it was very tiring and beside I thought that I should distance myself from her a bit as Hélène's return drew near. Geneviève called on Tuesday to ask what day she and Jean-Marie could spend some time with Catherine and Bobby. I suggested Thursday; they agreed and said that they would be here before lunch.

Wednesday, Thursday and Friday seemed like an eternity, waiting for Sunday. Marie-Jeanne had little time to eat, much less to prepare a meal. One lunch that she missed at my place she explained simply as 'I forgot.' I see a nervous fear growing in her; it disquiets me. I assume that it is because she thinks that her years of work in the forest may be thought of as amateurish or that she could not make it understandable. Less likely but also a concern was that her condition was the result of the impending return of Hélène and that her suspicions that there was a relationship between her daughter and me would prove to be correct.

All along I had thought that my affair with Marie-Jeanne was reckless seeing that it was Hélène that I loved, but Marie-Jeanne threw herself at me in such a playful manner that in my mind it was as though we knew that it was only recreation. My brief affair with Kaly did not bother her; she thought no more of it than a competition of sorts. If Hélène says she loves me, we will have to tell Marie-Jeanne. I cannot know how that would affect her. She could not accuse me of using her or deceiving her or even making a fool of her. We never asked for or received a commitment from each other but I know that she would be hurt. I know that she had hope that I would fall in love with her. It's not as though I didn't love her at all, it's just that what I felt for Hélène was compelling and what I felt for Marie-Jeanne was satisfying.

What a disaster it would be if she lost me to her daughter and the University rejected her work. That thought made me sad for her; that would be too much. I think I would feel guilty to have been the cause of part of it. I felt helpless, like a leaf driven by the wind, a man to whom fate has offered another chance to feel the depth of love that I knew with Laure-Anne. Marie-Jeanne and I both heard my mother say 'We do not chose who we love.' I believe it and I know that Marie-Jeanne does also; I hope that she will understand.

Saturday morning after Anne-Marie and I had our little battle of wits and words, and while I was having coffee in the garden, reading some notes that I had to turn into text, Marie-Jeanne came rushing through the house and plopped into a chair opposite me and gushed.

"Guess what?"

"You've discovered a new species?"

"Not yet. The University accepted my petition and wants me to meet with a board of review on the 26th. That gives me ten days to prepare."

"That's wonderful! Are you ready for it?"

"No. They want not only my report but my notes too . . . at least two days before the board convenes. I'm scared to death."

"Is your data sufficient to draw the conclusions in your report?"

"Yes, more than enough. I made sure of that."

"Did you save all your notes?"

"Yes, I have boxes of them."

"Have you started on the report?"

"No. I've never done one. I don't know where to start. I don't know what should be put in or what should be left out. I can tell them what I've found but I don't know how explain the science."

"What are you going to do?"

"Hélène will have to help me. I don't see any other way and I have little more than a week to get it done."

"Is that a problem?"

"Not if she cooperates with me. She will cooperate, won't she?"

Whether she was alluding to the search for Erich or a suspected relationship, I could not tell but her message was clear: don't give Hélène a reason not to cooperate.

"I don't see why not."

"Good! Is there more coffee?"

She talked me into going out for dinner that night but to spare me some expense she ruled out the Italian restaurant. The Quatre Vents was risky so we took a short drive to Toul where we were unlikely to meet any old Resistance fighters. On the ride home she began to question me.

"Did you hear from Hélène?"

"No, not a word."

"That's strange; she usually calls at least once. I wonder why she wouldn't call."

"She's probably having a great time and forgot."

"Hmmm. What time does your daughter arrive?"

"The plane lands at ten."

"Are you planning anything?"

"Not the first day. All Eliane's kids know that she's coming; I don't know how many are going to visit but they know that she'll be here for a week."

We talked about what was planned for the week until we arrived at Marie-Jeanne's house.

"Do you want to come in for a while?"

"No, not tonight. Give me a kiss."

She kissed me politely.

"Hélène and I have a lot of work to do next week and you have your family. When will I see you?"

"When we are both done, I suppose."

"Yes, I suppose so. Good night."

"Good night, Marie-Jeanne."

Phillip Varady

Sunday began just like any other day, routine through breakfast then Mother and Eliane burst in with an armload of groceries apiece.

"You could help, you know," Eliane said. "There's more stuff behind the seats. And you could get a bigger fire going to cook lunch."

I went out to get the groceries and put more wood in the stove.

"And make more coffee," Mother advised.

The two women discovered that beyond the top three of any stack of china, no dish, cup, plate or saucer had been washed in nearly ten years. They blamed me and set me to washing them. The tiles in the garden needed sweeping, the furniture outside needed dusting, the refrigerator needed to be reorganized to hold everything they brought . . . and the list just grew and grew. A car pulled up and everyone panicked. It was Marie-Jeanne.

"Good morning. Can you use some help?"

What a question! We were all busy for another forty-five minutes and finally stopped for coffee. We sat at the kitchen table; the dining room table was set for lunch and never looked so nice. The crunch of gravel got us all on our feet and heading for the front door. We were all outside before Catherine got out from behind the wheel; I almost snatched her from the car.

"Papa, Papa, Papa."

"Oh, Catherine. I missed you so much."

We hugged so hard I was losing my balance and leaned against the car. We kissed and kissed and hugged some more until other hands were pulling on me.

"Let go of her," Eliane protested, "you're not the only one glad to see her."

I hugged Bobby and turned my attention to my three grandchildren whom I had never seen in the flesh. Michael approached me first and extended his hand.

"Oh, no, Michel. You are in France now and you must give your Grand-père les bises."

"Kisses?"

"But of course. Don't you kiss your Maman?"

"Just on the cheek."

"Well that's all les bises are but you do it on both cheeks. You don't really kiss; it's more like rubbing cheeks. Come on."

He was a bit wooden but got through it all right and was immediately set upon by his grand-aunt and great-grand mother. Jennifer extended both her arms and I picked her up.

"Maman says that I can kiss you on the lips because I'm a girl."

"That's very nice but I want les bises too. Okay?"

"Okay."

I got my three kisses and tried for three more and got them too . . . and a wonderful hug. Bryan had to be pushed a little and when I picked him up he was looking to his mother for help.

"How's it going, Bryan?"

"Okay."

"Do you know who I am?"

"Grand-père."

"Do you know what a Grand-père is?"

He shook his head.

"Don't you have another Grand-père back home?"

He shook his head again.

"The other one is grandpa," Bobby said.

"Ah, then Grandpa is your father's father and Grand-père is your mother's father. That's me! Do I get les bises now?"

I'll wager that he loves his other grandfather very much because I got my two kisses on the cheek plus one on the lips. Eliane took the children inside and we would have followed but I took Marie-Jeanne's hand and pulled her toward me and introduced her.

"This is my friend Marie-Jeanne. My daughter, Catherine and her husband Bobby."

They exchanged greetings and handshakes and we went inside. The first opportunity that Catherine had she whispered in my ear.

"She's beautiful, Papa. I love her hair."

And she was gone with a wink and a smile before I could say anything. I looked at them all from a distance as they were getting coffee or hot chocolate. All of them were wearing jeans and outrageous undershirts. One would think that it was a mandatory uniform in America. We walked around outside, went into the woods a little bit; Bobby and I unloaded his and Catherine's luggage from the car. Actually, it was a Ford station wagon that could seat eight. We were still going from one to another asking endless questions when I notice Hélène's red Renault coming down the lane. I took Catherine's arm and led her to the front door.

"There's one more person I'd like you to meet."

The smile that Hélène had on her face as she got out of the car disappeared when she saw us; Catherine's hand on my arm tightened.

"I know you," Catherine said with almost a snarl in her voice.

"And I will always remember you!" Hélène said with equal malice.

"Papa, what's *she* doing here?"

"*That's* your daughter? Do you know what she put me through . . . for years?"

"Do you know what she is? And what her mother did?"

"That would be me," Marie-Jeanne said from behind us. "So, you're the one who tormented my daughter."

"Oh, Papa, no. Those Nazi bastards killed my mother and she slept with them . . . and brings her German daughter up as though she was French."

"Catherine, shut your mouth," I snapped.

I took her arm and pulled her away.

"I *am* French, you idiot," Hélène called out.

By now everyone except the children were outside. I pulled Catherine around the corner of the cottage.

"What's wrong with you? How could you be so rude? How could you have been so cruel to that little innocent girl? She was five and you were eight."

"You're taking their side? How could you? They killed my mother! Don't you care?"

"*They* . . . didn't kill anybody. One man, one German soldier with a gun, being chased by an army killed your mother."

"And she fucked one of them and got that bastard German daughter."

"Don't you use that language with me!"

I gripped her by her arms and shook her once

"Those women are my friends and I want to marry one of them."

"Oh, Papa . . . noooo."

She began to cry. Hélène was leaving; Marie-Jeanne was with her.

"Didn't you love my mother?" Catherine sobbed.

"Oh, Catherine. I loved your mother more than I thought it was possible. Why do you think I subjected myself to loneliness all these years?"

"Find someone else."

"We do not chose who we love, Catherine. I cannot fall out of love because you don't like the woman."

"I won't accept it. I can't accept it. I can't, I can't"

"You must accept it or expect to or never see me again. I lost one woman that I loved and I'm not going to lose another. You can't ask me to do that."

"I won't accept it. I don't care. Let me go, Papa."

I didn't let her go. This had to be settled; I will not let her cause me to make a choice like this . . . or force *her* to.

"Let me go, let me go."

Eliane appeared from around the corner and put her face up against ours.

"Édouard, let her go. Let me talk to her."

"No, Eliane. I know you only want to help but you can't. Get Maman for me and let the three of us talk privately . . . please, Eliane. I know what I'm doing."

If I had just told her to go away she would not have done it but seeing that I was willing to have Mother help, she reluctantly did as I wished. Mother came around the corner and Catherine tried to get to her. I released her.

"Grand-mère, he wants to marry that woman. Tell him he can't do that. Not to *that* woman."

"Marry her, eh? Well, you were the first to know Catherine. Tell me why he can't do that."

"Because she's a whore . . . who slept with German soldiers."

"And how many German soldiers did she sleep with?"

"Grand-mère, are you defending her too?"

"If I'm going to be of any help I need to know just what it is that you object to. Would it make a difference if she slept with only one?"

"No, one was one too many."

"Can you call a woman a whore if she sleeps with only one man?"

"If he's a German . . . yes!"

"And what about the child? The child was born innocent; she had no part in her mother's choice of partner. Why should she suffer?"

"Because she not French . . . and she pretends that she is. She should go back to Germany and live with her father . . . if either of them even know who he is."

"Oh, Catherine, all that was so long ago. Why do you still feel this way? Can't you forgive and forget?"

"No! My mother is still dead and they did it. How can they ever be forgiven if she's still dead?"

Mother and I looked at each other. We both knew that we would have to tell the secret that we have kept all these years.

"Do you want to tell her or shall I?" Mother asked.

"You."

"All right. So, Catherine, the mother is a whore and the child is a worthless German bastard and neither one is worth a lump of shit. Is that right?"

Catherine was a bit startled at Mother's language and a bit confused as to what this was leading. She nodded her head slightly as a sign of agreement.

"Talk to me, Catherine. I need to hear you say it if you agree with me. If I'm being too harsh, tell me."

"No, you are exactly right."

"All right. Now, I'm going to tell you something and I want you to promise that you will never tell another living soul. This involves more than just you alone, and I . . . we can't have you thinking that if you want to tell someone that it's your business and you have the right to do so. Other people will be affected and it is not your prerogative to change other people's lives. Do you understand? Do you promise?"

Catherine was aware that she had forced something to be revealed and was duly impressed with the importance of it.

"Yes! Yes, I understand and yes, I promise."

"Your grandmother's a whore because she slept with a German soldier and your father is a worthless German bastard and neither one of us is worth a lump of shit. And if you treat us any different than Marie-Jeanne and Hélène, then you're a hypocrite and *you're* not worth a lump of shit. What are you going to do now?"

Catherine's head slumped forward as if she had suddenly fallen asleep. It bounced off Mother's shoulder and she stood erect with her mouth open and a blank look on her face. She didn't do anything; she just stood there, speechless . . . frozen. After a minute of this I became concerned. I took her shoulders and shook her gently.

"Catherine! Catherine?"

Her eyes were closing and she was going limp. I took her from Mother's arms and picked her up and carried her around to the door. Eliane and Bobby had gone in the house but immediately jumped up when they saw me. I put her on the sofa.

"Get me a cold wet rag," I told Eliane.

I caressed her face until Eliane got back. Bobby knelt by the sofa but remained motionless and quiet. I gently wiped her face with the cloth, calling her name softly. In a minute she opened her eyes and put her arms around my neck.

"Papa, I love you. Please let me love you."

"Do you forgive me?"

"There's nothing to forgive," she sobbed and began to cry loudly.

When she had finally cried herself out, she released me and clung to Bobby.

"What is it, Cathy? What's wrong?" he asked.

"I've made a mistake . . . a horrible mistake."

"What mistake?" Bobby asked.

"I . . ." She looked at Mother. "I hated . . . I was so full of hate . . . I was wrong."

"Okay, darling. It's all right."

Then Bobby began speaking to her in English and she nodded her head several times. None of us knew what he was saying but she began to smile even as her tears continued to flow.

"Okay," she said several times. "I'm okay. I'll be right back."

She got up and went to the bathroom.

"She's all right," Bobby said. "She's over it."

When she came out, the children clustered around her, concerned about her well-being. She assured them that whatever it was, she was over it and that she was 'okay.'

"I'm starving," she said. "Aren't we ever going to eat?"

Everyone relaxed and began to act normal again. Mother and Eliane headed for the kitchen to begin the meal.

"Hey, Beau-père," Bobby called to me, "you have a cold 'brewski' . . . or two?"

"No, but I know where to find some. How long before we eat?" I called out.

"Forty-five minutes!" Eliane replied.

"Okay. We're going to see Doub for a minute. We'll be right back."

Two quick beers and we were seated at the table ready when they were. After the meal, Bobby spoke to me privately.

"Pop, we've been awake for more than twenty-four hours. We need to close our eyes for a while. Don't let us miss dinner."

Phillip Varady

A shiver ran through me until I realized that he was calling me 'father' in American slang and not Popp, as if Catherine had told him our secret . . . but then she didn't know my father's name. While Bobby and Catherine slept, Eliane's second daughter, Joëlle and her husband Jean-Claude came over. They made a big fuss over the children and were talked into staying for dinner so that they could see Bobby and Catherine. It was a wonderful time watching Catherine and Joëlle relive old times. Catherine and Elisabeth were closer, both in age and friendship, Joëlle being four years younger than Catherine but they were both thrilled.

After Jean-Claude and Joëlle left, Catherine wanted to get her children to bed; I told her to let Bobby do it. He followed Eliane and Mother with the station wagon and she and I paid a visit to the Denisarts. I stayed in the car while she went to the door. Marie-Jeanne opened it and after a moment Catherine was allowed in and the door closed. Ten minutes later the three women were on the steps hugging and kissing. Catherine got in the car smiling.

"Okay?" I asked.

"Yeah. Better than okay."

I slept well. I could not say if it was because Catherine was here or because the secret had been shared with another person. I remember how good I felt when I told Jean-Marie only a part of it. After seeing how Catherine acted and reacted I began to wonder if I could tell Eliane but then remembered what Mother told Catherine: 'It is not your prerogative to change other people's lives.' It was more than *my* secret; it was Mother's also and at the time she told me about my father she specifically told me that she did not want Eliane to know.

I had my breakfast and quietly slipped out of the house. Catherine and Bobby should be caught up on their sleep by tomorrow. It felt good going back to work although I wished it was a week later. The weather was supposed to be nice but warmer the whole week with showers only on Wednesday night. I left the top down as I parked my Mercedes in the University parking. I wonder how many of my colleagues could guess who owned that car. It had been weeks since I was here last and I had a daunting stack of mail. I began going through it before I got to the real work of the day. I had not yet finished it when I had a visitor.

"Oiseau, are you a bastard or an idiot?" Kaly asked angrily, slamming my door.

"How was Crete, good?"

"Are you sleeping with both of them?"

"You look like you've got a little tan. Do they have beaches in Crete?"

"Oiseau, do you like living dangerously? I could not imagine a more sure way for you to wake up and find that one or the other had slit your throat. I know that I would do it, no matter which of them I was."

"You seem a little tense, Kaly. Do you have any vacation time left?"

"Stop it! If you don't give me an answer right now, I'm going to Hélène and tell her. This is not funny."

"Why didn't you tell Marie-Jeanne when you had the chance?"

"I wasn't sure if you were sleeping with Hélène."

"What makes you sure that I'm sleeping with Marie-Jeanne?"

"Because she practically admitted it."

"Well then, why don't you tell Hélène that her mother practically admitted to you that she was sleeping with me?"

"I think I will."

"Good. Was there something else?"

"You don't care?"

"She'll just think that you're making it up so you can steal me away from her."

"You're crazy, do you know that?"

"I'm crazy for you, Kaly. Come here! Let me put my hands on you."

I got up from my desk and came toward her. She backed up two steps but was stopped by the closed door.

"If you put a hand on me, I'll scream."

"Like you did that night?"

"No . . ." she smiled, just for a second, "Stay away from me."

She put a hand on me to keep me at a distance. I just smiled at her.

"You're not worried! She already knows! You told her?"

I said nothing.

"You're both crazy, maybe all three of you. Let me out of here."

I opened the door for her but didn't move, forcing her to brush by me to get out. I caressed her buttocks as she passed me. She took several steps down the corridor before she turned and shook a finger at me. I blew her a kiss.

Phillip Varady

I finished my mail and met with my colleagues to establish a time when we would divide the work and schedule classrooms and lecture halls; Tuesday morning was agreed on. I replenished my office supplies, checked with the bookstore on the availability of certain textbooks, and leafed through two new ones that were sent to me for consideration by publishers. After lunch at the cafeteria I went home.

I went through my mail hoping to find something from the investigator about Erich but there was nothing. I suppose if someone did not want to be found it would not be hard. Catherine left a note for me saying that Grand-mère would not be going with them and that we would have dinner at her house. I made a reservation for Saturday night for eight at the Italian restaurant. The man who took the call was familiar with my name and when I said 'eight' asked 'eight, Sir? Certainly!' I wonder if he expects me to bring seven beautiful women with me. With nothing else to do, I went to see Mother. She was dozing in front of the television. I leaned over her from behind the chair and put my mouth next to her ear and spoke softly.

"Hast du etwas zu trinken, Muti, und genuch für diese abend?"

She patted one cheek and kissed the other. She continued her conversation in German also.

"I'm glad that you brought that up. Catherine said that wine at dinner was all right but that Bobby liked a whiskey call Jacques Daniel and she liked vodka."

"I'll go to the market later and see if I can find some. How did you feel about telling Catherine our secret?"

"It wasn't hard to tell her, it had to be done. You can't have her hating your new wife, not true?"

"Yes, that's so. I didn't mean to say anything yet, not even to Catherine; it just slipped out. I haven't even asked the girl yet."

"Das Mädchen? Are you talking about Marie-Jeanne or Hélène?"

I squatted in front of her and took her hands in mine.

"Would it make a difference?"

"Yes, it would make a difference. One would be sensible and the other would tell everyone that you bumped your head . . . very hard."

I took one of her hands and put it on top of my head.

"Do you feel that?"

"I don't feel anything . . . oh, you're just teasing me. Well, Marie-Jeanne certainly looks young with that hair . . . such hair."

"I'll go to the market; I'll be right back. Do you need anything?"

"You could get some wine for dinner . . . red this time, yes?"

Our neighborhood merchant didn't have American whiskey so I took a short trip into Nancy. What Bobby liked was only one of two brands that the larger store carried and it was expensive. On my way back I thought about Mother's reaction. Suppose I said that I wasn't teasing her . . . then what? I'll have to tell everyone sooner or later and they will all have to live with it. *She hasn't said that she would marry you, Édouard.* A small detail that will be taken care of in a week or so.

The family got back late in the afternoon with bags full of souvenirs of Nancy. Eliane looked worn out.

"It's like driving a truck, that car," she said. "I'm a nervous wreck."

"Have a little drink," I said, displaying the whiskey.

"*Oh, wow!* Jack Daniels," Bobby exclaimed. "Come on, Aunt Eliane, you've got to try this. Get some glasses."

Eliane and I were talked into sampling some, which Bobby poured into brandy glasses but put his in a wine glass so that he could add some ice.

"I would never dilute cognac with ice, why do you do it with whiskey?" I asked.

After Eliane and I tasted it we switched to wine glasses and added ice. Catherine put some vodka in a glass of orange juice . . . it didn't make sense to me why someone would make it so that they couldn't taste the thing that they wanted. The children showed the things they had for souvenirs; I was told that the shirts were not considered underwear but tee shirts, and they all had one as a souvenir except Michael. I asked him why he didn't want a souvenir of Nancy.

"I'm not wearing a tee-shirt with a girl's name on it."

"Ah, Michel, in a few years you will be writing girls' names on your arm."

He was not ready to admit any attraction to the opposite sex.

"Grand-père, don't call me Michel; my name is Michael."

"Yes, I know but in French it is Michel."

"But in English Michelle is a girl's name."

"Michèle is also a girl's name in French but we don't make too much of that kind of thing. In fact, your mother's Grand-père is coming to see her on Thursday and his name is Jean-Marie. What do you think of that?"

"French people are . . . *weird.*?"

"What is *weird*, Catherine?"

"Strange . . . odd, maybe peculiar."

"Sure, that's why we're French, so we can be *weird*. Now let me talk to your mother and father a little. Okay, Michel?"

"Okay, Grand-père, but all my friends call me Mickey . . . could you do that?"

"Sure . . . Mickey. All *my* friends call me Oiseau."

"Now that's *really weird*."

We had a little time yet before dinner and I walked with Bobby and Catherine into the backyard. This concerned only them.

"Your grandfather and another man formed a company that became very successful; he married the other man's daughter. A part of that man's inheritance came to me through your grandmother and your mother. I sold some of it but I still have a house in Paris and one share of stock in the company. That one share represents one per cent of the company and is worth much more to the owners than its share of the profits. Your grandfather controls fifty shares and a company run by his second wife's family controls the other forty-nine. You can see why they both would want it.

I signed an agreement that I would not vote my share as long as I owned it but if I transferred ownership to Catherine or she inherited it, she would be free to do as she wishes. Rochefort, the other owner will make what will seem like incredible offers but as soon as you sell them the share they won't need you. You can make deals for your vote but don't sell. I won't take the income from the share; that's yours. Last year it paid about fourteen thousand dollars per share but I expect with Rochefort money in it, by next year it could double."

"Papa, that's so nice of you. Thank you."

"Yes, Beau-père, I don't know what to say. Why does Catherine's grandfather want to speak to us?"

"If they're nice to you they hope that you'll be nice to them when you control the share; so will Rochefort. I don't know what they might offer; just remember why they are doing it. I know that they're family but business is business."

Eliane came out of the house with a crème de menthe for me and when Bobby wasn't looking I emptied the whiskey in a rosebush. The children were chased out of the house until mealtime and with a little prompting they all shared something that they liked about Nancy and about France. Bryan stayed close to his sister who would supply the word in French when he said it in English by mistake.

After dinner and the children's bedtime, we sat at the table asking the Gustavsons questions about Wisconsin and the family there. Bobby wanted to change the next day's itinerary to include a ride past the army base in Toul where he spent two years and another look at the house in Vaucoleurs that he and Catherine rented when they were first married . . . for the kids, he said. Eliane liked the idea because she thought that there was not enough in Verdun to spend the whole day.

When Bobby and Catherine and I were back at the cottage, ready to go to bed, I asked them if they minded if I knew more about their financial condition and what they hoped to do in the future. Catherine seemed reluctant but once Bobby started talking, she joined in. Regardless of what Jean-Marie might offer, I began to make plans of my own. A phone call and a lie would get things moving, I'm sure.

Tuesday was exhausting with each of my colleagues vying for some advantage or trying to avoid some nuisance. I have been doing this for almost twenty-five years and was better at it than most but my heart wasn't in it. I loved to teach but all the other things that I needed to do were tedious. Professors should have assistants who could take care of all the boring administrative necessities. We finally finished at three in the afternoon. If the whole family went today I planned to enjoy a beer or two at the Quatre Vents. First, though, I called Shlomo.

"I'm glad to hear from you, Édouard. I'm sure you know all about what happened to the business."

"Yes, and I'm sorry that it went so badly for you although I have some news but I don't know if it's good for you or not."

"I have no more interest in Thouvignon et Compagnie."

"Oh, I didn't know that they changed the name."

"Well, considering the Rochefort's reputation . . . you know what I mean, don't you? . . . it was not a surprise."

"No, I suppose not but this is not about the company. I am telling you this as family and I can tell you no more than this: I received an offer for the house last week that was more than what you offered. I told them that you had offered to match any offer that was made and they said that there were other things that you could not match. When I asked what they were, they said that if I was serious they would have a tax attorney meet with me."

"I know what they're doing . . . you do too. They've got a judge somewhere."

"Well, that's not all. Today I received another offer with the same vague promises and told them that I would consider it and later, out of curiosity, I discovered that it was exactly ten per cent higher. So, I am thinking that the people that made the second offer knew exactly what the first offer was. What do you make of that?"

"That's nothing. Someone in one firm is being paid to pass this kind of information to the other. I wouldn't be surprised if my original offer was discovered the same way."

"Well, Shlomo, I'm in no hurry to sell but if no other offers are made I think I'll let it go by Christmas."

"Édouard, if no other offers are made . . . take the money. If my people want it and can still see a profit . . . I'll call you back. We have spies too, you know. We know who else was interested in the property. And Édouard . . . I really appreciate your call. You're a much more decent person than Jean-Marie."

"Well, keep in touch, Shlomo . . . and good luck."

I drove to Eliane's to see if Mother went with them or not. She wasn't there but before I went to the café I stopped by to see Marie-Jeanne. I knew that I had been cold to her and to make up a bit I thought to encourage her and learn of her progress. She was excited when I arrived and brought me to her desk to show how much she had finished. She began to describe what she was doing while I stood behind her, looking over her shoulder at the different forms and charts that she was working on. It was not really interesting to me but she had such an enthusiasm about her as she told it that I noticed a side of her that I had never seen before. Unconsciously I put my hands on her shoulders and would not have known it except that she stopped speaking and covered my hands with hers.

"I miss you, Édouard."

"Hmmm."

She got up and hugged me. I held her close. *Why am I always worried about hurting her? Why do I keep giving her hope?*

"I won't keep you from your work. I'll stop in again."

I went to the Quatre Vents and had my two beers, one with Doub and Jeami. While he was telling me about his vacation Biston showed up and took his usual seat but said nothing. That's the way Biston was, quick to forget . . . especially his embarrassments.

The Swans of Lorraine

When I got home I discovered that they all were there and that dinner was already on the stove. My time was monopolized by the children, all of them competing for my attention to tell me about what they had seen today. As they excitedly related what it was that impressed them, I looked in their eyes and I saw, not Catherine or Bobby, but the child itself. I never saw this with Catherine, I always saw Laure-Anne in her eyes and I suppose it distanced me from her. I loved her, that's for sure, but maybe I loved her because she was all that I had left of Laure-Anne.

The children were not going to let me drift off into thought and would take my hand or tap my arm when they wanted more than their share of attention. Mickey and Jennifer hardly allowed Bryan to speak so I picked him up and sat him on my lap, asking him direct questions. He had a habit of omitting the *pas* that follows the *ne* in the negative and I would stop him and repeat it correctly. After about ten times he learned to use it and for the rest of the evening he would look at me and loudly say it no matter to whom he was speaking. The three of them became individuals that day.

After dinner when Mother and Eliane had taken them home I asked Catherine to sit alone with me in the garden while Bobby watched television. I spoke about her mother and her early childhood, trying to express my feeling for her through the years and after a half-hour I summed it up.

"I love you, Catherine, I always have but I think I never showed it much."

"You did, Papa. Sometimes when you were talking to me I would catch you looking into my eyes as if I were something wonderful and precious. I don't think you knew that you showed it but I'll never forget that; it helped me endure not having a mother."

Some things were better left unsaid. We went back into the house but I stopped her in the kitchen, out of sight of Bobby, and looked into her eyes. I didn't see Laure-Anne, I saw Catherine . . . something wonderful and precious. I took her in my arms and the tears began to flow. Catherine did not allow me to cry alone.

"Ten years is too long, darling."

"I know, Papa. That's why you gave us carfare, isn't it?"

I thought that she was speaking of the tickets that I had sent and nodded.

"You think that you have me completely figured out, don't you?"

"You're such a straightforward, uncomplicated person. You could have said when you promised us the money that it was so that we would come to France more often but you let us arrive at that by ourselves. Don't you think we figured that out? We saw right through it. Bobby and I talked it over and we decided that we would use part of the income from the share to come every year. Is that all right?"

"Why do you make your father cry so much?"

Wednesday is the day that I would have preferred to take off but my department was still getting organized and my absence would be missed. The carnival in Épinal would have been the perfect place for me to enjoy my grandchildren. The morning was tedious, working on the curriculum. We adjourned for lunch a little past eleven o'clock and I went back to my office. I called Hélène.

"What time do you go to lunch?" I asked.

"What time do you want to go to lunch?"

"Any time that we can talk privately"

"We usually go about noon . . . I can meet you in a half-hour."

There was nothing on my desk that required immediate attention. I decided to leave now but then my phone rang; it was Eliane.

"I've been trying to reach you all morning," she said.

"I haven't been in my office all morning. What's happening?"

"We're in Épinal with Elisabeth and her kids. Your grandchildren are thrilled to meet with their cousins and I called to tell you that we wouldn't be home until after dinner. Catherine wants to see Pierre so we'll follow Elisabeth home and visit for a while. Will you be all right?"

"You're asking a man that has lived by himself for ten years if he can open a can of soup so that he won't starve to death, if he'll be all right?"

"So, you'll be . . . okay?"

"Yes, I'll be 'okay.' Until later, eh?"

Those children will have her speaking English before long.

I drove quickly to the lab and waited at the door to the cafeteria; we went through the food line together. Being ahead of the crowd we found a table that was apart from other diners. We sat on opposite sides for appearances.

"I miss you." I said when we were seated.

She made a kiss with her lips.

"I miss you too. How is everything?"

"It's wonderful. I can't deny that but without you . . ."

"When do they leave?"

"Sunday morning. I hope that I can survive until then."

"I thought about you every day. It was very different without you . . . knowing that I couldn't be with you when I wanted as if you were only minutes away."

"Will you come to my place on Sunday? Not for breakfast; they leave about nine o'clock."

"I'll be there. I've just planned the day."

"Really? What are we doing?"

"It's a secret. It's special. It's exciting."

"So, you will torture me until then, eh?"

She reached across the table and took my hand and stared at me very seriously. She waited a few moments before she spoke.

"I'll make up for your suffering."

I had to smile, guessing what her implied meaning was. She knew what I was thinking and returned the smile, confirming my guess.

"How's your mother's report coming along?"

"We've got a complete report but it needs to be formalized. Most of it is hand written and needs to be typed. I brought home some forms and graph paper and showed her the acceptable way to show results. By Friday she should have it finished and I'll go over it to see if her science is correct. She's very meticulous, very precise."

A chorus of greetings announced the arrival of the Corsican gang.

"Ah, let me see how good my memory is. Christiane . . . Isabelle . . . and Hoa. How was the water in Corsica?"

Hoa and Isabelle sat on either side of me, rather close, I thought, and Christiane next to Hélène. They all seemed to be conspirators, as if Hélène had told them about us.

"She hasn't told you yet, Professor?"

"No, not a word. We were talking about her mother."

"Did you all decide to eat early?" Hélène asked.

"I saw you pass by Chem and I thought it was later," Hoa explained.

"Christiane, let me guess," I asked slyly, "you were the one who answered the phone when I called the lab, weren't you?"

"Yes . . . she was," Hélène said. "And so they all came to see you again but I don't know why they would do that . . . unless . . ."

Phillip Varady

It was very flattering and a bit romantic. I don't know if Hélène said anything or if her friends only suspected. No one was talking . . . except about Corsica.

When I got back to my campus after lunch I forced some issues to get them settled and badgered my colleagues to work late so that we could get this done today. That would leave tomorrow for each of us to work on our own schedules at our own pace. That way I didn't need to come in at all.

The sky was dark gray when I came outside; rain was threatening and I put the top up. I was about to leave but had nowhere to go, unless Mother had not gone to Épinal. It began to rain lightly on the way to Laxou and it was dark by the time I drove by her house; there were no lights on. I continued on to the cottage and briefly thought about dropping in on Doub as I went by his house but decided on a hot bath instead.

A piece of bread, a chunk of ham with mustard and a glass of Moselle were dinner. I brought some clean clothes downstairs in case Catherine and Bobby came home while I was soaking. I relaxed in the tub with a glass of Rémy sitting on the floor. When I had sipped it all I went to bed.

The Swans of Lorraine

Chapter 12

A good night's sleep and a pleasant dream make a person have a positive outlook the next morning. The rain had passed, it was sunny and warm and everything outside was wet. I brewed a pot of coffee and would have warmed some bread but there was no fire in the stove; I just tore off a piece and ate it while waiting for the coffee. As I poured my second cup I felt good; ordinarily I would be halfway to work at this time. The thought went through my mind, not the first time, to retire from teaching and find something to do that I liked. I couldn't think of anything immediately; maybe when I did I would think more seriously about it.

I heard the flop-flop of bare feet coming down the stairs. It was Catherine and as she turned to come into the kitchen I thought that I would spill my coffee. She was wearing a light blue garment that began below her shoulders and ended just below her hips and was almost transparent.

"Oh, shit!"

I can't recall ever seeing my daughter move that quickly before. She was back in two minutes wearing jeans and a tee shirt.

"Papa, I didn't know that you were still home. Why didn't you say something?"

"Something like, 'Hey, you look just like your mother?' "

My attempt at humor embarrassed her and she was at a loss for words for a few moments.

"No. I meant why you didn't let us know that you would be leaving late or have the day off. Which one is it?"

"I'm taking the day off. I didn't know until late yesterday; there wasn't any way I could have let you know and besides, I didn't even think of it."

She poured a cup of coffee and buttered some bread for both of us.

The Swans of Lorraine

"Papa . . . do I really look like her or were you just being funny?"

"No, that's pretty much the way she looked, except . . . maybe you have a little bit bigger belly."

We ate in silence for a few minutes.

"Are you really going to marry that woman?"

"Does that woman have a name?"

"Marie-Jeanne."

"No."

"No? I thought you said that you were going to marry her."

"I meant the other one . . . Hélène."

"Oh."

We ate some more bread. She didn't believe me . . . I think.

"Papa, do you still think of my mother?"

"Yes. Not so much now but she was all I thought about for years. I always made comparisons . . . the way other women looked or dressed, the sound of their voice, the way they did things . . . things like that."

"Do you compare that woman to her?"

"Catherine, if you're going to talk about her, use her name. No, I don't make comparisons any more, besides . . . well, never mind."

"Because my mother was so different?"

"Yes, exactly."

"Why did you wait so long?"

"Someone's here."

I got up and went to the door with Catherine right behind me. It was Eliane.

"Papa, why did you wait so long?"

"I'll tell you later. Good morning, Sister. What brings you around so early?"

She kissed us both and went to the kitchen and poured some coffee. We came back to the table and sat with her.

"I need a vacation to recover from your children," Eliane said. "Don't they ever slow down or stop eating?"

"Maybe they'll wear themselves out today," Catherine replied.

"What's going on today?"

I thought for a moment that Catherine forgot that Jean-Marie and Geneviève were coming.

"I'm taking the three American super-children swimming at the pool in Nancy. Elisabeth will meet me there with her two and she's bringing Sylvie along. I'll bring Sylvie back here and Philippe will come over later for dinner. Catherine is going to follow me home with the station wagon and bring Maman back in my car. Is all that clear?"

Eliane finished her coffee and she and Catherine left. Bobby came downstairs and joined me with two cups of coffee and more bread as I was wiping the garden furniture. I asked him about yesterday's travels.

"The Americans are long gone; it's a French base now but we could still see my barracks from the road and the warehouse where Catherine and I worked. The house in Vaucoleurs looked the same and we spoke to the people that were living there. They said that when the Americans left all the rents in the area went down; I don't think that they knew I was American."

"What about Verdun?"

"The town was nice but the war memorial was very moving. When did they build it? I don't remember ever seeing it."

"It opened about three years ago. I was there at the inauguration."

"The kids didn't understand, except maybe Michael. He asked some questions that I couldn't answer. We saw a photo of Catherine's grandfather and what was left of his company. They must have lost ninety per cent of their men."

"More like three hundred and ninety per cent if you count replacements. I use two textbooks that include that photo; it's become a classic."

We talked about what the average American soldier thought about serving in France and what the French thought about them in their country. Catherine came in with two sacks of groceries and Mother put my mail on the telephone table. They enjoyed coffee while Bobby and I put everything away. We all sat together only briefly afterward because Catherine wanted to know more about Mother's trip to Munich and suggested that they move into the kitchen to clean shrimp for lunch, and to speak privately, I assumed. The Thouvignons arrived at ten o'clock looking a bit different. More casual I'd say.

Geneviève was wearing an absolutely vividly colored, eye-catching blouse, a pair of jeans and heels. Jean-Marie had his shirt opened two buttons more than usual with a gold chain showing but it was his white shoes that made him look really different. We greeted one another and when Catherine and her grandfather embraced I was very touched; it pleased me to see the genuine affection that they had for each other. Jean-Marie asked me to leave Bobby alone with him and Geneviève for a while to get to know more about him; no business, he promised. I thought I would join the women in the kitchen but was chased out. I wandered out the front door.

It was amusing to see three Mercedes 280SL's parked together, especially when they were blue, white and red . . . or red, white and blue . . . very patriotic. I thought about the conversation that Catherine and I had earlier and why I didn't want to answer her question about why I had waited so long.

For a while it was because I was grieving, then because I felt guilty about abandoning Laure-Anne and the memories of her. After that I think that I was afraid to love again, fearing another tragedy that I would not survive. Even today my greatest fear is that after committing all that I am to another woman, that I will be robbed of the love that I want and need in return. I thought of Bobby and Catherine, with their three children, working hard to make life a success . . . and that thing that Catherine was wearing this morning . . . apparently their ardor has not diminished. That's what I want, and by God, I will not go to my grave without having it again. Only a few more days to wait.

"Papa, come in, they're ready."

Catherine and I joined the others in the garden. Bobby looked at ease, which I took to mean that he knew that he made a good impression on them.

"First of all," Geneviève began, "this is all about the one share of Thouvignon et Compagnie and cheese. A little history will explain what is going on. Your grandfather secured a contract with a chain of supermarkets, not a very big one . . . only a hundred and twenty stores, to carry our complete line of products. This upset Rochefort because one of their companies was the previous supplier. Then with these added markets we were able to negotiate the exclusive right to distribute the most popular brand of Dutch cheeses in France. We had been selling this brand for close to fifty years, so we were old friends to the Dutch. I say 'we' because I was in Rotterdam closing the deal two days before we arrived here . . . just ahead of Shlomo . . . to do business."

"And Shlomo didn't know it," I offered."

"No, we forgot to tell him. Well, then we were in a position where we could force other chains to accept some of our products if they wanted to continue offering their customers that brand of cheese. Rochefort lost business again as a result. When Shlomo put his shares up for sale, Rochefort snatched them up. If they couldn't get their cheese business back at least they could share the profit that *we* were making on it. However, no one stands against Rochefort very long without a strong bargaining point. What did you call it, Bobby?"

"An ace in the hole, *une carte maîtresse*."

"Yes, well the ace in the hole is that one share. Rochefort cannot move against us directly without it but that is not to say that they will do nothing. I sent my Uncle François, who runs Rochefort, a note about Bobby and last week he came to me with some news and an offer. They are now evaluating cheese producers in Wisconsin in the range of five to eight million dollars annual gross revenue. A year from now they will make offers to buy one out. They project some months of negotiating and closing the deal and a transition period when they will replace some of the management with Rochefort people. Of course this includes the Director . . . in America they would call him the CEO . . . and they would like the new one to be Bobby."

Bobby and Catherine were very excited, saying things in English that I could not understand but which I could imagine. When we were all calm again I tried to gain some perspective on this offer.

"Geneviève, you say 'we' and 'they' meaning Thouvignon and Rochefort but the deal is from Rochefort and yet you speak as a Thouvignon. Can you explain?"

"My uncle asked me to extend the offer and I agreed but I am more a Thouvignon than a Rochefort. The deal is a good one for Bobby and Catherine. It's not a gift, he will have to work for it and be competent and, family or not, if he can't do the job he will be thrown out."

"Do you think I'm qualified?" Bobby asked.

"No, not at present but they will try to remedy that. They want you to go back to school and get your degree in Business Administration. They expect that you will attend full time and take a full schedule of classes. Are you willing to do that?"

"I don't know if I can. I'd have to give up my job and work part time."

"I thought as much, so following your father-in-law's instruction . . ."

Geneviève produced a check.

"Ordinarily these checks aren't issued until 15 October but Jean-Marie agreed to advance it to you. The actual amount may vary slightly and we will make up the difference. This year's dividend per share in dollars amounts to thirty-two thousand dollars; next year we project about forty-five thousand."

"Thirty-two thousand," Bobby mumbled as he took the check. "That's twice what I'm making now. I guess I can afford to quit."

"What's Rochefort's plan here, Geneviève?" I asked.

"Production will gradually move away from the common types of cheese produced for the American taste and focus on French cheeses. They expect to make an impact first in the Canadian markets and then the American in a year or two. When the Rochefort brand name becomes established they will start production of the Dutch types. They expect their cheese sales in North America will cut into the Dutch export market. Whether or not it forces a re-negotiation of Thouvignon's contract is not the point, although that is part of it. More importantly it is to prove that Rochefort will not be pushed around."

"What I meant when I asked was what Rochefort's plan was for Bobby."

"If he can do the work, they'll give him all the benefits of a director and integrate him in the Rochefort corporate family. Those benefits will reflect the company's income and production increases, so will the salary. They want him fully Rochefort. When the share passes to Catherine's control, they will make an offer to buy it. The offer should be in the range of . . . this is difficult Édouard; it depends on how long you live. If we suppose another thirty years . . . about one and a half to two million."

"Dollars or Francs?"

"Dollars!"

No one said anything. I believed that Geneviève was being honest with us but there remained some nagging doubt that not everything was said.

"What happens to Bobby when Catherine sells the share?"

"They may replace him if the only reason he kept his job was nepotism but I reckon by that time he won't need Rochefort anymore. He'll be sixty, a good age to retire and spend one's fortune, eh, Édouard?"

She had a point, a very good point. I had much more than that now. Bobby and Catherine agreed and I went for some Rémy for a toast. I brought Mother out to share it with us.

"Who will propose it?" I asked.

"Me," Catherine said eagerly. "To family!"

"To family," we all replied.

Everyone hugged everyone.

"Will someone tell me what's going on?" Mother protested.

Catherine and Bobby went back in the kitchen with her. Jean-Marie and Geneviève were silent and satisfied.

"All right, you two," I said, "there's something you're not telling me. Out with it."

"Édouard, it's so obvious. I didn't think I needed to tell you," Geneviève said.

"What? It may be obvious to you but not to me."

"I wish you good health, Édouard," Jean-Marie said, "And may you live to be a hundred."

"And hold on to your one share until then," Geneviève added.

She poured another cognac for us and raised her glass.

"To my sons, Paul and Georges. May they be as wise as their brother-in-law Édouard?"

Mother's seafood lunch was delicious. She knows that I prefer seafood because no one dares ask for red with it. Surprisingly Geneviève volunteered to help Catherine clean up when Jean-Marie and Mother went for a walk in the woods. Bobby and I sat in the garden and speculated about his corporate future; we were both guessing. We talked about school, him going and me leaving. Bobby seemed like a different person; I wondered if it was the money. I know it changed me; I became more assertive, ruder, more confident and worry free. Catherine brought out my mail when she served the coffee. I only glanced at the sender's names but withdrew two envelopes and excused myself.

Upstairs at my desk I opened the first and found a bill for services rendered in the search for my father. In the second was a report on Erich. He was killed in action in a town named Heilbronn on 11 April 1945. It gave the last known address of his widow in another town named Pirmasens and asked if I wished to find her. Included was another bill. I put the two bills with my checkbook and the report in my pocket.

Geneviève had mentioned that she and Jean-Marie had planned to stay long enough to see the great grandchildren and Eliane but not for dinner. She was just getting off the phone when I came back down and followed me out to the garden. Jean-Marie and Mother had returned.

"Is everything all right?" I asked.

"Oh, yes. I called my uncle to tell him that Bobby and Catherine agreed to the proposal. He wants to see them before they return to the United States."

A chorus of negative responses followed.

"Don't worry," Geneviève continued, "I told them that you had not seen your family in ten years and that it would be difficult in any case. He asked what would be the earliest date possible; he would like about three hours of your time."

"If I'm in school it wouldn't be until Christmas."

The thought of it brought smiles to Catherine's face and mine also.

"It would be the first Christmas that we didn't go to my parents' house." Bobby said.

"So, that would be nine times that we were at your parents' house and this would be only the second that we were here. What do you think, dear?" Catherine replied.

So it was settled at that moment. Bobby would call Geneviève and she would set it up with her uncle when the dates were known. There was an air of celebration in the cottage; everything seemed right with the world. Then Eliane arrived and the children came running through the back door into the garden. Catherine gathered them together to meet Jean-Marie and Eliane brought me into the house to meet Sylvie. She was grinning like a mad woman and when I looked at Sylvie I knew why and couldn't help grin myself.

"It's nice to finally meet you, Sir."

"No, no, no, you don't call me Sir; soon you will be calling me Uncle."

"Is there something funny about me that amuses you?"

"Well, it's not that you're funny looking, in fact you're beautiful; it's probably only a coincidence."

"What's that?"

"Are you Berber?"

"My mother is. Could you tell?"

"Yes, my sister and I know a woman . . . and if you wore a hajib . . . well, anyway she looks exactly like you; perhaps we know your mother. Is her name Fariza?"

"No, it's Tafsut."

"Ah, wouldn't that have been something. Listen, Sylvie, do you like a little mischief?"

"Yes, sometimes."

"Go outside to that man talking to the children and tell him that I said that he knows your mother and would he please tell you about how that came about. And when he can speak again send him to me."

She had that look in her eye. This was going to be precious.

"Édouard," Eliane cautioned, "What are you going to do if he has a heart attack?"

Well, he didn't but his eyeballs came close to falling out of his head. In the end we had a good laugh over it; even Geneviève after we explained a bit. The Thouvignons left and Philippe arrived. Philippe was the closest thing I had to a son and I favored him for it above his sisters. I let him and Sylvie know that they could have the honeymoon of their choice.

The feeling of celebration carried over into dinner. We might have continued longer but both Philippe and I had to go to work in the morning. When Eliane took Mother home, Bobby followed with the children. Philippe and Sylvie went home and I went to the Denisarts.

"Hello, Oiseau," Hélène greeted me at the door. "I didn't think I would see you for a while."

I didn't speak. I took her in my arms and we kissed.

"Who is it, Hélène?" Marie-Jeanne called out.

"It's Oiseau," she said as she moved me toward the kitchen

Marie-Jeanne was typing her notes. The stack of hand written documents was small and the typewritten one was large.

"Good evening. Do you always work this late?"

"I'm near the end. I could finish tomorrow except for Hélène's corrections. What brings you around?"

"They found him!"

I gave the letter to Hélène. Marie-Jeanne was furious. I made a sign with my hand for her to be patient and in less than a minute Hélène gave it to her mother. Marie-Jeanne read it and showed no expression on her face. She gave it back to Hélène.

"So, it's over," Marie-Jeanne said to us.

"Thank you." Hélène kissed me on the cheek. "I'm going to bed."

Marie-Jeanne was still mad at me.

"You had to do it, didn't you? You had to please her. It doesn't matter that he's dead; what matters is that you did as she wanted not as I wanted."

"I was hoping that they couldn't find him. They were going to send me periodic reports as they went to greater lengths to find him. My plan was to give her all the reports except the last one. I reckoned that if it looked hopeless that she would quit."

Marie-Jeanne wasn't satisfied.

"Listen, if I didn't help her she would have done it on her own. She was the one who called these people. I took it out of her hands and made her feel comfortable with the way I was handling it. What would you have me do? Just say no?"

She sighed with exhaustion and threw her hands up.

"Come, sit on the sofa with me. I know that I'm working too hard."

We moved to the next room and got cozy. She put her head on my chest.

"I need her cooperation the next two days and then I'm done. I'm glad this thing with Erich is over; it was affecting everything I did. I shouldn't be angry with you; you handled it all perfectly. I'm very thankful."

She lifted her head and looked at me. She wanted to kiss me and I pulled her a bit closer. Our lips touched for a few seconds.

"Édouard, I miss you. I want to be with you."

I didn't know what to say so I kissed her again.

"I love you, Édouard. Have I told you that before?"

"Yes, I think you have."

"Does it matter to you?"

"Of course it matters to me. I would do anything for you."

"Anything . . . You should go home; you have to work tomorrow. I need sleep too. Édouard . . . call me when you would do *everything* for me."

Friday morning on the way to work, I almost fell asleep. I had not realized how tired I was. I couldn't remember dreaming or lying awake; something was bothering me. Consciously, I was anxious about being with Hélène on Sunday and wanted to see her today. The more I worked that morning, the more I thought about retiring. I could do anything I wanted but there was nothing that I wanted to do. My book was merely an exercise in collecting facts, which made it boring; there was no passion in it.

I called Hélène.

"Can you get away for a few minutes and meet me somewhere?" I asked.

"Not this morning. We're setting up to test for toxins in fish from the Sarre. There was a bad chemical spill in Sarrebourg. We may have to come in tomorrow. Maybe this afternoon sometime; shall I give you a call?"

Phillip Varady

"No, I can't concentrate on my work; I'll be going home soon. Maybe you could come over tonight; Catherine and Bobby are taking the kids to a concert."

"Oh, yes I know. Hoa and I have tickets. Why don't you come?"

"No, that's not my kind of music; I'd hate it."

"What about tomorrow?"

"It's their last full day; we're going out to eat in the evening. I'll suffer through it until Sunday."

"All right, until then."

I called Marie-Jeanne.

"How's the report coming along?"

"Hélène corrected it and I have about twenty pages to retype. I should be done by dinner. I can't believe it; seven years of work reduced to about a hundred pages. If they don't like it I think I'll shoot myself."

"Marie-Jeanne, about last night. I didn't mean to . . ."

"Not now, Édouard. I'm very busy."

"All right, some other time."

I called Catherine. No one answered.

I called Eliane. Mother answered.

"Is Catherine there; no one answered at my place?"

"Bobby picked up the children about a half-hour ago. I thought he was going back your house."

"Is Eliane there?"

"No, she went to Elisabeth's for the day. She said she wouldn't be home until after dinner."

"All right, I'll find them. See you later."

I left the University with nowhere to go. I wanted to be with someone, almost desperately. I decided to go home and wait. When I got to Doub's house I saw my grandchildren in his yard playing with *his* grandchildren. Jean-Yves and his wife, Sonia were visiting and Catherine evidently brought her family there to visit also. I drove to the cottage and went to my room to see if I could fall asleep. Apparently it was easy.

"Papa, are you awake?"

"Yes, Catherine. I must have dozed off."

"I'm making lunch. Are you hungry?"

"Yeah, I'll be down in a minute."

I sat on the bed and wondered how it was that yesterday was such a great day and today I feel so lonely. Everyone has their own life to live and for the most part I am not in it. It seems to have always been that way but I don't mind as long as there is one person that can fully share their life with mine. Laure-Anne was such a person; I hope that Hélène will be another. Although the roles are reversed, I hope the outcome will be the same. Laure-Anne was persistent until our souls were entwined and now I'm the persistent one who believes that I can do the same to Hélène. Her hint of intimacy on Sunday was not proof that I had accomplished anything but she must have reached some point on the way to that goal that she would make love with me.

Downstairs I was called out to the garden to eat. Catherine and Sonia were feeding their six children in the dining room so I joined Bobby and Jean-Yves outside.

"Hey, Jean-Yves, how's it going?"

"Good, Oiseau, we had a great week at the lake."

"Did your father do anything beside drink beer?"

"Not unless you count farting."

"Ha ha. So, you two guys got to know one another?"

"Oh, I had to," Bobby said, "after Catherine introduced him as 'my old boyfriend' and then waited a few seconds before adding 'when I was four years old.'"

Sonia brought out our plates and gave me les bises.

"Nice car, Oiseau. I hear you're giving them away."

"If you play your cards right, Sonia, I'll put you on the list."

She patted my cheek then kissed it.

"Do you have any chilled white?"

"Yeah, there's a bottle of Moselle . . ."

"I've got it." Catherine said.

She had the bottle under her arm, three wine glasses and a beer glass in her fingers and another plate.

"Doub and Nadine are here?"

So, we four men spent the afternoon in pleasant conversation while three women ran around trying to keep six children from having too much fun. I stopped feeling so alone. The Vinchelins left at five and I let Catherine use my car to get Mother. We ate by six and Bobby, Catherine, Mickey and Jennifer were gone by seven, they were meeting Philippe and Sylvie at the Exposition Park. The concert was from eight to midnight.

Bryan kept Mother and me amused until he went to sleep about eight-thirty. Mother dozed off a half hour later. The television kept me company until I fell asleep. Catherine woke me when they got home and

Phillip Varady

I went upstairs. While I lay in bed waiting for sleep to come again, one thought kept running through my head: *one day closer, two more sunrises until . . . until I stop being so afraid.*

I got up early and had breakfast alone on Saturday. It was quiet and sunny and the warmth on my back was pleasant as I faced the woods watching birds soaring in and out of the trees. I loved my cottage and thought that in spite of my wealth that I would not live anywhere else. The place could use some improvements though. Maybe it was time to get rid of the wood stove and modernize the whole kitchen while I was at it. I would need the floor torn up to run the hot water into it . . . and while I was at it, have a wine cellar put in. And if I had a cellar I could have a heating system installed. Since part of the bathroom floor had to be torn up, I might as well modernize that room too. The outside needed some work and maybe I could have some of the trees cut in front of the house and replace it with grass so the kids could play there. Yes, I think that I'll do it as soon as I find a place to live for a month or so.

I heard Anne-Marie speaking behind me but not to *me*. Bobby and Catherine came outside to join me; I was not even aware that they were up. Both of them were wearing their usual uniform, jeans and tee shirts. After a little conversation I decided to make an improvement in their wardrobe.

"Catherine . . . the restaurant that we're going to tonight is a bit fancy. Do you have something nice to wear?"

"I have a white blouse and a black skirt."

"Bobby, do you have something?"

"A sports jacket."

"Hmmm. Excuse me for a minute."

I called Eliane.

"Eliane, do you have an evening dress?"

"Not one that will fit me."

"And Maman?"

"You're joking!"

"Well, we're all going shopping. When can you both be ready?"

"Now! Can I leave the children behind?"

Well, we left no one behind. An eight-passenger station wagon was the perfect vehicle for a family shopping trip. I had to convince them all that what they liked was not too expensive and to stop looking at the price tags. We spent the afternoon making plans for Christmas and a possible visit by some or all of us to Wisconsin. The grandchildren and I took a walk in the woods when Eliane and Mother went home to dress and their parents took a bath. We had a wonderful time expressing ourselves to each other. They have become an inseparable part of me.

The children were the last to bathe being the least likely to sit quietly until it was time to go. When we arrived at Eliane's house we took photos of this well dressed family. We may never be this elegant as a group again. Eliane's choice of evening dress showed me that she was dressing with an eye to attract attention. There may be some hope for her after all. Mother on the other hand looked timeless in a jade green dress, à la chinoise. She amazes me. She looked sleek, being slimmer than her daughter.

When we arrived at the restaurant I asked everyone to wait outside for a minute while Catherine and I went inside. I wanted to tease the maître d'hôtel and I was successful when he was impressed at my ability to escort yet another beautiful woman.

Once we were all seated I let him know the truth that this was my family; he appreciated my familiarity. I had to explain to the children that if they wanted to act like French children when they were in France that they had to learn how to eat correctly. That meant that they had to look at a French dinner as an event to be enjoyed and savored . . . not as something to be rushed through so that they could return quickly to the television. A little conference with Bobby and Catherine allowed me to order wine for them, a watered down glass of Rosé. There would be no cola on this table.

It was fully forty-five minutes before any food was on the table and then that was only the appetizer. We talked among ourselves and did not leave the children to sit silently; we engaged them in our conversation in a meaningful way to show them they were a part of this family and that this was the place for them to contribute to the bond that tied us together. Wisely, we did not let the children sit next to one another, which reduced the tendency to exclude the adults and communicate only among themselves.

The meal was a wonderful conclusion of their visit. It was times like this that we will remember, if not in specific then as a small piece that goes into grand memories. All the children fell asleep on the short ride home. Bobby, Eliane and I each carried one of them to their beds and got their fancy clothes off them. When we got back to the cottage I would have wanted to stay up for a while but we were all tired and went to bed.

Sunday, glorious Sunday, has finally arrived. I am emotionally torn knowing that the sadness of my family's departure will be balanced by the joy of the arrival of the object of my desire. Bobby picked up the children before seven o'clock to allow me almost an hour to say good-bye; their flight left at 9:02. The sorrow of leaving was tempered by the knowledge that they would spend Christmas here. This comfort was enjoyed by all of us. The tears were held back until the last minute when Jennifer was the first to let her emotions rule. She clung tenaciously to my neck when I was about to place her in the wagon expressing her desire to stay. Bryan just cried; only Michel remained silent although not dry-eyed.

Bobby was different; he seemed happy to go but I knew that it was because he had a great adventure waiting for him back home. I remember the last time that I said good-bye to him when his guilt for taking away my only child was palpable. This time he was the head of a family that was part of a larger family, making us equals on a certain level. He expressed with unspoken gratitude what I had done for him and his family by the look on his face and the warmth of his embrace.

"Beau-père, this visit was priceless. It was a blessing to all of us and I want more. I want to come back as often as you will have us."

"Well, I could build a house for you right there."

"Don't tempt me. Will you really come to Wisconsin?"

It had only been a thought without details but I changed that.

"Yes, definitely. Let's say next June for sure unless it's sooner. I want to thank your parents for the fine son they raised."

"That will work both ways. My parents keep telling me how lucky I am to have Catherine. There is a debt that I owe you that I can never repay. You've filled your daughter with love and she fills me with it."

Well, he finally let a few tears flow. He thought by embracing me again that I wouldn't see them but Catherine came outside just then and forced him to let go of me so that she could have me. She brought me back into the house.

"Papa, you've been so wonderful to us. I'm sorry that we stayed away so long. The kids loved it here, they . . ."

I put a finger on her lips.

"I know. You don't have to tell me . . . they told me."

"Okay, then I'll tell you how much *I* loved it here."

She put her arms around me and her head on my shoulder. We remained like that for a minute. It felt so good to hold her; I wanted more.

"I love you so much." I said.

When I realized that those were the last words that I spoke to Laure-Anne, I began to cry. Catherine couldn't resist and cried with me. After a while I separated us to look in her eyes.

"Do you know what I see when I look in your eyes?" I asked her. She shook her head.

"I see Catherine. She used to be a little girl that I loved but she isn't that any more. Now she's so much more to so many more people. I think if I looked for that little girl I would not have any trouble finding her. I think that the offer of a hug and a kiss would tempt her to show herself again."

"Oh, Papa."

I got my hug and kiss.

"If it were not for Bobby, I would have regretted every day I was away from here."

"That's just as it should be."

"And Papa . . . I wish you every happiness with Hélène."

"Oh, I didn't think you believed me."

"I believed you; I just didn't know what to say. Later, I thought that I didn't have anything to say. You have just as much right to love *her* as anybody. I hope that she loves you as much as my mother did."

"Yes, wouldn't that be wonderful."

"Is she waiting in the bushes for us to leave?"

"I think I spotted her across the lane hiding behind a tree."

"Okay, I get the message. We'd better get going."

"Give me a kiss."

She gave me one more kiss and we walked to the wagon. When they were just about to pull away, Jennifer asked for and got the last kiss. I watched the lane long after they were out of sight. It comforted me to know that they will return at Christmas. Once having tasted the sweetness I can no longer go without it.

I showered and shaved, put on some clean clothes and sat at the kitchen table, waiting for Hélène. The phone rang; I looked at my watch, it was 9:02.

"Hello."

"Are they gone?"

"Yes."

"I'll be right there."

I waited at the doorway for her. When I saw her car appear I looked at my watch again; it was 9:05. I was amused when she got out; she looked just like an American with her tee shirt and jeans. As she walked toward me I watched her breasts move under the thin fabric. She stood in front of me and we both stared at each other's eyes, looking for that sign of commitment that would assure each of us that we have indeed reached that point of no return.

Her eyes sparkled. I put my hand on her cheek and slid it around to the back of her neck and drew her to me. Our lips touched, just for a second, then again, and again. She kept her arms at her sides, allowing me to continue as I wished. I put both hands on her face and kissed her again, longer this time, much longer, then released her. She put her hands behind my head and kissed me the same way. When she was done I put my arms around her and held her tightly. I found the bottom of her tee shirt and moved my hands under it, sliding them over her smooth skin upward on her back. I was sure of her intentions. I wanted to see her face and reached her shoulders to pull her away.

"I'm ready," she said simply.

"Let's go upstairs."

"No. Do you have a blanket?"

I went inside and took one from under the staircase. I held it up to her. She came in the front door and led me out through the rear.

"Where are we going?" I asked.

"I know a place in the woods. My mother used to bring me there sometimes. I think she and my father made love there."

We began to walk down the *sentier*. There could be only one place like that. I gave her no indication that I knew where we were going.

"What kind of place is this?"

"It's beautiful there. You could walk by it and not see it at all. You have to know where to step off the *sentier*."

We walked one behind the other on the narrow pathway. I could see the place ahead where we should turn but she didn't and we walked past it for a short distance. She stopped and looked around; she was lost.

"What are you looking for?" I asked.

"There should be a large tree where we turn but I don't see it."

I let her go ahead a few more steps while I went the other way.

"There's a rotten stump of a large tree here," I called out.

She hurried back and stepped off the *sentier*. When we went a few steps into the woods I could see the willows. After a few more steps we could see the grassy clearing.

"Oh, it's here," she cried and ran ahead.

She stood in the middle and turned slowly, surveying the entire area. When I approached her she took my hand and turned me around with her.

"Isn't this beautiful?" she asked.

"Yes, it is. It's incredible."

"And nobody knows it's here except us."

She took a step backward and found the spring and fell, landing on her buttocks. I helped her up and we both laughed.

"Ow, that hurt and my ass is all wet!"

She kicked off her shoes and removed her jeans. I slid my hand inside her panties and caressed her cheek.

"Does that feel better?"

"Mmmm, I think I hurt *both* sides."

I doubled my effort. After a minute she wiggled away and spread the blanket. She kneeled on it and patted it where she wanted me to sit. I sat.

"I want to show you something."

"What?"

"My scar."

She took hold of the bottom of her tee shirt and pulled it off over her head. Her breasts were beautiful. The scar tissue was smooth and a bit shiny where it had stretched but for the most part it wasn't as bad as I had imagined. The nipple on her left breast had not developed correctly and was flat and undefined with scar tissue surrounding it. I put my fingertip on her clavicle where the scar began and traced its path across the tip of her breast. She shuddered.

"Did that give you a chill?" I asked.

"I don't know why but it's so much more sensitive than the other."

I moved my finger back and forth over it and she put her hand on mine. I put my mouth over it and caressed it with my tongue. She moaned and pulled my head against her breast.

"Ooooh, Oiseau, you are the first to do that. You make me feel so good. Make me feel good everywhere."

She pushed me down on the blanket and kissed me passionately, covering my body with hers. I rolled her over and held her.

"Hélène, I love you so much."

"Get undressed."

A fear gripped me.

"Do you love me?" I asked quietly in her ear.

She didn't answer immediately. I raised myself and looked into her eyes.

"Oiseau, I want to do this . . . yes, I love you."

"Will you marry me?"

"Do we need to talk about that now? I want to make love to you."

I got off her and lay on my back. My dream was shattered, my hope gone. She brought her face over mine.

"Oiseau, I have never felt with any other man what I feel for you. Is it not enough that I want to make love to you?"

"No. I need more than that, I want more than that."

"Give me time."

"Time is not the answer. I've been a fool."

"No, don't say that. You've been so good to me, so good *for* me. You're the first man that did not turn away from my scar."

I raised myself a bit and she moved to let me sit up then knelt beside me.

"You're beautiful . . . your breasts are beautiful . . ."

My fingers caressed her face then moved downward and followed the roundness of her breasts.

". . . if you allow that scar to ruin your life, then *you* are the fool."

She lowered her head and spoke softly.

"You don't know what some men said when they saw this."

"It didn't matter to me; it won't matter to another man . . . one that you can love."

She sat, leaning back against me. I put my arm across her chest, my head on her shoulder.

"What do we do now?" she asked.

"We start over. We keep looking."

We sat like that for a while. For me it was a lie; I did not believe that I could start over or that I would keep looking. Hélène was young enough to find love. In my heart I sincerely hoped that she would succeed. She tapped my hand and I took it as a request to let her get up.

The Swans of Lorraine

We both stood and faced one another; she put her arms around my waist and I held her.

"What shall we do with each other?" she asked.

"What do you mean?"

"What will we be to each other now?"

"I could be your father and you could be my daughter."

She smiled at that thought; I smiled too.

"One thing though . . ." I said.

"What is that?"

"I can't let my daughter go half-naked in front of me."

She turned her back to me and got dressed. I gathered the blanket and we walked slowly hand in hand back to the cottage, to her car.

"Are you going to be a good father to me?"

"The best!"

"Give me a kiss."

I gave her a fatherly kiss.

"Don't you neglect your child," she cautioned.

"I won't, I promise."

I watched her go and I was overwhelmed with loneliness. It was almost like I felt when Laure-Anne died but nothing could ever be like that. I was empty, without hope of ever finding love again. I went to my room and lay on the bed . . . and waited. I felt like dying . . . I should talk to Eliane; she would know . . . I didn't care. I waited . . . some time passed and I waited more. Something will happen, something will change. The phone rang . . . I ignored it. A while later it rang again and I got up. It stopped before I got there. It was getting dark; it must have been Eliane wondering where I was and if I was coming to dinner. I was hungry but had no interest in making something to eat. I got in my car and drove to the end of the street where Hélène lived. Her car wasn't there. *What are you doing, Édouard? Do you want her now?* I didn't know what I wanted; I wanted help. Except for Eliane, I could think of no one to go to. *Will you tell her what a fool you've been?* I've been a fool before. *Will you get help from a sister who cannot find a man for herself?* I don't know. I drove toward Eliane's house.

As I passed the church I saw a priest closing the doors. It wasn't the same priest; this one was much thinner. I stopped the car and hurried to the door, which was now shut. I beat on it with my fist. I suppose I was upholding a Jannot family tradition by turning to God as the supplier

Phillip Varady

of last resort. The door opened and I was face to face with a young man in priests' clothing.

"Come in," he said.

"You're new here."

"I've been here for a month."

"I don't come regularly."

"How can I help you?"

We were inside and he closed the door behind us. He sat in the last pew and motioned for me to sit with him. His youth discouraged me; an older priest would have had more experience with people like me. I didn't want to make him think that he was useless; I sat.

"I have a problem . . . about love. What do you know about that?"

"I'm an expert in that field."

"Really!" I smiled at him. "And what makes you an expert?"

"I know all about love . . . God's love. Human love is only an inferior imitation and a bit more difficult to understood."

"I have never heard this before. Perhaps you can explain."

"Does God lack anything?"

"No, I don't suppose that he does."

"You've heard that God is love?"

"Yes, I've heard that but that doesn't mean anything to me."

"If I said that loving was giving, would that mean something to you?"

"Yes, I can understand that. So God gives, is that it?"

"Yes, and God only gives, he never takes because he lacks nothing and needs nothing. Human love is imperfect and lacks something. So those who experience human love, experience both giving and taking. The closer they are to God's love, the less they take and the more they give."

I liked this priest. He has taught me more in one minute than all the rest of them have taught me in my whole life.

"What you say makes sense, Father. I'm confused about what happened to me today. The woman that I loved didn't love me and we parted and now I'm empty. If I was being God-like why am I suffering?"

"You say that you loved her, which is to say that you were giving. What was it that you were giving?"

"Everything I have, everything that I am."

"And what did you require of her? What did you lack? What were you going to take from her?"

"What I required was a mutual relationship. I lacked her love. I could take nothing from her that she was not prepared to give."

"Maybe you should persist. God gives us many things and for the most part people ignore him. But God doesn't give up on those people; he continues to offer. He knows that if people can see his love they will respond to it. We usually respond to love given with love returned."

"But *she* didn't. It wasn't in her. I couldn't *make* her love me."

"Hmmm. How would you characterize your love? How much of it was to fulfill her needs and how much of it was to fulfill your desires?"

His question was like a slap in the face. I was full of desires and the greatest of those desires was that she love me. She knew that I had wealth and that I would love her but that obviously was not her need. I had no idea what her need was. I had never even thought about it.

"I think that you've found the problem, Father. I never thought about her needs. Why is that?"

"Because you were heading for destruction. Saint Paul speaks about those heading for destruction whose God is their belly. The belly only takes in, only considers what its needs are and never gives out . . . that is only true, of course, if you exclude what comes out the other end, which no one wants anyway. But God says that it is out of the heart that come the true riches of life. God fills our hearts with love and expects that at some point we will realize it and love him in return. When someone constantly gives from their heart, deep inside they believe that the person they love will respond."

"So, I should persist?"

"You should continue to love her with the love of God, which is to say, continue to bless her by meeting her needs as much as you can. But to continue to try to make her love you in a romantic way may be futile. This is where my expertise fails; this is a mystery to all men. It's sad when the love we give is not returned. Saint Paul said he wept for those people whose God was their belly because they could not see and thus did not return God's love."

"Well, I can sympathize with Saint Paul. I can't think of a way to hurt a person more than by not returning their love."

"And yet it is done all the time. People do it to God, to their parents, their friends and like the woman you spoke of, to those that love them. When it happened to us, we become more aware of the sadness we cause in others when we do the very same thing."

"Sometimes, Father, only sometimes. If I hadn't spoken to you I would not have been aware that I'm guilty of the same thing for which I'm seeking help."

"Then you are in a perfect position to bless someone, having known both sides."

"Father, you've been a great help. I've got to go to her now. I'll be back; I want to talk to you again. Good night, Father, and thank you."

I rushed from the church and drove back the way I came. From the circle I could see Hélène's car in front of the house. I drove home and called. Hélène answered and I hung up. I waited a half hour and called again; Marie-Jeanne answered.

"It's me, Édouard. How are you?"

"I'm good, and you?"

"Good. I'm good too . . ."

A short silence followed.

"Is the report finished?"

"Yes, it was finished yesterday. Hélène is going to submit it tomorrow. She found out that Kaly is a member of the board of review."

"Oh, I didn't know that. That might work in your favor."

"Yes, it might . . . "

I didn't know how to express why I called except by telling her what I wanted but what *I* wanted is exactly what I didn't want to ask for.

"Did you want something, Édouard? Did you only call to ask about the report?"

"No. Would you like to come to my place for a while?"

"I don't know . . . it's late."

"Just for a while . . . please."

"What's on your mind?"

"I thought we could talk . . . have a little drink."

"Couldn't we do it tomorrow night?"

"We could but this is important."

"What's important?"

"If you come, you'll find out."

"And we'll talk, is that it?"

"Yes, that's it."

"Anything else?"

"If you want."

"If I want . . . all right. I'll be there in a few minutes."

She did not sound enthusiastic. I rushed upstairs to get a clean shirt and back down to wash up a bit and put on a drop or two of cologne. I put the Rémy and two glasses on the table in the parlor. When I looked around for anything else to do, Marie-Jeanne was standing in the doorway. She was wearing an old pair of jeans and a tee shirt that had 'Corsica' and some smaller writing on it.

"How long have you been here?"

"A minute or so."

"Where did you get those clothes?"

"From Hélène. She thought that you might like it."

"I've never seen you wearing jeans."

"I'll take them off if you don't like them."

"No, no. Come in, have a seat. Would you like a little shot?"

"Sure."

We sat on the sofa and I poured two drinks. We sipped a little and relaxed.

"Hélène told me what she did. Is that why you called?"

I swallowed hard. I never would have thought that Hélène would reveal anything of what happened today. I felt as though I was one step from destruction.

"I didn't think she'd say anything. Did you come here to tell me what you think of me? Go ahead; I deserve every bit of it."

"Oh, it's not so bad. You're not the first man who was taken in by a pretty girl but at least this one promised me that she would reimburse you as soon as she had the money."

The money? I had no idea what Marie-Jeanne was talking about. I took another sip of cognac. I had to find out what Hélène said.

"What made her tell you?" I asked.

"I knew it was you that she called this morning . . . and then she sneaked out without saying anything. When she came back later I told her that I wanted to know what was going on . . . if she was sleeping with you. She just laughed. I tried to slap her but she grabbed me and held me and swore that there was *nothing* going on. I told her that I didn't believe a word she said. That's when she told me about the investigator. I had no idea that they were so expensive. She was so desperate to find her father . . . She said that you had the bill sent here so I wouldn't find out."

"Yeah, I'll go upstairs and get it."

When I got to my room I sat on my bed to let my heart slow down. What a clever girl Hélène was but she should have told me what she said

Phillip Varady

before I spoke to her mother. I retrieved the bill and gave it to Marie-Jeanne.

"Oh, my God. What was that girl thinking? She can't come up with this much money. Ooooh, you knew that, didn't you?"

Marie-Jeanne sprung off the sofa and sat astride me, facing me.

"Did you think that if you were nice to her and paid for this that you had a chance with her . . . to sleep with her?"

"Oh, please, Marie-Jeanne. Do you take me for a degenerate? Sleeping with a mother and daughter? What kind of person do you think I am?"

"She said that you had a twinkle in your eye and that's why she had to see you this morning to make sure that you didn't have any fantasies."

"Me? Fantasies? You don't give me enough credit. Do you know that? I knew what she was doing and I was amused by it. That's why I had a twinkle."

"She said that she kissed you a few times and that you were getting . . . ah . . ."

"I wasn't getting anything. I just let her think I was."

"Really? Why would you do that?"

"It's simple. If she thought a few kisses would get her what she wanted she wouldn't be tempted to go beyond that."

"Beyond that? Just how far did you think she might go?"

"Oh, there's no telling. I'm handsome, charming, irresistible, rich, handsome . . . did I say handsome already? But I'm not voluptuous, definitely not voluptuous."

"You, Édouard, are such a fraud. You didn't know a thing about it until she told you. You would never have called me unless your guilt drove you to it. Tell me that I'm wrong."

"Would you like more cognac?"

"She had you completely fooled, didn't she? She had your tongue dragging in the dirt and that's why you were so cold to me. Come on, tell the truth. Admit it!"

"You know, it's very warm in here."

"You're sweating because you're guilty."

"Let me up, I've got to go to the bathroom."

"You're going to piss in your pants unless you tell me."

I was so lucky. I had come out of this mess without a scratch. Marie-Jeanne was in a good mood and she was here with me. I laughed at it all.

"All right. Your daughter must be a wonderful actress to be able to fool someone so completely. Am I forgiven?"

"Yes, you foolish old man. So, is this why you called me . . . to tell me about your degenerate feelings for my daughter?"

"No. I wanted you here to tell you that I love you."

Her smile vanished; she seemed frozen for a second.

"Say it again."

"I love you."

"Say it again."

"I love you."

"Can you say it with more feeling?"

"No."

"All right. That's a good start. Do you want to kiss me or something?"

"Yes."

"Are you waiting for something?"

"I told you . . . I've got to go to the bathroom."

She started to get off my lap and I pushed her down on the sofa and kissed her. We were at it for a few minutes when she suddenly got up and ran to the bathroom.

"Oh, I just made it," she said when she returned. "You can go now."

When *I* returned she handed me a full glass of cognac.

"Can I sit on your lap again?"

"Sure, come on. Can I take off your tee shirt?"

"Sure, anything else?"

I waited until she was in place and I had her tee shirt off.

"Can you sit straight and lean forward . . . maybe stick your chest out a little. Ah, yes, just like that."

I teased her . . . she laughed, but she enjoyed it as much as I did. We found time to finish our drinks. She knew what to expect this night but I had to make her break our rule about us sleeping in our own beds; I could not let her speak to Hélène before I did. We went upstairs, got undressed and got into bed. I had Kaly's technique as my ace in the hole.

"Do you want to try something different?" I asked.

"That depends. How different?"

"It's not a different act; it's only a different way to do it."

"I'm not going to regret this, am I?"

"No, no, here, just turn this way a little and . . . a little more. All right now let me get here . . . now you roll a little . . . lift this up . . . higher."

"Are we going to make love like this?"

"No, I've got to put this here . . . all right, we're ready."

"You're joking . . . tell me you're only joking."

"No. Watch . . . How's that?"

"Oh, that's not bad. Oh, oh, what did you do?"

Our tempo slowly increased until I knew that she could not last much longer.

"I've got to ask you a question."

"Oh, oh, Ahhh. What? Oh, oh.

"Will you . . . uh, uh, uh . . ."

"Oh, oh, talk faster . . . oh, oh, Ahhh . . ."

". . . marry me?"

"Oh, oh, yes! Yes, yes, yes, yes . . .oh, oh, oh . . . you bastard! Oh, oh, aaaaaah."

Sometime later when Marie-Jeanne had regained her composure and began to get dressed, I put the second part of my plan into action.

"What are you doing?"

"I'm getting dressed, what did you think I was doing?"

"Why are you getting dressed? I wasn't finished."

"There's more?"

"Well, you know . . . it's always better the second time."

"It's after midnight."

"And . . . ?"

"If I don't get back to the house, Hélène will know what happened."

"I think it's time she knew, don't you?"

"I'm not going to tell her anything. What are *you* going to tell her?"

"That she should get accustomed to living alone."

"You want me to move in with you?"

"If it's what *you* want?"

"Hmmm. Not right away but soon. Right now I want something else."

"What's that?"

The Swans of Lorraine

"I want you to show me that thing again."
"Sure but you know I'm a little tired. I'll have to go slower."
"Yeah! I like slow."

Chapter 13

I was very careful when I got out of bed the next morning. I dressed quietly and went downstairs to make coffee. I was drinking my first cup and watching the clock; Hélène began work at eight o'clock. At two minutes past the hour I reached for the phone . . . and it rang. I snatched it up lest Marie-Jeanne awake from the noise.

"Hello," I said quietly.

"Oiseau, it's Hélène. Were you waiting by the phone?"

"No, I was about to call you. I need to tell you what happened last night. That was some story you fabricated. I wish I knew it in advance of your mother bringing it up. Do you know how close to homicide she would have been if I said the wrong thing?"

"Then I was right about you."

"About what?"

"You really loved *her* and you only wanted *me* for sex."

"You know that's not true . . . besides, you wanted it more than me."

"Yes, and I'm happy now that we didn't do it. Are you happy too . . . Papa."

"Stop that. You make me sound like a degenerate. Yes, I am very happy."

"Good. Now tell me what happened. I have work to do."

I quickly repeated every word of conversation that we exchanged concerning her fabrication.

"So, why didn't she come home?" Hélène asked.

"She was too tired from celebrating our engagement. Call back in a half hour."

I hung up the phone and then took it off the hook and left it lying there. I went upstairs and pulled the covers off Marie-Jeanne.

"Get up, woman! I've got to go to work and I'm already late."

"Just because you have to get up doesn't mean that I have to. Give me that sheet."

I grabbed her ankles and started pulling her off the bed.

"All right! I'll get up."

I released her and waited. She sat on the edge of the bed but didn't get up.

"I'll carry you downstairs like that unless you get up."

"Is this the way our marriage is going to be? I don't get up early."

"Well, I could retire and we could both sleep late or you could get that job and we both get up early."

"You have no sympathy."

"Yes, that's so. Oh, by the way, Hélène called, said she'd call back in a half hour. Something about your report."

"What! Why didn't you say something?"

While Marie-Jeanne was slipping into her clothes, I went downstairs and put the phone back on the hook. It began ringing almost immediately.

"Answer the phone," she shouted, coming down the stairs.

"It's not for me," I replied, casually.

"Hello . . . Yes. What's wrong with the report? . . . Édouard said that you called to tell me . . . Yes! . . . Yes . . . Yes . . . Well, I don't know that yet. We didn't have time to talk about it . . . We were busy . . . No, not all night but we had to get some sleep . . . Wait one minute, I'll ask him."

"Are you taking us out to dinner tonight?"

"If you'd like."

"He said yes . . . Yes . . . Yes . . . Italian . . . Neither do I but I have a plan . . . No, I'll meet you . . . Good. Until later."

"Coffee?"

"I should be mad at you but since I'm making you spend your money on me, I'll be nice . . . but I'm warning you, when it's all gone, things will be different."

"Then I have nothing to fear, eh?"

"Oh, you don't know. There's so much I could spend it on."

"I've got more than you could spend."

"Really?"

"Trust me."

"How much?"

"Well, if you were married to me, you would know."

"Then let's do it."

I took her in my arms.

"There is nothing that would please me more but I want *both* our daughters to be here when that day arrives."

"Do you want to marry on Christmas?"

"No, a day before, a day after. It depends on what day Catherine comes. I'll have to wait for Bobby to call with his schedule."

"When are you going to tell them?"

"They're not home yet. I'll call them when we come home from the restaurant. Do you want to talk to them?"

"Sure."

"Are you going to stay here tonight?"

"Sure."

"Good. I've got to go to work. Give me a kiss."

"Leave me some money."

"For what?"

"I liked the dress your mother bought and I want to get one like it."

"Sure. Anything else?"

"Hélène says that she has nothing to wear either."

"Sure. Are you done?

"Are you going to buy me a Mercedes?"

"Sure. What color?"

"White."

"Good. We'll pick it up tomorrow. Anything else?"

"Yeah. Give me a kiss."

"Sure."

I took Marie-Jeanne in my arms but she began to laugh and I couldn't kiss her.

"Do you want a kiss or not?" I asked.

"You are so funny."

"Why do you say that?"

"Sure, sure, sure. I'll be content to get the kiss."

Well, she got her kiss and then I threw a thousand francs on the table.

"I'll pick you up at six."

I walked out of the cottage without looking back. When I got to my office I worked furiously on my schedule so that I could take Friday off. Marie-Jeanne's board of review convened on Wednesday and I reckoned that they should be able to reach a decision by Thursday. I wanted to take

Marie-Jeanne to Paris for the weekend to celebrate. One more piece of business to take care of was a call to Jean-Luc.

"Hello Jean-Luc. This is Professor Jannot."

"It's so nice to hear from you again, Professor. What color do you want this time?"

"White. We'll pick it up tomorrow around noon. Is that all right?"

"Yes Sir. It will be ready."

"Good. I'll see you then."

"Professor?"

"Yes, what is it?"

"Are you finished now?"

"No. I'll have one more but I need to ask her what color she likes."

I had a good day, getting more done than I expected. My plans for Paris were cancelled when the department head scheduled a meeting for Friday afternoon. I was thrilled when I got to Marie-Jeanne's place and saw her in her new dress; a red copy of the Chinese style that Mother had worn. Hélène then came downstairs looking very provocative in a short white strapless dress that revealed quite a bit of her scar. Both Marie-Jeanne and I were surprised but we complimented her and encouraged her.

I felt decadent when I walked into the restaurant with two beautiful ladies. I had a secret wish that Kaly would be there but she wasn't. The three of us felt completely at ease with one another now that the reason for suspicion and uncertainty that I had caused was removed. When we got back to Marie-Jeanne's place she ran inside to get a change of clothes. As I walked toward my car Hélène followed me.

"You've made her very happy, Oiseau," she said.

"She makes *me* very happy. *You* make me very happy too. I'm surprised that you wore a dress like that. Have you gotten over something?"

"It was your idea . . . one button, then another, except I decided to go all the way all at once. I feel good about it. It's me; it's what I am."

"Oh, I think you are more than that and some lucky man will soon discover it."

"I should be as lucky as my mother. Is there another man like you somewhere?"

"No, unfortunately. I'm the best there is but if you search long enough you may find someone that comes close."

"Do you remember what you told me when I asked if you would feel different toward my mother if I were not in your life?"

"Yes. I said that she would have to be the most important person in my life for me to do what I have just done."

"And is she?"

"Yes. She is that."

"So, what you're saying is that you got over me in less than a day?"

"That sounds so shallow but it's true."

"So, I was right. You only wanted me for the sex."

That seemed terrible but true. I was ashamed to admit it and hesitated to answer but Hélène was smiling. She wasn't disturbed by this. I was going to admit it since there seemed to be no condemnation attached to it but I realized that there was more to it than only that. It slowly became clear.

"Oiseau, I'm only teasing. Don't be so serious."

"No, it's not that. Something you said to your mother in that story you invented, you said that you came to the cottage to make sure that I had no fantasies. That's exactly what I was doing . . . trying to make a fantasy come to life. Sex was part of it without a doubt but it was more than that. I was robbed of my young wife . . . I felt cheated. You came into my life . . . I could have my young wife back. Not another Laure-Anne, not someone who would continue for her but someone with whom I could start all over, experience the joy of discovery, be awed by the way love deepened as we became one. But it was a fantasy because I can't start over. I can love again but I can't erase twenty-six years of the past and start over. "

"So, what are you doing with my mother?"

"Life goes on. I could have fallen in love with your mother eighteen years ago if I allowed myself but I wasn't ready. It was there . . . it was already in me and she brought it back. We wouldn't have had any problem at all except for her young, beautiful, sexy daughter who came between us."

"Oh, so now you blame me for everything."

"Absolutely!" I joked. "Aren't you amazed at the power that you have over men?"

We continued to amuse ourselves with jokes and flattery until Marie-Jeanne came out. I had only minutes to think of a way to tell Catherine that I was going to marry a different woman while that woman was listening to the conversation . . . well, at least my half of the conversation. I didn't put it off but called the moment that we entered the cottage. Before she said hello I could hear her shouting at the children.

"Hello, Catherine. Is something wrong?"

"Papa! No, I'm trying to get dinner started and your grandchildren are acting like they were tied up for a week."

"So, you got home all right?"

"Yes, no trouble. How is everything?"

"Wonderful. I have a beautiful woman here who wants to speak with you when I am finished."

"Did you ask her to marry you?"

"Yes."

"And?"

"And she said yes."

"I'm so happy for you, Papa. When are you going to do it?"

"We thought that we would wait until sometime around Christmas so that both our daughters would be there."

"Both daughters? You're marrying Marie-Jeanne!"

"But of course."

"But you said . . . Papa, you're terrible. You did that on purpose, didn't you?"

"Did what?"

"You let me think that the girl that I tormented was going to be my step-mother."

"Wouldn't that be something?"

"Oh, sure! I don't know why I ever believed you. You'd have more luck sprouting wings. Okay, let me talk to her."

I gave the phone to Marie-Jeanne and poured two glasses of cognac and waited on the sofa for her. After a while she called out to me to find out if I wanted to talk on the phone again but I didn't. She was excited when she joined me.

"Mickey asked me if I was the pretty woman with the funny hair and Jennifer asked if I was the woman with the pretty hair."

"And Bryan?"

"He didn't want to talk to me."

"He probably would have called you the pretty woman with the pretty hair . . . the same as what I would call you. You looked superb tonight."

"And you looked so handsome. I suppose that I'll have to get accustomed to other women throwing themselves at you."

"Yes, that will be a problem but right now I only want one woman to throw herself at me. Let's have a sip."

We sat and talked and sipped. She fell asleep in my arms and after a while I joined her. I can't say that I loved her the same way that I loved Laure-Anne; one cannot be compared to the other. I know that I gave as much of myself to her as I did to Laure-Anne but perhaps that was because I was wiser now and knew that it would please Marie-Jeanne, which was my goal. I think Marie-Jeanne knew what I was doing and tried to outdo me; sometimes I let her and sometimes I didn't.

The next day I called her to pick me up at the Mercedes dealer saying that my car had to be repaired and that I needed a ride home. She didn't suspect anything until after she arrived and I asked her to bring the registration for the Renault into the office. When she did and asked why, Jean-Luc gave her the keys. Whereas Eliane was ecstatic, Marie-Jeanne had to sit down. She had a hard time filling out all the paperwork and said hardly a word through it all. When she was done, she got everything she wanted from the Renault and Jean-Luc lead her to the Mercedes parked next to mine. After a ten-minute explanation and examination of every feature, both Marie-Jeanne and Jean-Luc were satisfied that she was ready to go.

"Are you going to follow me home?" she asked.

"Yes, I'm done for the day."

"Let's go to your place; I need a drink . . . maybe two or three."

With that she started the car and took off, pulling into traffic, tires screeching and her hair flying in the wind. She was out of sight before I left. When I reached the cottage she was sitting at the kitchen table with a glass of Rémy in her hand.

"What kept you?" she asked.

"Common sense, perhaps."

"So, you weren't joking, were you?"

"You'll have to learn to believe me . . . all the time."

"So then, you really have some money, eh?"

I took out my checkbook and show her the balance: over seven hundred thousand francs.

"Why are you still working?"

"I ask myself that every day."

"You realize how difficult this will be for me."

"What will?"

"It might take me years to spend all that."

"Do you think that Hélène might want a Mercedes?"

"You may as well ask."

I did but Hélène declined saying that she and her friends often went places together in one car and she didn't want to change things . . . yet.

Marie-Jeanne was very confidant when she sat for her board of review and came home with a positive feeling. She said the one thing that made her feel so good was her ability to explain the science involved in her project. It was not until the following week that the board made its decision. They recommended a degree in Biochemistry rather than Biology, like Hélène's, and required that she successfully complete one semester in the various disciplines at the level that would normally be sufficient to warrant the granting of that degree. The same day she enrolled for the fall term.

I received notification that my application for the expedition to French Polynesia was rejected; it was not as devastating as I thought but it was still a disappointment. That evening Hélène informed us that her application was accepted along with those of Hoa, Christiane, Isabelle and four others from the University of Nancy. Of the thirty-one people selected for the expedition, our school with eight members was the highest of any other including the Sorbonne. I think we have made a name for ourselves. They would leave France the last week in February for six to eight weeks.

Mother left for Munich in good spirits. We had a party for her the night before and she expressed her gratitude to everyone for their concern and well wishing. It was only when I put her on the train that she told me that she was frightened to meet my father after all this time but that she would do it anyway. We would hear nothing from her at all, no letter, no phone call, nothing . . . until the third week of October when Eliane received a post card that read simply *'Munich, c'est belle. Maman.'*

Favier, the son, informed me that all the legal work was done and that there were now four building lots behind Doub's house in the names of my three nephews and nieces and their mother; all had given me their power of attorney. The town rejected the application for naming the lane and instead widened it, paved it and said that it would carry the name of the street that ended at Doub's house. So now I have my own number on the rue de la Toulose. As if to add insult to injury, now that they established their claim to the area, they laid out a new street perpendicular to mine only fifty meters from my door going into the woods to the south then turning east to join an existing street. Appropriately, they named it rue des Forestiers. There goes my privacy!

Just when I was about to lose some privacy, Eliane wanted more. She again stated her desire to move to Nancy to get it. A few well-chosen questions and she admitted that she was seeing someone and that if anything would come of it, she would rather have her own place without Mother. Without telling her, I ordered the construction of a house on the lot closest to me. If she moves to Nancy I will have Mother move to the new house . . . not to mine. Marie-Jeanne moved in with me that week. I also had an area cleared in front of the cottage thirty meters square with a stand of trees separating it from the road. We would have firewood for years to come.

Marie-Jeanne was delighted beyond words when the University published her report. I had not read it before but I read it then. Her conclusions showed a deteriorating condition throughout the area and revealed the sources of some problems and reasons for her recommendations. Her meticulousness and well thought out sampling procedure, plus the length of time that it covered was instrumental in having sixty-five hundred hectares of the Forêt de Haye declared a Domaniale reserve; what Catherine would call a National Forest.

During the same phone call that I informed Catherine of Marie-Jeanne's accomplishment, she informed me that they would arrive in Paris on Monday, 21 December for Bobby's afternoon meeting with François Rochefort. He reserved a room for them at the Hôtel Royal Monceau for that night and extended an invitation to dinner at his home. We could expect them in Laxou about noon on Tuesday. Marie-Jeanne and I then decided to marry on Wednesday. When I called Jean-Marie to invite him, he accepted immediately and asked to spend Christmas with us also. It seems that his older son Paul was getting married two weeks earlier and he offered his place in Saint Martin to him for his honeymoon. They would wait until January to go there.

Marie-Jeanne and I picked a restaurant in Nancy where we would have the reception after the wedding. We chose one that had a reputation for the superior way that they prepared Lorraine's special dishes. Next we wrote invitations to our friends, family and associates. The total came to fifty-eight. Marie-Jeanne suggested that we round it off at sixty and wrote one more invitation to Calypso Xenakis and friend.

A month after Mother's first post card, Eliane received another, but this time in German. Marie-Jeanne and I had just sat down to eat when Eliane burst into the cottage.

"What is this?" she asked excitedly.

"It looks like a post card," I said.

"I know it's a post card, you idiot! What does it say?"

"It says, '*Ich wurde zu heim durch 4 oder 5 Dezember sein. Maman.*'"

Marie-Jeanne could not contain her laughter and neither could I. Eliane waited impatiently until we calmed down and then waved it in my face.

"Édouard, you're so funny. About as funny as walking into a door. If you don't translate this right now, I think I'll strangle you."

"All right. She says 'I will be home by 4 or 5 December.'"

"That's what I thought it said. Why doesn't she tell us something? What has she been doing all this time? Why did she write in German?"

"Obviously she's been very busy; too busy to write and she's probably forgotten how to speak French."

"I don't know why I bothered to come here," Eliane sighed.

It was puzzling and we all wondered about the length of her visit. There was nothing we could do but wait. The waiting ended on the evening of 4 December when Eliane brought Mother to the cottage. She had taken a taxi from the train station and had arrived only minutes ago. We were still preparing dinner and made enough to feed us all. I let Eliane and Marie-Jeanne ask all the questions, all the innocent questions.

Mother stayed at the hotel for the first month then was a guest at the home of a new friend named Klara. As often as she was asked how she met this woman or why she would invite her to stay at her home, Mother gave some vague answer like, 'She's just someone I met' or 'She was so friendly.'

She obviously had a wonderful time and told of the many places she went and the things she did. When the two women thought that they had worn her out, Eliane offered to take her home. Mother told her to go because she wanted to talk to me about something. Eliane left and Marie-Jeanne went upstairs. I had an idea who this Klara was and did not like it.

"Is Klara his wife?"

"No, his sister."

"So, you met him."

"Oh, yes. Yes, we met."

"Are you going to tell me about it?"

"Hmmm, not tonight but I will tell you everything."

"Did you tell him about me?"

"Yes, he was thrilled to hear about you. I gave him your address and he said that he would contact you if you didn't object. Do you?"

"No . . . no, I don't object. Does he want to meet me?"

"He expressed that desire but again he said only if you had no objection."

"When would he want to do it . . . and where?"

"Well, I suppose you two can arrange that after he contacts you. I'll write to him and tell him how you feel about it."

Mother answered many questions that I asked concerning him but none about her feelings for him. When I asked if she had met his wife, she said that she was tired and that we could speak more about her visit at another time. Then she asked me to take her home. At her house she hesitated before getting out of the car.

"When you meet him, you will meet his wife."

With that cryptic statement she went inside. It left me wondering if the three of them had become friends. After all he and Mother were together before he married the first time; what would prevent them from becoming friends. But then would she accompany him to France to meet *me*. Perhaps he was counting on me coming to Germany . . . of course, and bring Mother back for another visit. That was a great idea; Marie-Jeanne could come with me.

The next day I explained to Mother what the unfinished house down the street was for. She and I walked through it that evening and then went to talk to Eliane. She told her daughter that she wanted to move there, with or without her and thought that as soon as it was furnished she would do it. Eliane was surprised but agreeable to her moving . . . by herself.

"Ah, something is happening, eh, Eliane?" I said.

Eliane would not say but it was the way that she said nothing that gave it away.

"Don't tell me that there's a reason you want to be alone?" Mother asked.

"No . . . it's just that the house is new, it has everything modern. You're just a short walk from Édouard and Nadine is right there."

Mother went to Eliane and looked closely at her.

"You're a year younger than Marie-Jeanne," she said.

The next Saturday Mother and Marie-Jeanne went shopping for furniture to be delivered when the house was finished. When we were at Eliane's house the next day for dinner, my fiancée advised me that *our* new furniture would be delivered in a week. I didn't mind but later when we were home Marie-Jeanne asked very seriously if I thought that she was spending too much of my money. I told her that I would let her know in a day or two.

Monday I called Patrick Ulrich to ask how much was in the special account he had set up for me to receive dividends and other income. I was amazed when he said about two and a half million francs. He quickly explained that most of it came from Shlomo for the sale of the house in Paris. I told him to deposit two hundred thousand francs in my checking account and that I would stop by to see him soon to pick up some checks. Two days later Marie-Jeanne opened a piece of mail from my bank that contained the receipt for the deposit. She waved it in my face.

"Where did this come from?" she demanded.

"I think the bank sent it."

She started laughing.

"You know, Eliane was wrong . . . you're much funnier than walking into a door."

"I would tell you but then there would be absolutely no surprises left for our wedding night."

"You'll pay for this, you know."

"I can afford it."

Saturday morning while Marie-Jeanne and I were having coffee with Anne-Marie, the furniture delivery arrived. I told Anne-Marie to take the laundry and go and paid her for the day. The men moved our old bedroom furniture into the south room and brought up the new carpet first. Every piece downstairs was replaced including all the curtains and drapes. A new addition was a Persian rug for the parlor. Marie-Jeanne has excellent taste; she just never had the means to buy quality furnishings. We spent the rest of the day moving our clothes from the old to the new. We decided to leave everything in the south room except my desk, until after the holidays.

At a meeting with the contractor for the new house, I was assured that even if it were not finished by Christmas, the master bedroom, bath and kitchen would be. He felt certain that if he had his men work overtime it could all be done. I asked him how much extra it would cost and when he told me I tried to look like I was in agony but agreed. I told him that I would have the furnishings delivered on the 19th.

My thinking was that if Mother did not move in immediately, perhaps we could offer it to Jean-Marie and Geneviève for the few days that they would be here. Mother said that she would call them and that she and Eliane would stock the house with groceries and household items. I was informed that the Thouvignons preferred to stay at a hotel in Nancy; no explanation was offered.

One evening that week, I paid a visit to the young priest who helped me find my way out of the situation I had put myself in. We had a very good talk and he inspired me quite a bit. I asked him to perform our wedding, which pleased him greatly but when he began to impose conditions, I told him that we would have only the civil marriage instead. He was disappointed but wished me well.

Monday morning, the 21st, the University was closed and we were all getting ready for many events. A call came from Bobby; they were in Paris and were going to get some sleep. He would call me in the morning when they got on the road. Instead of taking the train, they had decided to rent a car . . . not a station wagon. Tuesday, in time for lunch, the Gustavsons and the Thouvignons arrived together. They had arranged it beforehand, Geneviève and Catherine in the Mercedes and Jean-Marie and Bobby with the children in the rental car.

When we had finished our homecoming we unloaded Catherine's and Bobby's luggage and then Bryan's when he insisted on sleeping in my house. Mickey and Jennifer preferred to stay with Eliane, much to her dismay; Mother loved it.

Bobby and Jean-Marie rode together so that they could discuss Rochefort's deal on the way here, where Bobby divulged the conversation he had with François Rochefort. Jean-Marie was wary but Geneviève said that her uncle would be very open and honest with family. François was pleased with him and warned him to do his best in school. He was very impressed with Bobby's knowledge of retail operations. *Very* impressed, Bobby emphasized and added that François spoke of the possibility of a better position in retail sales, possibly in Québec or France, seeing that he was fluent in French.

Marie-Jeanne received many compliments for the new look in our home. One item that everyone said was an important change was our new dining room table that would seat twelve. After lunch I asked Marie-Jeanne, Eliane and Mother if there was any way I could relieve the burden of cooking for so many people so often. Eliane jokingly suggested taking everyone to the Quatre Vents for every meal but they all said that it was not so bad because it was fun doing it together. Half of our family went to Nancy to do some shopping, mostly the women, while the rest of us laid about enjoying the company.

Bobby took my car for a few minutes and returned with a case of beer. I had his bottle of whiskey but he said that it was better in the evening. I think that my little talk to the women caused them to agree with me a bit because they came home with two large sacks of Chinese food. The children were delighted; the women were also because not only did they not need to cook but also avoided cleaning up by serving the food on paper plates. Our evening was like our afternoon, sitting and talking, moving from one knot of people to another. Jean-Marie and Geneviève were the first to leave, then I drove Mother home. When the children got sleepy, Eliane left, putting Jennifer in the narrow space behind the seats. Finally Catherine carried a sleeping Bryan upstairs and Bobby followed.

Marie-Jeanne threw a few pillows on the floor in front of the fireplace while I poured two small cognacs. We got comfortable lying on our sides facing each other, enjoying the warmth of the fire.

"What a perfect day," I observed.

"I feel like an orphan," Marie-Jeanne said.

"What do you mean?"

"My family is one other person. My mother was an only child; at best I could call two of her cousins who don't even care if I'm dead or alive. Look at your family; it keeps getting bigger and bigger."

"Do you want to have more children?"

"Ha! How much have you had to drink? No, certainly not. It's just that you have this luxury, this blessing of family. I like it and want to be part of it and they all love me and I am so overwhelmed by it all. I know that I'll be a grandmother someday but for now I'm content with *your* grandchildren, especially Bryan. Do you know that he told me, that the reason he wanted to stay here was because he wanted to be where I was?"

"He told me the same thing."

"No he didn't. You're just saying that."

"No, really. He said, 'I want to stay here because my new grand-mère lives here.'"

"Oh, how sweet. Ask Catherine if we can keep him."

"Give me a kiss."

"Don't start. We need to get some sleep tonight."

"Giving me a kiss won't give you insomnia."

"No, but if I give you a kiss you'll put your hands on me and then I'll give you another kiss and you'll start taking my clothes off and then we'll be up all night."

"All right, give me a kiss good night and go upstairs. I'll put some wood on the fire and I'll be up in a minute."

She kissed me; we finished our drinks and she left. It took a few minutes to get the fire right for the night and by the time I got to bed, Marie-Jeanne was sleeping. How wonderful it must be to be able to fall asleep so quickly; what peace of mind she must have. She was so sure of me, so sure of my love for her. When I thought about it I realized that I was just as sure of her love. I loved her with all that I had and all that I was. I have felt this before . . . and it was ripped away from me. *Dear God, not again, never again, I beg you.* I got into bed and snuggled behind her, putting one arm over her. I buried my nose in her hair, inhaling the fragrance. *Please, God.* I slept.

I awoke to the sound of the telephone. By the time it stopped ringing I was aware that I was alone. I got dressed and went downstairs to discover that I was the last one up. Besides the aroma of coffee, I smelled bacon. Catherine was cooking and everyone else was eating.

"Want some bacon and eggs, Papa?"

"Sure, why not. You can give me an English lesson too."

I went to the bathroom and when I got back my plate was ready. How can people stuff themselves so early in the day? I suppose that I could skip lunch.

"Who was on the phone?"

"Aunt Eliane. She wanted to know if she should bring Mickey and Jennifer here. I told her that she could keep them until the wedding."

"And she thanked you profusely."

"Oh, Papa, they're not that bad."

"Well, not this one. Come here, Bryan and give me les bises."

He came to my chair and we rubbed cheeks.

"Do you know what will happen today?"

"Uh huh. You and Grand-mère are getting married."

"And do you know what that means?"

"Uh huh. That's what a boy and a girl do when they love each other."

"Yes, that's right. You'll do okay, Bryan."

"Grand-Mère, will you marry me too?"

"Oh, Bryan. A girl can marry only one boy and Grand-père asked me first. Maybe you could ask Aunt Eliane."

"Uh uh, she shouts too much."

The morning passed much like that. We watched a little television, drank coffee, shined shoes and everyone took a bath. When we got hungry we ate leftover Chinese food. We sat around ready to go but it was too early. I had asked Marie-Jeanne to wear her red Chinese style dress but she refused saying it wasn't dignified. She bought a black dress that was more modest on top and had long sleeves. At 2:30 Bobby, Catherine and Bryan left to pick up the other two children. At 2:50 Marie-Jeanne and I left for the town hall.

We were the last to arrive. The entire family was there besides a handful of my colleagues and all of the friends that we invited. After we were all in the meeting room, the official came in and proceeded with the ceremony. This was not like the first time; this was so useless. I didn't feel different at all. This was only the official recognition of what had already taken place. When I looked at Marie-Jeanne I could see that she felt the same way. So, we smiled and said the words and made everyone happy. We signed the register and Doub and Nadine signed as witnesses. Everyone cheered, everyone kissed us, and everyone followed us to Nancy.

We had engaged a few musicians for some dance music but they wouldn't be here until four o'clock. Dinner was at six and we had the hall until ten. People stood in small groups enjoying a drink and the conversation. When the dancing began I noted many odd partnerships, the most unusual I thought was Doub and Marie-Jeanne. When Jean-Marie asked Mother to dance, Geneviève asked me. She was totally opposite from what I had first thought of her. Jean-Marie was indeed lucky. Kaly was there with a friend but that didn't stop Marie-Jeanne from getting her to dance with me, they were both smiling so much that I nearly refused. René must have thought that he was in heaven, dancing with all four of the Corsican gang. Only Hoa was with someone.

Phillip Varady

The food was a testimony to the restaurant's reputation although I thought that they rushed us a bit. When the coffee was served Marie-Jeanne and I were called to the dance floor and we had our first official dance together. She asked me while we were dancing, why they said 'official' when it was our first dance ever. I hardly saw her again until it was almost time to go and we stood at the door together. I felt very proud of her when she said good night to my colleagues. They had all heard that her report had been published and most made mention of it. They treated her as an equal and she loved it.

When we got back to the cottage we were alone. Catherine and Bobby were probably at Eliane's house putting the children to bed. I put some wood in the fire and we waited for a while but then reckoned that they were going to let us have the place to ourselves. I had no idea where they would sleep but assumed that they had found a bed somewhere.

When Marie-Jeanne and I were finally in bed we held one another until the chill went out of the cold sheets. With two heavy quilts over us, it would be very warm in a minute or two. We touched and kissed and she rolled me on my back and lay on top of me and held me tightly.

"I'm ready," she said.

When I tried to proceed she held me tighter.

"Let me loose a little."

"You have to keep your promise first."

"What promise?"

"You were going to tell me how much money you have."

"Do I need to do that right now?"

"Do you want to sleep alone on your wedding night?"

" Well . . . I'm a millionaire."

"I knew *that*. Exactly how much money does my millionaire have?"

"More than enough."

"I want to know how much."

"What difference does it make?"

"If it doesn't make any difference, why don't you tell me?"

"You won't believe me."

"All right, I promise that I'll believe you."

"More than a million."

"Two million?"

"More."

"Five million?"

"More."

"Ten million?"

"More."

"I don't believe you."

"But you promised."

"You're just playing with me."

"I've got twenty-eight million."

"You expect me to believe that?"

"No, but you promised."

"Well, I promised to believe you but you've gone too far."

"All right, I'm going to make to make two statements; one is as true as the other. If you can't believe one . . . don't believe the other. I love you and I have twenty-eight million francs."

Marie-Jeanne didn't say anything for a while; I could understand why. After sufficient time had passed, I put my hands on her buttocks and moved her back and forth, to stir her into action.

"This is terrible, do you know that?" she said.

"No. How can it be terrible?"

"I'll be an old woman before I could possibly spend it all."

The morning of the day before Christmas was quiet. Everyone would eventually come here but that would be at dinnertime. Eliane was to help Marie-Jeanne make lunch for the eight of us, so we counted on being alone for a few hours. After our first cup of coffee I brought in enough firewood to feed both the stove and the fireplace for the entire day. When I sat again at the table, Marie-Jeanne had brought out some brioches and butter for me. Strangely we had little to say but she smiled at me quite a bit.

"Where do you want to go for our honeymoon?" I asked.

"I thought our trip to Wisconsin was going to qualify as a honeymoon."

"Oh, no. We wouldn't have any privacy at all."

"Well, then we'll go somewhere after that. It doesn't matter."

"I'm going to take a sabbatical after this term is over . . . maybe quit altogether."

"And do what?"

"I don't know but I'll have a whole year to think about it."

"Are you going to finish your book or start another?"

"No, I think I'm done writing; it isn't worth the effort. First thing I'll do is consult with a builder and work out a plan to modernize the cottage."

I explained to Marie-Jeanne all the changes that I wanted and she agreed. I was pleased when she informed me that the cottage had a cellar whose entrance was closed when the present bathroom was built, a year before Laure-Anne and I occupied it. Now, in order to use it again, we decided to have a new bathroom built upstairs and leave only the hot water heater, toilet and sink downstairs.

"Where will we live while all this is going on?" Marie-Jeanne asked.

"We could live in the new house even if Mother decides to move into it also. It would only be for a month or so."

That sounded like a workable solution and we lapsed into silence again, reading the wedding cards we received last night.

"When do you start work?" I asked.

"As soon as the grades are posted, I suppose."

"Do you know where you'll be working?"

"I don't think that has been determined yet."

"I have an idea. We could take a honeymoon in Tahiti for three weeks while the expedition is on the other island. With your recent report to recommend you, I don't think that they would turn you down as a non-salaried volunteer."

"I like that idea. Does it have any chance of success?"

"Sure. As soon as we go back, you ask the department head or have Hélène ask, and I'll call my friend at the Sorbonne. If we can do it, it would be the perfect time to do the remodeling. Doub can keep an eye on things for me."

As lunch approached and the family began to arrive, we told them of our plans. They all wished us well. We discovered that Catherine and Bobby slept in Mother's bed and that Mother had stayed in the new house; a permanent move, she said. The Thouvignons arrived in mid afternoon and gradually all of Eliane's family also. All the women gathered in the kitchen to prepare our evening meal and the men stood around the fireplace to discuss my remodeling ideas and my honeymoon plans. The meal was a buffet style and one sat where one could. Long after coffee was served, Eliane was gently pushing me toward the front door.

"Someone just drove up," she said.

"So, you could have just let them in."

"It's your house . . . you should greet them yourself."

When I opened the door I thought Eliane was pushing me out but I suppose she was as anxious as I to see who else would be joining us.

"René! Well, come on in and join us for a drink or two."

"Happy Christmas, Édouard . . . Eliane."

"Let me have your coat."

"Happy Christmas, René. I'm glad you decided to come," Hélène said behind us.

Rene took off his coat and handed it to me and took Hélène in his arms and gave her a kiss. The two of them were grinning as though they had just let us all in on a big secret.

"René and I have been seeing each other for two months. I finally showed up for my dental appointment and one thing led to another and well, here we are."

Hélène brought René around to meet everyone and I brought his coat upstairs. When I came down I waited for an opportunity to speak to her quietly.

"René? Of all people, why him?" I asked her.

"He's very nice, he's good looking, makes good money . . . he's very attentive to me and . . ." then she whispered in my ear "maybe I prefer older men, eh?"

"Well, there's something to that, isn't there. I wish you both the best."

I reached into my jacket for an envelope, actually four of them, and gave her the one with her name on it.

"Happy Christmas, Hélène. Wait until you get home to open it."

"Thank you, Oiseau. What is it?"

"I sold some property and I wanted to share it with my daughter."

"You're so sweet, Papa."

She gave me a kiss and we joined the others. I found Catherine and Eliane and gave them envelopes too, with the same request. Then I gave the last to Mother but she opened it in spite of my request.

"A half million francs? Édouard, where did you get all this?"

"Shlomo sold the house in Paris. I don't need the money and I wanted you to have it. I'm sure that you can find a use for it especially now that you're living by yourself."

Eliane had seen Mother open her envelope and came to look at what she was holding.

"Édouard, mine too?"

"Yes. Please don't say anything."

"All right," she said quietly.

I could see headlights in front of the house and excused myself. "Someone else is here," I explained.

A car was parking some distance away, of necessity since there were already eight other vehicles there. I waited just outside the door, not being able to determine whom it was in the darkness other than that it was a man. Someone closed the door behind me, no doubt to keep out the cold air. As he approached the cottage, the light coming through the windows illuminated his features but I did not recognize him. At last he stood in front of me.

"Hello, Édouard. I am Rheinhold Popp."

He was the same height as me and our eyes looked into one another's. He wasn't smiling; his arms were at his sides. I studied his face; it was so different from the photo in the yearbook. *What do I do now? What do I say?* I wanted to hug him.

"I have been waiting for this day for I long time," I said.

"I have been waiting longer than you . . . son."

He extended his arms to me and I embraced him.

"Oh, Father, Father. How good it is to say that word to someone."

I wanted to hold him but I wanted to look at him too. I realized that I was crying and I didn't want him to see it; I held on to him.

"Your mother says that you look like me a little. If we went inside I might get a better look at you."

Reluctantly I released him and wiped my face; he did the same. I pushed the door open and Mother was right there waiting for us. She embraced and kissed him; he was whispering to her.

"*Französisch jetzt, ach,* now you have me doing it. French now, ja?"

He removed his hat and coat. Everyone was looking; all conversation had ceased. His hair was all white, his face a bit gaunt. He was trim, in good shape for his seventy-five years. He looked casual in a gray knit sweater. Mother took his hand and brought him into the parlor. We were all waiting.

"Everybody . . ." she called out, "I would like you all to meet and to welcome Rheinhold Popp who for the last twenty-two days has been my husband. We have decided to live in Laxou in our new home just down the lane."

The silence lasted no more than a second and then the room was filled with words. The sound of the voices was joyous, heartwarming . . . full of exultation. The family gathered around them as I stood holding his hat and coat. I placed them on a chair and sought Marie-Jeanne. When I had her hand I approached them; he was still looking at me. We waited patiently until we could get closer. Finally we were together.

"I would like you to meet Marie-Jeanne who for one whole day has been my wife."

They embraced and kissed and exchanged greetings. Eliane was at my side and brought Catherine forward to stand in front of him. Eliane took my hand.

"Catherine," Eliane said slowly, "I would like you to meet your grandfather."

Catherine exploded with excitement and threw her arms around him; Eliane put her arms around me.

"Maman told me the day she got back. Édouard, I love you so much."

The room was abuzz with excitement as Mother confirmed the news. Catherine's children came forward to meet their other great grandfather. When it seemed that everyone had greeted him, Mother took him by the hand to where Jean-Marie and Geneviève were patiently waiting. I had not considered that two former enemies were now to greet one another as polite friends. Catherine, not having had enough time to share with her new grandfather, followed.

"Ah, Captain Thouvignon, a pleasure to finally meet you, Sir"

"A pleasure General, a long awaited pleasure."

They clasped hands . . . but only for a second and then embraced each other. I was amazed. When they separated they both looked at me and smiled.

"We were professionals, your father and I, in the first war." Jean-Marie said. "We did our job, we had respect for our enemy and they for us."

"We realized," my father said, "that it was our governments which wanted to destroy each other but we, as human beings, knew that when it came down to it, it was man to man and we acted like men, not animals. It was a contest, much like a prize fight; you test your skills against another and if you win or lose, you do not hate your opponent . . . you respect him."

"Just because France triumphed we did not think of our opponents as unworthy of respect; in fact we still feared and respected them," Jean-Marie said.

"And just because the French managed to get the Americans to come in on their side, which is really why they triumphed, we thought no less of them as brave soldiers," my father retorted.

"Ah, General, I can see that we have much to talk about, much that we are not in agreement on."

"Captain, I was still a captain in the first war, so we were equals then. Let us forget about rank and use our Christian names."

"Agreed, Rheinhold. And there is one thing that we can agree on now without controversy and I know that you are with me in this."

"And what is that, Jean-Marie?"

"We have a beautiful and charming granddaughter."

"You two had better not leave until I can find a camera," Catherine said.

It was obvious now that Mother and Eliane had been preparing for this event for some time. I thought that it was Providence that inspired me to have a home built for Mother, and now as it turned out for both my parents. The evening was planned to end about midnight but it was closer to two o'clock before we forced the last guests out.

Jean-Marie and Geneviève accepted Rheinhold's invitation to stay at *their* home for a few days. Marie-Jeanne and I were invited to breakfast on Christmas morning. It was generally acknowledged that the entire family would go to Mass first, not only to celebrate the birth of Christ but also to give thanks for a family that had suffered great loss and deprivation and one that had persevered and had been blessed beyond measure.

Saturday morning we said good-bye to the Gustavsons and the Thouvignons. They were all invited to François Rochefort's home for the evening. The return flight to Wisconsin would depart the next morning. My parents took Marie-Jeanne and me to dinner in Nancy at a German restaurant, which I never knew existed. We did not want the evening to end having grown so accustomed to having family around us. It was there and then that I announced my decision to submit my resignation, effective the last day of this semester. My father and I had fifty-two years of catching up to do.

When at last our door was locked against the world and Marie-Jeanne and I once again had our home to ourselves, we considered all that we had been blessed with since we had encountered one another last July. It was almost unbelievable, much more than pure chance. We felt awed by it all . . . very humble, which I felt was appropriate. There was one last thing that I had assigned to myself, to cut loose the past and to give to my wife the token of my total commitment to her. Of course I expected to have a little fun amid the seriousness of it.

"Are you sober?" I asked Marie-Jeanne.

"Yes, relatively so. Why?"

"Well, do you think you could have a bit of cognac with me by the fire?"

"Aren't you tired; don't you want to go to sleep?"

"Yes, yes. This won't take very long and it needs to be done."

"What? Are you starting a new Jannot tradition?"

"No, nothing like that. Come on, get a little shot for us so that we can go to bed."

"And do what?"

"Sleep, I promise . . . if you want."

"Well, I certainly do. All right but this better not take too long."

"Just minutes, I swear."

While she was getting the drinks I threw a few pillows on the floor in front of the fireplace and stretched out on them. The fire was still burning brightly and the heat at close range was more than comfortable. I moved the pillows back a bit. When Marie-Jeanne brought the drinks she sat alongside me and gave me one of the glasses. I drank mine down and she followed, no doubt to get this over with quickly.

"Come on and sit on me," I said.

"No funny stuff; we're going to bed to sleep."

"Yes, yes, I promise."

She pulled up her skirt a bit and straddled my hips. I began to unbutton her blouse.

"What are you doing? You said no funny stuff."

"This isn't funny stuff; it needs to be done. Trust me."

She smiled, thinking that I was an absolute liar but she let me continue. After I had her blouse completely unbuttoned, I removed it. Next I removed her bra.

"So, this is not funny stuff, eh?"

"No, absolutely not, and in a minute you'll agree with me."

"If it wasn't for the nice feeling the fire gives me, you'd be here alone."

Phillip Varady

"All right, woman, I'm ready. Put your hands behind your back, close your eyes and give me a kiss. One kiss and then we're through."

"You know . . . you're either insane or a liar."

"Shhhh, kiss me . . . and not a quick kiss."

She leaned forward, almost laughing, put her hands behind her back and when she had her lips close to mine she closed her eyes. With my thumbs I removed the gold chain from my neck and slipped it over my head and on to hers, putting my hands at the back of her neck so that she would not feel the weight of it. We had a very nice kiss.

"Since I didn't buy you anything, that's my Christmas gift to you," I said, still holding her.

"Well, that was very nice . . . not too expensive but the thought was sweet. Do you want to tell me why I had to get half naked?"

"You'll find out when you sit up."

She sat up and the birds nestled between her breasts. She looked at them, then at me, then pulled her hair out from under the chain and stuck her chest out.

"They're beautiful," she said.

"Yes, they are. So are the birds."

She laughed and gave me another kiss.

"I love you Édouard Jannot . . . more than anything."

"I love you Marie-Jeanne Jannot . . . more than anything. *Deux oiseaux, joint ensemble à jamais.*"